Lucian trusted no one.

If not for his wealth and name, they'd all be gone in a second. He'd learned that the hard way.

What about Megan? The beauty seemed to radiate goodness. He could almost believe she truly cared about helping this town. Was it real? Or a clever act designed to make him lower his guard?

He resented this present circumstance that was beyond his control. As empty as his life in New Orleans had become, it was familiar.

Frustration surged. If not for this young lady, he would've already put the house up for sale and be out of this backwoods town.

"Let me make myself clear, Miss O'Malley. I plan to do everything possible to find a way around that stipulation."

Anger flashed in her eyes. "And let me assure you, Mr. Beaumont, I will do everything I can to fight you."

He blew out an aggravated breath. He was beginning to wish he'd never heard of Gatlinburg, Tennessee. And Miss Megan O'Malley.

Karen Kirst

His Mountain Miss
&
The Husband Hunt

LOVE INSPIRED
INSPIRATIONAL ROMANCE

LOVE INSPIRED®
INSPIRATIONAL ROMANCE

ISBN-13: 978-1-335-23987-7

His Mountain Miss & The Husband Hunt

Copyright © 2020 by Harlequin Books S.A.

His Mountain Miss
First published in 2013. This edition published in 2020.
Copyright © 2013 by Karen Vyskocil

The Husband Hunt
First published in 2013. This edition published in 2020.
Copyright © 2013 by Karen Vyskocil

Recycling programs
for this product may
not exist in your area.

This edition published by arrangement with Harlequin Books S.A.

For questions and comments about the quality of this book, please contact us at CustomerService@Harlequin.com.

Love Inspired
22 Adelaide St. West, 40th Floor
Toronto, Ontario M5H 4E3, Canada
www.Harlequin.com

Printed in U.S.A.

CONTENTS

Karen Kirst was born and raised in east Tennessee near the Great Smoky Mountains. She's a lifelong lover of books, but it wasn't until after college that she had the grand idea to write one herself. Now she divides her time between being a wife, homeschooling mom and romance writer. Her favorite pastimes are reading, visiting tearooms and watching romantic comedies.

Visit the Author Profile page
at Harlequin.com for more titles.

HIS MOUNTAIN MISS

I will turn their mourning into gladness;
I will give them comfort and joy instead of sorrow.
—*Jeremiah* 31:13

To my parents-in-law, Pavel and Julie Turon,
who have brought such joy into my life.
I'm blessed to know you both. I love you!

A big thank-you to my editor, Emily Rodmell,
for all her hard work and dedication.
This series wouldn't be possible without you!

Chapter One

❧

May 1881
Gatlinburg, Tennessee

"Who are you, and what are you doing in my house?"

Jolted out of her concentration, Megan O'Malley dropped the books she was holding, and they thumped to the gleaming wood floor. She twisted around to face the unexpected visitor whose voice she didn't recognize. Odd, she hadn't heard the doorbell. Mrs. Calhoun normally announced company.

The stranger standing in the parlor's wide entryway was definitely not a local. Even dressed in their Sunday best, the men of Gatlinburg couldn't come close to imitating this man's elegance. Glossy black Hessian boots encased his feet and calves. Muscular thighs stretched the dove-gray trousers he wore taut, and underneath his black frock coat, the silver-and-black paisley brocade vest hugged a firm chest. The snowy white, expertly arranged cravat at his throat resembled a work of art.

Nothing was out of place. No lint on his coat. Not a single speck of dust dared cling to the mirrorlike surface of his boots…which was why his hair seemed to her untamed. It was glorious hair, really, thick and lustrous and wavy, the dark brown layers kissing his forehead in a manner that must irk him so.

His eyes, she noticed at last, were watching her with marked suspicion. He did not look pleased.

His black gaze raked her from head to toe and back up again, his frown deepening at the sight of the flower circlet adorning her loose curls. Megan experienced a spurt of self-consciousness. In preparation for the children's story time, she'd dressed the part of a princess, complete with a flowing white gown and fingerless lace gloves.

Unsettled, she clasped her hands behind her back and adopted what she hoped was a casual smile. "Hello, I'm Megan O'Malley. You must be new in town. Is there something I can help you with?"

He didn't deign to answer. Instead, he surveyed the airy room as he stalked towards her, circumventing the wingbacked chairs arranged in a semicircle about a plush Oriental rug. Fit and athletic, he exuded an air of command. Of authority. He struck her as a man accustomed to giving orders as opposed to taking them.

A wrinkle formed between his brows. Haughty brows, she thought. His was an arrogant beauty, with razor-sharp cheekbones and a harsh jawline. His nose was unremarkable, medium size and straight. The fullness of his mouth and the small dimple in his chin offset the harshness of his features.

When he stopped very near, his sharp-edged gaze cut into her, demanding answers. "Would you be so kind as to tell me what you're doing in my grandfather's house?"

A great trembling worked its way up her body. *This* was Charles's grandson? It couldn't be, could it?

"Lucian?" she whispered.

He sketched a bow, his gaze narrowing. "*Oui.* Lucian Beaumont, at your service. I take it you were well acquainted with my grandfather?"

"Charles was a dear friend of mine."

Sadness gripped her. How she missed the gentle, insightful older man, their lively conversations about life and love, music and books. Theirs had been an unlikely friendship brought about by a mutual love of literature. To Megan, he'd been a substitute grandfather.

"I see." And yet, it was perfectly clear that he didn't. Resentment came and went in his expression. "He passed away nearly three months ago. Why are you here?"

"I could ask the same of you." She met his gaze squarely, a rush of indignation stiffening her spine. "Why did you wait until now to come? In all these years, why didn't you visit Charles just once?"

The rift between Charles and his daughter, Lucian's mother, Lucinda, was common knowledge among the townspeople. He'd been dead-set against Lucinda's marriage to New Orleans native Gerard Beaumont, had rashly threatened to cut her out of his life if she went against his wishes. A threat he'd lived to regret. After their elopement, Lucinda and Gerard left Tennessee and settled in New Orleans, never to return.

A muscle in his jaw jumped. His already cool manner turned glacial. "That is none of your concern, Miss O'Malley. As to what I'm doing here, I happen to be the new owner of this house. And despite my repeated inquiries, you've yet to tell me what you're doing here."

He gestured to the chairs and the books scattered behind her.

The story time! The hand-painted, gilt clock on the fireplace mantel showed ten minutes to five o'clock. She glanced out the window overlooking the front lawn. The children would start arriving soon.

Turning her back on him, she bent and hurriedly began to gather the books she'd dropped. "Every Friday afternoon, we have story time for the children. They'll be here any minute."

To her surprise, Lucian crouched beside her, his tanned hands deftly assisting her. "Children? Here?" They reached for the last one at the same time, his fingers closing over hers. A frisson of awareness shot through her, and she was suddenly conscious of his knee brushing hers, his bold, sweet-smelling cologne awakening her senses. Megan had the absurd notion to lean closer and sniff his clothes. Instead, she snatched her hand back. His eyes as black as midnight, he held the book out to her, waiting.

Flustered, she took it from him and pointed to the cover. "*The Princess and the Goblin* is our story for today. In case you haven't noticed, I'm the princess." She touched a finger to her crown of daisies.

"I noticed." He held her gaze a moment longer. Then, with a fleeting touch on her arm, he assisted her to her feet. "How long has this been going on?"

"About a year," she said, hugging the books to her chest. "Your grandfather wholeheartedly approved."

"So this was your idea?"

"Yes."

His open assessment put her on guard. He didn't

know her, yet he regarded her with a healthy dose of distrust.

"Here are the refreshments, Miss Megan." Mrs. Calhoun entered the room with an oval tray piled high with strawberry tarts, stopping short when she spotted Lucian. Her mouth fell open. "Oh my!" Her gray brows shot to her hairline. "You look so much like Charles did when he was younger that I was momentarily taken back in time. Mr. Lucian, I presume?"

Setting the books aside, Megan took the tray from the older woman's hands and placed it on the credenza beside a crystal pitcher of lemonade. Turning, she caught Lucian's arrested expression before he smoothed all emotion from his face.

He regally dipped his head. "I'm afraid you have me at a disadvantage, *madame.* I—"

"Of course you wouldn't know me." She chuckled as she mopped her brow with a handkerchief. "I'm Madge Calhoun. My husband, Fred, and I came to work for your grandparents when your mother was just a baby. We live in the little house on the back side of the property. I do the cooking and cleaning, and Fred maintains the grounds."

"I see."

Her expression clouded, the lines about her eyes becoming more pronounced. "I sure was sorry to hear of Lucinda's passing. And now Charles… I keep expecting to hear him coming down the stairs asking me what's for dinner. Hard to believe he's gone."

At his low hiss, Megan's gaze darted to Lucian. A flash of regret on his face, of deep-seated pain, mirrored what was in her own heart. Was his grief entirely for his mother? Or did he—too late—understand what he'd given up by refusing to mend things with his grandfather?

The doorbell chimed. "Oh, our first visitor." Mrs. Calhoun stuffed the handkerchief back into her apron pocket. "It's probably Ollie Stevenson. He comes early in hopes I'll relent and give him a treat before all the others get here. Of course, I never do, but he's a persistent little fellow."

As soon as she'd gone, Lucian turned to Megan, his voice low and urgent. "How many children are coming?"

"On a good night, we have about twenty."

"Twenty." He visibly swallowed. "And how long will they stay?"

"About an hour. Why do I get the feeling you don't like children, Mr. Beaumont?"

"In my world, children do not normally mingle with adults. I've little experience with them."

"And yet—" she smiled sweetly "—you were once one yourself."

His lips didn't so much as twitch. "Miss O'Malley, I will absent myself for the duration of your…story time. It's obviously too late to cancel. However, I'd like a word with you immediately afterward. There are matters we need to discuss."

He pivoted on his heel and strode out of the parlor before she could respond. Cancel? Matters to discuss? Somehow, Megan sensed she wasn't going to like what he had to say.

The children's excited chatter, punctuated by Megan O'Malley's lilting voice, ultimately drove Lucian out the back door and into the flower gardens. He strode along the winding stone path, past gurgling fountains and whimsical marble statues and wildflowers in every imaginable shape and hue, unmindful of his destination. His chest felt too tight. He needed air. Distance. In that house, unwanted emotions crowded in without his consent, nipping like rabid dogs at his tenuous hold on his composure.

He abruptly swung about to glare at the two-story, gabled Victorian, the late-afternoon sun bathing its yellow exterior in soft, buttery light. The stained-glass windows glowed like fine jewels. White wicker chairs situated along the porch invited a person to sit back and relax, to enjoy the view of the blue-toned mountains rising above the valley.

Had his mother sat and rocked on that very porch? Explored these gardens?

Reaching out, he fingered the velvet bloom of a purple hyacinth. Of course she had. Lucinda had been born in one of the upstairs rooms, had spent the first eighteen years of her life here. Until his father had happened into town and turned her life upside down. He frowned. No good would come of revisiting his mother's unhappiness and regrets. Releasing the petals, he turned and continued walking in the opposite direction of the house, purposefully moderating his steps.

He concentrated on his breathing. Blanking his mind, the heavy feeling in his chest slowly began to recede. The air here was fresh and clean. Pleasant, even. A far cry from the humid, salty tang of New Orleans, the rush of the mighty Mississippi and steamboat blasts and lusty cries of the dock workers. His home.

Over the course of the past year, Lucian had learned to avoid his darker emotions, to push aside grief and loss instead of dealing with it. A coward's way, he admitted. But it meant survival. And right now, that was his only goal. To keep his head above the waters of disappointment and disillusionment that was his life.

This house and all it represented threatened to suck him under. He could not—*would not*—allow that to happen. He would sell it to the first reasonable bidder, no matter if it was at a loss. Money was not the issue here. Ridding himself of this burden was. The sooner the better.

Quiet footfalls against the stones registered behind him. Megan O'Malley.

Wearing that filmy, bridal-like gown, with flowers intertwined in the white-blond curls hanging nearly to her waist, she seemed to him a sort of woodland fairy, as insubstantial as a dream or a figment of his imagination. He blinked, wishing her far from here. But she kept coming, her movements graceful and fluid. She was beautiful, radiant even, with dewy-fresh skin that invited a man's touch. Inquisitive eyebrows arched above large, expressive eyes the color of the sea. Straight, flawless nose. Lips full and sweet like a ripe peach.

In New Orleans high society, Megan O'Malley would be a much sought-after prize. Thankfully, he'd learned his lesson where innocent-seeming beauties were concerned. He was immune.

The determined jut of her chin gave him pause. Made him wonder if she was going to prove an obstacle to his plans.

Boots planted wide, he clasped his hands behind his back. "Story time over already?"

"I cut it short today. I saw the last child out myself, so there's no need to worry you might bump into one later." Amusement hovered about her mouth, but her eyes were watchful. "So, what do you wish to speak to me about?"

He gestured to the metal bench to his right. "Would you like to have a seat?"

"No, thank you. I'd rather stand."

"As you wish. Miss O'Malley, I'm not sure exactly what sort of arrangement you had with my grandfather, but I'm afraid it must come to an end. You see, I'm here to oversee the sale of this property, and in order to do that, the house must be kept in excellent condition for potential buyers. I can't have strangers, especially children, traipsing in and out doing who knows what sort of damage. I'm sure you understand my predicament."

"Actually, I don't." Her pale brows collided. "Charles assured me that the children, and indeed the townspeople, would always have access to his home. In addition to the weekly story times, we host once-monthly performances open to the community."

"He meant while he was alive—"

"No." She shook her head, curls quivering. "He meant *always*. In those last months when he was growing weaker, he spoke of how he wanted our endeavors to continue after his d-death." Her blue eyes grew dark and stormy, her distress a palpable thing.

Lucian couldn't help but be suspicious. What had been her true motivation for befriending the old man? Had she assumed that, because of the rift in their family, neither he nor his father would come to claim the house? That after Charles's death, she would have unlimited access to it?

"Must you sell?" She stepped closer, tilted her head

back to gaze imploringly up at him. "Charles wouldn't
have wanted it to go to strangers."

"What he wanted is no longer relevant," he retorted,
years of animosity born of rejection rising up within
him. His only grandfather hadn't wanted anything to
do with him, so why should he care about the man's
wishes? "I am the owner now, and I will do as I see fit."

Sidestepping her, he stalked back towards the house
to order his valet to unpack enough clothing for the next
week. Hopefully, that was all the time it would take to
find a buyer.

"What kind of unfeeling man are you?" Megan called
out after him, voice shimmering with indignation.

Lucian stopped dead in his tracks. Pivoted on his
heel. Smiled a cold smile. "Unfeeling? How I wish that
were the case! For without feelings, one could avoid a
plague of problems, wouldn't you agree? Good evening,
Miss O'Malley."

He left her there in the garden to see herself out, lips
parted and eyes full of reproach. If he felt a pinprick of
remorse for his less-than-stellar manners, he shoved it
aside. This wasn't about her. This was about unloading emotional entanglements. He couldn't allow her or
anyone else to distract him from his goal.

Chapter Two

Megan hesitated before the imposing mahogany-and-stained-glass door, her finger hovering above the doorbell. Gone was the eager anticipation that had marked her past visits to Charles's home. Now there was only sadness. And dread. That Lucian Beaumont's behavior had marred her pleasant memories of this place stoked her ire.

In her left hand, she clutched the missive that had been delivered to her cabin shortly before lunch. What could he possibly have to say to her? He'd made his intentions plain last night. Charles's wishes meant nothing to him. Though it was a stretch, she could somewhat understand why he wouldn't care about helping her or the townspeople. They were strangers, after all. But Charles was family. His only grandfather.

A grandfather he hadn't bothered to come and meet, despite repeated invitations to do so.

Recalling the anguish in her friend's eyes as he spoke of his failed attempts to bring his daughter and grandson back to Gatlinburg, Megan blinked away tears. Nursed the grudge she'd harbored towards his estranged family. Knowing what she did, she shouldn't be surprised by Lucian's selfish disregard of everyone else's needs but his own.

The door swung inward, and there stood the object of her turmoil, looking coolly refined in a chocolate frock coat, tan vest and pants, and the ever-shiny black Hessians. Her gaze was drawn once again to his hair, the dark, unruly waves at odds with his neat clothing and stiff manner.

His black gaze bored into her, making her want to squirm. "Miss O'Malley, I see you received my message."

Walking past him into the entrance hall, she was glad she'd chosen to wear one of her best outfits, a deep blue fitted jacket with layered skirts that skimmed the tips of her boots. Her mass of curls, too heavy to be piled on top of her head, was restrained at her nape with a matching ribbon.

"No princess attire today?"

"No, that was strictly for the children's benefit."

Glancing up, she caught him gazing at her hair with a look akin to disappointment. She blinked and it was gone. Must've been a trick of the light.

"I see."

There was that phrase again. She gritted her teeth, fairly certain Lucian Beaumont did *not* see the true picture at all, his outlook tainted by cynicism.

"You wished to see me?"

"Actually, Charles's lawyer is the one who asked for you. He arrived this morning from Sevierville and wishes to speak with us about the will." He motioned for her to precede him. "He's waiting for us in the office."

"But Charles never indicated that I'd be included. I can't imagine why he would've done such a thing."

Lucian's steady gaze assessed her. Perhaps gauging her sincerity? "You indicated the two of you were close. Most likely he wanted to leave you some things to remember him by. Your favorite books, for instance."

Megan's thoughts were a jumble as they passed through the hallway to the rear corner of the house where the office was located. She hadn't spent much time there, as she and Charles had preferred to use the library or, weather permitting, the back porch or gardens. Like the rest of the house, this room was richly appointed with dark wood furniture and plush throw rugs. However, there were personal touches here. Artifacts from his travels littered his desk. Photographs lined the bookshelves. Even his scent lingered in the air, a blend of sandalwood and lemon. For the second time that afternoon, Megan blinked away moisture gathering in her eyes.

"Mr. McDermott," Lucian addressed the man standing at the window, "may I introduce Miss Megan O'Malley?"

The distinguished older man smiled a greeting as he moved behind the desk. "How do you do, Miss O'Malley? I'm pleased you could join us. Won't you have a seat so we can begin?"

She looked to Lucian, who indicated she take one of the two chairs facing the desk. On the low table between them rested a silver tea service.

"I had Mrs. Calhoun prepare a pot of Earl Grey," he commented as he lowered his tall frame into the chair beside her. "Would you care for some?"

"Yes, please." Hopefully the warm liquid would

ease the sudden dryness in her throat. But when she attempted to pour herself a cup, her trembling hands managed to spill the brew, splashing it onto the tray and table. "Oh," she gasped, embarrassment flooding her cheeks.

Half expecting Lucian to react with irritation, she caught her breath when he stilled her attempts to mop it up with his large hand covering hers, slipping the napkin from her suddenly nerveless fingers to do the job himself. Then he poured her a second cup, adding sugar and cream when she indicated her preferences.

"Here you are." His enigmatic gaze met hers briefly as he settled the cup and saucer into her hands. "I believe we're ready now, Mr. McDermott."

"Charles summoned me here approximately six months before his death to add a stipulation to his will."

Beside her, Lucian went as still as a statue. Tension bracketed his mouth. "What sort of stipulation? I was under the impression from your letter that the house is mine."

Mr. McDermott nodded. "Indeed, it is, Mr. Beaumont. However, there's a condition attached." His thoughtful gaze settled on Megan. "As you are aware, he and Miss O'Malley were involved in various community projects. Charles felt strongly that these should continue under her guidance after his death."

Megan quickly swallowed her mouthful of tea and set it aside before she dropped it on her lap. The storm brewing on Lucian's face was on the verge of being unleashed, tempering her anticipation. This was not going to be pretty.

"Get to the point, McDermott," he practically growled.

"If you do not allow her to continue use of the house as stated in the will, you will forfeit and ownership will transfer to Miss O'Malley."

Megan's mouth fell open.

Lucian clutched the chair's armrests, knuckles white with strain. Megan sensed his control on his temper was slipping. "That's ludicrous!" he pushed through clenched teeth. "How am I supposed to sell it, then? What potential buyer would agree to have their house available to the whole town?"

"Not many, I agree—" the lawyer began gathering his papers into a neat pile "—but then, Charles didn't intend for you to sell it. He wanted to keep it in the family."

"She's not family," he gritted out.

"True, but it was plain to see he cared a great deal about her. If you refused to honor his wishes, at least it would go to someone close to him. Mr. Beaumont, I got the feeling that your grandfather wanted you to stick around for a little while. Maybe he thought the town would grow on you and that you'd decide to stay."

His grip on the armrests tightened. It was a wonder the wood didn't snap in two. "That will never happen."

Standing and rounding the desk, the lawyer shook her hand and nodded at Lucian. "Yes, well, it would seem the two of you have much to discuss. I'll let myself out. Good day."

Battling outrage and disbelief, Lucian shoved to his feet, paced to the fireplace and leaned his weight against the marble mantel, his back to the room. He'd known the old man was controlling and manipulative, but this… Closing his eyes, he forced himself to take deep, calming breaths. The tightness was returning to his chest.

He didn't have to hear Megan's approach to sense her nearness. The faint scent of roses wafted over. "Lucian—"

He stiffened at the soft, irrationally pleasing sound of his name on her lips.

"Mr. Beaumont," she began again, "I had no idea what Charles was planning. I realize this will make things difficult—"

"You mean impossible," he interrupted, turning to face her. "He's made it impossible for me to sell this house." He fisted his hands. "I don't know exactly what he expected me to do. I have a life waiting for me back in New Orleans. I can't stay here indefinitely."

Her brow furrowed. "I can't claim to know his reasons, but I'm certain it wasn't his goal to make things difficult for you. That wasn't his way."

"Oh, wasn't it? He certainly made things difficult for my mother when he cut her out of his life."

He'd witnessed her tears, the brokenness caused by Charles's need to control those around him. Even now, he was attempting to control Lucian from beyond the grave. Unbelievable.

"Is that why you never came?" she demanded, eyes brimming with accusation. "Because you couldn't forgive him for what he did to your mother?"

"How could I forgive someone who wasn't sorry?" He didn't tell her Charles hadn't wanted him here. It was too painful to put into words.

"But he *was* sorry." She took a step forward, intent on convincing him. "He regretted pushing her away, I know it."

For a second, Lucian got lost in her impossibly blue

eyes. She seemed to sincerely believe what she was saying. He, on the other hand, wasn't that naive.

"It hardly matters now," he pushed out. "They're both gone. And I'm left here to deal with the whims of a manipulative old man."

She bristled. "Since you're obviously so eager to leave, why don't you?"

"You'd like that, wouldn't you? Me out of the way so you can be free to come and go as you like? That was probably your goal all along. Why else would a young lady like yourself willingly spend time with a man three times her age?"

The color waned and surged in her cheeks, and when she spoke, he had to strain to hear her. "Your accusations are not those of a gentleman, sir. Charles was a fine man. Good and wise and generous. He was like a grandfather to me, something you couldn't come close to understanding."

Whirling away, she strode from the room with her head held high. Lucian sagged against the wall. What was supposed to have been a relatively short and simple visit to East Tennessee was proving to be anything but.

At the conclusion of the church service, Megan and her sisters, Nicole and Jane, joined their good friends, Cole and Rachel Prescott, in the shade of a sugar maple's sprawling branches. The Prescotts' one-year-old daughter, Abby, grinned at Megan and extended her arms, wanting to be held. The sweet little girl had captured her heart the moment she was born. Megan supervised her from time to time, and she liked to think of herself as a favorite auntie. Taking her from Cole, she hugged her close. It wasn't Abby's fault that her dark hair and eyes reminded her of a certain haughty gentleman.

Her heart squeezed, remembering Lucian's hurtful words and the blazing suspicion in his eyes. She'd spent a restless night, reliving their conversation again and again. He was a hard man. Arrogant and close-minded.

"So what do you think Mr. Beaumont will do?" Concern marked Rachel's expression.

Megan shrugged. "I don't know. He doesn't want to stay, yet he won't agree to leave me in charge." She gave a dry laugh. "And the last thing he'd want is for the house to go to me. He doesn't trust my motives."

Cole's hazel eyes turned quizzical. "What motives would those be?"

"He thinks the only reason I spent time with Charles was to ultimately gain control of the house, like I'm some kind of opportunist."

Fifteen-year-old Jane placed a comforting hand on her shoulder. "We all know that's not true. Despite his advanced years, I found Charles a delight to be around. He always had interesting things to say." Sometimes Jane and Kate, their cousin Josh's wife, had accompanied Megan on her visits.

Rachel nodded, pushing her heavy sable waves behind her shoulders. "The man is obviously hurting, and he's lashing out at you."

"But he doesn't even know me," Megan exclaimed, inexplicably bothered by this stranger's poor opinion of her. "He just assumes the worst."

Cole placed an arm around his wife's shoulders. "His attitude has nothing to do with you, Megan. Something in his life has skewed his thinking. If he spent a little time with you, he'd quickly come to see his error."

Megan wasn't so sure. Lucian seemed to *want* to believe her capable of such underhanded behavior. And anyway, it wasn't as if he was going to stick around long enough for it to matter. The only time the two of them would be spending together would be to figure out this mess.

Seventeen-year-old Nicole, who'd been leaning against the tree trunk with a bored expression, straightened and brushed off her bottle-green dress. "I'm starving. Can we leave now?"

Megan was used to her younger sister's sour attitude, but it had gotten steadily worse since their mother, Alice, and Jane's twin, Jessica, had departed last week for Cades Cove. Their oldest sister, Juliana, was due to deliver her first baby any day now. Of course, they'd all wanted to go, but there simply wasn't enough room in her sister's cabin. Too many people milling about would overwhelm the new parents, anyway.

She aimed a reproving frown her way. "If you'd rather not wait for us, you're welcome to go on ahead."

Jane, ever the diplomat, offered to go with her.

Megan watched the two girls, so different in both appearance and temperament, head arm in arm down Main Street. Then her gaze encountered her friend, Tom Leighton, striding in her direction wearing a determined look.

With a smile at Rachel and Cole, she returned Abby to their arms. "I guess I should go, as well. I'm keeping you from your lunch."

"No, you're not—" Rachel smiled as she spoke "— but I can see a certain gentleman is intent on snagging your attention. Whenever you need to talk, our door is always open. Come over anytime."

"Thanks, I appreciate that."

Megan watched the couple stroll to their wagon, Cole holding Rachel close to his side, his smile bright enough to rival the sun. She was thrilled to see her friends happy at long last. Cole and Rachel had very nearly lost each other, but God had brought them back together in their darkest hour.

"Megan, I'm glad I caught you."

"Hello, Tom." She smiled at the tall and lean barbershop owner, genuinely happy to see him. His easygoing personality made it easy to relax in his presence. "How are you, today?"

"Better now that I'm talking to you." He grinned, dimples flashing. "Josh invited me to join you for lunch at his parents' house. Care to walk with me?" He held out his arm.

She felt a flash of momentary irritation. Her cousin Josh insisted on pushing his best friend and her together, and she didn't like it one bit. While Tom was an extremely nice man, she wasn't interested in more than friendship. There was no spark, only casual affection.

Growing up, she'd envisioned a dashing hero, her own personal knight in shining armor sweeping into her life and fulfilling all her childhood dreams. Older and, she hoped, wiser at twenty years of age, she realized the impossibility of those expectations. No man could be *everything* she needed and desired. God alone could be her all in all. Still, the romantic, idealistic side of her hoped for a man who would challenge her, thrill her, cherish her.

So far, that man had yet to materialize. She was beginning to fear he never would.

Suppressing a shudder, she met Tom's hopeful gaze. "I'd love to, but I'm going home for lunch."

"Are you sure I can't change your mind?" His smile held a tinge of disappointment.

"Not this time." She wasn't in the mood for a crowd today, even if it was family. Her mind was too full of Lucian Beaumont.

"All right, but at least let me walk with you part of the way." He lifted his hat and fluffed his brown hair, a habit that left him looking like a ruffled little boy. An adorable one, at that. How could she refuse him?

Placing her hand in the crook of his arm, she smiled her thanks. His conversation managed to distract her, at least until they passed the turnoff for Charles's house. What was Lucian doing right this minute? Had he decided how he was going to handle the stipulation?

Friday would be upon them before they knew it. If he was not planning on honoring Charles's wishes, she needed to know sooner rather than later. The children deserved to be told ahead of time, as did the people preparing for the poetry recital coming up. She would visit him first thing in the morning, she decided. No reason to delay what would surely be an unpleasant confrontation.

If Lucian Beaumont thought he could run roughshod over her and this town, she would soon prove him wrong.

Chapter Three

Rounding the curve in the tree-lined lane leading to Charles's house, Megan was presented with an unobstructed view of the gardens spreading out behind it. Against the backdrop of gray skies, the lush grasses seemed greener than usual, the vibrant flower patches more vivid. Tree branches swayed in the rain-scented breeze.

And there, in the midst of everything, sat the lord of the manor. Eating his breakfast and perusing a newspaper as if he hadn't a care in the world. And looking entirely too at home, she thought peevishly. He was a worldly-wise gentleman, wealthy beyond belief and accustomed to the conveniences of city life. He didn't belong in her quaint mountain town.

Determination spurred her across the lawn.

When he noticed her approach, he set aside the paper and stood up, his expression carefully neutral. "To what do I owe the pleasure of this visit, Miss O'Malley?"

His voice, like sweet tea and molasses rolled into one, shouldn't please her, but it did. His accent was deeper than hers, almost like a song with its French undertones. She wondered what it would sound like if he was actually happy.

She stopped a distance away, the round, white metal table between them. "We don't stand on formality here. Why don't you call me Megan?"

"As you wish, Megan. Please, call me Lucian." His eyes seemed to impossibly darken. He gestured at the food spread out on the table. "Have you eaten? You're welcome to join me."

His invitation was born out of politeness, no doubt ingrained from birth. It was clear he didn't really wish to dine with her.

"No, thank you. I've already had breakfast." If you could call a cup of coffee breakfast. She couldn't eat when she was nervous.

"Some tea, then?"

"Yes, thank you."

Coming around to her side, he scooted out the chair for her and poured her tea, stirring in cream and two spoons of sugar.

"You remembered," she blurted.

"Yes" was all he said as he placed it in front of her.

When he was seated, he rested one arm on the table, the other fisted on his hip in a relaxed position, waiting for her to explain the reason for her visit. His black gaze was too direct, sharp, for her to be at ease. His masculine appeal didn't help matters.

Smoothing her skirts, she took a calming breath. "I came this morning because I'd like to know what you've decided about the house."

"I haven't yet."

"Until you do, are you going to allow the story times to continue?"

"Do I have a choice?" he responded evenly, one dark brow arched.

Megan truly didn't want to goad him, to argue, so she said nothing. Sipped her tea.

"Tell me, *mon chou,* why is this so important to you? Reading to other people's children?" His gaze swept her curls, which she'd again restrained with a single ribbon. "Dressing like a princess?"

"What did you call me?"

Lucian looked startled, as if he'd made a slip. He waved it aside. "Later. For now, I'd like to hear your answer."

Perhaps Kate knew French and could tell her what he'd said. An heiress from New York City, she must've learned other languages.

"Living off the land is hard work. As early as four or five years of age, children begin helping with chores. Depending on each family's situation, there can be little time for a child to relax and just be a child. In addition to this, many families can't afford books. Since Charles has a vast collection and ample space, he and I decided the children would benefit from a weekly story time. Not only would it be fun for them, but also educational." She leaned forward, warming to her topic. "Books expand horizons. They entertain, inspire and enrich lives. I enjoy reading to them. Dressing the part merely adds to the experience."

"And the strawberry tarts and lemonade? What purpose do they serve?"

She smiled then. "Incentive for them to sit still and listen. Treats are reserved for those children who behave."

"I see."

That phrase again. She wanted to shake him.

He was studying her, obviously trying to decide if he believed her. No one had ever doubted her sincerity before. It was not a pleasant feeling.

A raindrop splashed on her arm. Then another. She glanced up at the rain-swollen clouds overhead. "I think we're in for a shower."

The drops began to fall harder and faster.

Lucian surged to his feet and, circling the table, took hold of her hand. "Let's make a run for it!"

"The dishes—"

"Forget them," he ordered as the clouds opened up, releasing a torrent.

Tugging on her hand, they made a dash for the back porch, surging up the slippery steps to stand, breathless and soaked to the skin, beneath the sheltering roof. The rain pounded the earth in an unrelenting assault. Lucian dropped her hand. His unfathomable gaze met hers. His hair was plastered to his head, his face slick with rainwater. Megan shivered. Her white eyelet blouse clung to her body, as did her robin-egg-blue skirts. Before she could guess at his intentions, he'd shrugged out of his coat and stepped close, settling it across her shoulders and pulling it closed. His heat and exotic cologne enveloped her.

"Th-thank you."

"Are you warm enough?"

She nodded, suddenly tongue-tied.

Several wet strands clung to her face, and before she could brush them aside, his fingers were there. Warm and featherlight. His fingertips skimming her cheek set off sparks, shimmers of light through her body. Her breath hitched.

What was happening to her?

She didn't like this arrogant man, his polished manners and jaded view of life.

Thank goodness he moved away so she could breathe again. Resting one hip against the railing, he stared solemnly out at the rain. Without the formal coat, he looked more approachable. The white shirt molded to his athletic build, his biceps straining the thin material where he'd crossed his arms.

Stop staring, she chided herself. His outward appearance may be attractive, but it hid the darkness he held inside. The turmoil she'd glimpsed on his face the few times his control had slipped. Who was he, really? All she'd ever known was that he hadn't cared enough about a lonely old man to make the journey to see him before he died. That was hard to forgive.

Lucian's instincts were normally right. People in his circle tended to be shallow and self-centered, motivated by greed and the lust for power and increased social standing. He trusted no one. Not even his so-called closest friends, for he knew that if not for his wealth and the Beaumont name, they'd be gone in a second. He'd spent a lot of years wishing things were different. Eventually, he'd come to terms with the state of affairs.

Until Dominique. The seemingly innocent, sweet-natured girl had resurrected his hope, his longing for something real and pure. He'd thought she was different from the conniving, scheming vipers trying to win his favor. He was wrong. In fact, she'd turned out to be worse. Much worse. And he'd fallen for her act—hook, line and sinker.

Shoving the humiliation aside, he focused on the

blonde beauty beside him. Megan fairly radiated goodness, the depths of her sea-blue eyes clear and honest. Listening to her impassioned speech a moment ago, he could almost believe she truly cared about helping the children of this town. Was it real? Or a clever act designed to lower his guard?

"How did all this come about?" He circled a finger in the air. "With Charles, I mean."

"It started with a simple invitation to borrow books," she said as her features softened into a smile of remembrance. "He was a bit reclusive, your grandfather, coming to town only for church services and an occasional visit to the mercantile to catch up on local news. It was there that he overheard me complaining that I'd read everything I could get my hands on more than once, and that I longed for new reading material. He remarked that he had a houseful of books. I was welcome to borrow as many as I liked.

"My first few visits, he left me to my own devices. Then one day, he seemed particularly down. I joined him in the parlor—uninvited, mind you—and we wound up talking for hours. He wanted to be a writer. Did you know that?" Huddled inside his overlarge coat, her pale hair clinging to her skin, she looked small and vulnerable. Sadness tugged at her mouth.

"No, I didn't." He forced himself to look away from her, to watch the continuing storm that mirrored the one inside him.

It sounded as if she and Charles had shared a special bond. Of course he hadn't been privy to his grandfather's dreams, his likes and dislikes, or anything else remotely personal. He had never even met the man! The spurt of jealousy took him by surprise.

Why should he care? Charles had written his mother and him off years ago. They had ceased to exist in his grandfather's mind. This will stipulation only served to prove Charles's dislike, one final thrust of the dagger. It hadn't been enough to ignore Lucian during his lifetime. He'd had to go and complicate matters with this house, just to underscore his loathing.

"He tried his hand at poetry," she continued, "and he even penned a couple of short stories. I think it kept the loneliness at bay, if temporarily."

He chose to ignore the censure in her voice, the unspoken questions.

"Lucian, your grandfather was a good man. He—"

"Stop. I do not wish to discuss him anymore today."

"But—"

"Megan, don't." He shot her a warning glance.

"Fine." She jutted her chin. "Then how about we address the poetry recital coming up?"

"Poetry recital?"

"You know, when people stand up and recite poetry by rote?"

"I know what it is," he told her drily. "How many people are we talking about?"

"We average between twenty-five and thirty."

He sighed. Thirty strangers parading through his house. He didn't like it. Resented this present circumstance that was beyond his control. As empty as his life in New Orleans had become, it was his home. Comfortable and familiar. Predictable. He knew what to expect from those around him, and they him.

Frustration surged. If not for this young lady, he would've already put the house up for sale and been well on his way out of this backwoods town.

"By all means, proceed with your plans as you've always done."

Surprise flickered.

"But let me make myself clear—I plan to do everything possible to find a way around that stipulation."

She jerked her head back. Anger flashed in her eyes. "Why am I not surprised? You don't care about the children or the people of this community." Yanking off his coat, she thrust it at him, and he fumbled to catch it before it fell to the floor. "You care only about yourself—" she poked him in the chest "—what you want and what you need. Well, let me assure you, Mr. Beaumont, I will do everything I can to fight you on this."

Then, to his shock, she pivoted and dashed out into the rain. Though it had slacked off, the rain was still steady. Did she plan to run the entire way home?

"Megan!" He rushed to the top step. "Wait!"

He wasn't sure if she heard him or not. She didn't hesitate, didn't slow down, just kept going. Across the grass and down the lane, until she disappeared around the bend.

Shoving his hands through his hair, he blew out an aggravated breath. The woman was a danger to his sanity. And control? Hah! She had him so mixed up, he couldn't tell up from down.

He was beginning to wish he'd never heard of Gatlinburg, Tennessee.

Chapter Four

Lucian couldn't in good conscience allow Megan to leave without some sort of protection from the elements. Ignoring the fact he was dripping water all over the floors, he went inside in search of his umbrella. Seizing one propped against the wall, he tossed his coat on the hall table and hurried back out into the rain. There, at the end of the lane, was a flash of white and blue.

As he sprinted across the sprawling lawn, bits of mud splashed up on to his boots. His pristine, clean-as-a-whistle boots. And since, in his haste, he hadn't bothered opening the umbrella, his vest and shirt were now soaked. He ground his teeth together. If the woman had an ounce of sense…

Drawing closer, he noticed she'd slowed, her head bent and shoulders hunched. Her heavy skirts impeded her progress. His annoyance evaporated at once, and he was glad he'd followed her.

"Megan, wait!"

She ignored him. Still angry, obviously. The woman certainly had spunk. She didn't fawn all over him like the young socialites in his circle, which he found refreshing. It was growing tougher to stomach their batting eyelashes, coquettish smiles and honeyed words. Their thinly veiled attempts to garner his favor.

Megan, at least, gave the *appearance* of being straightforward with him.

Opening the umbrella, he caught her upper arm and moved to bring them both beneath its cover.

"What are you doing?" she demanded, eyes still smoldering and chin lifted in defiance.

She was strikingly beautiful, even more so when angry. With his finger, he outlined her chin, dislodging the water droplets. "Has anyone ever told you that you have a stubborn chin?"

Her lips parted. "Actually, you're the first."

Lucian dropped his hand. He really needed to stop touching her. He wasn't what one would consider an affectionate man. In fact, Dominique had complained at his lack of attention. Accused him of being an ice sculpture. He'd shrugged off her comments.

So why would he be any different with Megan? Why did he feel compelled to connect with her every time she was near?

Releasing her arm, he offered her the umbrella handle. "Take this. It doesn't look like the rain will let up anytime soon."

Her pale brows rose. "You followed me in order to give me this?"

His smile was grim. "Despite popular opinion, I'm not completely unfeeling."

"I—" She paused, her brow furrowed. "Thank you."

When she shivered, he pressed the handle into her hand. "You should go. Too much longer in this weather, and you'll become ill. Good day, *mon chou*."

He pivoted on his heel before he touched her again or made another inane remark about her person. *Not smart, Beaumont.* As the cool rain slid over his skin, he reminded himself of his purpose. He couldn't allow Megan to distract him, or worse, trick him into giving her control of the house.

As soon as he got out of these wet clothes, he was going to sit down and draft a letter to his lawyer. One way or another, he would find a way to rid himself of Charles's house and all the emotional baggage that went with it.

Friday afternoon, Jane handed Megan the basket of tea cakes. "Are you sure you don't want me to come with you? What if he's hateful?"

Megan touched the red silk jacquard scarf tied about her head. It was a bit too snug, but she didn't want to take it off. The kids would enjoy her pirate costume. She could only imagine what Lucian's reaction might be. "Lucian can be difficult, that's for sure, but he isn't hateful."

Infuriating, yes. And bewildering. The man made it practically impossible to stay mad at him! Scooping up the umbrella he'd loaned her, she recalled their exchange and how his nearness, the intensity of his black eyes, made rational thought impossible.

"Would you mind opening the door for me?"

Clearly not convinced, Jane complied. "When will we get to meet him? Do you think he'll come to church on Sunday?"

"Oh, I hope he does." Nicole looked up from her latest sewing project, violet eyes shining. "From the way you described him, Megan, he sounds like a dream.

Just think, a wealthy aristocrat in our midst. All the way from Louisiana!"

Megan couldn't help but smile at her younger sister's enthusiasm. Nicole was enamored with the idea of big-city life. As soon as she had enough money saved, she planned to open up a clothing boutique in the city of her choice.

Not Megan. She loved East Tennessee, the mountains and streams and forests. The peace and quiet, the fresh air and space to roam. To daydream. She couldn't imagine being content anywhere else.

She hesitated in the open doorway. "How about I ask him outright whether he plans to or not? That way your minds will be at ease." And hers, as well.

"Yes, do!" Nicole urged.

"Only if he's in an agreeable mood," Jane cautioned.

Lucian, agreeable? She didn't expect him to be, not with her and the children invading his territory. *I can handle whatever he dishes out. I have to. For the kids and the town.*

"I'll see you both later." She turned and headed out into the late-afternoon sunshine, soaking in the hum of life all about her. Birds chirping. Squirrels darting up and down the trees on either side of the lane. The breeze swelling through the tree canopy far above her head. Ah, spring. Her favorite time of year. If only it could last forever.

If only Charles was still here. Waiting for her and the children with eager anticipation, his weathered face smoothing into a welcoming smile, the loneliness in his eyes fading for the short time they were there. It was highly unlikely that Lucian would welcome them. If anything, he would take himself off to another part of the house in order to avoid their presence. That was fine by her. Why wouldn't it be? She didn't care one way or another.

However, standing on his front porch a quarter of an hour later face-to-face with the man, she realized that was a lie. Lucian Beaumont was not the sort of man who inspired indifference. Quite the opposite, in fact. The strong emotions he invoked within her were foreign to her experience. Sure, her sisters and cousins sometimes irritated her, but they'd never made her furious enough to want to punch something. And yes, she was naturally curious, but she'd never been driven to discover the inner workings of a person's mind. And never, ever had she felt this crazy, inexplicable, overwhelming attraction to a man.

Well, you're just going to have to control yourself, because he is not hero material. Far from it.

"Here's your umbrella." She thrust it at him, uncharacteristically flustered.

He, on the other hand, appeared coolly poised in a deep blue cutaway coat and vest, a brilliant sapphire tiepin nestled in the folds of his snowy white cravat. Black pants and his Hessians completed the ensemble. Way too formal for the occasion and even for the town, but she supposed that was the way he was accustomed to dressing in New Orleans. And he pulled it off beautifully, she had to admit. Masculine and formal. In control.

Except for the hair. There was no taming those luxurious, dark brown waves that insisted on falling forward to rest on his forehead.

"Merci." He stepped back to allow her entrance, his intense gaze sweeping her scooped-neck white blouse,

full black skirts and wide black belt that accentuated her waist. "Where's your eye patch and wooden leg?"

"Isn't this enough?" She pivoted in the entryway and indicated her scarf.

After looping the umbrella on the coat stand behind him, he settled his hands on his hips and appraised her appearance. "You need an eye patch. The wooden leg, not so much, but definitely some gold jewelry—loot from the legion of ships you've besieged." Amusement shone in the depths of his eyes.

Was he *teasing* her? Her palms began to sweat. "I'm, uh, fresh out of gold. Sorry."

"That's too bad." He tipped his head towards the basket dangling from her fingers. "May I take that for you?"

"No, thank you." She tightened her grip. She didn't want him to discover the tea cakes now and forbid the children to have them. Better to wait until the book had been read to pass them out. He wouldn't be around to intervene.

"As you wish." The amusement faded, replaced with a subtle knowing.

His open scrutiny unleashed a flurry of butterflies in her middle. "I always come half an hour early to set up the chairs and get my books in order. May I?"

"By all means." He motioned for her to precede him into the parlor on their left. Megan stopped just inside the room.

"I took the liberty of arranging the chairs for you."

"Oh."

"This is the way it was set up last week." He stood close beside her, his exotic scent stirring the air. "Did you prefer it done another way?"

"This is fine. I—"

"Well, hello there, Miss Megan." Mrs. Calhoun entered the parlor bearing a tray of delicate-looking pastries and fresh strawberries. "Doesn't this look delectable? I was all prepared to make a batch of sugar cookies when Mr. Lucian suggested I do something special. I'm so glad he did. The children will enjoy these."

Mouth hanging open, Megan's gaze followed the older woman's movements. *Lucian* suggested? But—

Mrs. Calhoun spotted her basket and pointed. "Oh, what do you have there? More goodies?"

"Y-yes." She avoided looking at Lucian. "My sister and I baked tea cakes."

"That's wonderful," she said, bustling over to take it from Megan, "they'll go fast." To Lucian, she said, "That Jane O'Malley has a way with food. Her twin, too. Whenever there's a church social, folks flock to the table to try and snag a sampling of their desserts. There's never enough to go around, though."

When they were alone once more, Megan finally looked at him. Spread her hands wide. "I don't understand. Why are you being so…agreeable?"

Folding his arms across his wide chest, the corners of his mouth turned down. "Just because I don't happen to like the situation I find myself in doesn't mean I should make things difficult for you. What did you expect I would do? Blockade the door?"

"No, not that." She shook her head. "But neither did I think you would help me."

His dark brows winged up. "My grandfather didn't?"

"He was too feeble to do any heavy lifting," she said defensively. "As to the other preparations, he left everything to me and Mrs. Calhoun. Which was fine by me," she rushed to add.

Dropping his arms to his sides, Lucian's expression turned pensive. "I must inform you that I've written my lawyer asking him to find a way around the stipulation."

She wasn't surprised. Still, disappointment spiraled through her, as did a prick of anxiety. "I doubt he'll be successful."

But what if he somehow found a way? A loophole of some sort?

"We'll have to wait and see, won't we?" His gaze flicked to the window behind her. "For now, it appears you have an early arrival."

Turning, she spotted Ollie Stevenson trudging up the lane, gesturing and talking to himself. She suppressed a mischievous smile. "Would you care to greet him? I have to retrieve my book from the library."

"Me?" He followed on her heels. "How about I go and get Mrs. Calhoun?" A slight undercurrent of anxiety wove through his words.

With a dismissive gesture, she shot over her shoulder, "She's busy getting the drinks. Don't worry, Ollie doesn't bite. Not often, anyway."

Leaving him behind, she heard him mutter something about her enjoying this. A thrill lightened her step. Upsetting Lucian's reserve could become addictive. Good thing he couldn't see the wide grin splitting her face.

Lucian had initially intended to secrete himself in Charles's study for the duration of the evening. Those plans changed. Megan knew children made him uncomfortable and yet she'd purposefully left him to face the unpredictable creatures alone. Well, two could play at that game.

One arm propped against the mantel, he couldn't stop a satisfied smile as he recalled her dumbfounded reaction to his announcement that he'd be sticking around to observe story time. If her frequent, darting glances his direction were any indication, his presence made her nervous. Good. Served her right.

Ollie, the precocious, persistent seven-year-old whose earlier stream of chatter had given Lucian a headache, kept raising his hand despite Megan's calm assurances that there'd be time to ask questions later. He had to hand it to her, the woman had a seemingly endless supply of patience. And she was an adept storyteller. Her lilting, musical voice pulled one into the adventure, her enthusiasm transferring itself to the audience.

Watching her, Lucian's gaze was naturally drawn to her white-blond hair. Rays of waning sunlight slanted through the window to glisten in the loose curls, and his fingers itched to bury themselves in the silken mass. *Careful, Beaumont. She's as pretty as a picture, for sure, but you've no idea what lies beneath the surface. Remember Dominique.*

How could he ever forget? She'd convinced him of her sincere affection, had even claimed to love him, while all along she'd been biding her time. Holding out for the true prize—his father. Why settle for the son of a shipping magnate when she could have the man with all the power?

His chest seized up, and he absentmindedly rubbed a flat palm over his heart in an effort to soothe away the discomfort. The smothering sensation had started not long after his mother's death a year ago. Had worsened a few months later with Dominique's trickery. Being in this house didn't help. There was no escaping his grandfather's indifference and worse, the constant reminders of his mother and the fact she was lost to him forever.

When he glanced up and caught Megan looking at him with concern creasing her brow, he dropped his hand. There was nothing to worry about. At least, that was the family physician's conclusion, who'd declared Lucian fit as a fiddle. Mentioned something about anxiety and getting more rest. Right. Lucian wasn't one to sit around. When he wasn't working in the shipping offices or attending social functions, he was at the country estate, hunting and fishing and assisting his staff with repairs and the like. Lately he'd entertained passing thoughts of leaving the city behind to take up permanent residence there. But the prospect of rattling around in that big manor all alone stopped him from seriously considering it.

Just then, a small hand slipped into his, startling him out of his reverie.

Straightening, he stared down into the pixie face of a little girl he'd noticed simply because she reminded him of Megan with her long blond hair and big blue eyes.

"I'm Sarah." She didn't smile, only studied him with a seriousness that unnerved him.

Lucian glanced around the parlor, belatedly realizing Megan had finished the book. She and the parents were assisting the children swarming the dessert table.

"Uh, hello."

What did one say to a child? Her warm fingers clutched his, and he marveled at their fragility. If he had to guess, he'd say she was about five or six.

"What's your name?"

"I'm Lucian."

She scrunched up her nose, which only made her look more adorable. "Huh?"

Squatting to her level, he repeated, "My name is Lucian."

Reaching out, she touched the tip of her finger to his sapphire tiepin. "That's sparkly. I like pretty things. Can I have it?"

He cleared his throat to cover a chuckle. There was no guile in this little one's eyes, merely simple curiosity. "Well, I doubt you would have use of it. It's for gentlemen, and you are a lady."

She seemed to ponder that for a minute. He held his breath, wondering what he'd say if she insisted. He had no experience with this sort of thing.

"Are you Mr. Charles's son?"

He jerked his head back at the unexpected question. "No. I'm his grandson."

Tilting her head, a tiny line appeared between her fine eyebrows. "Mr. Charles was a nice man. Are you nice, too?"

Lucian sucked in a breath.

"Sarah," Megan said as she appeared at their side and placed a gentle hand on the little girl's shoulder, "wouldn't you like a treat? They're going fast."

With a nod, Sarah slipped her hand from his and hopped to the table without a backward glance. Lucian stood, grateful for the intervention and wondering what Megan had seen in his face that had induced her to take mercy on him. Could she read his moods that easily?

"She didn't intend to make you uncomfortable."

"I know." He watched her at the table, solemnly debating what to put on her plate. "Is she always that serious?"

A heavy sigh escaped her. "She's had a rough year. Her ma died in childbirth, as did the baby. Her father hasn't coped well."

Lucian's mouth turned down. Such a tragic loss couldn't be easy for a young child to process. His gaze returned to Megan to find her studying him with an inscrutable expression. One pale brow quirked.

"So, are you?"

"Am I what?"

Her voice went soft. "Are you a nice man?"

He exhaled. "That's impossible for me to answer, Megan."

She stepped closer, smelling of roses and, more faintly, strawberries. He clasped his hands behind his back, away from temptation.

"Well, I'll answer it, then. I think you *are* nice."

His jaw went slack. Pleasure reverberated through him, followed quickly by misgivings. "I'm astonished you'd say that, considering."

"You're simply acting under false assumptions concerning your grandfather." Her blue eyes darkened. "And me."

"Is that so?" He fought the pull of her innocent appeal.

"Don't go all haughty on me," she challenged, not in the least fazed. "We're going to have to discuss this sometime." Her mouth softened as genuine confusion settled on her face. "I'd really like to know why you didn't come to see him. You don't strike me as someone who'd deliberately hurt another person."

Lucian didn't often find himself without a ready response. Megan thought he was nice? If that was her true opinion, then she was one of the most charitable women he'd ever met. So was she really that bighearted? Or just very clever?

Chapter Five

Megan could tell she'd shocked him. No doubt he wasn't accustomed to anyone questioning his behavior, especially females. New Orleans socialites likely tripped all over themselves to gain his favor, to be linked with such a man as he—wealthy, influential, articulate, *gorgeous*. Not her. She may be a romantic at heart, but she wasn't about to allow herself to be impressed by superficial charms.

She wanted to know the man beneath the brooding reserve and smooth manners. His innermost thoughts and feelings. His motivations. And she wasn't sure if that was possible, or even wise.

Abbott and Ivy Tremain, grandparents of one of the kids, took the silence stretching between them as a sign to interrupt.

"Mr. Beaumont," Abbott interjected, thrusting out his hand, "it's an honor to finally meet you."

As Abbott introduced himself and his wife, Lucian shook his hand and nodded to Ivy. "Likewise. Please, call me Lucian."

Was Megan the only one who noticed the tension

jumping along his jaw? She mentally kicked herself. She shouldn't have brought up the volatile subject while the house was crawling with guests.

"Lucinda, Ivy and I grew up together. Your mother was a delightful girl. Fun to be around."

"Oh, yes." The attractive brunette nodded with a nostalgic smile. "She was as sweet as could be. Growing up, she never caused Charles a bit of trouble, and so we were all taken by complete surprise when she up and ran off with Gerard. Terrible time, that was."

Megan's stomach dropped to the floor. Lucian's face appeared carved in stone, his eyes as black as the forest on a moonless night. Beneath the blue coat, his shoulders went rigid.

Oblivious to his turmoil, Abbott continued, "Charles was never the same after that, was he, my dear?"

She shook her head sadly. "He missed her something fierce. I know a lot of folks around here hoped she'd come back and visit, but she never did."

"But we're glad Charles's grandson is here, at long last," the older man said with a grin. "How long are you in town for?"

Megan held her breath. Would he tell them about the will stipulation? If he did, the whole town would be buzzing about it within the hour.

"I'm not certain." Their gazes locked, but she couldn't tell what he was thinking. "For a couple of weeks, at least."

"Good, good. It's awful nice of you to continue your grandfather's traditions. The children really enjoy themselves when they come here." Abbott cocked his head at Megan. "This young lady is a gifted storyteller."

Lucian's dark brows met in the middle. "Yes, she certainly is."

Now, why didn't that sound like a compliment?

"She's going to make some lucky man a fine wife someday," Ivy piped up. The sly wink she sent Lucian's direction made Megan long to run for the door. Her cheeks grew hot. She kept her gaze trained on the colorful rug beneath her feet.

"I believe Tom Leighton's already figured that out," her husband joked.

Enough humiliation. "If you'll excuse me, I should go and help Mrs. Calhoun with the cleanup."

Leaving them to their conversation, she attempted to bury her embarrassment by seeing to the children's needs, wiping crumbs from sticky fingers and chocolate-rimmed mouths, refilling drinks and trying to ensure the furniture didn't get soiled. Though she refrained from looking directly at Lucian, she noticed many of the parents had drifted over to chat with him. She swallowed back concern. Was it too much to hope no one else brought up the subject of his mother?

A frown pulled at her lips. What if he found this evening so unpleasant that he did decide to blockade the door next time?

No. She sincerely believed that, despite his intentions to thwart Charles's wishes, Lucian was a good man. Misguided, definitely. A bit selfish and stubborn, maybe. But didn't everyone have faults? His actions tonight had softened her opinion of him. He didn't have to lift a finger to help her, but he'd anticipated her needs and acted accordingly. He'd suffered through Ollie's onslaught with fortitude, nodding at all the right times and answering the boy's questions with careful consideration. Watching his gentle interaction with Sarah, Megan's heart had squeezed with a curious longing. A longing she didn't dare examine.

Lucian is not responsible for these feelings, she assured herself. *It's just that, with both Juliana and Josh reveling in wedded bliss, you're dreaming of your own happy-ever-after.*

Besides, Lucian Beaumont didn't strike her as a man who believed in such a thing. He wouldn't willingly be any girl's knight in shining armor.

Lucian bade good-night to the last guest and, closing the door, sagged momentarily against it. He'd survived his first story time. While this evening had had its trying moments, there'd been interesting ones, as well. What surprised him most was how friendly everyone had been. It seemed Megan was alone in feeling betrayed by his absence all these years.

Going in search of her, he found her scooting a heavy wingback chair across the thick multihued rug towards its rightful place beside the settee. He strode to intercept her.

"I'll take it from here."

"That's all right. I'm used to doing this without help."

He placed a stalling hand on her shoulder. The warmth of her skin beneath her blouse, the slender grace of her, prickled his palm. He had the ridiculous urge to knead the stiffness from her muscles. "I don't mind. You've been on your feet for most of the night. Why don't you sit and rest for a few minutes?"

Her red scarf askew, she reluctantly nodded and, moving away from his touch, settled on the settee. Her hands folded in her lap, her gaze followed his movements as he quickly replaced all the chairs. The lamplights cast a cozy glow about the room, which, with its navy-blue-and-green accents and dark walnut woodwork, gave it a masculine feel that was echoed throughout the house. He wondered if it had ever had feminine touches, or if Charles had removed all reminders of his late wife and his absent daughter.

When he'd finished, she asked, "How do you think it went tonight?"

Standing in the middle of the rug, arms crossed, he gave her his frank opinion. "I think the kids are fortunate to have someone who's willing to give of their time and energy on their behalf."

Her chin went up. "I enjoy it." There was force behind the words.

On this point, he didn't doubt her. He'd seen her nurturing touches, the easy care of the children as if they were her own. Affection like that couldn't be faked.

"I know you do."

Surprised relief flickered in her eyes before her lashes swished down, cutting off his view. She began to pluck at the ruffles on her skirt, her trim, shiny nails winking in the light. "I noticed many of the parents made a point to introduce themselves to you. Was everyone...welcoming?"

The hitch in her voice lured him closer. *She must be thinking of the Tremains and their guileless comments.* He eased down beside her on the cushion, a respectable twelve inches away, and rested his palms on his thighs. "They were indeed."

Welcoming and genuinely glad to meet him. Effusive in their praise of Charles. He'd had trouble reconciling the man they'd described as *good as gold* with the cold,

unfeeling grandfather he'd envisioned all these years.
The discrepancy troubled him. If Charles was the man
they made him out to be, why had he ignored his own
family? If he regretted the rift he'd created with his
pigheaded stubbornness, why hadn't he come to New
Orleans and attempted to make amends? It wasn't as
if he couldn't afford to travel. And his health problems
hadn't presented themselves until recent years.

He looked up to find her studying him, trying to decipher his thoughts.

"I received several supper invitations," he continued,
"as well as a request to come to church on Sunday."

Interest bloomed in her expression. She angled towards him. "Will you come?"

"I haven't been to church in more than a year," he
admitted. "My mother and I used to attend services together. Then she became ill, and I…" He shook his head,
reluctant to think of his beloved *mère* and her swift
decline, the bloom of health stolen from her without
warning and without mercy. His wealth had garnered
her access to the best medical care available, yet in the
end, it hadn't mattered. No amount of money could've
prevented her death.

His utter helplessness had nearly destroyed him.

"I understand how it would've been difficult for you
to go, especially since it was something the two of you
did together."

Megan's compassion threw him off-kilter. He'd gotten precious little of it back in New Orleans. In the
face of his grief, his friends and acquaintances hadn't
known what to say, so they'd avoided the subject altogether. And his father, well, he'd been relieved at his
wife's passing. Gerard was finally free of the unsophis-

ticated mountain girl he'd made the mistake of marrying all those years ago. To him, her love and adoration had been a burden. An embarrassment.

His hands curled into fists. Shoving down the familiar anger and bitterness that thoughts of his father aroused, Lucian nodded. "I couldn't bring myself to go alone. Besides, all those years I'd gone in order to make her happy. After her passing, there didn't seem to be any more reason to go."

Megan's brow furrowed in consternation. "What about deepening your relationship with God? Learning more about His Word?"

"Relationship? With God?"

"Haven't you ever shared with Him what's on your heart? Your hopes, dreams, failures? He already knows, of course, but He wants us to express it through prayer."

He'd prayed before, on occasion, but it had been brief requests for help. Nothing like what Megan was talking about. "You speak as if God cares about the details of your life. I don't see Him that way. While I believe He exists and that He created this world for our use and pleasure, I find it difficult to imagine He'd bother Himself with our problems."

"David wrote in Psalms, 'O Lord, you have searched me and you know me. You know when I sit and when I rise; you perceive my thoughts from afar. You are familiar with all my ways. Before a word is on my tongue you know it completely, O Lord.' Does that sound like a God who can't be bothered with us?"

The gentle curve of her smile, the utter lack of judgment in her eyes, compelled him to be truthful. "It sounds like you're much better acquainted with the Scriptures than I am. In fact, I can't recall the last time I opened a Bible." He thought of his mother's black Bible tucked safely in his trunk, a tentative link that eased somewhat the ache of her absence.

"It's not too late to start," she said encouragingly.

His gaze fell on a small portrait on the side table, one he hadn't noticed before. Standing, he stepped around her and picked it up, fingers tight on the gilt frame. His grandparents, Charles and Beatrice, in the prime of their lives. And his mother, who looked to be about eight years old, dressed in a simple dress and her dark hair in pigtails. She wasn't smiling. No one really did for portraits. But her eyes were clear of the familiar shadows, and curiosity marked her rounded face. How might her life have been different—better, freer, happier—if Charles had handled the whole situation differently?

"Tell me something," he said quietly, still staring at the images. "Did my grandfather believe as you do?"

"Charles loved the Lord," she answered, matching her tone to his, perhaps sensing the turn of his mood. "He tried to model his life after His teachings, a life pleasing to Him."

Replacing the frame with a bit more force than necessary, he pivoted to glower down at her, unable to mask the cold fury surging through his veins. "Then surely God wasn't pleased with his coldhearted treatment of his own daughter. And what of his only grandchild? He didn't even acknowledge my existence! Isn't there something in there about loving your neighbor as yourself?"

Surging to her feet, Megan adopted a fighting stance—shoulders back, chin up, hands fisted. A not-so-friendly pirate. "And what of your mother's behavior? She refused Charles's numerous pleas to return. He desperately wanted to meet you, Lucian. How could she deny him that? How could you?"

He snorted. Sliced the air with his hand. "What are you talking about? What pleas? The night before she married my father, Charles warned her that if she went through with it, not to bother coming back. Ever."

"Charles apologized more than once for his past behavior. He sent letters begging her to come and visit. To bring you so that he could spend time with you. Show you around town, introduce you to all the townspeople, take you fishing. She flat-out refused. Charles didn't tell me why."

Lucian turned away, shoved a frustrated hand through his hair. No. No, this couldn't possibly be true. His mother wouldn't have hidden such a thing from him.

"I don't know anything about any letters," he ground out.

He startled when her fingers curled around his biceps, a slight pressure. "Lucian—"

The chime of the doorbell derailed her train of thought. "Would you like me to get that for you?"

"No." He straightened, and her hand fell away. "I'll get it."

He didn't recognize the brown-haired, green-eyed man on the other side of the door. "Good evening. May I help you?"

He looked to be about the same age as himself, maybe a year or so younger, and was dressed like the local men in casual pants, band-collared shirt and suspenders. While his expression was pleasant, his eyes were assessing, his fingers crushing the brim of his hat he held at his waist.

"Evenin'. The name's Tom Leighton. I own the barbershop on Main." He stuck out his hand. "You must be Charles's grandson."

He shook his hand. "Lucian Beaumont."

"Pleased to meet you." His gaze searched the entryway. "Is Megan still here? I came to walk her home."

"Yes, she is." Lucian stepped back and motioned him inside. "She's in the parlor."

Following Leighton, Lucian ignored a twinge of dislike. He had absolutely no grounds for such a reaction. He didn't even know the man. *It bothers you that he appears to have a relationship with Megan.* The banker let slip earlier that Tom Leighton saw Megan as a prospective wife. Question was, how did she feel about that? Did she want to marry the barbershop owner? Were they courting?

As the two exchanged greetings, Lucian watched her expression carefully. Was her smile a bit forced? Her eyes a little tight? Or was he being ridiculous? He puffed out an irritated breath. Definitely ridiculous.

He had absolutely no romantic interest in this woman. Or any other woman, for that matter. The misery of his parents' mockery of a marriage had carved deep scars on his heart, creating within him an aversion to anything resembling an intimate relationship. He would not repeat their mistakes. He would marry because it was expected of him to produce heirs and further the Beaumont legacy. For duty and social connections, not fickle emotions or fleeting attraction.

He'd had a near miss with Dominique. Had begun to entertain the notion that perhaps pure love could exist for him, that he wouldn't have to endure a marriage that was more business arrangement than anything else.

Thank goodness she'd revealed her true nature before his heart had succumbed.

Watching Megan, he reminded himself of his charted course. She was a diversion, and, albeit delightful and intriguing, one he didn't want or need.

"Tom!" Megan wasn't sure why his arrival had disconcerted her. It wasn't unusual for him to show up to walk her home. She'd been so immersed in the conversation with Lucian, deeply attuned to his turmoil, that the interruption had thrown her.

"I had a couple of late customers. I wasn't sure if you'd still be here." He seemed a touch nervous, which was unlike him. He lowered his voice. "How'd it go?"

"Wonderful."

Surprise flitted across Tom's face. "Really?"

Movement beyond his shoulder meant Lucian had entered the room, holding himself back, his dark gaze hooded.

Stepping to the side in order to include him, she touched Tom's arm in a silent request for him to turn around. "You've met Lucian already?"

He nodded curtly. "Yes."

The two men regarded each other in silence. She glanced askance at her friend. He was normally talkative and friendly, even with strangers. Why was he acting like this?

She cleared her throat. "Tom is a close friend of the family. We've known each other practically from birth. He and my cousin Josh used to take great pleasure in tormenting me."

Laughter erupted from Tom, and, ignoring her arched brow, he slung an arm around her shoulders.

"Like hiding frogs in your lunch pails." Tucking her close to his side, he grinned at Lucian. "Made her so mad, she could hardly speak. But she'd eventually cool off and talk to us again. Megan and I know each other *very* well, almost as well as an old married couple. We have a lot in common."

"Sounds like it," Lucian responded drily.

Stunned and irritated by Tom's familiarity, his insinuations, Megan shrugged off his arm as unobtrusively as she could. "Well, I believe we should be going." Before he embarrassed her further.

She paused before Lucian, wishing they could've finished their conversation. Hating to leave him to deal with his confused anguish alone. Longing to reach out and comfort him. He seemed in desperate need of a hug. "Thank you for everything."

He stared at her for so long that Tom approached and took hold of her arm.

"Ready?"

She jumped, having forgotten for a split second that there was anyone else in the room besides the two of them. "Y-yes, I'm quite ready. Good evening, Lucian."

His nod was almost imperceptible, his low drawl a caress. *"Bonne nuit, mon chou."*

It wasn't until they'd reached the end of the lane that she rounded on Tom.

"Why did you do that?"

He held up his palms. "Do what?"

"You know perfectly well what." She jammed her hands on her hips. "Why did you try to make Lucian believe something about us that isn't true?"

Grasping her upper arms, he peered down at her with

an intensity he rarely displayed, making her stomach clench with dread.

"I can't deny that I *want* it to be true. Surely you know by now how I feel about you, Megan." His green eyes blazed with conviction. "I would like to court you properly."

Megan squeezed her eyes tight. What could she say that wouldn't hurt his feelings? She'd been so careful not to encourage him!

"If you don't open your eyes, I'm going to take it as an invitation to kiss you."

"Don't you dare!" Her eyes popping open, she wriggled out of his grasp and strode briskly down the lane. He easily kept pace with her but didn't speak, allowing her time to sort through her response.

When she stopped at the split-rail fence that signaled the beginning of her property, he stopped, as well, expectant.

"I can't think about this right now." She took the coward's way out, opting to delay what would be an extremely difficult task, one that would alter their friendship forever. Feeling lower than pond scum, she rushed ahead to explain, "I'm in charge of my sisters while Momma is away, you know. This is the first time in the twins' entire lives that they've been apart, and Jane is having a tough time of it. Nicole is even more unpredictable than usual, and now I have the issue with Charles's house to contend with. I'm sorry, but I—"

"It's all right." He held up a hand. "This wasn't the best time to spring my feelings on you, but I'm not sorry it's finally out in the open. Take all the time you need."

His consideration made her feel even worse.

"Thanks, Tom," she murmured, toeing the grass with her boot.

"Just remember, I'll be waiting."

With a slight smile and a tug on his hat's brim, he turned and walked back the way they'd come, headed to his farm on the opposite side of town. Sagging against the fence, she watched until the shadowed lane swallowed him up. *I don't know what to do, God. I need to be clear with him about my feelings, but I can't bear the thought of wounding him. He's been such a dear friend.*

Friend. That's all he'd ever be. All she'd ever want him to be. Tom was easy to be with, funny and interesting, as well as dependable and an all-around great man. But he wasn't the man for her.

Thoughts of Lucian crowded in, prodding her. Sure, he could make her tremble with merely a look. Release a storm of butterflies in her tummy with the slightest touch. Stir her heart with emotion. Despite all that, he wasn't the one for her, either.

Chapter Six

Lucian missed his predictable life. His comfortable routine. Coffee and croissants in the estate gardens, mornings at the waterfront overseeing his family's shipping offices, afternoons devoted to social responsibilities and evenings dining and dancing with the upper crust of society. Every day was pretty much the same, and he liked it that way.

The inactivity here was killing him. Too much time on his hands. Time to think.

Megan's assertions had circled through his mind like ravenous vultures until the wee hours of the morning. The prospect that his grandfather hadn't been indifferent, had actually yearned to meet him, weakened the grip of resentment in his soul. But it also brought heartache and disillusionment. For if Megan was right, that meant his mother had lied to him. He couldn't bear to entertain such an idea, so he forced his thoughts elsewhere...to another tangled coil.

Tom and Megan. Megan and Tom.

He kept picturing them in his parlor, tucked together like two peas in a pod, all the while wanting to protest that *he* should be the one holding her—not some back-woods mountain man. Okay, that wasn't exactly fair. Tom Leighton seemed nice enough, appeared to honestly care about her.

These feelings have nothing to do with Megan, specifically. You're accustomed to women throwing themselves at you, and now that you've encountered one who doesn't, you don't have a clue how to react. She's a challenge, that's all. One he wouldn't pursue, for both their sakes. Not only were they from disparate worlds, they had different expectations where relationships were concerned. A man would have to be blind not to know Megan O'Malley craved what many other women in the world craved—love and romance and happy-ever-after. He'd seen it in her eyes, that starry, hopeful light not yet dimmed by betrayal or misfortune. She wanted it all… adoring husband, bouncing babies and a cozy home. He wasn't prepared to give that to anyone, especially her.

He still hadn't made up his mind about her. Whether she was the genuine article or an exceptional counterfeit.

His fingers closed over her reticule.

He'd noticed the lacy, beribboned article lying on the entryway table this morning. Megan had left in such a hurry last evening that she'd accidentally left it behind. He'd toyed with the idea of allowing his valet to return it to her, but in the end, his curiosity about her home and family had won out. Getting directions had been a simple task. As Charles Newman's grandson, the locals accepted him more readily than he expected they would a complete stranger.

Now on his way to the O'Malley farm, he found himself wondering what he'd find there. He knew nothing about her family, except that she had a cousin named Josh. Had her parents grown up with his mother? Did they, like Megan, think he was heartless for staying away all these years?

This lane was unfamiliar, the forests on either side thick and endless yet somehow welcoming.

Amid the sea of coarse bark and lush green leaves, splashes of vivid pink caught his eye. Phlox. The delicate flower blanketed the forest floor in this particular area, a pleasing respite from the verdant landscape. Farther on, yellow lady's slippers decorated a mossy slope. And later, white-and-pink painted trillium. The peaceful, majestic beauty reminded him of his estate outside New Orleans. Not that these mountains could compare to his beloved lowlands, but he felt the same sense of serenity here, of freedom and completeness, that he did there. Curious.

By the time he'd reached Megan's farm, his mind was blessedly clear.

Taking the worn path veering from the lane, he passed a fair-sized vegetable garden and a crude, open-air shelter fashioned from four sawed-off tree trunks topped with a slanting, wood-slat roof, under which sat a wagon. The barn, while sizable, had seen better days. Boards were warped or missing altogether. Beyond sat a corncrib and smokehouse in much better condition. Diagonal from the barn, its roof sheltered by the branches of a towering magnolia tree, sat a two-story, shingled-roof cabin with a long, narrow porch running the length of the dwelling. Stacked river rock formed the supports. Flowers spilled from crates on either side of the door, spots of color in the porch's shadow. Two rocking chairs waited, still and silent, for someone to relax and enjoy the view.

Nearing the barn, Megan's voice drifted out through the open doors, and he stopped to listen.

"Mr. Knightley," she all but crooned, "we can't go for another jaunt in the woods today. It's almost time for supper."

Lucian frowned. Who was Mr. Knightley? Another suitor? Treading silently, he edged closer to the shaded opening, craning his neck for a glimpse of her and her companion.

"How about tomorrow afternoon? If the weather co-operates, that is."

There was no response. Seeing a flash of her blond hair, he moved into the barn itself and saw that her Mr. Knightley was in fact a beautiful bay dun.

"Bonjour."

With a gasp of surprise, she pivoted his direction. Her eyes were huge and dark. "Lucian! I didn't hear you come in."

"That's a fine horse you have there." He advanced farther inside, noting the neatness and order, garden-ing tools and pails stacked in one corner. A dairy cow shifted in her stall as he passed. Fresh hay littered the earth floor.

When he reached her side, he placed a hand on the horse's powerful neck, inches from where hers rested. She didn't speak at first, simply stared at him as if try-ing to absorb the fact that he was actually here, on her property. The air around them shimmered suddenly with energy, sharpening his senses. She was so very close. Adrift in blue eyes that reminded him of the mysterious ocean deep, Lucian found his ability to speak failed him. As did his common sense.

He covered her hand with his own. Edged closer. Inhaled the faint rose scent that clung to her. Captured a wayward curl and wrapped it around his finger.

"Lucian?" Her whisper caressed his neck.

His heart thundered inside his chest. "Has anyone ever told you that your hair is like moonlight?" he murmured, his gaze freely roaming the silken mass. "So pale it practically glows luminescent?"

Her peach-hued lips curved sweetly. "Actually, you're the first."

That smile nearly felled him. His gaze homed in on her lush mouth, and he bent his head a fraction. Her breathing changed. He stilled.

What was he doing?

"I'm sorry. I—" What could he say? That he'd temporarily forgotten all the reasons he mustn't fall prey to her charms?

Uncoiling his finger, he put distance between them. Focused on the horse. Mr. Knightley. "I take it you're an admirer of Jane Austen? *Emma,* in particular?" Averting his face, he grimaced when his voice sounded more riled bear than human.

Megan didn't move. "Y-yes, I am as a matter of fact. You're familiar with her works?"

"You sound surprised." He dared a glance at her, watched her expression change from bemused to contemplative.

"Not surprised, exactly. *Pleased* would be a more apt term. Some men consider female authors inferior and, as such, unworthy of their attention."

"And here I thought you'd be surprised that I read at all."

Lifting a shoulder, she averted her gaze and stroked her horse's neck. "Charles mentioned he'd passed his love of books on to Lucinda. I surmised she taught you to do the same."

Lucian didn't respond. She was right, of course. His earliest memories were of sitting on his mother's lap, snug and warm, listening to bedtime stories. She'd read to him until he'd learned to do it for himself. Growing up, he'd passed countless afternoons hidden away in their estate's library, immersed in one adventure or another.

"I have to admit, I never did warm to Emma and her matchmaking. I prefer *Mansfield Park*."

"Indeed?"

"Megan—" they turned as one at the feminine intrusion barreling into the barn "—what's taking you so…long?"

The raven-haired beauty's momentum faltered when her wide-eyed gaze encountered him. She pressed a hand to her chest. "Oh, I didn't realize we had company."

Once Megan made the introductions, Lucian nodded in greeting, surprised that, besides their striking eyes, the sisters didn't share any other physical similarities. He instantly recognized the calculating gleam in Nicole's, having witnessed it in scores of other young ladies' gazes. What schemes was this young minx entertaining? He had a feeling she caused her poor parents a fair share of grief.

"Supper's on the table," Nicole announced brightly,

smoothing her lace-and-ribbon-embellished purple skirts. "Please say you'll join us, Mr. Beaumont."

He glanced at Megan, uncertain of her feelings on the matter. He wanted to accept, not because he was particularly hungry, but because his curiosity had only increased in the time he'd been here.

Her hesitation lasted a fraction of a second before good manners kicked in, and she smiled her agreement. "Yes, please do. You can meet our younger sister, Jane, and taste her fine cooking. It's simple fare," she hastened to add, "nothing like you're used to, I'm sure."

"Not all of my meals are seven-course fanfares," he said leaning towards her, a slight smile playing about his lips. "In fact, when I'm out hunting, I sometimes make do with a can of cold beans and hard biscuits."

"I can scarcely believe it," she responded with mock horror. "Lucian Beaumont, lord of the manor, eating out of a can? What would people say if they knew? I hope you at least had a fork and weren't forced to use your fingers."

Lord of the manor? Was that how she saw him? As some stuffy stick-in-the-mud?

"Well, beans aren't on the menu tonight, thank goodness!" Nicole said with relief. "Jane's fixed pot roast and all the trimmings. Let's go eat before it gets cold."

With a shrug and a smile, Megan fell into step beside him, explaining the whereabouts of her mother, Alice, and sisters Juliana and Jessica. There was no mention of a father, which meant the man had either abandoned his family or passed on. The question would have to wait until later.

Preceding Megan into the cabin, he stepped into a rectangular, low-ceilinged room crammed with furniture. Oval-backed chairs surrounded one long, chocolate-brown settee and a yellow-gold fainting couch. Two oversize hutches monopolized the wall space opposite him, while sewing baskets, fabrics and supplies occupied a low table in the far corner. To his left, impossibly steep stairs disappeared into an opening in the second floor. Beyond the living area, he glimpsed a narrow passageway that contained the dining table laden with dishes and, past that, the kitchen.

The rich aroma of succulent meat and fresh-baked bread hit him. His mouth watered. Perhaps he was hungrier than he'd thought.

As he understood it, until recently, six females had shared this cabin. That number was now at five. Despite the crowded nature of the space, they did a remarkable job of keeping it clean and clutter-free.

Auburn-haired Jane, he found, did resemble Megan to a degree. While her hair and eyes were different, she had the same cheekbones, nose and chin, though that last part lacked her older sister's stubbornness. That could be due to her young age. Jane exuded the same gentle sweetness, but she lacked Megan's spark, the inner fire that drew him unwillingly to her. *Ignore it or fight it. If you don't, you could wind up getting burned.*

Beside him at the table, she was unusually quiet. She didn't have to utter a word, however, for him to be aware of her every movement. Did she resent having him here?

He should've felt awkward, outnumbered as he was by unfamiliar females. However, the delicious meal and the younger girls' eager inquiries about city life put him at ease, as did the realization that Nicole didn't have her sights set on him. In fact, the thoughtful glances she slid between he and Megan indicated she had ideas about the two of them.

Pity she was bound to be disappointed.

Tonight Jane's pot roast didn't melt on Megan's tongue. It was difficult to chew and even harder to swallow, and it was all *his* fault. Every time Lucian shifted in his seat, his shoulder brushed hers and her stomach took a dive. Once, when his knee bumped hers, she nearly toppled her lemonade. His masculine presence filled the room, robbing her lungs of air. All she could think about was that scene in the barn. He'd almost kissed her! The worst part was the acute disappointment she'd experienced when he didn't. If anything, she should be relieved.

Kissing Lucian would have disastrous consequences. One kiss from him and she'd be planning their wedding. Risking a sideways glance, she tried to imagine him in formal black wedding clothes. His unruly waves slicked back…

Lowering her gaze to her still-full plate, she swirled the potatoes through the gravy with her fork. *Have you forgotten the children? He's made it plain he seeks to circumvent Charles's will. I guarantee he won't be quite so attractive if you have to cancel story time and explain to them that their fun is over.*

Besides, his home was hundreds of miles away. If she allowed herself to get close to him, to care for him, he'd take a part of her heart with him when he left. Could she endure that? Pining hearts made for great fiction…why else would she have pored through the pages of *Pride and Prejudice* half a dozen times? She wasn't so certain she wanted to experience it in reality.

"Megan," Jane's voice intruded, "would you like a slice of pie?"

"No, thanks." She dredged up a smile, laying her fork aside when she noticed everyone had finished. "I'll help clear the dishes."

Rising, she began to stack them.

"Jane and I will clean up," Nicole protested, rising and taking the plates from her hands. "Why don't you and Mr. Beaumont have a seat on the front porch while we dish up dessert?"

Megan stared. Nicole didn't volunteer to do anything unless it suited her purposes. What was she up to?

Lucian stood, as well, and placed a hand against his flat stomach. "That was a fine meal, ladies. I enjoyed this evening very much. Thank you for your generous hospitality."

Jane flushed. They'd all noticed he'd eagerly accepted second portions. "It was our pleasure, Mr. Beaumont."

After inviting her sisters to call him by his first name, he turned that intense focus on her, waiting for her to lead the way. Where they'd be alone again. Her nerves zinged with equal parts anticipation and dismay. Would he touch her again? She hoped not. Really, she did.

Outside, darkness blanketed the land, obscuring the distant mountain peaks. Moonlight cast the yard and outbuildings in a muted glow, glancing off the treetops while the thick forest below remained cloaked in impenetrable blackness. The nearby stream's hushed journey over and around moss-covered rocks formed a backdrop to the cicadas' calls and frogs' songs. The night air was pleasant against her skin, not too warm and not too cold. Perfect.

Lucian stared into the night, one shoulder propped against a wooden support. She moved to rest her back against the one opposite, arms crossed over her chest. She studied his proud profile, wondered if he ever truly let go and allowed himself to relax. Lost the brooding tension humming along his body.

"What's the city like at night?"

He didn't answer immediately. "The air is humid, almost sticky, and sweet with the scent of magnolias and beignets. Buggies and people roam the streets at all hours, the sounds of horses and wheels clattering over bricks, laughter and jazz flooding the night. It's a vibrant place."

If it was so wonderful, then why did he sound dissatisfied? Wistful for something else?

"What are beignets?"

"Fried dough dusted with sugar."

She smiled. "Sounds delicious."

"They are, indeed, especially when accompanied by café au lait. We use chicory in our coffee, which makes it stronger, more bitter than what I've tasted here." He angled his face to study her. "I think you'd like it there, Megan, especially the waterfront. The nonstop activity. Interesting characters. The boats and the water."

"I've yet to leave these mountains. Not sure I ever will."

He shifted so that his stance mirrored hers, his back against the support. "You surprise me. I would've guessed that a young lady such as yourself yearned for adventure, hungered to see the world you read about in all those books."

"I'll admit I've often wondered what other places are like. I'm realistic enough to know, however, the opportunity will probably never arise." She shrugged. "That's all right with me. I'm content right where I am."

"The mountains are all right," he agreed offhandedly.

"Just all right?" She dropped her arms, indignation pushing upward. "How can you say that—"

"There's no need to get huffy, *mon chou,*" he responded, amusement deepening his accent. "I was merely teasing. While I prefer the lowlands, I can't deny East Tennessee is lovely. In fact, it sort of reminds me of my property outside New Orleans. The landscape is vastly different, of course, but the feeling I get is the same. A feeling of freedom. Free of constraints, of expectations. I can let down my guard there."

During supper, she'd found his descriptions of his life in the Crescent City fascinating, if somewhat confining. The thought of all those strict social rules and expectations, not to mention the head-spinning whirl of parties and engagements, made her break out in a cold sweat. Made her grateful she wasn't part of a prominent, wealthy family like the Beaumonts.

No wonder he was coiled tighter than a copperhead about to strike. How much time would it take for him to let his guard down here?

"Do you go there often?"

He paused. "Not nearly as often as I'd like."

"Have you ever considered leaving the city behind?"

"I have." He heaved a sigh. "This last year, especially."

Because his mother was gone.

Lying in bed last evening, she'd prayed for him, asked God to comfort him as he sorted through the truth. His instinctive denial, his difficulty in accepting that his mother might've deceived him in this matter, revealed how deeply he'd loved her. Treasured her, even. Recalling his pained denial, outrage had bloomed inside Megan. How could Lucinda betray him that way? Deny both men a chance at a close relationship? She couldn't begin to understand the woman's reasoning or motivations.

With tears wetting her pillow, it had dawned on her that she no longer blamed Lucian for not visiting Charles. Lucinda had led him to believe his grandfather was apathetic. And perhaps worse. Her actions had inflicted deep hurt on two men. Charles, her friend and substitute grandfather. And Lucian, someone who, if the circumstances were different, she could come to care a great deal about.

But they're not. Remember that. He's not the hero you've been dreaming about your whole life.

Needing to divert her treacherous thoughts, she grasped blindly for a change in subject.

"Did your house sustain any damages last night? I trust you didn't discover any handprints on the furniture." She hoped he didn't detect the breathless strain in her voice.

"I didn't find any when I inspected the parlor in the morning light."

Oh, why did the man have to have a sense of humor

beneath that brooding reserve? Where was the haughty arrogance she despised?

"No misplaced children after I left?"

"No," he said with mock sternness. "I can assure you that if I had, I would've brought them straight here for you to deal with."

"Aw, but look at how well you handled Ollie and Sarah."

"If you dare to leave me alone with that boy again, there will be dire consequences."

She couldn't hold back her laughter, the thrill his subtle teasing sent rushing through her.

"Go ahead. Laugh. You think I'm jesting when in fact I'm completely serious."

"Right." The tremor of humor belied his words. Holding her stomach, she laughed harder, recalling his look of strained patience when dealing with the boy.

When Lucian pushed away from the post and stalked towards her, black eyes burning, the laughter died in her throat. Uh-oh. Every nerve ending stood to attention. What were his intentions?

He came very close, clasped his hands behind his back even as his upper body bent towards her. A good three to four inches taller than her, his broad, muscled chest and capable shoulders blocked the moonlight. His nearness didn't trouble her in the least. She welcomed it, felt sheltered by him. She pressed her arms tighter around her middle to keep from reaching up and weaving her fingers through his brown locks, from pulling him to her. *That would be unwise. Extremely unwise.*

That didn't mean she didn't long to do so. This enigmatic man tugged at her heart, her soul, like the pull of the moon on the ocean's waves.

"Has anyone ever told you that your laugh is like a song? A merry tune brimming with unbridled enthusiasm?"

"Has anyone ever told you that you've a heart of a poet?"

Surprise flashed across his face. "No. Never. It must be your influence." His gaze roaming her face was like a physical touch. "You are so incredibly beautiful." His warm breath fanned her mouth.

Her lungs hung suspended. Was he going to kiss her?

The door opened then, and Nicole appeared, interrupting them a second time. Megan didn't know whether to be irritated or relieved.

He straightened, his eyes hooded. Unreadable. The air whooshed from her lungs. Why did she feel as if she'd just missed something special?

"Dessert's on the table," Nicole announced brightly, unaware of what she'd interrupted.

"I, ah, am sorry to have to decline, after all." Lucian backed towards the steps. "But it's later than I realized. I need to be going."

"Oh." She blinked, glanced between them. "Next time, then."

"Good evening."

"Wait!" Megan ducked inside for a kerosene lamp. Their fingers brushed as she handed it to him and an unexpected pang shot through her. There was such strength and warmth in those hands. Gentleness, too. "To light your way," she said.

His features tightened briefly. "Thanks."

Then he turned and walked away. And Megan was

glad she was smart enough to know not to fall in love with the man. Something deep inside warned that it wouldn't be the happy-ever-after kind of love. More like the Romeo and Juliet, tragic kind of love. For them, there could be no happy ending.

Chapter Seven

Standing in the flower garden Monday afternoon, Lucian turned at the sound of angry footsteps.

"Cabbage?" Megan marched his direction, her pastel-pink skirts skimming the stone path and swiping the blooms unfortunate enough to be too near the edge. "*That's* what you've been calling me?"

"Good afternoon." He gestured to the clear blue skies overhead. "Nice day for a stroll, isn't it?"

Her pink blouse, with fitted bodice and flared sleeves, delineated her slender waist, while the delicate hue enhanced her pale beauty. Her skin glowed with health and vitality. She'd captured the top layers of her curls in a pink ribbon at the back of her head, while the rest cascaded down her back. A silver ribbon choker encircled her neck, a small cameo brooch in the center. She was a delicate rose of incomparable beauty, but not without a few thorns.

Reaching his side, she jammed her fists on her hips. The color in her cheeks matched the red tulips planted along the back porch. She wasn't going to let this go.

"I spoke to my cousin's wife Kate today. You know,

the one from New York? She studied French, so I asked her what *mon chou* meant." When he didn't immediately respond, she narrowed her gaze. "Well? Care to explain in what way you believe I resemble a cabbage?"

"She's right. It does mean that." She opened her mouth to speak, but he held up a hand. "It's also slang for…little pastry."

One pale brow arched in a way he was coming to adore. "That's supposed to make me feel better?"

"Actually, yes." And because he didn't trust himself not to do anything rash, like he very nearly had last night, he pivoted on his heel and began to stroll away from the house. As expected, she followed.

"Why?"

He sighed, uncertain if he was strong enough to maintain self-control. To keep things between them platonic. Businesslike would be even better, though at this point, all but impossible. No other woman had ever gotten under his skin like this one.

Waving a hand in dismissal, he drawled, "You know, your skin is like heavy cream and your eyes the hue of blueberries. Your lips—"

"I get the picture," she spoke up hastily.

Silence stretched between them, their boots striking the stones and birds twittering in the trees filling it. He was glad she was behind him, unable to see the struggle in his expression.

"How was church yesterday?"

"Good." She hesitated. "Though I'm not sure I appreciated the onslaught of questions about you."

That brought him around. His brows met in the middle. "About me?"

"Yes, you." She met his gaze openly. "This is a small

town, remember? People are curious about Lucinda's son, Charles's grandson."

He absently rubbed his chest, so accustomed to the pressure he was beginning not to notice it. "I'm sorry you were put in an uncomfortable position on account of me."

"It wasn't that bad." Concern flooded her gaze. She touched his wrist, her fingers lingering against his skin. "Are you all right? I've noticed you doing that a lot."

He lowered his hand, forcing her to drop hers. "It's a habit." Turning, he resumed walking. This time, she fell into step beside him.

"You aren't having chest pains, are you?"

"No, nothing like that. Just pressure and sometimes an uncomfortable tightness. My physician checked me out and declared me healthy. Said I needed to slow down for a while." He skimmed the flowers with his flattened palm, an ironic smile on his lips. "Stop and smell the roses."

Sensing her regard, he turned his head to meet her probing gaze.

"It appears this trip could accomplish that, if you'd let it."

"You don't understand." He stopped short to face her, throwing his hands wide. "I don't *want* to be here. I don't want that house," he confessed, jabbing a finger at the yellow structure visible in the distance. "This garden. I don't want to meet people who knew my mother, to listen to them say how sad they are that she never came back. How my grandfather regretted how he handled my parents' marriage. How he died all alone, with no one to comfort him."

He passed a shaky hand over his face. Frustration

and sorrow churned inside him, and he wanted to rail at someone or something, needed to release these emotions before they consumed him. But his mother wasn't here to explain herself and neither was his grandfather.

"No one blames you," she said quietly, his grief mirrored in her face. "I'm sorry for the things I said before. I made assumptions about you, about your motivations, that I now know were wrong." Slipping her slender hand in his, she gently squeezed. "Charles wasn't alone at the end."

"What?"

Her lips trembled. "I was with him. So were Mr. and Mrs. Calhoun. He was ready to meet Jesus. He went peacefully."

"That's good to know," he scraped out. He felt raw inside.

What if everything he'd ever believed about the man was untrue, distorted by deception? All those years wasted harboring resentment. Feeling unworthy. Outraged on his mother's behalf, hurting for her. Had he been wrong about it all?

He held on to her hand like a lifeline. "Did he ever say anything about me?"

"A few times."

"I see."

"He loved you, Lucian," she said, pressing closer, "but it was a painful subject. In many ways, your grandfather was a very private man."

Nodding, he swallowed hard. He shared that particular trait.

"Lucian—"

Reaching up, he cradled her cheek with his hand, skimmed his thumb along the petal-soft skin. Battled the urge to find comfort in her arms. "I wish I knew what to believe." *Who* to believe.

Everything in him screamed Megan was trustworthy. That she was a good person. That the compassion in her eyes was real.

"I'm sorry you're struggling with this."

Inhaling, he dropped his hand and stepped back. "You truly believe he wanted us here?"

"I do."

He nodded, glanced out over the gardens, not really seeing anything.

Megan felt helpless in the face of Lucian's anguish. She would like nothing more than to hold him, but she didn't dare. *Father God, please bring the truth to light somehow. Give him clarity and closure. Help him to see how much You love him.*

"I have an idea," she ventured softly. "You haven't seen much of the town yet, have you? Why don't we take a walk? It will do you good to get your mind off things."

The questions in his eyes shouted his mistrust. "Why do you want to help me? I haven't changed my mind about the house. If my lawyer finds a way around that stipulation, I'll take it."

It hurt that he still didn't trust her motives, but she understood it wasn't about her. Not really. "I'm praying he doesn't. But if he does, I'll just have to trust God to open up another way for us to minister to the children and the community." She hadn't answered that other question. Couldn't. Not without alerting him to the fact he was fast becoming important to her.

As for the house, she couldn't find it in her to be angry. Not now that she realized everything it represented for him, the upheaval, the painful reminders. She just wished there was a way to meet everyone's needs. Perhaps, if he came to trust her fully, he might agree to leave the house in her care so that he could return to New Orleans.

Assessing her, he appeared to come to a conclusion. "At least you're honest." He held his arm aloft. "Very well—let's go exploring."

Walking arm in arm down Main Street with Gatlinburg's latest arrival caused quite a stir. Because news traveled fast here, a good majority of folks would know of Lucian's connection to the town. Some stopped whatever they were doing to stare unashamedly, speculation in their gazes. Speculation about Charles's grandson. And about the two of them.

Lucian tilted his head, speaking for her ears alone. "Do I have dirt on my face? Something on my shirt, perhaps?" He paused and ran a hand over his coat and vest, inspecting his front.

His hair fell forward, softening his features. Making him look...vulnerable. "There's nothing wrong with your appearance," she said wryly.

"Then why is everyone staring?"

She smiled. "You're big news around here. They're wondering, how long is he in town for? Is there a chance he might stay? What does he think of Gatlinburg? What's he like?"

"All that, huh?"

And more. Most likely, they were wondering what, if anything, was going on between the two of them. "Make no mistake, dinner conversations will be lively tonight."

Lucian didn't comment. The tension sparked by their

earlier conversation yet lingered in the stiff set of his shoulders and the lines about his mouth, but his eyes were not as black, his expression less formidable.

"Does the attention bother you?"

He shook his head. "No. I'm accustomed to it, though not while walking down the street, I admit."

Megan experienced an unwelcome spurt of jealousy. He was referring to the balls and social engagements he attended nearly every evening. With his wealth, social standing and devastating good looks, of course he'd have scores of girls vying for his attention.

Her fingers tightened on his sleeve. This wasn't good. She mustn't start thinking of Lucian as hers. He wasn't. Never would be.

"Does it bother you?" he asked, guiding her closer to the storefronts to avoid a collision with a group of men.

"Not really." She smiled in response to their friendly greetings. "Besides, it's simple curiosity. Nothing malicious."

Pulling back on his arm, she urged him to stop. His glance was questioning.

Gesturing to the plate-glass window beside them, she said, "Recognize the name?"

"K. O'Malley Photography and J. D. O'Malley Furniture." One black brow lifted. "That's an interesting combination. Your cousin and his wife?"

"Would you like to go inside and meet them?"

"Certainly."

The shop's interior was divided into two separate areas—Kate's studio on their right and Josh's furniture on their left. Neat and organized, the place was a feast for the eyes. Landscape photographs of New York and Tennessee lined the walls, as did examples of personal portraits—couples and families and babies. In the back, an oversize black curtain hid the log walls and rough-hewn floorboards where a settee and two chairs were set up, along with her camera and equipment.

In an effort not to overcrowd the space, Josh had chosen his finest pieces to showcase his work. Customers had the option to buy the inventory or put in special orders. A gleaming cherry dining set, an intricately carved walnut hutch, a writing desk and a few other pieces were situated about the area with enough room for folks to meander and touch and inspect.

The bell above the door jangled, and Josh, who seemed to be comforting Kate, looked up.

"Megan."

His lips quirked up in a welcoming smile, but he couldn't quite hide his worry. Immediately, concern washed over her. Kate lifted her head from his shoulder and, hurriedly wiping her eyes, stepped out of the shelter of his arms. Attempted a smile.

"Megan, hi." She eyed the man at her side with interest.

"We can come back another time—" Megan began, unhappy they'd interrupted a private moment.

"No, that's all right." Clasping Josh's hand, Kate pulled him forward. "We'd like to meet your friend."

All the while making the introductions, she tried to guess what was the matter with her best friend. She hadn't noticed anything unusual about Kate's behavior, although, now that she thought about it, she *had* been quieter than normal these past few weeks. A touch withdrawn. The joy and pride that had been a constant on Josh's face ever since their wedding last fall was still there, but he seemed distracted. Concerned for his wife.

Please, Lord, don't let it be anything serious. If anyone deserved happiness, it was Kate.

Threading her arm through Kate's, she addressed her cousin. "Josh, could you show Lucian around? I'd like to speak with Kate for a few minutes."

"Sure."

She looked to Lucian for approval. "Do you mind?"

"Not at all." His mouth eased into an almost smile, his expression thoughtful.

Once inside the small storage room in back, Megan took Kate's hands in hers. "What's wrong?"

Since finding love with Josh, the petite, refined lady who'd known more than her fair share of loneliness and heartbreak had blossomed into an outgoing, confident woman with a ready smile and infectious laughter. Today, though, her wide green eyes were filled with unshed tears. She looked miserable.

Megan's heart squeezed with compassion. "Why are you so upset? Are you ill?" She held her breath, braced for bad news.

"No, nothing like that." Freeing one hand, she smoothed dark chocolate wisps away from her forehead. Her luxurious mane, normally trained into an elaborate twist, was caught back in a simple bun. "Although, I'm afraid something may be wrong with me."

"What do you mean?"

Kate's cheeks grew pink, and her lashes swept down. "I—I'm afraid I won't be able to have a baby. Josh and I have been trying since the wedding, and, well…" She trailed off, worried her lower lip.

"Oh." Relief swept through her that Kate wasn't facing a health crisis. "It's early yet. You've only been married a little over six months."

"But look at how quickly it happened for Juliana and Evan!" she protested. "What if I can't give Josh a son or daughter? For so long, I dreamed of having a family of my own, and now that I've found Josh, I want that dream to become a reality. I want a little boy with his daddy's honey-colored hair and blue eyes. And a little girl I can teach to take photographs and cook and read…" Her eyes welled up again. "What if God doesn't think I'd be a good mother?"

"Don't think that way, Kate," she admonished with a gentle smile. "You are the most nurturing, kind, loving woman I know. You'll be the best mother ever! God knows the desires of your heart. Just keep praying and waiting on Him. I'll pray, too."

She nodded slowly. "I have been. I suppose I'm impatient."

"God's timing isn't always our own," Megan agreed, thinking of her own longing for a husband. "What's Josh saying about all this?"

Her quick smile lit up her lovely features. "He's been very supportive, very patient with me. He's my voice of reason, something I desperately need right now."

"I'm not surprised. He loves you so much." Last fall, when Kate left Gatlinburg to return to New York, Megan had worried the pair would never find their happy ending. She thanked God that Josh had come to his senses and gone after her.

"I've been truly blessed." Kate paused, reflective. "Not only do I have a husband I dearly love, I have new friends and family. I need to remember my many blessings instead of focusing on what I don't have."

"There's nothing wrong with wanting things," Megan

said, "but you're right—if we focus too much on what we don't have, it can affect our outlook."

Kate gave her a quick hug, then leaned back to smile at her. "Thanks for being such a dear friend, Megan. I think of you as a sister, you know. I love you."

A lump formed in her throat. "I love you, too."

Thank You, Lord, for bringing this delightful woman into my life. Kate's friendship eased the ache of Juliana's absence.

Turning speculative, Kate rested her hands on her hips. "Charles's grandson is certainly a distinguished gentleman. You failed to mention how utterly handsome he is!" Her brow furrowed. "He does seem a bit haughty, however. Is he a cold man?"

Megan rushed to his defense. "That was my first impression of him, too, but he's not at all that way. Actually, he's quite kind. Lucian's a good man—he's just… going through a rough patch right now."

"It sounds as if you've learned a lot about him in a short amount of time."

"You could say that."

Strange—she couldn't recall what life was like without him around. There was a connection between them, one she hadn't experienced with anyone else. One she must ignore, must fight against. At the very most, they could be friends. There would be risk involved, of course, but she was certain she could withstand the temptation to care for him more than was wise. He was only here temporarily, after all.

"Be careful, Megan," Kate warned. "I wouldn't want to see you hurt."

"Don't worry. I'm perfectly aware that Lucian isn't the one for me."

"Hmm." She moved to the door. "Well, I believe we've left them to their own devices long enough, don't you?"

To Megan's relief, the men were involved in a deep discussion about furniture. Josh winked at her, continuing to talk as he placed an arm about Kate's shoulders. She took it as a sign that he liked Lucian, which pleased her. Both were businessmen, so they had something in common. Lucian searched her face as if trying to ascertain if everything was all right and, apparently satisfied, returned his attention to Josh. His stance was relaxed yet focused.

Twenty minutes later, they were back on the boardwalk.

"Do you want to return home?" she asked.

"Not unless you do."

Shielding her eyes with one hand, she scanned the blue sky above. No clouds. Good. "I can show you our favorite picnic spot, if you'd like. It's a twenty-five minute walk from here."

"I'd like that."

They were quiet as they left the town behind, each lost in their own thoughts. Walking side by side in the forest, Megan was acutely aware of his commanding presence. There was no compulsion to fill the silence with inane chatter.

Spotting one of her favorite birds, she tugged on his sleeve to stop his forward progress, pointing to a branch above their heads. "Do you see that?"

He tipped his head back to study the elegant golden-hued bird with a splash of red on its wings.

"That's a cedar waxwing," she told him, suddenly reminded of a verse she'd read the night before. "'Look at the birds of the air; they do not sow or reap or store away in barns, and yet your heavenly Father feeds them. Are you not much more valuable than they?'"

His gaze turned quizzical. "That sounds familiar. Is it from the New Testament?"

"The book of Matthew. And Luke writes, 'Are not five sparrows sold for two pennies? Yet not one of them is forgotten by God. Indeed, the very hairs of your head are all numbered. Don't be afraid; you are worth more than many sparrows.'"

"You've memorized quite a bit of Scripture."

"That's true, but you're missing the point." She spread her arms wide. "Since God took the time to create an astonishing array of creatures for His pleasure and ours, don't you think He'd care about us, who are created in His image?"

His mouth lifted in an indulgent smile. "*Oui,* it would make sense." He didn't elaborate, however, leaving her wondering if she'd gotten through to him. When he resumed walking, she had no choice but to follow. He shot her a sideways glance. "Thank you, Megan."

She stepped around a large hole in the ground, likely a gopher's. "For what?"

"For caring."

Uncertain how to respond, she merely nodded and averted her gaze. When they reached the forest's edge, she paused in order for Lucian to take in the view. A wide, sweeping green field sprinkled with clover lay before them, and in the distance, a tree-lined river meandered through the valley. On the far side of the river, green hills and pastures gave way to the mountains, rounded peaks shining in the sun.

Inhaling the fresh, sweet-smelling air, he wore a look of appreciation. "I can see why you like it here."

"Our families come here to relax. My ma, aunt and uncle normally sit and talk while the rest of us swim or fish or play games."

He held out his hand. "Want to walk to the river?"

Placing her hand in his felt like the most natural thing in the world. The sun warmed their skin and the light breeze teased their hair as they crossed the field.

"Your cousin is an astute businessman," he said after some time. "I enjoyed our discussion."

"More importantly, he's a good man. He's like a protective older brother—irritating at times but always looking out for my best interests."

"His wife seemed upset when we arrived. Is everything all right?"

Megan hesitated, not because she didn't trust him but because it was a delicate subject. How to say it? "Kate is eager to start a family."

His grip on her hand shifted so that their palms fit snugly together, his fingers firm and sure. He shot her a sideways glance. "And it's not happening as quickly as she'd like?"

Heat rushed into her cheeks. "Exactly."

"I see."

Oh, dear. In this moment, she didn't resent that phrase quite so much.

They stopped at the river's edge and stood on the low, gently sloping bank, their boots sinking slightly in the soft earth as they watched the clear water tumbling past. Thousands of tiny rocks littered the riverbed, all shapes and sizes and colors. Pond-skater bugs pushed across the surface. Fish the size of her thumb darted back and forth.

Lucian didn't release her hand. She'd hoped he wouldn't, relishing the connection although she knew she shouldn't.

He turned to her. "How many children do you want?"

"Me?" The question startled her. "Oh, I don't know. Five or ten." A laugh burst forth when his jaw dropped.

"Surely you jest!"

"I love kids. I'll take as many as the good Lord sees fit to give me."

He shook his head in wonder. "I noticed you seem to have a way with them." He asked quietly, "Is Tom the lucky man?"

"What? Tom and I? No."

His face inches away, his dark gaze pierced her. "I got the impression that the two of you are more than friends."

"I don't feel that way about him."

Was that relief in his eyes?

Breaking eye contact, they stood and gazed at the scenery. After long moments of silence, she asked, "What about you? How many do you want?"

Hitching a shoulder, he spoke matter-of-factly. "I need a son to carry on the Beaumont name. If my first-born is a son, then I'll have only the one."

His detached attitude made her feel slightly nauseous. "You make having a child sound like a duty," she accused.

His gaze sharpened, his jaw hardened into marble. "That's because it is. Unlike you, I won't marry for love or some other fickle emotion. I'll do so because I have a responsibility to my family to further the Beaumont legacy."

Snatching her hand from his, she lifted her chin. Why was she so angry? "Let me guess—only the brightest, richest, most well-connected young debutant will do?"

His eyes shuttered, he jerked a nod. "That's the way things are done in my world."

"Then I'm glad I inhabit a different one." Trembling now, she hitched a thumb over her shoulder. "We should probably be heading back."

Without a word, they retraced their path. Only this time, the silence was strained, heavy. As disheartening as it was, she'd needed this reminder of their vast differences, not only in their stations but their outlooks. While she envisioned marriage as a union of hearts, he saw it as a cold, emotionless business arrangement. She could never live that way, and it saddened her that Lucian would choose such a life.

Rounding the base of a live oak, he nearly trampled a patch of pink heart-shaped flowers. He stopped short. "What are these?"

"Bleeding hearts." Joining him in the shade, she gently traced a petal. "There's a legend associated with them," she said offhandedly. "It involves a tale of a young man's quest to win the love of his life."

He cradled one flower against his flat palm. "Is it an interesting story?"

"I'll let you be the judge of that." Snapping one off, she removed the two pink petals and, balancing them on her hand, lifted them up for his inspection. "A young man fell deeply in love with a wealthy and beautiful maiden and, in an effort to win her love, gave her extravagant gifts. The first gift consisted of two rabbits to keep as pets."

One black brow snaked up as he eyed the petals. "I see the resemblance. Let me guess—she didn't want them?"

"Oh, yes, she did. She accepted the gift, but rejected the giver." Pulling out the white inner petals, she said, "He didn't give up, though. Next, he gave her a pair of silk slippers. The finest money could buy."

"Well, I know for certain she kept those," he drawled. "What woman would turn down a pair of shoes?"

"You're right—she did. But she still wasn't interested in him. Desperate now, he spent the last of his money on a pair of extravagant earrings." She showed him the question-mark-shaped stamens.

Lucian outlined her palm with his fingertip. "It didn't work, did it?"

His light touch and husky voice sparked shivers along her skin. Her gaze caught in his, she shook her head. "No."

"What did he do?"

"He had no more gifts to give," she murmured, unable to maintain eye contact, "and no way to win her love, so he took his knife and plunged it into his heart." Placing the stamens side by side, she created the heart shape. The green pistil represented the knife. "They say the first bleeding-heart plant sprung up in the spot where he died."

All of a sudden, she wished she hadn't told the story. Just as there was no hope for the mythical characters, there was no hope for her and Lucian.

When she started to drop the disassembled flower onto the ground, he stopped her. "May I have that?"

"Of course." When she'd transferred the pieces to him, he placed them in a handkerchief and, folding up the sides, tucked it into his pocket. He didn't offer an explanation. And she didn't ask for one.

At the lane leading into town, she stopped to bid him goodbye. She resorted to twirling her hair, a nervous habit she'd developed as a small child and one she'd mostly abandoned. "I need to get home and help the girls with supper."

His hands at his sides, he stood tall and straight and formal. "Thank you for showing me around. I know you have responsibilities to tend to."

The solemn expression on his handsome face, the weariness in his dark eyes, called to her. How she yearned to throw her arms around him, to pull him close and smooth all the cares from his brow. She ruthlessly squelched the urge. Heartache lay down that path.

"I was happy to," she said in all honesty.

He sketched a bow. "Until Friday evening."

"Yes, I'll see you then."

She watched him go, his long, sure strides carrying him quickly in the opposite direction, his shiny Hessians winking in patches of sunlight. A solitary figure with the weight of the world on his shoulders. Megan desperately wanted to be the friend he needed. But at what price?

Chapter Eight

In Charles's study Tuesday afternoon, Lucian refolded the letter and, sliding it inside the top desk drawer, let his head fall back against the leather chair. Stared at nothing in particular. His lawyer had written not to impart news, but to reassure Lucian of his efforts to find a way around the stipulation. Upon seeing the return address on the envelope, he'd assumed it meant his stay here in Tennessee was coming to an end. Not another delay. Apparently the gentleman hadn't been able to give the matter his immediate attention as he'd been wrapping up a delicate legal matter.

He needed to leave and *soon*. He had work and responsibilities. A life to resume. With nothing pressing calling for his attention here, his mind was free to wander down paths he'd rather not explore.

He'd spent the better part of the day searching his mother's and grandfather's rooms for clues, anything that might shed light on the status of their relationship in recent years. He'd rifled through this desk, examined the bookshelves. No letters. Nothing. No way to know what, if anything, had transpired between them.

The lack of evidence was telling in and of itself. Besides a couple of photographs, Charles hadn't kept anything near him that would remind him of his estranged daughter. And there certainly wasn't anything here linked to Lucian.

Going from room to room, touching their belongings, he'd felt like an intruder.

Pushing to his feet, he crossed to the single window, taking in the sweeping view of property, the flower gardens and beyond, the forest and distant mountain peaks. He could easily picture Megan there, a vision in pink. Had it been only yesterday that she'd stormed up to him, demanding to know the reason for her nickname?

Hands curling into fists, his nails bit into his palms. Megan was the primary reason he couldn't afford to stay much longer. The alluring country-miss was dangerous to his peace of mind, to his goals. Too much time in her company, and her naive dreams about love and marriage might start to make sense.

He'd purposefully shocked her yesterday, spoken plainly about his expectations all the while knowing her views were in complete contrast to his. The censure in her beautiful blue eyes had stayed with him the rest of the day and long into the night. Of course a romantic like her would find his businesslike approach to marriage difficult to swallow. A man such as he—practical-minded, cynical, uninterested in love and without a single romantic inclination—could never meet her high expectations, would only disappoint her.

His housekeeper poked her head in the door. "Mr. Lucian?"

He turned and motioned for her to enter. "Mrs. Calhoun. What can I do for you?"

Although in her mid-sixties, the woman had boundless energy and could accomplish more than ten men put together. A hard worker, she was pleasant without being intrusive. He appreciated that.

Her shoes squeaking on the polished floorboards, she held her folded apron in her hands. "I'm off to the mercantile. Is there anything in particular you need?"

"Not that I can think of."

"All right, then." She made to leave.

"Uh, Mrs. Calhoun? If you give me a list, I'll go for you," he blurted, unable to shake the restlessness plaguing him. Needing *something* to do, he was even willing to do her shopping for her. If she didn't accept his offer, he was going to go find Fred and help him weed the gardens.

"Well… I do have a new recipe for buttermilk pie I'd like to try out. I could do that while you went to town. Are you sure you don't mind?"

"Not at all." Moving around the desk, he pointed out, "I'm not used to having this much time on my hands."

"Rest isn't always such a bad thing, you know. I suspect you don't get much of it back home."

Shrugging, he brushed aside her words. "I prefer to keep myself busy." So he didn't have to face his problems. To think about this past year and all its disappointments and losses. The glaring mistakes. *Coward,* a taunting voice accused.

Shaking her head in motherly concern, she sighed, turned and led the way to the kitchen where she handed him a slip of paper.

"Is this everything?" He scanned the ten items.

Retying the apron around her ample hips, she instructed, "Give the list to Emmett or his wife. They'll gather everything for you. Don't be surprised if you have to wait a little while. They fall behind sometimes, depending on how many orders they have to fill. Besides, I'm in no hurry." She thumped a bag of flour on the work surface, alongside a bowl. "And if this here recipe of Juanita's is any good, you can have a slice of pie when you get back."

Smiling, he rubbed his stomach. "I don't see how Fred has managed to stay fit after all these years eating your cooking. Our chef could learn a thing or two from you."

Though she waved away his compliment, she fairly beamed. "He works it off doing all that yard work."

"Ah, I see." He glanced out the window to where Fred was trimming bushes with a wicked-looking pair of shears, sunlight bouncing off his sweat-slicked bald head. "If I'm here much longer, I'll have to join him if I don't want to go home stouter than I arrived."

"It's been a pleasure having you here." She held a spoon aloft, gazing at him with disconcerting nostalgia. "It's almost like having Charles here again." Then she turned her attention back to her recipe.

He didn't know what to say to that. He supposed it would be strange for the elderly couple to work here with no one around. They'd been here for most of their lives, were here while his grandmother, Beatrice, was still alive, and his mother was small.

Slipping the paper in his pocket, he asked as casually as he could manage, "Were they a happy family? Charles and Beatrice and my mother?"

Lifting her head, she gave him a surprised smile. "They were very happy."

"Good." Bittersweet relief curled through his body.

At least they'd had a taste of happiness before…well, before his grandmother died and his father came and ruined it all. "I'm glad."

He left then, before he peppered her with more questions. Waving to Fred, he went to the barn to hitch up the wagon. His valet was there mucking out stalls.

Lucian stopped short. Laughed at the sight of the normally fastidious gentleman sweaty, his hair mussed and bits of hay clinging to his pant legs. "You must be as in need of a diversion as I am."

Smith didn't stop what he was doing. "You would be correct, sir."

Still smiling, Lucian went about his business, glad to be doing something as simple as hitching horses to a wagon. He had to admit, it beat sitting in the stuffy shipping offices pushing papers across his desk and having his father assess his every decision as if he hadn't a clue what he was doing.

It didn't take long to reach Main Street. Pulling up in front of Clawson's Mercantile, he glimpsed a flash of blond hair through the window. Megan? Setting the brake, he jumped down to the dusty ground and stepped up on the weathered boardwalk. Who else could it be? No one else in this town had hair the color of moonlight.

Anticipation humming along his veins, he opened the door. The bell clanged above his head and she looked up, full lips parting. The eager welcome surging in her wide eyes buoyed his spirits. Apparently she'd set aside her irritation.

"Lucian?"

"Good afternoon, Megan." Sweeping off his black hat, he tucked it beneath his arm and, shoving his unruly hair out of his eyes, approached the wooden shelves lined with personal items such as combs, mirrors and shaving supplies.

Refreshingly lovely as always, her simple, unadorned dress would have been deemed boring were it not a pleasing aquamarine, its exact hue putting him in mind of the sea he loved but couldn't handle. Dratted seasickness.

"What are you doing here?" Her quizzical gaze slid to the wagon outside.

"I'm running errands for Mrs. Calhoun." He lifted a finger to touch the porcelain doll she clutched to her chest. "I didn't realize you still played with baby dolls," he teased, arching a mocking brow.

The witty retort he expected didn't surface. Instead, regret pulled at her mouth as she replaced the frilly-dressed doll on the shelf. "I'm on my way to Owen Livingston's to deliver food. I'd like to purchase this for Sarah, but it will have to wait."

He finally noticed the cloth-lined crate at her feet. "Are they ill?"

"No, but it's hard for him to manage the farm chores and still find time to cook. From what I understand, he's not an experienced cook, anyway. Ever since Meredith died, the ladies of our church have taken turns taking food to them twice a week."

"How long ago did she die?"

"Six months."

So the loss was still fresh. What a nightmare for Livingston and his small daughter. To have lost not one, but two cherished loved ones at the same time. A wife and mother. An innocent baby.

Sympathy clogged his throat. "It appears your towns-folk take care of their own."

"You're right about that." She lifted her chin a notch. "Like any other small town, we have our not-so-great moments, but I have to say I'm proud to be a part of this community."

He could tell she meant it. Unlike Nicole, who'd made it clear she found small-town life confining, often declaring her intention of leaving it behind, Megan loved her life. She didn't care about fashion or fancy houses or money. She cared about people. That much was plain in how she chose to spend her time…whether it was entertaining little children or preparing and delivering food.

How could he have ever doubted her integrity?

Heart beating out a warning, he forced his attention away from her. It wasn't easy. Not now that he'd come to his senses and could see her as she truly was…compassionate, sensitive to others' needs, a heart full of love.

He picked up the doll. "How about I purchase this for Sarah?"

"I can't ask you to do that."

"You didn't." He guessed she didn't have enough money for such a splurge. How to put this to her without hurting her pride? "I think a little girl who's missing her mommy might be cheered by a gift such as this. You're right to want to give it to her."

"But it won't be from me if you pay for it."

Leaning closer, he suggested softly, "Why can't it be from the both of us?"

"You have a soft spot for her," she stated with sudden clarity. "Don't try to deny it."

"If I do have one—and I'm not saying I do—it's because she reminds me of a certain sassy storyteller," he said, gently tapping her nose.

The bell clanged as another patron, a skinny, awkward girl who looked to be in her teens, entered the mercantile. Straightening, Lucian dipped his head in greeting as Megan offered her a quiet hello. The girl smiled shyly before darting to the fabrics' section.

Get a hold of yourself, Beaumont. Have you forgotten your surroundings? No wonder the girl acted embarrassed...you were too near Megan, touching her in a familiar manner right here for all the world to see.

Megan was looking far too pleased with herself, like a cat with a big bowl of cream.

"What?"

"I thought you said you didn't like children."

Wagging a finger, he passed the doll to her and lifted the crate. "No... I recall saying I have no experience with them."

Walking beside the shelves towards the long counter where the Moores measured out goods and calculated totals, Megan fell into step with him, a huge smile on her face. Her eyes sparkled with friendly challenge. "If it's to be from both of us, that means you'll need to come with me to give it to her. I'm heading over there now."

"We can take my wagon," he agreed smoothly, sliding the crate onto the counter so that he could retrieve the paper from his pocket. "Let me give them Mrs. Calhoun's list and have them wrap up Sarah's doll, and then we can go."

"Fine with me."

Ruthanne Moore exclaimed over the doll, chattering

endlessly as she wrapped it in crisp white paper. At long last, they escaped outside, the humid heat that made it difficult to breathe preferable to the stuffy confines of the mercantile and the speculative glances of the proprietress. He stowed their belongings in the back. Ran a finger beneath his stiff cravat where it stuck to his damp throat.

"Today seems hotter than usual."

Megan huffed a laugh as he assisted her up onto the wooden seat. "This is nothing. Wait until July. You won't want to go outside after eight o'clock in the morning."

He wouldn't be here come July, he wanted to remind her. But that would only chase away her smile, and what was the point in that?

At the turnoff leading to the Livingstons' homestead, the front wagon wheels hit a dip that jostled Megan. Pitching sideways, she very nearly landed in Lucian's lap. Without a moment's hesitation, he put an arm around her. Anchored her to his side.

"You all right?" His warm gaze assessed her, strong hand settling heavily on her waist.

Licking suddenly dry lips, she nodded. He was looking at her as if seeing her for the first time…the same look he'd given her in the mercantile. There'd been a flare of *something* in those shrewd black eyes. Insight maybe? Whatever it had been gave her hope. Was he finally coming to realize she wasn't out to gain possession of his house or anything else that belonged to him?

She would have gladly remained this way for the rest

of the afternoon. Tucked in the shelter of his arm, inches away from his firm jaw shadowed by a hint of a beard and his generous mouth, infused her with tingling delight. His nearness was more exciting than any adventure she'd ever read, more thrilling than any romance put down on paper. This was real. *He* was real. Better than any hero her imagination could've constructed.

You mustn't think that way, Megan. It isn't wise. While Lucian was certainly hero material in the minds of New Orleans socialites, he wasn't *her* idea of a hero. Her hero would marry for love instead of duty. Her hero would want children to love and cherish, not simply to carry on a family name. She couldn't afford to forget that.

As the cabin came into view, she pulled away, the heat of his hand lingering long after he'd removed it. Sarah emerged from the darkened doorway dragging a bucket behind her. A black dog trotted beside her, pink tongue lolling. Lucian frowned at the little girl's untidy braid and smudges of dirt on her cheeks.

Sarah stopped and stared. Her mouth formed a little O. "Miss Megan! Mr. Lucian!"

Megan climbed down without bothering to wait for Lucian's assistance. "Hi, Sarah." Bent with her hands perched on her knees, she pasted on a smile for the little girl's benefit. The sight of the two crude grave markers beyond the barn had sucked the joy from the day. "Where's your pa?"

"Fixin' a fence."

Her blue eyes were large in her thin face as she watched Lucian pat the dog's head. Lips pursed, his sharp gaze swept their surroundings. The farm was showing signs of neglect. Weeds threatened to choke out the vegetable plants in the small patch of garden beside the cabin. Dirt streaked the window panes. Without Meredith to help him, it appeared Owen was falling steadily behind.

Megan held out her hand. "Why don't you take us to him so we can let him know we're here?"

Dropping the bucket, Sarah placed her tiny hand in hers. So solemn. Megan wished there was something more she could do to help the devastated family.

"Are you coming, Mr. Lucian?" Sarah held out her other hand.

A startled look, quickly masked, flashed across his face as he took her hand. The trio bypassed the barn and passed through the wide field to where Owen was struggling to do a chore better suited to two men. Shrugging quickly out of his coat and looping it over the fence, Lucian rushed to assist him, grabbing hold of the other end of the heavy post.

Surprised, Owen's puzzled gaze shot between Lucian and Megan. The men had met at story time but hadn't spoken at length. From his reaction, he plainly hadn't expected the smartly dressed gentleman to willingly assist in menial labor.

"You looked as if you could use some help," Lucian grunted by way of greeting. "Just tell me where you want this."

Owen barked instructions. Together, they worked to repair the fence. Nonplussed, Megan stood there and watched. If one were to discount Lucian's green paisley vest, tailored shirt and extravagantly tied cravat, which were more suited to a well-appointed drawing room than an isolated mountain farm, one would have no trouble believing he was accustomed to getting down in the dirt and working with his hands. His back and shoulder muscles rippled beneath the taut cotton; his biceps strained the material. This was no idle aristocrat.

Realizing she was gawking, Megan suggested to Sarah that they return to the cabin so she could bring the food inside out of the direct sun. The one-room dwelling wasn't filthy, exactly, but it needed attention. And, since Lucian was occupied, Megan immediately set to work, sweeping the floors while waiting for the water to heat, which she'd use to clean the work surfaces and stack of dirty dishes in the basin. She settled Sarah at the table with a slice of buttered bread and a glass of milk. The little girl didn't chatter like most five-year-olds. Instead, she sat silently observing Megan, her gaze occasionally lighting on the wrapped package. Megan bit back a smile, anticipating Sarah's reaction to Lucian's gift.

Beneath his aloof demeanor beat a compassionate heart.

By the time the men returned, the kitchen fairly sparkled and not a speck of dirt lingered on the floors. When Owen's gaze settled on Sarah, nestled in Megan's lap with a book, her face scrubbed clean and hair brushed and rebraided, embarrassment, guilt and gratitude marched across his rugged features. The ever-present sorrow lurked in his eyes.

"You didn't have to do this, Megan," he said gruffly.

"I didn't mind."

He worried the hat in his hands. "Appreciate it." Nodded to Lucian, who was standing slightly behind him.

"You too, Beaumont. I was about ready to give up when you arrived. Thanks."

Lucian's smile eased the austerity of his features. "I ought to be thanking you. You saved me from yet another tedious day of staring at the walls. I'll be back tomorrow, if you don't mind."

Both men's clothing were dirt-stained, but they'd washed up at the outside well. Their faces and hands were clean, their hair wet and slicked back from their foreheads. Lucian's cravat was now stuffed into his pocket.

Owen's mouth turned down. "I can't afford to pay you."

"I don't want your money." He held up a palm. "Trust me, I'd be doing it as much for myself as for you. I need the distraction."

"I don't know."

Lucian appealed to Megan. "I thought you said this community helps each other out."

"We do." To Owen, she said gently, "You know you'd do the same if the situation were reversed. You should let him help you."

Kneading the back of his neck, he jerked a nod. "Okay. If you change your mind…"

Lucian stuck out his hand. "I won't."

Shaking hands, Owen remarked lazily, "You won't be wearing clothing like that tomorrow, will you? I'd hate to feel responsible for ruining those fancy duds."

Lucian chuckled. "I think I can find something more appropriate to wear."

Megan urged Sarah off her lap and stood up. "Before we go, Lucian and I have something we'd like to give Sarah."

Looking wary, Owen slipped his hands in his pockets as she waved Lucian over to the table and gave him the package. "You give it to her."

"Why don't you?" he whispered, brows raised.

"Are you afraid of a five-year-old girl?" she whispered back.

"Of course not. That's ridiculous." Taking it, he pivoted and, walking slowly to where Sarah stood with wide-eyed anticipation, crouched to her level and held it out. "For you."

Gingerly, her tiny fingers peeled back the paper. Her gasp of wonder made all three adults smile. "A dolly!" Carefully, she touched the blond ringlets and the silky blue dress.

"Look, Papa!" Dashing to his side, she lifted it for him to inspect.

He cleared his throat. Smiled and smoothed a tender hand along his daughter's hair. "She's beautiful. What will you name her?"

Sarah bit her lip, staring intently at her new gift. "Megan."

Pushing to his feet, Lucian arched a brow at Megan. Owen looked surprised. "Well, I suppose that's a fitting name, seeing as how she brought it to you."

"She looks like her."

"Oh. Yes, I suppose she does. What do you say, Sarah?"

Hugging the doll to her chest, she looked at Megan and Lucian. "Thank you."

"You're welcome."

"We should get going." Lucian looked to Megan. "I have that order to pick up for Mrs. Calhoun."

As they made to leave, Sarah rushed over to give them each a hug. Although clearly discomfited, something like affection shone in Lucian's gaze.

Once again perched high on the wagon seat, she gazed at his profile. "That was a nice thing you did back there."

He shrugged. "What about you? From Owen's reaction when we walked through the door, that cabin must've been in dire need of a cleaning."

"Yes, well... I know him. You, on the other hand, are a visitor. Once you leave Gatlinburg, you'll probably never see him again."

He gave her a sideways glance. "So that means what? I should only help people I know?"

"No, of course not." She spread her hands wide. "I just— It was unexpected, is all."

"I was being honest back there. I'll go mad if I don't find something to fill the hours."

He could remedy that if he'd only entrust the house to her and go home. But she didn't say that out loud. The thought of him leaving, of never seeing him again, troubled her.

"You seemed to know exactly what to do. Have you fixed a fence before?" Doubt rang in her voice.

"More times than I can count. I have the estate, remember?"

"Don't you have hired men to do that?"

"I do. However, I like fixing things. Working with my hands. I never aspired to manage our family's shipping empire. I wanted to be a ship captain, toiling on the open sea, not cooped up in an office all day. Physical labor gives me a sense of accomplishment that signing a contract or reviewing ship inventory lists doesn't."

"Why didn't you become a ship captain?"

"Seasickness. As a teenager, I spent a lot of time down at the docks and on the ships my father owns. My father didn't approve of my wish to captain my own ship, but I was determined. Shortly after my fourteenth birthday, I snuck aboard a ship departing for New York. One long, agonizing day and night later, I realized the futility of my dream. I couldn't move without getting violently ill."

Megan stared at his profile, absorbed in this glimpse into his past. She could imagine him as a young teen, determined and intense even then, coming to grips with the loss of his dreams. "Was your father angry?"

His laugh was harsh. "Angry? He thought the whole thing quite amusing. Said I got my just deserts for defying him."

"So now you oversee things from a distance."

"Yes."

"I'm sorry it didn't work out for you."

He lifted a careless shoulder. "It wasn't meant to be."

"What about when you're in the city? Do you fix things there, too?"

"Oh, no. My father would have a fit of apoplexy. I spend a large part of my free time at my gentleman's club boxing. Or fencing."

Megan could only stare. "Boxing? Isn't that a brutal sport?" No wonder he was in top physical condition.

"It can be. Lucky for me, I've only ever suffered the occasional black eye and busted lip." He ran a fin-

ger down the length of his straight nose. "No broken
nose. Yet."

His rakish grin transformed his features. Irresistible.

Forcing her gaze straight ahead, Megan retreated into
silence. Attempted to make sense of these new revelations. There was certainly more to Lucian Beaumont
than she'd given him credit for. And that made it even
more difficult not to care for him.

Chapter Nine

Since Megan had insisted on taking a bundle of Owen's and Sarah's clothing to her aunt for mending, Lucian convinced her to let him take her there in his wagon. No point in her toting it across town. She waited patiently while he retrieved the supplies from Clawson's and delivered them to the house. Mrs. Calhoun came outside and invited her in for a slice of pie, but as it was nearing supper time, she declined. Having encountered the sweet aroma permeating the kitchen, Lucian promised he'd eat a slice upon his return. All that hard work had stirred his appetite.

His clothes might be dirty and his body weary, but he felt terrific. The best since his arrival, actually. This was a good kind of tired. Plus, he'd come away knowing he'd helped a man in need. Recalling Sarah's reaction to the doll, his chest squeezed. Maybe because of her resemblance to Megan or maybe because—like him—she'd recently lost her mother, the little girl had somehow wormed her way into his heart. He hoped the gift would bring her a measure of happiness.

Megan sat quietly as he guided the team along the

shaded lane. It was cooler here, the profuse, overhead canopy a barrier against the sun. They'd crossed the wooden bridge spanning the Little Pigeon River a quarter of a mile back, so they'd be coming upon the turnoff to Sam and Mary O'Malley's place shortly. He'd passed it before on his way to Megan's. Apparently the two properties were adjoining but Sam and Mary's cabin was situated closer to town.

"There it is." She pointed to a break in the trees.

The first thing Lucian noticed when they emerged into the clearing was the picturesque view, quaint cabins and outbuildings nestled in a verdant valley and framed by sprawling mountains. The main cabin was a two-story structure with a porch running its length and a massive stone chimney scaling one end wall. Blue-and-white gingham curtains hung in the sparkling windows. On the opposite side of the clearing, tucked beneath the trees, sat a one-room dwelling also with a porch. A large barn dominated the space between the two structures, along with a corncrib, chicken house and smokehouse. Neat rows of vegetables comprised a good-sized garden.

"Who lives there?" He indicated the small cabin.

"Nathan. Josh built it for himself and his intended bride—Kate's sister, Francesca. When Kate arrived in her stead, Josh moved back in with his parents so that she could have the cabin. When they got engaged, Josh decided to build a larger one. He doesn't like to admit to being sentimental, but I think he did it to spare Kate's feelings. He wouldn't want to live with her in a home originally intended for himself and her sister," she said with a knowing grin. "Their home is located behind my aunt and uncle's house, beyond the apple orchard."

"Wait." He was having trouble reconciling this revelation with the obviously head-over-heels-in-love couple he met the other day. "Josh was supposed to marry Kate's *sister?*"

Her expression took on a dreamy quality. "Yep. It's a rather complicated story. Here's the short version— Francesca married another man and Kate came here to deliver the news. Josh eventually came to realize that Kate had all the qualities he'd been searching for in a wife, and they fell in love."

"Just like that, huh?"

She rolled her eyes. "I told you, it's complicated. Theirs was not an easy road to happiness."

"I'm sure you enjoyed observing it firsthand."

"It wasn't as enjoyable as you might think," she remarked, swaying in the seat as he guided the team to a stop beside the porch. "There were times I questioned if they would end up together. It was all quite stressful, let me tell you." Squinting, she jerked her chin. "Look, there's Nathan."

As usual, she didn't wait for him to assist her down. As his boots touched the ground, he reminded himself she wasn't the helpless type. Nor was she the type to manipulate the situation to her advantage, pretending to be helpless so that he'd be forced to help her at every turn.

The tall, dark-headed young man striding across the yard resembled Josh in height and build. Similar facial features, too. Only this man was clean-shaven, unlike Josh, who sported a mustache and goatee, and his eyes were an odd silver instead of blue. He smiled broadly at Megan, yet his eyes were assessing when his gaze met Lucian's.

"Nathan, this is Charles's grandson, Lucian Beaumont. Lucian, Nathan is the middle son. Don't let his quiet nature fool you. He's as stubborn as the rest of us." She elbowed her cousin in the ribs.

His response was to tuck her against his side. He stuck out his free hand. "Nice to meet you."

The two men shook. "Ma's got supper on the table. Why don't you join us?"

The way Nathan said it made it sound almost like a challenge.

"I wouldn't want to intrude. Besides, I'm not exactly dressed for dinner." He indicated his wrinkled shirt and grass-stained pants. He wasn't even wearing a cravat, for goodness' sake. And who knew what his hair looked like. As usual, it was hanging in his eyes.

Megan laughed. "Trust me, you'll fit in. You don't look any different than Nathan here. Uncle Sam, too, I'm sure."

"She's right," Nathan agreed.

While Megan was looking at him expectantly, her cousin retained his watchful air. Did Nathan regard all strangers with a dose of suspicion, or was Lucian's association with Megan the cause? She'd mentioned the O'Malley cousins had grown up together and were practically like brothers and sisters. Lucian wouldn't blame the man for being protective.

He had two choices. Eat with the O'Malleys and spend a little more time in Megan's presence. Or eat at the house. Alone.

"All right, then, I accept."

Reaching in the wagon bed, he retrieved the sack of clothes and followed them inside.

The cabin was roomier than Megan's. On their right was a wide staircase made up of smooth, white pine boards, same as the floorboards. An oversize stone fire-place dominated the living area, family portraits lining the mantel. Kate's work, perhaps?

Tossing her bonnet on the side table, Megan motioned for him to follow her. Windows lined the dining area, providing a sweeping view of the front lawn. The succulent smells emanating from the kitchen filled his nostrils. His stomach rumbled. Lunch seemed ages ago.

Megan introduced him to Mary O'Malley, who welcomed him like a long-lost relative. The type of lady who immediately put a person at ease. Sam, Josh and Kate entered through the kitchen door just as he and Megan were handed platters to carry to the dining table. Like his wife, Sam was friendly, with a bespectacled gaze that seemed to miss nothing.

Lucian didn't have a chance to feel self-conscious. The lively bunch swept him along to the table, seating him beside Megan and around the corner from Sam. Mary and Nathan sat opposite. Josh occupied the opposite end from his father, with Kate on Megan's other side.

"Is Caleb joining us tonight?" Kate asked, indicating the one empty chair.

"I don't think so," Sam said in a subdued voice. Mary's mouth pinched with worry.

Megan placed a hand on Lucian's sleeve and leaned in close, her shoulder bumping his. "Caleb is the youngest brother. You'll meet him later. I hope."

He nodded, wondering what she meant. What Caleb's absence meant. Family trouble?

As soon as the blessing had been said, conversation surged as platters passed around the table. Chicken and dumplings. Pickled beets. Green beans. Fried potato cakes. The food melted in his mouth. He could quickly grow accustomed to this.

He liked Megan's family. Like Josh, Sam was well-spoken and intelligent. A solid, practical man. Humble, too. A quality Lucian didn't encounter often in his world. Nathan didn't offer much to the conversation, but when he did, there was quiet wisdom laced with humor. Lucian intercepted his probing gaze more than once. What did he see between himself and Megan that bothered him? Lucian had made a conscious effort not to touch her. Or lean too close. Or whisper in her ear.

When the women began to clear the table, Nathan offered to show him around. Lucian accepted. He was interested in seeing the farm. Curious, too, if the other man would confront him with whatever was bothering him. A half an hour later, he had his answer.

Lounging against a barn stall, Nathan tossed a hay sliver to the ground and turned his enigmatic silver gaze on Lucian. "There's something you should know. Megan is family, and I make it my business to watch out for family. I've noticed the way she looks at you." His gaze narrowed. "And the way you look at her. Seems to me you're more than friends, which doesn't make a whole lot of sense seeing as how you're not sticking around here."

Lucian didn't speak for a moment. Exactly *how* did Megan look at him? *Focus, Beaumont.* "You're right— we are friends. But that's the extent of our relationship." He could not allow it to develop further. "I like your cousin. I respect her. The last thing I'd want to do is cause her harm."

Nathan pushed upright, crossed his arms. Set his jaw. "You *like* her? Correct me if I'm wrong, but I was under the impression that you suspected her of selfish motives where Charles and that house are concerned. Accused her of things she's incapable of doing."

"I can't deny that I misjudged her." He held Nathan's gaze. "I was wrong."

"Have you told her that?"

"No, not yet." He sighed and lowered his gaze to his boots. She deserved an apology. "But that's something I plan to remedy."

Nathan considered that a long moment. Relaxing his stance, he jerked a nod. "Good. Oh, and Beaumont?"

"Yes?"

"Megan is a one-of-a-kind girl. Folks around here wouldn't look too kindly if you were to hurt her in any way."

"I understand."

No use telling Nathan his warning wasn't necessary. Any punishment the townspeople might mete out wouldn't compare to Lucian's own guilt and self-recrimination were he to cause her pain.

Megan was ensconced in the rocking chair, exhausted from the day's chores and enjoying a moment's rest when Lucian and Nathan emerged from the barn. Keeping the chair in motion with the toe of her boot, she observed the two men as they headed her direction. They weren't speaking, and the waning light made it impossible to read their expressions. She'd noticed the looks Nathan had sent Lucian, looks that troubled her. Sometimes Nathan took his role as protector a bit too seriously.

Her gaze naturally strayed to Lucian. Slightly taller than her cousin, Lucian's posture, the way he carried himself, commanded respect. Restrained strength combined with rakish good looks equaled devastating appeal. He was so incredibly handsome. And far, far out of her reach.

Climbing the porch steps, Nathan asked, "Where is everybody?"

Megan stood and smoothed her water-stained skirt. There was nothing she could do about the dirt clinging to her hem. "Josh and Kate went home, your ma is already mending Owen's and Sarah's clothing and Uncle Sam is reading his Bible."

Lucian paused on the top step, one hand resting on the handrail. "I'll give you a ride home, if you'd like."

"Thanks." She gave Nathan a hug. "Good night."

"Take care."

Lucian was quiet during the short ride to her place. When he halted the team, his warm fingertips grazed her knuckles. "Allow me to help you down."

Puzzled, Megan waited as he came around to her side and lifted his hands. Setting her hands on his shoulders, he gripped her waist and swung her down. His fingers tightened when she would've pulled away. Pulse jumping, she searched his features, barely visible in the low light cast by the kerosene lamp.

"Lucian?"

"Please, I have something to say." His voice was gruff, apologetic, as his hands dropped to his sides. He didn't move to put space between them, however. His heat and closeness were reassuring. "When I first arrived in town, I accused you of a lot of things, none of them good, and now that I've gotten to know you…well, I realize you aren't the type of person who would take advantage of an old man. Or anyone else, for that matter.

I know what a conniving, manipulative woman is like and, frankly, you're not it. I'm sorry, Megan. Will you forgive me for my utterly absurd error in judgment?"

Megan couldn't think to respond. He was apologizing? Admitting he'd been wrong about her?

"Aren't you going to say something?" he said at last.

"I, uh, wasn't expecting this. Of course I forgive you."

"I mean it. I shouldn't have rushed to judgment like that."

"I made assumptions of my own, remember? It happens. But I'm glad we're past all that now."

"Me, too." He sounded as relieved as she felt. Glancing at the cabin, he said, "I should get going. It's been a long day. I have a feeling I'm going to fall asleep the second my head hits the pillow."

When he made to move past her, she snagged his hand. "That comment about manipulative women… what did you mean by that?"

"Only what I said. You have a good heart. Nathan was right," he responded as he squeezed her hand. "You're a one-of-a-kind."

"Whoa. You and Nathan talked about me?" She wiggled her hand free. "Did he put you up to this?" If the apology wasn't his idea, it meant nothing.

"I didn't need Nathan or anyone else pointing out what I had already figured out myself," he said with a hint of asperity. "Yes, your name came up in the course of conversation. He cares about you, you know."

"I know." Still…

"That apology was mine alone. My thoughts, my words." His tone brooked no argument. And honestly, was he really the type of man who'd do something purely because someone else suggested it?

"All right. I believe you."

With a speaking look, he circled around the horses and climbed up onto the seat. *"Bonne nuit, mon chou."*

"Bonne nuit."

A tentative happiness settled in around her heart. Lucian's trust in her was responsible for that. Only his mention of manipulative women hampered it. Why had he refused to offer an explanation? She wasn't naive. A man like him wouldn't lack for female attention. So who had tried to hurt him? And why did she suddenly want to strangle the unknown perpetrators?

Chapter Ten

"I'm off for the day." Mrs. Calhoun poked her head in the study door late Thursday. "Your supper is warming on the stove. Don't leave it there too long," she said with a smile, "else the potatoes will get soggy and the creamed corn will cease being creamy."

Lucian turned from the window. "I'll remember. Thank you."

"Is there anything else you need before I leave?"

"Actually, I was wondering if you could answer a few questions for me." These past few days with Owen and Sarah had kept his own family in the forefront of his mind.

Her wrinkles became more pronounced. "I'll do my best."

Coming around the desk, he leaned his weight against the edge so as not to tower over her. Embarrassed to be involving her in private family matters, but determined to find answers, he forged ahead. "Did my grandfather ever mention wanting my mother and I to come and visit?"

Resting a hand on the back of a chair for support,

Mrs. Calhoun regarded him with regret-filled eyes. The subject obviously troubled her. "After your mother left, Charles became a different man. He spent much of his time closeted in here or in the library, preferring to be alone. I'm sorry, I wish I could help you, but he didn't speak with me or Fred about what happened. We wanted to help. And although we made it clear we were available if he needed a listening ear or a shoulder to cry on, he chose not to come to us."

Disappointment gripped him. "He apparently didn't have a problem opening up to Megan."

Her face smoothed, brightened. "Her friendship brought a bit of joy back into his life. I'll always be grateful."

"You didn't think it strange?" he felt compelled to ask. "A young woman spending time with an elderly man when she could be out doing a hundred other more exciting things?"

"Megan is a helper by nature, a nurturer. The type of girl that, when she sees someone in need, drops what she's doing and rushes to their aid. In Charles, she saw a hurting, lonely old man."

"So she befriended him."

"Yes."

Lost in thought, he trod back to the window and leaned against the frame.

Perhaps he *should* leave the house in her hands. Even if he did find a way around the stipulation and put it up for sale, who knew how long it would take for a buyer to materialize? He could be tied to this place indefinitely. A shiver of alarm worked its way up his spine. No, he couldn't have that.

"Mr. Lucian?"

He jerked around, having forgotten the other woman's presence.

"You seem to be a fine man. I'm certain Charles would've been proud." A warning worked its way into her eyes. "But you'll be returning to New Orleans soon, and I'd hate to see Megan hurt. She's a very special young lady. The townsfolk wouldn't look kindly on anyone who took advantage of her kindness."

Lucian stared. She thought he was like his father? Capable of sweeping an innocent girl off her feet and wresting her from the only home she'd ever known, only to revile her the rest of her days? Once settled into married life, Gerard had come to resent Lucinda's lack of social connections, of town polish and upper-class education.

He spoke stiffly. "You have no need to worry on that score, *madame*. I have no intention of engaging in a passing indulgence and absolutely no designs on Megan O'Malley."

Oh, didn't he? Hadn't he nearly kissed her twice already? Did he not think of her practically every moment?

Shoving the hair off his forehead, he softened his stance. "Your concern is understandable. The last thing I want to do is cause problems for her."

Lips pursed, she studied him, gave a brisk nod. "Well, now that I've said my piece, I'd better get home. Fred will be wanting his supper."

Preoccupied, he bade her good evening. Before he could change his mind, he sat down at the desk and, locating a sheet of blank paper, began to write. His lawyer probably wouldn't understand his instruction to cease and desist, but it made all the sense in the world to him.

Leaving Megan in charge meant he could go home and put this unhappy chapter behind him. His mother and grandfather were gone, their secrets buried with them.

What's done was done.

Running again? an accusing voice prompted. *When are you going to face your problems head-on? The grief will follow you wherever you go, you know. You can't avoid it forever.*

"There are no answers here," he grumbled aloud. No way to discover if his mother had, in fact, deceived him. And, coward that he was, wasn't he glad of that? Relieved?

No, this was the best way for all involved. The house would stay in the family, which meant the next Beaumont generation could come and visit one day. Learn about their ancestors. Perhaps even take up residence here.

Lucian would not return. But he'd never forget this place...or Megan.

By the time Friday afternoon rolled around, Lucian was certain he'd made the right decision. Owen had told him not to come today because he had errands to tend to, so he'd meandered aimlessly about the house. All this free time was making him antsy. And fanciful. He'd caught himself entertaining thoughts of Megan, wondering what it might be like if she were mistress of this house, picturing the two of them together sharing breakfast in the garden or playing a game of chess in the parlor. Holding hands in the moonlight, stealing kisses beneath the stars...

The doorbell rang. He blinked, threaded fingers through his hair. He really needed to get back to New

Orleans. Perhaps even begin his search for a wife. There were a number of young ladies who'd made their eagerness to fill the position clear and who'd meet his qualifications perfectly. They wouldn't marry him expecting anything other than financial security and his good name. Easy enough expectations to meet.

Steeling himself to face Megan, to resist the pull she had on him, he left the study and made his way to the front of the house. Wall sconces threw soft light against the floral papered walls. His boots striking the hardwood echoed throughout the cavernous Victorian. Lucian couldn't wait to see her reaction when she learned he was giving her charge of it.

But when he swung open the door, it wasn't her waiting on the porch. A silver-haired man dressed in an inexpensive brown sack suit and a woman whose jet-black hair belied her age stood smiling at him.

"Mr. Beaumont?" The man, who topped Lucian by about three inches, stuck out his hand. "I'm Reverend Monroe and this is my wife, Carol."

"How do you do?" His nod encompassed them both. Spying the cake in her hands, he stepped back. "Would you like to come in?"

In the entry hall, Mrs. Monroe lifted the plate. "Would you mind if I take this to the kitchen? I know the way."

"Certainly. *Merci beaucoup.*"

The reverend accompanied him into the parlor. Lucian offered him a seat, but he declined, regarding him with wise eyes that seemed to have the ability to pierce a man's facade. Lucian forced himself to meet the man's gaze without flinching.

"I'd intended to come much earlier to welcome you

to town, but Carol's sister and her family have been visiting. How are you settling in?"

"The truth is I'm not here for much longer. This was to be a short business trip. Due to unforeseen circumstances, I've stayed longer than I'd originally planned. But I'll be leaving next week." He pursed his lips together. Why was he blathering on like this? He had nothing to hide.

Except, this was a man of God. Could he somehow sense Lucian had fallen away? That he hadn't darkened the door of a church in more than a year? And that he kept his mother's Bible close but never opened it?

The reverend's expression revealed sincere regret. "I'm sorry to hear that. I was looking forward to getting acquainted. Your grandfather was a faithful member of our congregation. A fixture on the front row in all my years of preaching in this town. Every Sunday on his way out the door, he'd shake my hand and tell me he was praying for me."

Emotion clogged his throat. Hearing that his grandfather was a praying man made the emptiness inside yawn wider, a cavern that refused to be filled. A yearning for something he couldn't pin down.

Mrs. Monroe joined them then, saving him from having to reply. "I left your cake with Mrs. Calhoun. The children will be arriving soon for story time, won't they?" She nudged her husband. "We should get going."

"I'd actually like to stay."

At his unspoken question, Lucian said, "Please do. A few of the parents stick around and help serve the refreshments."

Mrs. Monroe beamed her approval. "I think it's wonderful how you've allowed the town to continue using this place. You're a generous man, Mr. Beaumont."

If they only knew… He realized suddenly that Megan could've easily spread the word of his original intentions, turning the tide of the town's opinion against him. It would've been a strategic move, a way of putting pressure on him. But she hadn't done it. Further proof of her selflessness, her kind and humble spirit.

He glanced at the mantel clock. She was late, which wasn't like her. Had something happened? Was she ill? Crossing to the window, relief spread through him at the sight of her coming up the lane. He squinted. What on earth was she wearing?

Anticipation she shouldn't be feeling danced along her nerve endings, hammered her heart against her rib cage and lengthened her stride. In the past few days, she'd thought of little else besides Lucian and the many reasons she mustn't care for him. Since she was a daydreamer by nature, often preoccupied with her thoughts, her sisters hadn't noticed anything out of the ordinary.

Her life was good—like a rich chocolate cake. Plain. Unexceptional. But good. Lucian's presence in her life was like sweet, decadent icing on that cake. His presence added depth and excitement and meaning. Paired together, the two created a delicious concoction.

Well, you'd better get used to cake without icing, because Lucian isn't sticking around. He has a life to get back to. A perfect, beautiful, spoiled young debutant to choose.

That put a damper on her anticipation.

Climbing the steps, a scowl twisted her mouth. She really was a foolish, naive girl. Her wayward heart had actually entertained the notion that he could come to care for her. *Her.* A simple mountain girl who would stick out like a sore thumb in his glittering world. She didn't know the waltz. Or which fork to use. When she laughed, it wasn't a polite twitter but a full laugh that would no doubt shock polite society.

Josh was right. She read too much. This was real life, not fiction.

The door opened before she could press the bell. Instead of admitting her, Lucian crossed the threshold and pulled the door closed behind him.

The humor warming his black eyes to melted chocolate robbed her lungs of breath. He was always so serious and somber that this unexpected lightheartedness made him seem like an entirely different man.

Folding his arms across his strong chest, straining the shoulders of his gray, pin-striped coat, he looked her up and down. "Who are you supposed to be? Or should I say what are you?"

She smoothed the furry pelt covering her hair, the one Nicole had fashioned into a sort of headdress for her. It was hot and itchy and tended to pitch forward into her eyes, but the kids would love it. "Tonight's story is *Little Red Riding Hood.* Can't you guess who I am?"

Eyes twinkling now, his head fell back and he laughed, a rumbling, husky sound that tickled her ears. The unrestrained curve of his generous lips, the flash of white teeth, the glimpse of happiness in his otherwise stern face, evoked an intense yearning deep within her. A yearning to see this man happy more often. To see his smile. To hear his laughter.

Oh, wow, she was in way too deep. She couldn't start caring about his happiness!

"Ah, *mon chou,* you are something else." Grinning, he shook his head. "I've never met anyone quite like you."

She didn't have a response to that. So she simply gazed at him, soaking in this new Lucian to remember later, after he'd gone. Gradually, the humor faded and was replaced with his customary intensity. Her disappointment was sharp.

"I need to talk to you about something." His gaze shifted past her shoulder to the lane. "Ollie and a few others are here. Later, all right?"

"Yes, okay."

What could he possibly want to talk about? Her stomach dipped. What if he'd heard from his lawyer? What if he'd found a way to circumvent Charles's wishes?

Her nerves were stretched taut throughout the evening. She rushed through the story and afterward had trouble making small talk with the parents. Distracted, that's what she was. Just when she thought they'd bidden good-night to the last of the guests, Tom showed up. She hadn't seen him since the previous Friday night, the night of their confrontation. As impatient as she was to learn Lucian's purpose, she couldn't bring herself to dash the cautious optimism on her good friend's face.

Tom may not be cake icing, but he meant a lot to her. *He* wasn't going anywhere.

Asking him to wait in the entryway while she gathered her things, she hurried to the parlor where Lucian was finishing the cleanup.

Picking up her reticule from the settee, she slipped her hand through the ribbon loop. "I'm sorry. Our conversation will have to wait. Tom's waiting to walk me home."

An empty pitcher in his hands, his gaze shot to the door and back. He didn't look pleased. "Do you have free time tomorrow?"

"Once I finish my morning chores. Do you want me to come here?"

He considered the matter for a moment. "Would you mind showing me some more of the area? I can ask Mrs. Calhoun to prepare a picnic lunch. My horse is in need of exercise," he tacked on.

An entire day with Lucian all to herself? The prospect eclipsed any dread of what he might tell her.

A smile bloomed across her face. "I'd like that."

"Magnifique." His answering smile, slow and easy, heated her inside and out. She would never, ever take that smile for granted. "Shall I meet you at your place, say, around ten o'clock?" he asked.

"I'll see you then." *Please let this night pass quickly!*

When he waved away her offer to help with the chairs, she rejoined Tom, ignoring the questions in his eyes. On the walk home, they talked of inane things— his customers, his ailing mother, Megan's impatience for news from Cades Cove. Nothing too personal, thank goodness. True to his word, Tom didn't press her or even mention their earlier conversation. But it was there nonetheless…a strange tension between them that hadn't been there before. One day soon, she was going to have to muster her courage and admit she wasn't interested in pursuing a romance with him.

Please, Lord, grant me wisdom and courage. Prepare his heart to hear what I have to say. I hate to think of what this will do to our friendship, but the longer I remain silent the harder it will be on the both of us.

She couldn't do it tonight. Not with her blood still

humming from the effects of Lucian's smile. Her body singing with excitement in expectation of their outing. Her words would tumble out a tangled mess, and she'd end up hurting him more than was necessary. Better to wait, to prepare. Frame her thoughts in the best way possible.

When he invited her to go fishing with him the following morning, she declined without telling him of her plans. Trying to cover his disappointment, he smiled and bade her good-night, waiting until she was safely inside the cabin before he left.

That night, she dreamed that Lucian, herself and Tom were seated around their dining table, a humongous chocolate cake in the middle. It all started out normally. They each ate their slice of cake while engaging in polite conversation. The next thing she knew, they were fighting over what was left of it, a fight that quickly turned into a full-fledged tug-of-war!

She awoke just as Tom smashed a gob of cake into Lucian's face.

What a strange, unsettling dream. One thing was certain—she would never look at chocolate cake the same way again.

"C'est magnifique." Sitting astride his most trusted and favored mount, Lucian rested his hands on his thighs, enjoying the view while waiting for Megan's Mr. Knightley to crest the hill. To their left, rounded peaks dense with trees reached for the blue sky, the undulating ridges stretching into the distance. On their right, the fertile valley dotted with cabins and other structures lay far below, a verdant oasis sheltered by the mountains.

Pulling astride, Megan patted her horse's neck and smiled over at him. She wore a sturdy, navy blue riding dress that made her eyes seem that much bluer and a stiff-brimmed bonnet in the same hue that hid her curls. He did not care for that bonnet, he decided.

"Your father is French, right? Is he the one who taught you to speak the language?"

"No, but it was important to him that I learn to speak it fluently, so he hired a native French tutor for me. Now my father and I converse strictly in French." His mother had attempted to learn but couldn't quite master it. He knew she'd felt left out whenever he and his father spoke together.

"That's why you slip so easily into it."

"*Oui, mon chou,* that's why."

A becoming pink stole along her cheekbones. "It's a beautiful language. I could sit and listen to you speak it for hours, even though I wouldn't have a clue what you were saying."

Pleasure spread through him at the revealing statement. "Is that so?"

Her blush deepened, spreading to her slender throat, and she turned her head, the bonnet's brim shielding her. He forced his gaze to the impressive scenery. This was to be their final day together. After lunch, he would tell her of his decision and his plans to leave in two days' time. The pleasure he'd experienced seconds ago twisted into something painful, and he realized with some shock that he'd grown attached to this young woman.

Better a quick break now than a slow, tortuous parting later.

He would enjoy this one day with her. Tuck the memory away for safekeeping.

"You didn't tell me what your horse's name was," she ventured, taking in his mount's sleek, muscled frame.

"D'Artagnan." He waited to see if she recognized Alexandre Dumas's character.

"*The Three Musketeers* is a favorite of yours?"

He smiled, not surprised she had. "I've lost count how many times I've read it. I could probably even quote parts of it."

Guiding their horses away from the main trail and into the woods, they discussed books they liked and ones they didn't. It was a lively, stimulating conversation, one he couldn't imagine having with any debutant in his circle. Megan's intelligence and observations impressed him.

"Why don't you try your hand reading to the children sometime? I'm certain they'd enjoy a change of pace—having a man read to them."

"I can't do that, Megan. I—" He stopped at the sight of her frown. "What is it?"

Pointing ahead, she said unhappily, "The meadow I wanted to take you to is beyond that stream, but it's too swollen to cross. I'd hoped to have our picnic there."

As they neared, Lucian gauged the width and depth. "It doesn't appear to be that deep. Our horses won't have a problem crossing."

Her gloved fingers gripped the reins. "It's the swiftness of the current that has me worried. I wouldn't mind walking across on those larger rocks, but on the back of a horse…" She shuddered. "I've seen too many men swept downstream when their horses lost their footing." Twisting in the saddle to study the land behind them, she said, "We can have our lunch here somewhere, and hopefully go to the meadow another day when the water level's lower."

But there wouldn't be another chance. Dismounting, he walked around to her side and held out his hand. "Don't worry, *mon petite,* I will get you to your meadow."

"I don't know—"

"Trust me."

With a quizzical smile, she placed her hand in his and allowed him to help her down.

"Wait here."

Vaulting into Mr. Knightley's saddle, he leaned down and, gathering D'Artagnan's reins, guided them both across the stream. As he'd suspected, it wasn't deep. They made it to the other side without a single misstep.

Megan waited for him on the opposite bank, white teeth worrying her bottom lip. Standing in a patch of buttery sunlight, she was a vision in blue, a burst of color amid the vast green landscape. He wished then for a camera or a canvas and paints, any way to capture this image to keep for all time.

Splashing through the cool water to reach her, he lifted her into his arms without a word of warning.

"Lucian!" she exclaimed, fingers clutching at his coat lapels. "What are you doing?"

"What does it look like I'm doing?" He grinned, re-entering the water. "Hold on tight."

Encircling his neck, she pressed into his chest. Hid her face in the hollow between his neck and shoulder. "Please don't drop me."

He tightened his hold about her waist, delighting

in her soft, warm weight. Her delicate scent. "I'll do my best."

Her response was to snuggle closer. Up on the bank, water sluicing from his boots, he was loath to put her down. But he did, slowly lowering her, steadying her. The undisguised yearning in her wide blue eyes did him in.

"This bonnet has to go." The unsteadiness in his voice took him by surprise.

Her brow puckered. "I realize it isn't fashionable or new, but it's durable."

"It wouldn't matter if it was fresh from the store or twenty years old, I still wouldn't like it."

Tugging on the bow beneath her chin, he undid the loops. When no words of protest followed her audible breath, he carefully lifted it from her head, stepping away only long enough to hook it on the saddle horn. Her white-blond mane shimmered in the sun's rays. Still not satisfied, he reached around and untied the blue ribbon at her nape. Curls cascaded down past her shoulders.

"Much better," he murmured.

Their gazes locked, she didn't move or speak, but her wishes were written there for him to see. Cradling her face, he skimmed a thumb across her mouth. "Has anyone ever told you that your lips are the color of ripe peaches?"

"A-actually no," she whispered, her hands coming up to grip his forearms. "You're the first."

"They haunt my dreams," he ground out, dipping his head and capturing them with his own. He slid his fingers into her glorious hair, cool, liquid silk whispering across his skin.

Ah, yes, she was as sweet as he'd imagined. So much so that his chest ached with the knowledge that she would never be his. A whirlpool of need, accompanied by emotion he couldn't identify, spiraled through him, and he deepened the kiss. Megan's arms looped around his waist to hug him close. Her mouth was soft and inviting, clinging with a tenderness that made him want to weep.

Chapter Eleven

In the haven of Lucian's arms, Megan felt protected. Cherished. And blissfully happy. Knowing it couldn't last, she savored every second, memorizing the feel of his broad chest, the leashed strength in his powerful arms, the delightful sensation of his fingers threading through her hair. His kiss was warm, insistent yet tender.

She'd been right about the effects. Already she was picturing herself in a beaded gown and flowers in her hair, pledging herself to this man. She was mentally sliding the ring on his finger when he literally jerked away as if burned.

Startled, she gripped the sides of his coat to stop his retreat. "Lucian?"

His hands resting heavily on her shoulders, he struggled to regain his composure. There was a vulnerability in his dark eyes that hadn't been there before. Regret pulled his mouth into a grimace. "I'm leaving Monday morning."

It took a moment for his words to sink in. "What? Why?"

"I'm leaving the house in your care. You may do with it what you wish, except sell it. I prefer for it to remain in my family."

When his hands fell away, she relinquished her hold. He moved downstream, leaving her to process the news. Denial ripped through her. She'd known this day would come, of course—she just hadn't expected it so soon.

"What about the lawyer?"

Head bent, his dark layers slid forward and concealed his eyes. Near his jawline, a muscle twitched. "I've written him to call off his search. It's clear you cared a great deal for my grandfather, and I have faith you'll take care of the house just as you've done in the months since his death."

Speechless, she scuffed the grass with her boot. The elation she should be feeling didn't come. Wasn't this what she wanted? Hadn't she prayed that he'd change his mind and let her use the house?

"I shouldn't have kissed you. Not when I have no plans to court you."

His blunt words chilled her to the bone, his cool reserve chasing away the warm and fuzzy feelings of a moment ago. Hugging her arms about her waist, she looked away. Couldn't risk him seeing how much this hurt.

"Look, I don't want this to ruin our last day together. I've enjoyed spending time with you, Megan." His voice deepened as he spoke. "I'd like to carry good memories back home with me."

Tomorrow he'd be preparing for his trip while she was attending church and having lunch with her family. They'd both be too busy to do much more than say goodbye. After tomorrow, she would likely never see

Lucian again. Sadness leached the color from her surroundings, muting the grass and rushing water and sky above. Even the birds' songs seemed to take on a hollow, mournful quality.

"If you'd rather return home," he continued into the lingering silence, "I'll accompany you. No hard feelings."

"I suppose we shouldn't let all that food go to waste." She waved a hand towards D'Artagnan's bulging saddlebags. "Not after all the trouble Mrs. Calhoun went to. And then there's the matter of your boots. You would've ruined them for nothing."

Water streaks marred the mirrorlike surfaces and bits of mud clung to the heels. She knew how their condition must irk him.

"You didn't ask me to carry you across. I did that all on my own." He shrugged. "It's nothing a little spit and polish won't fix."

"All right, then." Snatching her bonnet, she crossed to her horse and thrust her boot in the stirrup. "We have another quarter of a mile to go."

They rode the rest of the way in silence, giving her time to regain her composure, to marshal her emotions. Time enough to deal with them later. Like Lucian, she wanted things to be peaceful between them. If memories were all she would have, she wanted them to be good ones.

A break in the trees, a wide swath of sunlight streaming through the overhead canopy shone down on her favorite meadow. A thick carpet of grass intermingled with purple-and-blue wildflowers. Butterflies flitted above blooms. She soaked in the sight, remembered all the fond memories associated with this spot.

"How did you find this place?" Lucian unlatched the saddlebag containing their lunch.

Taking the quilt he held out to her, her gaze tracked the massive tree trunks up to their leafy branches far above. "My father and I discovered it long ago on one of our bird-watching hikes. We came here often. Sometimes Juliana would tag along, but for the most part, it was just he and I. He'd sit and play his harmonica while I read or made friends with the butterflies."

He straightened, a square, lidded basket in his arms. "Where is your father?"

"He passed away when I was young. Heart attack." Even after all these years, she still missed him. "Sometimes a man will walk past me on the street, and I'll get a whiff of the cologne Father used to wear. In that moment, the grief resurfaces and I long to tuck my hand in his again. See his smile once more. He had a great, booming laugh that shook the walls."

Lucian winced. Too late, she understood the wounds her words were likely to inflict on someone whose loss was still fresh.

He wore a grim expression. "Does it ever get easier?"

"Time helps. And lots of prayer." Making her way through the grass, she chose a good spot and, shaking out the quilt, bent to smooth it. He set the basket aside to assist her. "My father's passing was unexpected. One minute he was sitting on the porch, rocking and playing his harmonica, and the next he was gone. We didn't even have a chance to say goodbye. The shock would've devastated us were it not for God's comforting hand. 'Blessed are those who mourn, for they will be comforted.'"

The quilt smoothed, Lucian settled the basket in the

middle and waited for her to sit before lowering himself to the ground. Long legs stretched out so that his boots rested on the grass, he watched silently as she unpacked first the dishes and silverware, then the jar of tea and the food.

"I haven't found any measure of comfort in my mother's death."

Megan's hands stilled. His bitter grief hung in the air between them. Beneath the black coat that molded to his athletic build like a second skin, his back and shoulders were rigid. Anguish swirled in his eyes like an out-of-control tempest.

"You haven't allowed yourself to grieve, have you?"

"I'm not sure I know how. I have to be honest—I'm… angry at God for taking her. She was too young. And vibrant. If He cared about me like you say He does, then how could He take away my one true friend?"

"Oh, Lucian, I can't answer that." Heart heavy for his loss and his loneliness, she covered his hand with her own. "No one can fathom God's intentions or reasons. Why did my father have to die when he did? Why are precious babies taken from their mothers before they even have a chance to live? No one travels through life untouched by heartache, but God is there to help us. He promises to never leave us."

Flipping his hand beneath hers, he threaded his fingers through hers. "I carry her Bible with me everywhere I go. When I'm out riding, it's in the saddlebags. When I'm at home, it's on my bedside table. She cherished that Bible. Keeping it nearby helps me feel close to her."

"But you don't read it, do you?" When he shook his head, she suggested, "Maybe it's time you started. We keep Father's on the living room mantel so that we all have access to it. He wrote sermon notes in the margins and underlined important passages. It's a glimpse into what he was thinking, the things the Lord was teaching him. Perhaps Lucinda did the same."

His gaze flicked to his horse, standing in the shade with Mr. Knightley and nibbling on grass. "Perhaps you're right."

Disengaging her hand before she did something foolish, like pulling him into a hug, Megan focused on dishing out the fried chicken and potato salad. Lucian poured tea into the glasses.

"You know, I hadn't intended for this outing to become so somber. You're probably wishing you'd stayed home."

She handed him a filled plate and cloth napkin. "On the contrary. I'd much rather speak plainly than ignore the deeper issues. What would be the point in that?"

Funny. She hadn't felt that way the night before. With Tom, she craved the exact opposite. Had been relieved to speak of nothing of import, to avoid the one subject they needed to address.

Accustomed to giving thanks before meals, Megan said a silent prayer before picking up her fork. She wasn't as hungry as she should've been. In a hurry to finish her morning chores, she'd settled for a single biscuit slathered with blackberry jam.

When they'd eaten their fill and cleared away the dishes, Lucian asked if she'd mind reading to him. A little self-consciously, she agreed. He lay back, tanned hands folded on top of his chest, and closed his eyes. Before long, he was sound asleep.

Megan lowered the book to her lap. The harsh set

of his features relaxed in sleep, he looked ten years younger. And at peace. Watching the even rise and fall of his chest, her throat closed as unshed tears sprang up. Lifted trembling fingers to her lips. *Oh, Lord, I'm going to miss this man so.*

He was leaving, and there was nothing she could do to stop him. She felt helpless and a bit frantic. Desperate. Was this…love? Surely not. Surely it wouldn't hurt this much. Surely she wouldn't have been so foolish!

Jumping up, the book slipping from her lap, she strode across the meadow and into the forest's cool shelter, not stopping until she was certain she wouldn't cry. Lucian would see the evidence and seek to discover the reason. Better to wait until he was gone.

She'd have the rest of her life to cry over him.

Lucian stirred from his slumber, disoriented at first. Then he remembered. He'd drifted to sleep to the soothing sound of Megan's voice. Propping himself up on one arm, he scanned the meadow. Where was she? The book she'd been reading lay facedown on the quilt, some of the pages bent. Frowning, he righted it and got to his feet, turning in a circle to search the surrounding woods for a sign of her.

"Megan?"

"I'm here," she answered, as she ducked from behind his horse. "I've got most of the supplies packed away. We should probably be heading back."

Lucian rested his hands on his hips. Something was wrong. Beneath her bonnet's brim, her face was pale, without expression, and she was avoiding his gaze. Was she angry he'd fallen asleep? Suffice it to say, he wasn't exactly thrilled he'd wasted precious time with her.

"I didn't mean to fall asleep like that. I'm sorry."

She faltered and her lips softened. "I don't mind. You needed the rest." Then she passed by him without another glance. Turning, he followed and helped gather the rest of their things.

When they were about to mount up, he stopped her with a hand on her arm.

"Are you all right?"

The smile lifting her lips didn't quite reach her eyes. "I'm fine."

While he didn't believe her, he refused to argue. "Thank you for bringing me up here. For sharing your special place with me. I don't know when I've enjoyed myself more." It was the best he could give her without admitting how much she'd come to mean to him. She was a once-in-a-lifetime woman. *Yet you're going to turn your back on her.*

Her blue eyes grew luminous. "I'm glad. I—I enjoyed our time together."

Shaking off his hand, she climbed into her saddle and signaled her horse to head out. Lucian caught up to her, and they rode side by side, lost in thought. At the stream, he halted his horse but didn't dismount. Absorbed the magnificent view one last time.

Megan seemed as reluctant to move as him. Was she thinking about the kiss they'd shared? He longed to take her in his arms again. Glancing back at her, he was disappointed to find her face hidden from view. Dreadful bonnet.

"Lucian."

Staring at the ground, she held herself very still.

"Lucian, don't move."

He started to scan the ground. "What—"

Tension screaming from her body, she hissed, "There's a copperhead close to D'Artagnan's rear leg, and he's poised to strike."

Heart pounding, teeth clenched, his fingers tightened on the reins even as he forced his muscles not to react. Sweat popped out on his brow. The rushing water masked the sound of the snake's warning hiss. If his horse was struck, Lucian would be forced to put him down. He couldn't let that happen. Not to this loyal friend.

Megan was inching her hand towards her boot. "What are you doing?" he demanded softly.

She didn't answer, and he didn't shift in the saddle to look for the reptile. He was afraid that if he moved even an inch, D'Artagnan might sidestep. When she scooted up her skirts, Lucian averted his gaze. What on earth was she doing?

"Hold on," she ordered.

He did look then, shock reverberating through his body at what he saw. A gun. She was holding a gun. A mean, dangerous-looking weapon more suited to a lawman than a young lady like herself.

The sudden blast spooked the horses. D'Artagnan reared. Lucian felt himself slipping backward. In his haze of disbelief, he'd let go of the reins. Too late. He felt nothing but air as the hard earth rushed up to meet him. The sound of bones cracking as he landed echoed in his ears an instant before he registered mind-numbing pain.

Chapter Twelve

"Lucian!"

Megan watched in horror as he hit the ground, face contorting as he cradled his right arm against his body. Sheathing her weapon in her leg holster, she worked to calm her horse. When he'd settled, she scrambled down and, sidestepping the dead snake, sprinted to where Lucian lay on his side.

"I'm so sorry," she stammered, reaching out a hand to touch him only to snatch it back when he grimaced, burst forth with a slew of French. Pale beneath his tan, breathing fast, he held his injured arm tight against his midsection.

"The snake?" he pushed out through clenched teeth.

"Dead. But I'm afraid D'Artagnan bolted."

He closed his eyes. Muttered in French again.

Sick with worry, she went to her knees beside him, looking for evidence of other injuries. "Does anything else besides your arm hurt?"

He grunted a negative response.

"You didn't hit your head?"

"Non."

She skimmed shaky fingers over his scalp to be sure, then turned her attention to his arm. "We need to get that coat off so I can take a look at it. Check if the bone pierced the skin."

She prayed it hadn't. That would mean surgery and the potential for complications, as well as risk of infection. *Oh, God, please...*

"I don't feel any blood soaking through," he panted, wincing as she helped him into a sitting position.

"That's good. Is it the upper or lower part?"

"Forearm."

His hair hung in his eyes and bits of grass and dirt clung to his clothes. First she removed the sleeve of his good arm, then she moved around to the other side, sliding the material down as carefully as she could to avoid aggravating the injury. When he flinched and sucked in a harsh breath, she clamped down on her lip to keep from crying.

This was all her fault. She was the reason he was in such agony. *Berate yourself later. Right now you have to focus on helping him.*

There was no sign of blood, thank the Lord. But when she rolled up his sleeve, she noticed the swelling right away. And the beginnings of an angry bruise.

"I'll need to splint this."

The muscles in his jaw working, he nodded. His dark eyes bored into hers. "I know what you're thinking, and you can stop it right now."

Swallowing hard, she pulled her hands away. "If I hadn't shot at such close range—"

"My horse would be dead."

"Your horse is gone." And with him, Lucinda's Bible. His most treasured possession.

He looked away. "At least he's alive. Maybe…"

"As soon as we get to Doc Owens, I'll send for my cousins. They'll search for him."

"You did warn me. I just—" Perplexed, he shook his head. "Why didn't I know you were carrying a gun? And where did you learn to shoot like that?"

"I'll explain later. We need to get that splint on you and get you back to town as quickly as possible." Brushing the hair away from his face, she peered closely at him. "Are you dizzy? Nauseous? I've read the body can go into shock after an injury like this."

"I'm okay."

Of course he would say that. Strong and stubborn man that he was, he wouldn't be quick to let on how much he was hurting.

"Well, if you do experience any symptoms, tell me. I'm going to go find a stick."

It took her five minutes to find one the thickness and length she desired, another five to rip her petticoat into strips. He didn't utter a single sound as she wound the strips about his wrist and the area below his elbow, securing the stick. She used an extra-long length of cloth to fashion a sling.

When she'd helped him to his feet, he stepped over and toed the lifeless reptile with his boot. "Good shot."

Scooping his coat off the ground, she quickly folded and stowed it in the saddlebag. Leading Mr. Knightley over to him, she took in the pitiful picture he made, his right side all wrapped in her shredded undergarments. "How are we going to do this? You can't lead him, but if I sit in front, I'm afraid I'll accidentally bump your arm. The last thing I want to do is cause you additional pain."

A fine sheen of sweat was visible on his forehead.

"We'll just have to take that chance. I'll try to shield it with my good arm."

With one boot in the stirrup and a hand on the saddle horn, Lucian hauled himself up behind Megan. A wave of dizziness washed over him. His body went first hot, then cold, his arm one throbbing mass of pain.

Dear God, Megan insists You care about what happens to me. Well, I'm in a bit of a bind here. Not really sure I can make it to town without sliding off the back of this horse in a dead faint. She's already feeling guilty about this whole thing, so I can't exactly tell her how bad off I am. Can You help me stay upright? Please? For Megan's sake?

He didn't get a response. No inner voice acknowledging his request. No giddy feelings. Still, it felt good. And right. He hadn't prayed like that since he was a young boy, when he and his mother would pray together every night before she tucked him into bed. She was the one who'd taught him about God and about His son Jesus, had read the Scriptures to him. As he'd grown older, he'd lost interest in those rituals he'd considered childish.

Now he wasn't so sure he wasn't missing out on something vitally important.

Oh, and God, could You please bring my horse back to me? He and I go way back, and, well, I'd hate to lose him. And my mother's Bible. I'd like to have that back, too. I promise I'll read it this time.

The trek down the mountain dragged on interminably. Due to the slope of the land, he had to fight gravity, lean backward at a slight angle so as not to fall forward into Megan's back. The shade was both a blessing and a curse, depending on whether he was sweating or shivering. His body couldn't seem to make up its mind.

Megan had asked him only once if he thought he could make it. After that, she'd concentrated all her attention on guiding her horse so as not to jar his arm. Now, though, he needed a distraction. Something to focus on besides his screaming wound and occasional dizzy spell.

"Talk to me, Megan," he murmured. "Tell me about the gun."

Her backward glance gave him a glimpse of her eyes, huge and dark with worry, at odds with the determined set of her chin. Beneath her feminine softness and delicate beauty lay a brave soul, strong and courageous. He counted himself fortunate to be in her capable hands. Many other young ladies in her position would've fainted or indulged in a fit of hysterics.

"It was a present from Josh. After our father passed, he thought we needed to learn how to protect ourselves and our property should trouble arise. He taught all of us girls how to shoot. Except for my mother. She refused to learn."

"Why don't you wear a holster about your waist? Where did you have it hidden? In your boot?"

"Josh fashioned a leg holster for me." She hitched a shoulder. "I don't wear it around the cabin or in town. Just when I'm out exploring. You never know who might be passing through."

"Or what wild animals you might have to defend yourself against."

The horse stepped into a dip. Lucian's hand shot out and cupped her waist as a way to brace himself. She rested hers atop his, pressing hard.

"Are you all right?"

"Yeah." He wanted to curl his arm about her and pull her snug against him, but his busted arm prevented him. He settled for this small connection.

"Have you ever broken anything before?" She tilted to the left to avoid hitting a low-slung branch face-first.

He mimicked her action. The forest had thickened, the trees growing closer together here. She concentrated on navigating around gnarled roots jutting out of the ground.

"No, I haven't."

"So, thanks to me, you've just suffered your first broken bone." Her sigh was rife with self-disgust. "Great. Just great."

He gripped her waist a fraction tighter. "Stop blaming yourself. I saw the gun. I knew what you were planning. I should never have let go of the reins. This injury is a result of my own stupidity, Megan."

"You do know what this means, don't you?" Her voice was low and strained.

Of course he did. He opted for a lighter note. "That I won't be penning any poems for a while?"

"Lucian—"

"Stop the horse and look at me."

Easing back on the reins, she waited until they had stopped to half turn in the saddle.

He cupped her chin, forced her to look him square in the eyes. He spoke clearly and with conviction, determined to make her see reason. "What you did back there took guts and skill. I'll always be thankful you saved D'Artagnan's life. I'd rather him be roaming these mountains without me than lying dead from my bullet because of a snakebite." He jerked his chin towards his arm. "This is a temporary setback. So I'll have to postpone my return. So what? Trust me, New Orleans will survive just fine without me."

He refused to think about what a prolonged visit might lead to. More than anything, he was petrified he wouldn't be able to stay away from her, that he'd wind up hurting her. Megan was a true innocent, her pure heart untouched by the cynicism with which he viewed the world. He would not be the man to tarnish that well-spring of optimism or dash her dreams of a marriage based on mutual trust and love.

But when her lower lip quivered and tears welled in her great big eyes, his heart went butter-soft.

"Please don't cry over me," he pleaded on a ragged whisper, unable to resist pressing his lips to hers, if only to stop their trembling. *Sweet. And vulnerable.* He broke contact, reluctantly, and brushed away a tear that had escaped. "I'm not worth it, *mon bien-aime.* Surely you know that."

"Oh, yes. Yes, you are." Her fierce expression dared him to argue the point. In that instant, Lucian understood how precariously close he was to tumbling into love with this woman. Him. A man who'd sworn off love and all the complications that went along with it.

He grimaced, aching physically and emotionally. "How much longer until we reach town?"

"Another half an hour. Can you make it? Do you need to dismount and rest for a bit?"

The concern and caring in her gaze made him feel reckless. He gritted his teeth, willing himself to think of all that was at stake. His sanity, for one. And her heart—well, he couldn't very well risk that, could he? "I can make it."

Thankfully, she turned and nudged Mr. Knightley into motion once more. By the time they halted outside the doctor's home, Lucian was light-headed and weak from holding himself rigid in the saddle. Somehow he managed to dismount without landing on his rear in the dirt. Wouldn't that make a nice impression on the upstanding folks of Gatlinburg? Lucian Beaumont sprawled in the middle of Main Street trussed up in a lady's undergarments?

As Megan assisted him inside the neatly furnished parlor, he swayed. Sat down hard in the nearest chair and fought the unpleasant queasiness in his middle.

"I'll go get Doc," Megan assured him, rushing from the room.

All he could do was sit there and hope he wasn't about to embarrass himself by getting sick right there in the doc's parlor.

"I'd advise you not to travel for at least a month," the doctor announced as he washed his hands in the basin. "You need to give that arm plenty of time to heal. If you injure it further before then, there's no telling what kind of permanent damage you might sustain."

Lucian's eyes were closed. "I understand."

Perched in a chair beside the bed, Megan worried the material of her skirt. Having refused chloroform and put off the laudanum until he got home, he'd endured the doctor's examination and the wrapping of his lower arm in plaster of Paris without pain reliever. She'd remained at his side throughout the entire process, had felt each wince and grimace clear down to her toes. He was holding back on account of her. And it had cost him.

Tension bracketed his mouth, his clean-shaven jaw like carved stone. His brown hair was damp with sweat.

Wearing his usual stern expression, the doctor came and rested a hand on her shoulder while addressing his patient. "Count yourself fortunate to have had this one along. She did everything right, from the splint and sling to getting you here in a timely manner."

Lucian's lids lifted a fraction. "She was amazing out there, sir."

Megan dipped her head. Wasn't he forgetting something? Like how he wouldn't be in this predicament if it weren't for her? Guilt weighed heavily. She'd desperately wanted Lucian to stay, but not like this.

To Megan, he instructed, "Make sure he takes the laudanum as soon as you get him home. He's going to need lots of rest."

"Yes, sir." Rising, she briefly touched Lucian's hand. "Josh is waiting out front with the wagon. I'll go tell him you're ready to go. He can help get you settled."

"I'm not an invalid." Nostrils flaring, he swung his legs over the side of the bed and pushed himself into a sitting position with the use of his good arm. "I can make it on my own steam."

"There's nothing wrong with accepting a little help now and then, young man," the doctor chided.

Lucian dragged a hand down his face, then looked at Megan. "I didn't mean to sound ungrateful."

"I know that." He was in pain and trying desperately to hide it. The sooner he was tucked in bed, the better. "Ready?"

He stood, pausing for a minute to get his bearings. Ignoring her instinct to hover, she preceded him out of the room and down the hall, his footsteps heavy behind her. As they emerged on to the porch, Josh looked up from the book he'd been reading and snapped it closed. Pushing out of the rocking chair, he approached with concern marring his brow.

He gave Lucian a once-over. "Everything all right?"

"It could've been worse," Lucian admitted. "It wasn't bad enough to require surgery, thank goodness."

"Just the one bone was broken," Megan added.

"That's something to be thankful for." Eyeing the sling, he nodded and rubbed his goatee. "Nathan and Caleb are out searching for your horse. I'll join them as soon as we have you settled."

"I appreciate the help." Gratitude laced his voice.

Lucian rode in the back of the wagon, while Megan joined Josh on the bench seat. She couldn't help glancing back every few minutes to check on him.

"He's going to be just fine, you know." Her cousin shot her a knowing grin.

Frowning, she explained in a low voice about Lucian's plans to leave. How she was the reason he'd been forced to postpone his plans.

"Does he blame you?" Josh managed to look incredulous and irritated at the same time.

"No, of course not." She rushed to defend Lucian. "He's adamant that he's glad I did what I did and thankful his horse is still alive."

"Good." The tension left his shoulders. "For a minute there, I thought I was going to have a little chat with our friend."

Megan sighed and rolled her eyes. Who needed big brothers when she had Josh to defend her honor? And Nathan and Caleb? "You wouldn't dare."

"Um, yeah, I would." His blue eyes narrowed. "Any

man who dares to treat you or the girls in an ungentle-manly fashion will have to answer to me."

"Wasn't it you who taught us to stick up for our-selves?"

"I'm not implying you can't do that. I'm just saying that I won't ignore such behavior. With your pa gone…" He trailed off, shrugging.

She laid a hand on his arm. "I know you have our best interests at heart. You're more than a mere relative, you know. You're a true friend."

The tips of his ears turned red and his smile had an awkward tilt, but his eyes were warm as he curled an arm about her shoulders and hugged her close. "Are you trying to make a grown man cry, Goldilocks?"

"I would never do such an underhanded thing," she protested with a smile, adding on a more serious note, "Kate and I talked the other day. I'm praying for you both."

The amusement faded from his face. "Thank you."

"If you need someone to talk to, I'm here."

He only nodded, clearly troubled but not willing to discuss the subject. She knew him well enough not to push. When and if he wanted to talk, he'd let her know. Until then, she would continue to pray.

Josh didn't come inside the house, preferring to leave right away and join the others in their search. Mrs. Cal-houn didn't fuss over Lucian as Megan had feared she might. Although clearly concerned, she seemed to sense, like Megan, that he wouldn't welcome being coddled. He turned on the bottom step, his good hand propped on the wall for balance.

"Go home, Megan," he said gently. "It's long past supper time, and I'm certain your sisters are growing anxious. You need rest, as well. My valet will help me rid myself of these atrocious clothes and boots."

Her cheeks heated. Of course her helping him into bed was out of the question. Still, she would've liked to hang around until he was settled, to make sure he was comfortable. "I'm not that tired. I can wait down here—"

He ran his knuckles lightly down her cheek. "You're swaying in your boots. Go home and eat something. I'll still be here tomorrow if you want to check up on me," he said wryly, one black brow arched.

"All right, I'll go, but only if you promise to be a good patient and take the laudanum. You won't be able to truly rest if you're in pain."

His generous mouth curved, softening the aristocratic features. "I give you my word, Nurse Megan."

"I'm praying for you, Lucian." At his arrested expression, she ventured softly, "What? Has no one prayed for you before?"

"Only my mother," he admitted, his dark eyes swirling with emotion.

"Well, I know for a fact that as news of your accident travels through town, the number of people praying for you will grow."

"I should tell you something." He hesitated. "I prayed today like I haven't done since I was a young boy. A real prayer—not like grace before a meal or a quick plea for help. I really talked to God. Not sure if He heard me or if He even cares, but I did it. And it felt…good."

"Oh, Lucian, that's wonderful." She smiled tremulously. "He does care. I have that on authority of His Word."

He gazed at her without speaking, mulling over her words. "Yes, well, I just wanted you to know."

"I'm glad you told me. Good night, Lucian."

"Bonne nuit, mon chou."

With his whispered farewell lingering in her ears, she let herself out. Walking home, she pondered their conversation, her burden of guilt sitting a little lighter on her shoulders. If this delay accomplished only one thing—deepening Lucian's faith—then it was worth her guilt and even his momentary suffering.

God worked in mysterious ways. He had His reasons for allowing the accident to happen, reasons they may never understand. All she knew was that Lucian wasn't leaving as planned, which meant she wouldn't have to say goodbye right away. Had been granted a reprieve. What that meant for her heart she was afraid to find out.

Chapter Thirteen

Descending the church steps after the morning service, Megan felt a hand on her arm and glanced up into Tom's smiling face.

"Hey, pretty lady, can I have a moment?"

She smiled back. "Of course."

At the bottom, she stepped off to the side to avoid the stream of churchgoers heading to their wagons. He motioned for Jane and Nicole to join them.

"What are your lunch plans?" His eager gaze touched each of theirs.

"Leftovers," Nicole said with a sigh, her displeasure marring her perfect features. Wearing her smart green ensemble, a feathered hat perched atop her shiny black mane, she looked like an angry china doll.

"Why do you ask?" At nearly sixteen, Jane exhibited more maturity than her older sister. Her serene expression couldn't mask the telltale loneliness in her eyes. Megan wondered how Jessica was handling this separation, the twins' first. The more outgoing of the two, Jessica wasn't as sensitive as Jane.

Lifting his hat to fluff his hair, he hooked a thumb towards his wagon. "I took a chance and ordered a picnic lunch from Plum's in the hopes you three ladies would agree to join me. I thought about heading over to the river." He mentioned their family's favored picnic spot.

She'd planned to pay Lucian a visit immediately after lunch, but Tom had already purchased the food, and the look Jane shot her was hope-filled. Besides, a tiny part of her dreaded seeing Lucian. He had an awful lot of time on his hands. Time to think, to replay yesterday's events and the consequences. What if he'd finally come to the conclusion that she'd caused nothing but trouble for him since the day he'd first arrived? What if he was angry? What if—

"So what's it going to be, Megan?" Tom stood with his hands on his hips, waiting expectantly.

She took a deep breath. "We'd love to join you."

"Great." White teeth flashed in a wide grin that had no effect on her whatsoever. Nothing like Lucian's potent smiles.

She surreptitiously studied her friend, trying to study him objectively as a girl new to town would do. Dressed like the locals in pants, band-collared shirt and suspenders and boots, he was tall and lean and sturdy-looking. He was a tidy man, both in appearance and practice. He kept his barbershop spotless. His home, too. Attractive in an understated way, his green eyes were his only intriguing feature. Tom may not be the kind of man that would stand out in a crowd, but he was nice-looking in his own quiet way.

Why, oh why, wasn't she drawn to *him?* A local with no plans to leave. A man who knew where he stood with God, who lived to honor Him. A man who *wanted* to court her, who wanted a wife and children.

Why couldn't she be practical-minded? At times like this, she despised her romantic nature, her idealistic dreams of how her life should be.

Tamping down her frustration, and a childish desire to stamp her foot, Megan refocused on the conversation.

Jane was smiling shyly up at Tom. "It was very thoughtful of you to plan this outing, Tom."

His wink caused a blush to spread along Jane's cheeks. "I must admit to selfish motives, Janie-girl. It's not every day a man is blessed with the company of three lovely ladies."

"Don't you mean three of the loveliest ladies in Gatlinburg?" Nicole smirked.

"Tom," Megan interjected to save him from having to reply, "will you mind stopping at the cabin long enough for us to change?"

Amusement dancing in his eyes, he nodded, and, taking her hand, he placed it in the crook of his arm. On the drive out to her place, he made casual mention of Lucian's accident. Even if he hadn't heard it through the town grapevine, he would've learned about it in church this morning as Reverend Monroe had spoken of it from the pulpit, asking the congregation to pray. She skirted the issue in an effort to deflect personal questions. No way did she want to discuss her and Lucian's relationship—or lack thereof—with Tom.

Kind man that he was, he allowed her to steer the conversation into safer waters. He waited patiently in the wagon while the girls changed out of their Sunday best and into everyday dresses. Nicole, in particular, was happy to have a reprieve from kitchen duties. The only chore she enjoyed was sewing clothes, and she excelled at it. Everything else that needed to be done around the farm she considered beneath her. One would think she believed herself royalty rather than a simple mountain girl. Megan loved her sister, but sometimes she didn't understand her.

They weren't the only ones at the river. When they arrived, they discovered a handful of families scattered along the riverbank, enjoying the fine spring weather before it turned hot and humid and far too uncomfortable to lounge about in the noonday sun. Waving to familiar faces, they selected a spot in the flower-strewn field and set out their quilts and the mouthwatering food Mrs. Greene, the Plum Café's owner, had prepared for them. Ravenous now, their prayer of thanks was a brief one. Companionable silence reigned as they ate.

Children's delighted shrieks carried on the wind, punctuated by adult laughter. The meandering river trickled over rocks and occasional fallen logs, birds chirped and whistled. One family in particular caught Megan's eye—a sharply dressed man and his wife and their small toddler, a boy with a shock of dark hair the same hue as Lucian's.

Her heart constricted. Longing for the impossible sliced through her, left her bleeding and sore. She and Lucian didn't have a future together. They would never be that family—a loving husband and wife and children filling their lives with laughter and joy.

Despite this delay, Lucian would eventually return home. He would choose a suitable bride, perfect in every way, one who would dutifully provide him with his sole heir. Irrational jealousy gripped her, soured her stomach. She set aside her plate, sipping her lemonade in the hopes it would wash away the bitter taste in her mouth. It would serve him right if his future wife gave him a passel of daughters. How many until he gave up hope for a son? Six? Nine?

"I'm going for a walk," she abruptly announced, heartsick at the image of him and his ice queen surrounded by rosy-cheeked girls with black eyes.

Tom's forehead bunched in concern. Eyes crinkled at the corners as he squinted against the sun. "You haven't finished your lunch."

"I wasn't as hungry as I thought. I'll finish it later." She covered her plate with a cloth and placed it back in the basket, safe from flies and ants, then strolled down to the river's edge.

Watching the water flow past, she trailed a line in the damp earth with her boot.

Tom joined her after five minutes. "Want to tell me what's on your mind?"

She shrugged. "Nothing interesting."

He took both her hands in his. "We're friends, remember? No matter what happens between us, we'll always be friends first. I can tell something's bothering you. You haven't been yourself lately, and frankly, I'm a bit worried."

While his words indicated one thing, in his eyes she saw the hope for something more. "I'm just concerned about the girls. Jane mopes about the house missing Jessica, and Nicole…well, you know how she can be. Multiply that by ten. It's a big responsibility Ma placed in my lap, and she hasn't yet sent word what's happening with Juliana. We don't know if she's had the baby yet and if so, how they're both faring."

All of that *was* weighing on her mind. And it was all she was willing to share with him.

"I'm sure your sister and the baby are just fine. I

don't know much about females, but I'll help with your sisters in any way I can."

"That means a lot to me." She lightly squeezed his hands before pulling free.

A loud splash, followed by a woman's alarmed cry, startled them both. Tom whirled around. Lunged for the little boy who'd landed on his rear in the water. The one who'd reminded her of Lucian.

Noticing the tears welling in his eyes and the curl of his bottom lip, Tom picked him up and, heedless of the water dripping everywhere, hugged him against his body. "Hey there, little buddy. What's your name?"

Before he could get a word out, his mother rushed up. "Lenny! Are you all right?"

He wiggled to get down. Tom lowered the tyke to the ground so he could toddle over to his mother.

"Thank you," she said, taking hold of the boy's hand. "Stay close to Mama from now on, Lenny. Let's go dry you off." She led him back to their quilt.

"Cute little guy," Tom said with a grin, seemingly oblivious to his damp clothing.

"How many kids do you want?" Megan blurted, her gaze still trained on mother and son.

His brows lifted, "I think four is a good goal. What about you?"

"Ten."

"I can see that." He smiled and slowly nodded. "You're good with kids. You'll be a wonderful mother someday."

She didn't comment and, after moments of silence, he ventured, "Why do you ask, Megan? Are you…? Have you thought more about my courting you?"

Her gaze shot to his face alight with anticipation. Oh, no. What had she done? Thoughtless girl.

"Oh, Tom, no, I—I was simply curious. A friend and I were discussing the matter the other day, and Lenny reminded me of the conversation. I didn't intend to imply that I'd made a decision." Seeing his crestfallen expression, she decided she couldn't leave him hanging any longer. Not only was it unfair, it was cruel. "Actually, Tom, I don't need to make a decision. I—"

"Wait." He stepped closer. "I can see you're upset and worried about hurting my feelings. Let's not rush things. Like you said, you have a lot on your mind right now. I think it would be best if we waited until things have calmed down a bit to discuss this."

"But—"

"No buts." Smiling gently, he jerked his head towards the field where Jane and Nicole waited. "Let's rejoin your sisters. I promised them an entertaining afternoon, and I aim to deliver."

Megan woke before dawn Monday morning. Padding to the window in her bare feet, she pushed the curtain aside and peered into the silent darkness. *Where are you, D'Artagnan?* Josh and Nathan had stopped by after supper last night with unhappy news—two days of searching had gotten them nowhere. Lucian's horse was still missing, and it fell to her to tell him.

Her cousins couldn't take any more time away from their work to search, which meant D'Artagnan—and Lucinda's Bible—might never be found. *Lord, this is important to Lucian. Please lead his horse back safe and sound.*

Wide-awake and restless, she tackled her chores and

even made a simple breakfast of ham, eggs and toast, a task that usually fell to Jane. Then, unable to wait a moment longer, she set out for Lucian's house.

Mrs. Calhoun came to the door, wiping her hands on her apron. "He's in the garden parlor. Go on back and say hello. I'm in the middle of fixing breakfast."

"Sorry to interrupt you." Megan paused in the entrance hall to remove her bonnet and straighten her apricot skirts. "I know it's early, but I was eager to check on him." Only half-past eight. Not exactly proper visiting hours.

"No need to apologize, dear. Company will do him good. Fred and I hung around yesterday to see to his needs, but I caught him watching the door off and on. Probably hoping for a visit from you." Turning, she preceded Megan down the hall, stopping in the doorway leading to the dining room and, beyond, the kitchen. "I'll be along shortly with breakfast. Will you be joining him?"

"No, thank you. I already ate."

"A cup of coffee, then?"

"That would be wonderful, Mrs. Calhoun. Thanks."

When the older lady bustled off, Megan went in the opposite direction. Situated along the back of the house, the garden parlor was a long, rectangular room with high ceilings and a row of windows overlooking the rear porch and gardens. Done primarily in hues of cream, gold and sage, with occasional bursts of poppy-red and apricot, it possessed an airy, open feel that Megan found inviting. Botanical prints dotted the papered walls, and potted ferns flanked the windows thrown open to catch the floral-scented breeze. Gauzy drapes fluttered softly.

Advancing into the room, her steps muted by the

sage-and-cream-swirled rug, she spotted Lucian
stretched out on the sofa sound asleep. She rounded
the carved mahogany coffee table. Edged closer. He
was dressed more casually than she'd ever seen him.
No boots, of course. His stocking feet peeked out from
beneath chocolate-brown pants and beneath his sling,
he wore a loose cream shirt open at the neck, giving
her a peek of his smooth, tanned throat. A day's worth
of stubble darkened his jaw, his brown hair mussed.

Had he slept here the whole night through? From the
looks of him, he must've. Was Mrs. Calhoun right? Had
he been expecting her yesterday?

Bending at the waist, she carefully smoothed a lock
of hair that had fallen on to his forehead. When he didn't
stir, she gave in to the temptation to repeat the action,
trailing her fingertips lightly through the silky waves.
He sighed. Nestled his head deeper into the feather pillow, a small smile on his lips. Lips that had touched
hers, sparking dreams of a future.

Leaning down, she kissed his cheek, smiling when
his whiskers tickled her chin. She straightened, gasped
when her gaze encountered his confused one.

"Megan?" he said, voice raspy from sleep. "Am I
dreaming?"

Embarrassed, she acted as if he hadn't just caught
her kissing him. "*Bonjour,* Lucian. Did you sleep well?"

"*Bonjour,*" he responded slowly, his brow wrinkling.
"You speak French now?"

Twisting her hands behind her back, she said, "Kate
told me how to say that. Although, I can't pronounce it
quite like you do."

He struggled to sit up. Needing to distance herself
from his irresistible male presence, she backed away,

plopping clumsily into a nearby chair when her legs bumped against it. Lucian slouched against the sofa cushions, legs planted wide, one hand resting in his lap.

This rumpled version of him, unrestrained and a touch untamed, had a devastating effect on her equilibrium. Her heart jerked about in her chest in an uneven rhythm.

"Are you here because you're feeling sorry for me?" Raking her from head to toe, his gaze challenged her. "Or because your misplaced guilt became too much to bear?"

She hadn't expected an assault. "Why do you do that?" she demanded, chin lifting. "Why do you suspect everyone around you of ulterior motives? Couldn't I have come simply because I wanted to see you? To find out how you're feeling?"

"You didn't come yesterday." The slip in his customary confidence dispelled her ire.

"I wanted to, believe me, I—"

He held up a hand. "That was out of line. Forgive me. There's no need for you to explain." Lowering it, he appeared both stern and thoughtful, saying, "I suppose it stems from a lifetime of people befriending me on account of my last name, the wealth and power associated with my family."

Leaning forward, she studied the shadows of past pain in his eyes. "There's more to it, isn't there?"

Frowning, his gaze drifted to the floor. "There was a woman, Dominique. We traveled in the same circles, she and I, and crossed each other's paths quite regularly. Shortly before my mother's death, we were seated together at a friend's musical and, throughout the course

of the evening, found we had similar interests. We…
became close."

Megan sat stock-still, hands locked together in her
lap, insides withering. To hear Lucian speak of another
woman in this manner was like walking barefoot across
burning coals. *Dominique.* With a name like that, she
must be lovely and soft-spoken and well dressed, not a
single hair out of place.

He had courted Dominique. Yet, he'd made it clear he
wouldn't court Megan. She wasn't quite good enough,
was she? Didn't fulfill the lofty standards required of
the wife of Lucian Beaumont.

"I thought she was different from the rest. I believed
the extras didn't matter, that she was interested in *me*.
After all, she came from old money and was in possession of a pedigree even more stellar than mine." His
scowl was directed more at himself than anyone else,
as if *he* was to blame for the betrayal. "I misjudged her.
About a month after my mother's death, Dominique
came to the conclusion that she would be better served
if she aligned herself with my father. He's the one who
wields the reins, so to speak. The head of the family
and the shipping empire."

Megan's stomach dropped to her toes. This woman,
this Dominique, had betrayed him in the worst possible way. And at the worst possible time. What kind
of woman would do such an underhanded thing, especially when he was mourning the loss of his mother?

"I had to wonder if she'd been using me the entire
time to get to him."

Suddenly the pieces fit together like a well-written
horror story. His accusations and suspicions, his inabil-
ity at first to believe her motives were pure. Why dis-

covering that Lucinda, the mother he'd adored, might possibly have hidden the truth from him was so hard to accept.

"I'm so sorry, Lucian." Her jealousy and self-pity seemed very pathetic in this moment. She ached for this lonely, stoic man. "Did your father— What I mean is, did he—"

"Did he court Dominique?" he snorted. "No. And not due to any loyalty to me. No, he'd only recently rid himself of my mother. He wasn't about to tie himself to another desperate female."

"Is she the reason you don't want to marry for love?"

"The truth is, I'd rather not marry at all. Dominique made me forget, for a little while, a decision I made many years ago—that if I must marry, it would be a marriage based on social compatibility and companionship. *Not* emotions as changeable as the sea, as unstable as shifting sand beneath your feet. Dominique's betrayal turned out to be a blessing, really. Brought my goals back into focus."

He passed fingers over his injured arm beneath the sling and winced. "My parents' marriage was a disaster. Enamored of my mother's beauty and innocence, my father rushed them both into it without taking into account their differences. They had vastly different upbringings, as you know, which resulted in wholly different mind-sets. The physical attraction that had brought them together didn't last, at least not for my father. When he realized my mother wouldn't fit in his world, he made no attempts to hide his disdain. But no matter how ruthless he was, she never stopped loving him. Never stopped hoping they could recapture what they'd lost. She did everything in her power to change, to fit his idea of the ideal wife.... In the end, she only ended up losing herself." His expression grew fierce and his eyes blazed molten fire. "I refuse to live that way, to hurt a woman like my father hurt my mother. That's why when I marry, I'll make certain there are no attachments on either side. No feelings of any sort beyond common respect. That way, neither one of us will suffer."

Neither will he experience the joy of true love, she thought morosely, the satisfaction of shared dreams. The beauty of hearts in tune, woven together by God's sure hand. She wanted to argue with him. To plead with him to give love a chance. Just because Gerard and Lucinda's marriage was a failure didn't mean Lucian's would be. But he was a stubborn man, and she could tell by looking at him that he wouldn't be swayed on this. He was convinced that to marry for anything other than duty would be a grave mistake.

They made quite a pair, didn't they? The cynic and the dreamer. Lucian would not allow himself to love, and she...well, she would never stop yearning for it.

"I can see how a romantic-minded young lady such as yourself would have a tough time digesting all of this," he said with quiet intensity. "However, if you'd lived my childhood perhaps you would have an easier time understanding my point of view."

"I was blessed with two parents who loved each other." Her broken voice mirrored the state of her heart. Lucian's determination to live without love deeply saddened her. "So much so that my mother refuses to marry again."

Steps heralded the arrival of Mrs. Calhoun. "Breakfast is served." Sliding the tray onto the coffee table, she eyed Lucian. "I've prepared another dose of laudanum for you."

"Thank you." His gaze remained on Megan, and she knew without asking that he wasn't planning on taking it.

"Oh, it was no trouble. If you don't need anything else, I'll leave you two to your conversation." At his nod, she left them.

"How bad is the pain?"

He shifted beneath her scrutiny, unable to hide a sudden grimace. "Nothing I can't handle."

"Why won't you take the medicine?"

"I did take it that first night, as promised. However, I don't particularly enjoy the way my head feels as if it's going to topple from my body and as if I've swallowed a ball of yarn. I'd much rather deal with the discomfort."

"It would help you rest," she persisted.

"I'm not a man who needs a lot of rest," he muttered with a frown, even as he absently massaged the spot above his heart.

She was reminded of his doctor's recommendation to slow down. Lucian may not wish to take it easy, but this forced inactivity could turn out to be the best thing for him. He couldn't run from grief indefinitely. At some point, he was going to have to deal with his loss. And come to terms with Dominique's deception.

"I'm afraid my cousins weren't able to locate D'Artagnan."

He nodded. "I wasn't hopeful. Still, I'm grateful they were willing to try."

"There's still a chance he'll find his way back."

"I suppose. If he doesn't, I'm okay with that. I just

hope he finds himself a new owner soon. There're dangers out there."

Scooting to the edge of the cushions, he awkwardly lifted the coffee cup to his lips.

She pointed to the stack of johnnycakes drizzled with molasses. "Would you like my help with that?"

One black brow arched. He lowered the cup a fraction. "Are you offering to feed me?"

"It can't be easy feeding yourself with your left hand," she retorted, cheeks heating at the lights dancing in his eyes.

"I *have* nearly stabbed myself half a dozen times. And Mrs. Calhoun has had to sweep beneath my chair after every meal because the food doesn't seem to want to stick on my fork."

"Poor Lucian," she teased.

"As much as I'd like to take you up on your offer, I think I'd better get used to doing things a bit differently. I can't expect to have you with me for every meal, now can I?"

"I'll leave you to it, then." Standing, she slipped her reticule over her wrist. "I have to go."

"So soon?"

"My sisters and I are picking strawberries this morning to make into jam. Without Ma and Jessica here to help, canning it all will take longer than usual. Nicole and I aren't as handy in the kitchen as the rest of our family. We'll slow Jane down, I'm sure. Depending on how much we get done today, I may come back this evening and bring Jane. Would that be all right?"

"Only if you aren't too tired," he cautioned. "And bring both your sisters. We'll play chess or charades or something."

"How are you supposed to play charades?"

One side of his mouth lifted. "I'll be the guesser."

Tucking an errant curl behind her ear, she gave him a small wave. "Enjoy your breakfast, Lucian."

Leaving him there, she wished she didn't have to go, wished she could indeed share every meal with him. They were the foolish wishes of a careless heart. A heart that was falling for a man who wanted nothing to do with love.

Chapter Fourteen

Friday evening, Lucian found himself in a precarious position. Apparently he hadn't given adequate consideration to which chair he occupied for story time, for the moment he lowered himself into this one—set apart from the rest near the fireplace—the children had descended.

Sarah, the sweetheart, had climbed into his lap without a single word and snuggled against his uninjured side, her head a barely perceptible weight against his shoulder. Ollie had plopped down on the rug at Lucian's feet and was now pressed against his leg. Others whose names he couldn't recall had joined Ollie, crowding in so that Lucian was afraid to move for fear of crushing their little hands beneath his boots.

Megan, the little minx, was thoroughly enjoying his plight. Her attempts to curb her smile had failed, and of course, there was no masking the delicious glee in her beautiful blue eyes.

Sarah shifted, her fine hair tickling his chin. Small and warm, she smelled like sunshine and lemonade. His protective instincts kicked in, and he found himself wishing he could take away her pain. He knew the anguish of losing a mother. How much worse must it be for a young child?

Would he feel this way about his own child? He'd only ever considered having a son. Sweet Sarah spawned thoughts of a girl. One who looked an awful lot like Megan. It was a dangerous path to wander down... imagining what it might be like if he and Megan were to marry and have children of their own. She was a natural with kids. Nurturing and kind. Patient. Wise. There wasn't a single doubt in his mind that she would make an exceptional mother.

For some other man's children, not yours. A local man. Someone like Tom Leighton.

Why did that prospect hit him with the force of a direct blow to the gut?

If he shifted his head slightly to the left, he could see the man in question leaning against the wall, watching Megan with undisguised admiration and longing. Tom made no effort to hide his feelings. Did he comprehend what a treasure he had in her? If he succeeded in winning her, would he truly appreciate her?

Megan deserved to have her happy-ever-after. Lucian wanted that for her. Even if he couldn't be the one to give it to her, even if it wounded him to imagine her setting up house with another man.

Lucian couldn't afford to make the same mistakes his father had. He would not rip an innocent girl from the only home she'd ever known, separate her from family and friends and then subject her to a world that was oftentimes cruel and cold. Megan was a small-town girl through and through. She belonged here in East Tennessee with her mountains and the people she'd known her whole life and the children who adored her.

Besides, he wasn't exactly levelheaded when it came to her. With her around, his determination to remain detached, to hold his heart apart, disintegrated like parchment in flames into a pile of smoldering ashes. If he married her, duty would have nothing to do with it. And that would prove disastrous for them both.

"The end." Closing the book, Megan's warm gaze connected with his and her slow smile made him wish for the impossible.

The kids at his feet surged as one and descended on the dessert table. Sarah scooted off his lap and joined them at a more sedate pace.

Muscles stiff, he pushed himself upright. He'd learned to live with the persistent throbbing in his forearm, and, as much as he wanted rid of the sling, he knew it kept him from further discomfort. The one night he'd attempted to sleep without it, he'd flipped on to his side, pinning his arm beneath him. He'd awoken in agony. Worried he might have done further damage, he'd summoned the doctor the following morning, who'd examined him and declared him a fortunate man. He'd also urged him to take the laudanum before bed. Lucian had agreed to think about it.

Megan appeared before him, familiar concern lurking at the back of her eyes as her gaze touched on his sling. Nothing he said to try to ease her guilt seemed to make a difference.

"No costume tonight?" he asked, appreciating how her peach blouse enhanced her peaches-and-cream complexion. Her flawless skin glowed, her mass of moonlight curls skimming her shoulders and caressing her nape with every movement of her head.

Surely noting his approval, she blushed becomingly and locked her gaze on his cravat. "There wasn't time. We finished our last jars of strawberry jam about an hour before I was to leave to come here."

She'd brought him a jar, bless her. Chewing on her lip, she'd been a bit unsure of his reaction. As she'd pointed out, he could purchase the finest-quality jam from anywhere in the world. Touched by her humble offering, he'd assured her he would take it home and enjoy it on Cook's delicate croissants when he breakfasted in the estate gardens. It would remind him of her and her sisters, of the good times they'd shared. The trio had gifted him with their presence nearly every evening this past week, chasing away his boredom with laughter and good-natured teasing.

At that last bit, her smile had been tinged with sadness, a sadness that echoed in his own soul every time he thought of never seeing her again.

"If you don't have any objections, I'd like to stay for a little while after everyone leaves." She appeared pleased about something. Eager. "I have news to share."

He placed a hand on his chest. "*Moi?* Objections to your company? Never."

Her blue eyes shone with pleasure. "Good."

Tom approached with a glass of tea in each hand, expression pensive as he observed their interaction. "Evening, Lucian. How's the arm?"

"Not bad."

He passed a glass to Megan, who murmured her thanks. She didn't appear entirely comfortable in his presence. Why was that?

"I hope it heals quickly so you can return to New Orleans." Sipping his drink, he smirked.

"Honestly, Tom." Megan's brows lowered in rebuke.

"What? I'm sure the man has commitments to tend to. People eager to welcome him home. Don't you, Lucian?"

Lucian stiffened. How dare he disregard Megan's feelings on this issue? Didn't he know she blamed herself? Assuming his most imperious expression, he inserted frost into his response. "You're right, I do. However, I can't complain. I find I'm rather enjoying my prolonged visit. Megan and her sisters have proven to be delightful company, a most pleasant diversion from my plight."

Lowering the glass to his side, he scowled. "Is that so?"

His eyes narrowed in silent challenge. "Indeed."

"Well, that's…swell." He curled an arm about her shoulders, retaliating with a challenging gaze of his own. "Mind if I steal my girl away for a few minutes?"

"That's entirely up to her."

With an apologetic glance at Lucian, she said, "We'll talk later." Then she allowed him to lead her out of the parlor.

Lucian stalked in the opposite direction, seeking sanctuary in Charles's office before he gave in to impulse and punched something.

"I've never known you to be rude." Arms crossed, Megan waited impatiently for an explanation.

Tom walked to the porch railing and turned to face her without a trace of apology. He whacked his hat against his thigh. "What's going on between you and Lucian Beaumont?"

"We're friends."

He scoffed at that. "If you could see the way he looks at you…"

"And just how does he look at me?" she retorted.

"*Not* like a friend," he stated flatly. Pushing away from the railing, he shoved his hat on his head and stopped in front of her, settled his hands on her shoulders. "He's not the man for you, Megan. He's going home as soon as his arm mends. Do you really want to hang your hopes on a man who would willingly leave you behind?"

Megan didn't speak. He wasn't telling her anything she didn't already know. Still, to hear it spoken aloud gave it more weight. Made it more real.

He dipped his head to meet her gaze directly. "I would never leave you. You know that, right?"

"Tom, I—"

The door swung open, and Ollie and his parents appeared in the doorway. Tom dropped his hands. When they'd exchanged farewells and the trio had descended the steps and were making their way across the grass, he turned to her, more somber than she ever recalled seeing him.

"Will you allow me to walk you home?"

"Not tonight. I'd like to stay and help clean up."

Nodding, he attempted a smile. "All right. Good night, then."

"Good night, Tom."

More people streamed through the door, bidding her good-night. With one last glance at Tom's retreating figure, Megan slipped inside and went in search of Lucian.

She found him in the office, staring out the window at the gardens awash in fading pink-tinted light.

"I'm sorry about that." She stopped beside the desk and stared at his broad back, defined muscles stretching the soft cotton shirt. Because of the sling, he couldn't manage a vest or coat. Without them, he was less formidable. More approachable and yet, still elegant.

When he turned, there was speculation in his black eyes but he didn't mention Tom. "Are you all right?"

"I'm fine." It was an automatic response, not necessarily an apt description of her mental state. How could she *possibly* be fine? Her life was a mess. Her friend was hurting on account of her, and she'd yet to find a way to tell him how she truly felt. Even worse, she wasn't listening to her voice of reason where Lucian was concerned. She should steer clear of him. Instead, she seized every chance to be near him.

As was his habit now, he rested a protective hand over his injured arm. "Has everyone left? My curiosity about your news has reached tortuous heights."

The ever-so-slight curve of his generous lips lifted her spirits. His smiles were rare gifts, their effect on her unmistakable. Perhaps, it wasn't such a bad thing to focus on the here and now. To disregard the future. For now, Lucian was here with her. She should savor this time, for memories were all she'd soon have.

"You must be patient awhile longer. There were still a few people lingering about the dessert table."

He looked regretful. "It's the cream puffs. They're hard to resist."

She laughed. "You're right about that. If we start straightening up, they may get the hint and leave."

His expression brightened. "Let's go."

Placing his hand at the small of her back, he guided her through the house. The heat of his fingers burned through her dress, his touch protective and possessive at the same time. She liked it very much. *Too* much.

In the parlor, she moved away with a warning. "Your job is purely supervisory. I can handle the chairs on my own." Like she had before he came. And would after he was gone.

He didn't like that. "I'm not accustomed to standing by while a lady does all the work."

"Too bad."

Mrs. Calhoun and another man pitched in to help her rearrange the furniture. Out of the corner of her eye, she noticed Lucian piling dirty dishes on top of each other. He was determined to help one way or another, it seemed. By the time they'd righted the parlor, the last guest had left.

Lucian appeared at her side, his good arm aloft and eyes alight with anticipation. "Care to take a stroll about the gardens with me, my lady?"

Alone at last. A thrill pulsed through her as she curved her fingers around his biceps. "I'd like nothing better."

They exited through the rear door that led out to the porch. The humidity from earlier in the day had eased somewhat and the air, heavy with the scent of earth and grass and blossoms, was pleasant against her skin. Cicadas hummed. In the distance, a dog barked. Another splendid spring day was coming to a close.

Lucian led her along the stone path at a sedate pace, content to soak in the colors and textures of the plants and trees on either side. In this moment, he appeared completely at ease, his customary tension conspicuously absent. He seemed almost…happy.

"Have you ever considered leaving the city? Settling somewhere else?" she blurted. Like here?

He halted, looking down at her in question. "Not seriously. I've toyed with the notion of relocating to the estate, but there's no one out there but a handful of staff. It's a rambling old mansion, too large for a single person."

Slipping her hand free, she went to sit on a wooden bench beneath the rose arbor, arranging her skirts about her. He came and sat close beside her, his leg brushing hers.

His face was inches away, his dark gaze a caress. "Tell me your news."

"We finally received a letter today." Her joy overflowed into a huge smile. "Juliana had her baby—a healthy boy with a shock of black hair like his pa's. They named him James, after his late uncle. They're both doing great. Evan is over-the-moon excited. Ma wrote he hasn't stopped smiling."

Lucian's smile was curiously wistful. "Congratulations—you're an aunt now. Auntie Megan."

"I like the sound of that. I hope to go and meet him later on this summer, perhaps in August. Jane is anxious to go, as well."

"Not Nicole?"

"Nicole isn't what you'd call sentimental. And she doesn't get excited about babies."

"That may change. She's young yet."

"The twins are younger than her, yet they're more mature. I'm not sure if she'll ever grow out of her selfishness."

"Everyone matures at a different rate. Give her time."

"I hope you're right."

"Thank you for sharing your news with me." His low drawl wrapped her in cozy warmth.

He was close enough to kiss. Memories of that other kiss by the stream, of how it felt to be held in his arms, rushed in. Her fingers gripped his sleeve. She leaned closer, tilted her face up a fraction. Lost herself in his molten gaze. Waited for him to lower his mouth to hers in tender possession. Waited in vain.

His expression darkened. Frowning, he disengaged her arm and, surging to his feet, strode purposefully away from her.

Megan ducked her head. Hot color infused her face. How could she have been so bold? He'd made it clear he thought kissing her was a mistake. That other kiss on the horse had been an impulse, an attempt to comfort her and assuage her guilty conscience.

"It's getting late," he said without looking at her, his shoulders rigid. "You should go. I don't like the idea of you walking home in the dark."

Humiliated and hurt, she shot to her feet. "I can take care of myself, you know."

He turned, one brow arched. "Yes, I know. Humor me."

So, he wasn't really concerned for her welfare. It was an excuse to get her to leave.

"Fine. I won't stay where I'm not wanted."

As she passed by him, his hand snaked out and snagged her wrist. "Don't ever think you're not wanted, *mon bien-aime*," he forced out. There was a battle going on inside him, emotions warring on his face. "I'm trying very hard to protect you."

Slowly, he bent his head and brushed a light-as-air kiss on her cheek. Megan's heart kicked. Longing engulfed her.

"Lucian—"

He released her wrist and stepped back, his gaze once again hooded. "Go get some rest, Megan. You've been working hard all week, and the poetry recital is tomorrow night."

"Right. Good night, then."

"Bonsoir."

He did not accompany her inside. Unsettled, she hurried down the hall, her steps echoing through the silent, empty house. *This is what it will be like once he leaves,* she thought glumly. Strange and lifeless, as it had after Charles's death.

Tears pricked her eyes. Lucian's presence had assuaged somewhat her grief, lessened the impact of Charles's absence. All too soon, he would leave her, too.

What was she supposed to do then? Especially now that she knew she loved him?

Chapter Fifteen

Lucian relented and took the laudanum that night. His body needed the rest, as did his mind. The medicine would knock him out cold, granting him a reprieve from these persistent thoughts about Megan. Resisting her had drained him of every last drop of strength he possessed. If he expected to be in her presence tomorrow night without crossing the line of friendship, he had to get some sleep.

And perspective. Perspective was good. Remembering their differences was good, too.

Sliding beneath the cool sheets, he fell asleep listing them all.

When he awoke Saturday morning, it was much later than usual. After nine. Where was his valet? Smith should've woken him. The house was silent, so the reserved gentleman was either still abed, which was not his custom, or he'd gone to the stables. Mrs. Calhoun was off duty on the weekends, but she'd be coming in at some point today to help ready the house for tonight's event.

He awkwardly pushed himself up. As expected, his

head felt too heavy for his neck, his brain a bit foggy. Hopefully a large cup of coffee would fix that. Dressing took some doing on his part, despite the fact his injury dictated he wear less clothing. Unfortunately, Smith wasn't around to assist with the buttons, so he pulled the sides of his shirt closed as best he could and slipped the sling back over his head. The windows in this guest room overlooked the back of the property, and he looked out in search of his valet. No sign of him.

Exiting his room, his gaze strayed to his mother's old one directly across the hall. He had avoided it since that first week when he'd snooped through her and Charles's things searching for answers. He hesitated. *What did you do, Maman?* He hated the suspicions rifling through his mind, tainting his memories. He'd been ready to leave here without the answers he sought, but he had time on his hands now. Perhaps he should resume the search.

He strode to the door and pushed it open, paused on the threshold. White lace curtains hung at the windows and a pink ruffled bedspread adorned the bed where two dolls—one porcelain and one handmade—lay waiting. There was a small writing desk and chair and an oversize oak wardrobe. A small stack of fancy stationery and envelopes lay untouched on the desktop, and two paintings hung above the headboard. His mother's work? She hadn't painted at home. Something else she'd given up in an effort to please his father?

He walked to the wardrobe and opened the doors, fingering the dresses hanging inside. Good material, pretty yet simple in style, fitting for life in this quaint mountain town. Similar to Megan's and her sisters' clothes, in fact. He certainly hadn't seen his mother wear anything like this. She'd dressed the part of the ship baron's wife in gowns crafted by the most fashionable designers around, ears and neck dripping with jewels and hair styled just-so. Father must've brought someone in shortly after their wedding to transform the humble mountain girl into an acceptable lady of society.

Had she missed her old life at all? He wished now that he'd thought to ask her.

He couldn't picture Megan in his world. Found it nearly impossible to picture her amid the splendor and opulence of his family's mansion in the city. What a shame it would be to try to tame her natural beauty, to mold her into an unoriginal socialite with pretty manners and shallow conversation. No. Megan didn't need extravagant clothes or flashy jewels. She was perfect just the way she was—delicate and feminine in her softly flowing dresses, her white-blond curls tamed by a single ribbon. In his eyes, she was more beautiful than any other woman in the world.

With a heavy sigh, he pushed the doors back into place, thinking he should do something with the dresses. Perhaps donate them? He would seek Megan's advice. As Charles's close friend, she might have an idea what would've pleased him.

His grandfather must've left this room exactly as Lucinda had left it. Why? Had he ever entered it again? Or had it been too painful a reminder of all he'd lost?

Dear God, I'm so confused. Help me, please, to find the answers I'm looking for. And if there aren't any to find, help me to accept that. To find peace.

He hoped Megan was right. Hoped God was listening and that He cared.

Through the window, Lucian heard someone whistling a merry tune. From the sound of it, that someone was advancing up the lane. He pushed the curtain aside with a quiet swish and stared out. His jaw dropped. His horse! Squinting, forehead pressed against the cool glass, he studied the large, sleek animal. No question about it… D'Artagnan was home.

Hurrying down the winding staircase, his hand skimming the banister for balance, questions zipped through his brain suddenly cleared of all fog. Could it be true?

Out on the porch, he held on to the post and waited for the seedy-looking character leading his horse to reach him. When the man spotted Lucian, he tipped his battered hat up and studied him. "Howdy do. Would you be Lucian Beaumont?"

"Yes, sir." He descended the steps, stopping at the bottom, his gaze sweeping D'Artagnan in search of possible injuries. Relief expanded his chest when he didn't notice any. Dirt-coated, his mane knotted with debris, all he appeared to need was a good meal and thorough brushing down.

Impatient to greet his old friend, he moved closer and, skimming a palm along his neck, murmured in French. Snickering, D'Artagnan turned his head and nudged Lucian. Transferring his gaze to the wizened old man who, by the looks of him, was a down-on-his-luck drifter, he said, "I'm sorry, what did you say your name was?"

"I didn't." He grinned, shocking Lucian with his rows of straight white teeth, made brilliant against his sun-browned skin. "The name's Cyril Hawk."

"Mr. Hawk, where did you find him? And how did you know to bring him to me?"

Shrugging, he released the reins. "He wandered on

to my property last evenin'. I went through the bags and found a Bible. Can't read, so I brought him into town early this morning and showed it to Sheriff Timmons. Belonged to your ma, did it?"

Lucian nodded, gratefulness clogging his throat. Opening the bag, he clasped the large black tome and, lifting it with his good hand, held it against his chest. *Thank You, God.*

Cyril just stood watching him, wise understanding in his eyes.

"Do you live nearby?" he asked, voice gravelly.

He motioned over his shoulder. "About five miles south of town."

"Five miles?" He hadn't brought a wagon or second horse with him.

Noticing Lucian's confusion, he offered another grin. "I like to walk. Well, now that I've done my good deed for the day, I gotta be headin' back." He tipped his hat. "Nice to meet ya, Beaumont. You have yourself a good day."

"Wait."

Cyril paused midturn, bushy brows raised in question.

"I'd like to repay you for your kindness. Give me a moment, and I'll get you some money—"

He held up a hand. "No need for that. I was happy to do it. Golden rule and all that."

"I insist. You've returned something very valuable to me."

"Horses can be replaced."

Lucian gripped the Bible tighter. "This one can't."

Approval showing in his expression, Cyril said gruffly, "Your gratitude is payment enough, young man." Then he turned resolutely and headed back down the lane, whistling a vaguely familiar tune.

He watched until the stranger disappeared from sight. *I don't know if this was Your doing or not, God, but thank You.*

Because both hands were indisposed, he buried his face in his horse's neck. "Welcome home, buddy. Wait until Megan hears this."

Stationed in the parlor entrance, Megan was able to see the guests mingling inside and those just arriving. The house was abuzz with anticipation, chatter and the clinking of glasses echoing off the walls. Nervous excitement bubbled in her tummy. The turnout so far exceeded that of any previous poetry recital, and there were still fifteen minutes before time to begin.

Her gaze was drawn once again to the fireplace, to where Lucian stood sandwiched between the Moores and the Jenkinses, his air of command making him seem a foot taller than those around him. Wearing a black vest and evening coat beneath the sling, his rich brown hair somewhat tamed away from his face, he was easily the most handsome man in the room. His austere mask didn't fool her. She was well acquainted with the sensitive, hurting heart hiding behind it.

When she realized his attention was not on his companions but on *her,* his black-as-midnight gaze intent with undisguised admiration, her breathing quickened. Sparkling awareness danced along her nerve endings. Since the moment of her arrival, she'd sensed his perusal move with her about the room.

Wanting to look her best this evening, she'd borrowed one of Nicole's dresses. Crafted from exquisite ivory silk that brushed against her heated skin like cool water, bands of seed pearls enhanced the scooped neck and fitted waist and edged the short puffed sleeves. An intricate lace overlay adorned the full skirt, and along the hem, Nicole had stitched delicate gold-and-silver flowers. Kate had secured the top section of her hair with sparkly diamond pins—family heirlooms, she'd called them—allowing the remainder of her curls to tumble down her back. Judging from Lucian's reaction, the effort had been well worth it.

Megan shoved aside the inner warning that she was playing a dangerous game.

"Megan? Hello?"

With a start, she tore her gaze from Lucian and looked up into her cousin's amused face. "Nathan!"

Surprise spurred her to hug him. Low laughter rumbled in his chest, and she eased back, smiling. "What are you doing here? This isn't your cup of tea, so to speak."

"Would you believe I just happened to have free time on my hands?" He touched his still-damp brown hair.

"You? Free time? No, sorry. Not buying it." Nathan and Caleb stayed busy around the farm, neither one much inclined for social events such as this.

"I didn't think so." He sighed with mock defeat, his gaze straying to the crowd behind her and then back. "Josh and Kate were all set to come, but then she had a dizzy spell. She insisted it was nothing, but Josh urged her to stay home and rest. She's been awfully busy lately with people wanting their photographs taken, which is good for business but you know how Josh worries. Anyway, he asked me to come in their place. Wanted someone here to support you."

He shrugged, clearly perplexed. Nathan was a good man, caring and protective of his family, if a bit too serious and introspective at times. But he'd never been in love. Seemed uninterested in finding himself a wife and utterly oblivious to the single girls' attempts to snag his attention. Of course he wouldn't understand Josh's need to take care of his wife.

"I was with her earlier today. Now that you mention it, she did seem a bit more subdued than usual." Had she been feeling unwell and hadn't wanted to let on? Or was it her longing for a baby weighing on her mind?

Nathan squeezed her shoulder. "Don't worry, the bloom was back in her cheeks when I left. Josh was plying her with tea and cookies."

"If she's not at church in the morning, I'll pay her a visit afterward."

"I'm certain she'll be there." Searching the crowd once again, his gaze intercepted Lucian's and he tipped his head in silent greeting. "How much longer do you think he'll be here?"

Megan shrugged, tried to appear nonchalant. "A couple of weeks."

His voice deepened in concern. "Are you going to be all right?"

"Of course. Why wouldn't I be?"

"Don't try and pretend he doesn't matter to you. When I walked up, the two of you were locked in your own little world. You didn't even hear me greet you the first time."

Megan's cheeks burned. Were her feelings that obvious? Was Lucian aware?

She had to be more careful. He'd made it plain there was no room in his life for love. He would not be pleased to learn she had disregarded his wishes. Had foolishly allowed her heart to love him.

"Look, I didn't mean to upset you," Nathan said into the silence hanging between them. "I'm worried, that's all."

Twisting her hands together, she forced a bright smile to her face. She had the entire evening to get through. "You didn't." Glancing at the clock, she said, "You should go and find a seat. I—I remember something I need from the library."

His brow furrowed. "Megan—"

"I really can't talk right now."

Not daring to look in Lucian's direction, she hurried down the hall and into the blessedly empty library. The night was dark behind the curtains, and with only one lamp lit, the room was wreathed in shadows. She moved into them, taking refuge in the far corner against the bookshelves. She needed to clear her head. To regain control over her emotions.

Suddenly she wondered how she was supposed to stand up in front of everyone, Lucian in particular, and recite words of love without the truth shining through? Why, oh why, hadn't she picked something humorous? Or lighthearted?

One thing she knew—she must not look at him. Not even once. He'd see her heart's yearning and if he did… She shook her head. At best, he'd be disappointed. At worst, horrified. Repulsed.

The skin of her nape tingled then, the fine hairs on her arms standing to attention.

She whirled. "Lucian?"

He came towards her, concern pulling at his mouth. "You looked upset, so I followed you." He came very close, his expression difficult to read in the relative darkness. His broad shoulders blocked out what little light there was. "Are you all right?"

"Just a little nervous." *And going a little bit crazy worrying over you.*

"You're a natural storyteller. I'm confident you'll have them all mesmerized by your talent and grace. That is, *if* they can focus on your words." He gently tugged on a curl and watched it spring back into place. "You look absolutely breathtaking tonight, Megan."

She couldn't think straight with him standing so near. No matter what, she wouldn't repeat last night's mistake. Sidestepping him, she moved in the direction of the door.

Anger tinged with despair thrummed through her. He wasn't playing fair! Complimenting her in that smooth-as-velvet voice, touching her when he'd rebuffed her less than twenty-four hours ago.

"Can I get you a glass of water or something?" he asked, subdued. As if she'd given voice to her rebuff.

"No, I'm fine."

Closing her eyes, she recalled the expression on his face as he'd insisted he was trying to protect her. He'd been torn, conflicted. It hit her then. He was as drawn to her as she was to him. Oh, she was under no illusion that he loved her. He wouldn't be that reckless, not when he'd clearly outlined his goals and the way he expected his life to go. For him, the attraction was merely physical. The fact that she was different from the young socialites he was accustomed to made her interesting. A passing fancy.

Anguish wrapped its tentacles about her heart and squeezed, the pressure almost too much to bear.

He came up behind her but made no move to touch her. "Megan?" A thousand questions in one word.

Opening her eyes, she lifted her chin, determined he not discover her true feelings. Ever.

Turning, she shot him a smile that hopefully appeared genuine. "It's time to start the recital. Are you coming?"

His gaze narrowed. "I—"

"I don't mean to be rude, Lucian, but I don't want to keep everyone waiting."

She left him there, not stopping to see if he followed. It would be amazing if she made it through this night.

Chapter Sixteen

Lucian followed several steps behind, slipping into a vacant seat in the back row as Megan made her way to the front to welcome everyone and introduce the first speaker. He studied her as he'd done since the moment she'd arrived, captivated by her beauty and her innate sweetness. Her smile was fragile, the customary sparkle in her blue eyes conspicuously absent. Was she always this nervous before an event? He hadn't noticed her this way with the children, but adults were a different audience. Or was it something else entirely? They hadn't exactly parted on good terms the night before. He'd planned to speak with her before the recital, to share with her the good news of D'Artagnan's return, but there hadn't been time.

The matter plagued him as one by one, the people stood up and recited their selections. He tried to listen, really he did, but his gaze kept straying to Megan seated in the first row in between Nathan and a young lady he hadn't met before. Candlelight glistened in her curls, diamonds sparkling with every tilt of her head, the intricate beading on her bodice gleaming in the golden light. Her skin, he knew, was as soft as the silk dress she wore. He wished he was sitting there beside her, wished he had the right to cradle her small hand in his and reassure her fears.

At long last, it was her turn. The final speaker of the night. Standing there looking like a woodland princess in that gauzy, flower-embellished creation, her chin tilted in unspoken defiance of he knew not what, she cleared her throat and began to speak. Speaking quietly at first, her voice gained strength as she quoted Shakespeare's "Sonnet." He was familiar with the poem, of course, but hearing the words of love spoken in her lyrical voice affected him deeply. Made him wish love like that truly existed, love that didn't try to alter the other person, love that was unbending, unmovable, never shaken no matter what storms may come. She spoke with conviction and emotion, holding the room in silent thrall.

She didn't look at him. Not once.

He knew then that *he* was the cause of her discomfiture. He'd made her unhappy. How was he supposed to handle that?

When she'd finished, the audience burst into applause. With a strained smile, she thanked everyone for coming and invited them to help themselves to the refreshments laid out in the dining room. Lucian longed to go to her, to apologize for hurting her feelings, but he held back. How could he explain that, while he liked and respected her, he found it difficult to be near her? Megan made him forget lessons learned from childhood about love and the heartache that inevitably followed.

He clenched his right hand, gritting his teeth as razor-sharp pain radiated up his as-yet-unhealed forearm. This delay was going to cost him. The longer he stayed here, the less appeal his old life held for him. A dangerous thing. He needed to go home and begin his search for a suitable wife. Once he was married, he would banish all thoughts of Megan. Bury his memories of her. Erase Gatlinburg, Tennessee, from his consciousness.

As it turned out, he didn't get a chance to share his good news. Or apologize. She made certain they weren't alone and bade him good-night with Nathan by her side.

"Thank you for everything, Lucian," she told him with her arm linked through her cousin's. "The flowers were a nice touch." Her appreciative gaze wandered about the room, lighting on the freshly cut bouquets he'd asked Fred to assemble.

"I would call the evening a success, wouldn't you?"

Her eyes touched his only briefly. "Yes, I would." She addressed Nathan. "What did you think?"

"It wasn't a bad way to spend the evening." He winked at her.

"Good night, Lucian," Megan said softly, finally allowing her blue gaze to linger on his face. But he couldn't read her expression, and it bothered him not to know what she was thinking or feeling.

"Good night." *Mon bien-aime. My beloved.*

But he mustn't say that or even allow himself to entertain such a thought.

He shut the door behind them, leaning back against the polished wood and stained glass. After such a lively evening, the stillness of the house seemed magnified. Despite his reservations, he hadn't minded having a houseful of strangers. The townspeople had accepted him into their fold without question, most of them friendly.

As the silence settled over him like a heavy blanket, he felt his aloneness acutely. More than anything, he wished Megan could've stayed a little longer and discussed the night. He enjoyed their conversations, was intrigued by her intelligence and insight and wit.

Her leaving with Nathan was probably for the best, however. Might as well get used to not having her around.

This time, the heaviness in his chest had nothing to do with not getting enough rest and everything to do with the prospect of leaving her.

At the conclusion of Reverend Monroe's prayer, Megan turned to exit her pew and was stunned to see Lucian's familiar form slipping out the door. He hadn't indicated he would be here today. Surely this was a good sign.

Outside in the sunshine, she spotted him in the hillside cemetery, a solitary figure outlined against the blue sky studded with clouds. The stout breeze ruffled his hair and tugged at his coattails.

Nicole stopped beside her, pulling wayward raven strands away from her face put there by the wind. "Are you going to talk to him?"

"No, I don't think so." Although she wanted to. Badly.

Hadn't she made enough of a fool of herself around him lately?

Jane rushed up, breathless, gray skirts swirling about her boots. "The Nortons invited me to lunch with them. Do you mind?"

Jane, Jessica and Tori Norton were close friends. "Sure. What time do you expect to be home?"

"Tanner offered to bring me home later this evening."

Megan had long suspected Jane was nursing a crush on Tori's older brother. He was a nice young man, but at twenty a bit too old for her fifteen-year-old sister. Jane had a good head on her shoulders, but Megan worried she might get hurt.

"Fine, just be home before dark."

"Thanks, Megan." Jane bussed her cheek and dashed off in the direction of the other family's wagon. The Nortons waved to her. She waved back, then turned to Nicole.

"Well, I suppose it's just you and me."

"We could always invite Lucian to join us."

Risking another glance at the cemetery, she saw that he hadn't moved from his spot. What was he thinking? What did he think of the sermon?

"Not today."

Thankful Nicole didn't question her further, they walked in silence the rest of the way home. They spent a restful afternoon reading and playing chess. Lucian was never far from her thoughts, however. While she'd managed not to look at him while standing in front of the audience, the words she'd spoken had been all for him. Her love for him was like that poem. Unshakable. Accepting of their differences. A love that time could not erase.

That's why she hadn't wanted to risk being alone with him last night, why she hadn't approached him after church today. She was afraid he'd be able to see it in her eyes, this all-encompassing love. A love he would reject in a heartbeat.

She stayed away all that week.

And, although she had every intention of leading story time Friday night, she was stricken with a terrible headache shortly after lunch that afternoon. Nicole begrudgingly agreed to go in her place, not because she liked the kids but because she liked Lucian and his fancy house. She planned to live in an even grander house than that one day, she'd declared. When she returned later that night, she told Megan that Lucian had been even more reserved than usual. Downcast, even.

Guilt and worry immediately assailed her. Was Nicole exaggerating? Questions pummeled her mind. Was he getting enough rest? Was his arm healing properly? What must he think of her absence this week? Was she right to avoid him?

Saturday morning, his valet delivered a bouquet of delicate pink roses and a note. With trembling fingers, she opened it and read his fine script.

Dearest Megan,
While the children and I were grateful for Nicole's presence last evening, we missed you.
I hope this morning finds you much improved. If you have need of anything, please do not hesitate to call on me.
Your humble servant,
Lucian

By the time Sunday morning rolled around, she was desperate to see him.

Like the previous week, he occupied the last pew, slipping out at the final amen. Megan impatiently wound her way through the crowd and down the steps, relieved when she spotted him in the cemetery. She told her sisters not to wait. Walking up the hill with her skirts lifted off the ground, her pulse quickened in anticipation.

His back to her, he stood before two headstones, dark head bent.

"Lucian?"

He pivoted, the soles of his boots squeaking against the grass. "Megan." His obsidian eyes raked her from head to toe, searching for…something. His face creased in concern. "Are you well?"

Warmed by his gaze, she smiled. "I am." Lowering her skirts, she took an involuntary step closer. "I didn't have a lot of extra time this week. We stayed busy working in the vegetable garden."

"I see."

The line between his brows indicated he didn't. Was trying to work out if she'd stayed away for another reason altogether.

Before he could pursue the subject, she pointed to where he cradled his arm against his stomach. "How is your arm?"

"It's healing. More slowly than I'd like. On doctor's orders, I've been taking off the sling a couple of times each day and exercising my shoulder and biceps. He warned me I'd get stiff if I didn't."

His fawn suit coat hugged his athletic build to perfection, the pale hue lending his sun-bronzed skin a healthy glow. The noonday sun picked out highlights in his hair.

"Does it pain you?"

"Only if I make an unexpected movement or forget and clench my fingers."

Hating that *she* had put him in that cast, she only

nodded. Gazed at Charles's headstone and that of his wife, Beatrice, who'd died years before Lucinda left Gatlinburg. Megan came here sometimes to place flowers at his grave, to read to him and imagine him listening from his eternal home above.

Lucian followed her gaze. "When I was very young, I often wondered what they were like. Like Mother, my father was an only child and his parents died before their marriage. Charles was my only other living relative, and I was quite curious about him. My friends all had these wonderful tales of fun-loving grandfathers who took them fishing and hunting and grandmothers who plied them with chocolates and pulled them onto their laps for hugs and stories. As I grew older, I became more persistent in questioning my mother about him. I wanted to know why he never came to visit. Why we didn't visit him.

"When she told me Charles didn't want to meet me, I couldn't believe it. Why wouldn't a grandfather want to know his grandson? I thought something was wrong with me."

Hurting for the little boy that he had been, Megan slipped her hand into his larger one. His lean fingers closed around hers, mouth twisting in regret.

"On occasion, she'd relent and tell me about this place." He gazed out over the valley, the forested mountains seemingly close enough to touch. "I think…it's entirely plausible that my mother refused Charles's requests. It makes sense. She wouldn't have wanted to upset my father by coming back. Because of her feelings for him, she would've denied herself the chance to see her home again, to mend her relationship with Charles. If that meant lying to me— She would've done

anything, anything at all, to make my father love her."
Bitterness crept into his voice. "Love. Pointless, futile
emotion! It got her nothing but misery."

Pulling his hand free, he shoved his fingers through
his hair. Frustration hummed along his rigid muscles,
so intense he almost shook from it. *This* was why he
spurned love. He'd only ever witnessed its destructive
power.

"It doesn't have to be like that, you know," she said
urgently, curling a restraining hand about his upper
arm. "Love doesn't hurt when it's right…when God is
the foundation."

"What does God have to do with it?" His gaze probed
hers, sincerely conflicted.

"Why, everything! God *is* love. Apart from Him,
people are basically selfish, concerned only about our
own interests. But with God's help, we can put others'
needs and interests above our own. We can love sac-
rificially."

He studied her for the longest time, warring emotions marching across his face. Then he smiled such a
sad smile it rent her heart in two. "My sweet dreamer, I
wish I could believe in the kind of love you do. But I'm
afraid I've seen too much, endured too much. I'm jaded
and cynical and much too hard for the likes of you."

"No." Her grip on his arm tightened. "No, Lucian,
you just haven't had the right kind of examples in your
life. I know true love exists because I've seen it with
my own eyes. My parents had that kind of love. Aunt
Mary and Uncle Sam, too. Now Evan and Juliana. Josh
and Kate. Their relationships aren't perfect, of course,
because none of us are perfect. But they share a genu-

ine love and commitment to each other. It does exist," she repeated, determined he see the truth.

"I'm sorry. You won't succeed in convincing me."

Megan bit her lip. It wasn't enough to tell him so. He had to see the evidence with his own eyes. Spend time around couples who were committed to each other.

"Hey," he murmured, tipping up her chin, "you don't have to look so sad."

"Come to my aunt and uncle's with me."

His black brows winged up.

"Please," she added with a beseeching gaze. "Have lunch with my family."

"I am rather tired of my own company," he said ruefully.

"It will be crowded and noisy like last time. Nothing formal or fancy."

"Crowded and noisy sounds perfect." Lowering his voice to a whisper, he confided, "And to be completely honest, I'm not all that fond of formal or fancy." Covering her hand, he said, "Shall we?"

Happy he'd agreed, Megan smiled and allowed him to guide her down the hill and along a nearly deserted Main Street. As they passed Tom's darkened barbershop, she sensed Lucian's perusal. If he'd noticed Tom's absence this morning, he made no mention of it.

They walked in amiable silence, nature's springtime music a well-orchestrated symphony. Beneath the wooden bridge, the Little Pigeon River churned and crashed over mossy boulders, the hum of rushing water trailing them onto the tree-lined lane that led to her aunt and uncle's farm and, a mile and a half farther down, her own home. The dense forest on either side popped and cracked, branches swaying in the breeze.

Somewhere a woodpecker pecked. Thrushes and warblers whistled and cooed.

Sneaking a glance at Lucian, she wondered what he was thinking. Wondered if he would ever change his mind about love. About marriage. Would he ever learn to trust again?

And could *she* be the one to teach him how?

Chapter Seventeen

Rocking on the porch, Sam lifted his head at their arrival and gestured to an empty chair beside him. "Sit and rest a spell, Lucian. The gals will let us know when the meal is ready."

Grasping the door handle, Megan smiled her agreement. "It shouldn't take long."

As she disappeared inside, Sam commented, "Hope you brought your appetite. They tend to go overboard for Sunday dinner."

Smiling, Lucian lowered himself in the rocking chair. "Since I overslept and had to skip breakfast this morning, I'd say that suits me just fine."

"How's the arm?"

His fingers grazed the sling. "It's coming along. Doc wants me to wait two to three more weeks to travel home."

Sam gazed at him. "It's awfully generous of you to leave the house in Megan's care. Folks around here will be mighty grateful."

Lucian studied the older man, judged him to be about

the same age as his mother. "How well did you know my grandfather?"

"Charles? I knew him to be a fair man. Well liked. A responsible member of the community." He nudged his spectacles farther up his nose. "You probably heard that in recent years he didn't go out much. He came to church but didn't attend any functions. Why do you ask?"

"Megan said that Charles wrote my mother in an attempt to mend the rift between them. That he wanted to meet me. My mother didn't mention any letters. She… led me to believe Charles was indifferent. I'd like to know the truth. So far, I haven't found anything in the house that can shed light on their relationship. Or lack thereof. I plan to look through her things when I get back to New Orleans. Maybe I'll have better luck there."

"I'm afraid I can't help you with that. I *can* tell you this," he said as he waved his finger. "Family was extremely important to Charles. He adored Beatrice and Lucinda. Bea's death devastated him, but at least he still had your mother. They were very close. After she left…" He shook his head in regret. "It makes sense he would try to make amends. There's no question in my mind that he would've wanted to meet you."

Lucian trusted Sam's judgment. And Megan's. Granted, Charles could've said those things simply to gain her sympathy…but he didn't think so. As difficult as it was to admit, even to himself, it appeared his mother had misrepresented the situation. And, while he understood her reasoning, it hurt to know she'd deceived him. Her only son. Cheated him and Charles out of a relationship. It hurt bad.

"Kinda tough to be angry at someone who's not around to defend themselves," Sam observed offhandedly.

He stood and crossed to the rail, stared out across the yard. "Yes, well, she did it to make my father happy. Too bad it was all for nothing. She cheated not only herself, but Charles and me, as well." Bitterness encased his heart, dripped from his words. Didn't he have the right to be angry? Deceived by someone he'd trusted completely? This lie of hers…it had far-reaching effects.

"I'm sorry."

"Me, too," he murmured, turning as the door creaked open.

Megan's questioning gaze volleyed between her uncle and him. "Dinner's on the table."

"It's about time." Sam winked at her, pushed to his feet.

She looked at Lucian. Her gaze caught by something behind him, her face brightened. "Caleb!"

She swept past him. Turning, he spotted the youngest O'Malley loping towards the house, serious and drawn. When Megan threw herself into his arms, his head dipped, hat brim blocking his expression. He gave her an awkward pat on the back. "Hey, Meg."

Lucian shot a glance at Sam standing stiffly by the door, watching the exchange with pronounced lines about his eyes.

"I haven't seen you in weeks," she chided gently, stepping away to look full in his face. She tugged on his arm. "Come on—there's someone I'd like you to meet."

Lucian straightened from the rail, moved to the top step to intercept them. While the younger man matched him in height, he was bulkier than Lucian. His dark gaze flicked to Sam for an instant. Clearly happy to see her cousin, Megan made the introductions. Caleb angled his face to the side, but not before Lucian glimpsed a jagged scar near his eye. Hmm.

"Nice to meet you," Lucian said evenly as they shook hands.

"Likewise," he bit out. It was apparently a struggle for him to be civil. What was behind his absences? Didn't he help Nathan and Sam around the farm? Josh did what he could, but the majority of his time was spent building furniture and managing the store.

Sweeping off his hat, Caleb paused in front of his father. "Pa."

"You're just in time for dinner, son," Sam said with a strained smile as he held the door open.

Twirling a stray curl about her finger, Megan shot Lucian a meaningful look as they followed the men inside. This would no doubt prove to be an interesting meal. Everyone greeted Caleb with warmth. Warmth he had trouble accepting.

When everyone was seated and grace offered up, conversation progressed in fits and starts, the edge of tension palpable. The youngest O'Malley sat with his head bent, looking as if he wished he was invisible. Gradually, though, the mood eased.

With Megan at his side, Lucian savored the meal of roast chicken and mashed potatoes, assorted vegetables and fresh sourdough bread slathered with butter. The O'Malleys were a lively bunch. There was a lot of good-natured teasing going on. Hearing Megan's laughter, seeing her happy and relaxed, he finally understood her desire for a large family.

Perhaps if he'd grown up in such a setting, he'd want that for himself.

All through the meal, he surreptitiously studied Josh and Kate, who were seated directly across from him. Josh was affectionate with his delicate, dark-haired wife, constantly touching her hair, her cheek, whispering in her ear. Still in the newlywed phase, obviously. For some couples the phase lasted longer than others, he supposed. Watching them exchange secretive smiles, Lucian resented the fact he couldn't be so free with Megan.

Once, she'd caught him staring at the couple, and her smile had faltered, tremulous, fierce longing blazing in her expressive blue eyes...searing him with its heat, making him crazy to hold her. To lay claim to her. And then the panic had set in. He was close, dangerously close, to giving in to these forbidden feelings. To throwing caution to the wind and going down on his knees right here in front of everyone and begging her to stay with him forever.

Somehow, he garnered the strength to break eye contact. Did she notice the tiny beads of sweat forming on his brow? His uneven breathing?

All he had to do was think of his parents and know what a monumental mistake that would be. He told himself this was an infatuation. What man wouldn't be enamored of her natural beauty, her strength of character? Her compassion and wit?

What he felt for Megan was not love. Not even close. He was so confident of this fact that he thought nothing of asking her to accompany him back to his house later that afternoon. He had yet to tell her of D'Artagnan's return, and he decided it would be more fun to show her.

At the entrance to the barn, he put a hand out to stop her. "Close your eyes."

"What?" She laughed up at him, charming curls framing her face. "Why?"

"Just do as you're told, young lady," he admonished with a grin, too content to be properly wary. With an arched brow, she complied and he took her hand and led her deep into the barn's interior. "Keep them closed," he warned.

"I'm not sure I like surprises," she said smartly, her boots scuffing the dirt as she took halting steps, her free hand outstretched to catch herself if she stumbled. Of course he wouldn't let that happen.

"I guarantee you'll like this one."

When they reached his horse's stall, D'Artagnan came close and extended his head their direction. "All right. You may open your eyes now."

Lids fluttering open, she gasped. "What? He's here?" Her incredulous gaze volleyed between him and his horse. Stepping closer, she rubbed a hand down D'Artagnan's face. "Oh, Lucian, I can hardly believe my eyes! How did you find him?"

Enjoying her reaction, he stood still and watched her. "I didn't. A man by the name of Cyril Hawk found him on his property and brought him back to me. Do you know him?"

Her brows met in the middle. "No, I'm afraid I don't."

"He must not come into town very often, then. He wouldn't accept payment."

Megan paused in bestowing affection on the big animal, brow furrowing. "And your things? Were they in the bags?"

"Yes, everything." He nodded. "Including my mother's Bible." And he'd been reading it every day since, just as he'd told God he would. "You were right about the notes. I've found lots of underlined verses and words jotted in the margins."

"You've been reading it?"

"Since it's been a while, I decided to start in Psalms. I find them…comforting. Uplifting."

"This is a positive answer to prayer, Lucian. You see that, don't you?"

"I do."

"I'm so happy you got it back. And D'Artagnan, too."

Eyes shining, Megan threw her arms about his neck, burying her face beneath his chin. Stunned, he didn't move. He'd taken his sling off as soon as they'd arrived, so his injured arm hung awkwardly at his side. Her silky hair tickled his throat. He curled his good arm around her waist in a kind of half hug, anchoring her more firmly against his chest. His eyes drifted shut, and he inhaled her rose scent. Megan here, in his arms, felt right. Natural. Meant to be.

With a tiny, reluctant sigh, she lifted her head. Touched his every feature with her hungry gaze. He couldn't *not* kiss her. Unlike the kiss at the stream, this one was tentative. Gentle. Their lips clinging in tender reverence, his heart shifted, strained towards her as if it recognized its lifelong companion…its soul mate.

He lifted his injured arm and carefully sank his fingers in her curls, luxuriating in the weight and feel of it. What was a little pain if it meant he got to touch her crowning glory? Her fingers kneaded his nape and tangled in his hair. His heart felt as if it might burst from his chest.

With bone-deep regret, he lifted his head. If only he had forever to kiss her.

She unwound her arms, sliding them lower so that her palms rested on his chest. "I should go." Her eyes were a turbulent blue storm.

His fingers flexed on her slim waist. "Are you certain? We could go inside and play a game of chess. Or read." He liked that idea, the two of them together in the cozy library, sharing funny or interesting bits of the books they were reading.

"I can't." Extracting herself from his arms, she gave D'Artagnan a final pat. "Good night, Lucian."

He stopped her exit with a hand on her shoulder. "We should talk."

"There's nothing to talk about." She was avoiding his gaze, and it gave him a panicky feeling.

Dropping his hand to his side, he demanded, "Are you planning on avoiding me again this week?"

When she shot him a helpless look, he went on beseechingly, "My time here is growing short, *mon chou*. I'd like to spend it with you."

"I'd like that, too." But the pucker between her brows revealed her disquiet.

"Why don't you and the girls come for dinner tomorrow night?"

A weak smile was his reward. "What time do you want us here?"

"Six o'clock?"

"Okay."

Standing in the barn entrance, he watched her walk away. Watched until she'd rounded the bend and disappeared from sight, a yawning emptiness in his chest.

Odd…this didn't feel like a harmless infatuation.

Megan and her sisters dined with him every night that week. Nicole's and Jane's presence acted as a buffer, making it easier to maintain his perspective and eliminate any chances of acting rashly. For just a little while, the sprawling house would transform into something resembling a true home with laughter and conversation and the glow of friendship…far removed from the stiff formality he'd known at home.

For Lucian, the hours between breakfast and dinner stretched endlessly, and he found himself prowling about the property, counting the minutes until she arrived, her smile the only antidote to his lonely, restless state. Late Thursday evening, after they'd gone and the rooms once again stood silent and brooding, he wandered into the study to where his mother's Bible lay open on the desk. He sank into the chair. Scanned the pages of John.

Peace I leave with you; my peace I give you. I do not give to you as the world gives. Do not let your hearts be troubled and do not be afraid.

Troubled? That summed up his entire year. *God, I don't have this peace. Not about my mother and Charles. And definitely not about Megan.*

Resting his head against the soft leather, his eyes drifted shut. He was exhausted. A bone-deep, soul-weary exhaustion that stemmed from frustration. No matter where he turned, the answers he sought eluded him. And the situation with Megan…it was impossible.

With a sigh, he opened his eyes and stared at the polished copper ceiling tiles, his gaze falling naturally on the shelves opposite. There, wedged between the ceiling and the shelves, sat a wooden box. Lucian's lungs hung suspended. What was that? Standing, he crossed to that side of the room and cast about for something to stand on. His palms were sweating. Heart hammering. He had a funny feeling about that box.

Shrugging out of his sling, he dragged a chair over, and, stepping onto it, he balanced himself with a hand on the shelves. It was a stretch, but he managed to scoot it close enough to get a good hold and lower it without losing his balance. Anticipation zipping along his nerves, he carried it over to the desk and placed it in the center. Stared at it.

Don't get yourself all worked up. For all you know, Charles could've stored expensive cigars in there. Or photographs.

"Only one way to find out," he murmured, lifting the lid.

At the sight of the stack of letters all tied up with a black ribbon, Lucian sank into the chair. That was his mother's handwriting. Megan was right. Charles had been telling the truth.

His mother and Charles *had* been in contact.

It took a while for him to work up the courage to lift

out the stack, untie the ribbon and pull out that first letter. Then he began to read.

Strolling arm in arm towards their cabin, Jane was the first to spot Tom in the gathering dusk. At her nudge, Megan looked up. His lean body propped against a support, hat dangling from his fingertips, he was listening patiently to Nicole chatter as she rocked back and forth. Then she saw them and put her boot down to stop the motion.

"How was dinner? Did Lucian miss me?" To Tom, she declared, "We've dined at his house every night this week. One day I'm going to live in a house like that. Grander, even, in a big, bustling city where exciting things happen all the time."

Jane sighed long-sufferingly. This was nothing they hadn't heard before. "Of course, Lucian sent his regards. He's the consummate gentleman."

A shadow passed over Tom's face. Megan met his green gaze with a tentative smile. "Hello, Tom."

Leaping to the ground in one smooth move, he met them halfway up the path. "Hello, ladies." His smile held a nervous edge. "Care to walk with me for a bit?" His gaze slid reluctantly to her sister. "You're welcome to come along, Janie-girl."

Jane's lashes swished down, and, flipping her auburn ponytail behind her shoulder, she tipped her chin up in a signature O'Malley move. "Thanks for the invitation but I'm tired. I'm going inside."

As she and Nicole disappeared inside the cabin, Tom waited for her reply. She was tired, too, but wouldn't turn him away. He obviously had something on his mind.

Falling into step, they ambled past the cabin and, entering the woods, headed without speaking to the stream. Pink-washed light penetrated the trees. Darkness would descend soon, but they weren't going far and they knew this path by heart. It was where they came to fish or visit or simply sit and daydream.

Megan despised the uneasiness she felt around him now. Would it always be this way? Would things ever go back to normal?

Once there, he didn't lounge on a rock along the grassy bank or lean against a tree and toss rocks into the meandering water as he usually did. Instead, he paced like a caged panther.

"Tom, is something bothering you?"

"Yes." He stopped short, grimaced. Shook his head. "No." Coming towards her, he stopped a breath away. "Actually, I have something I'd like to ask you."

His demeanor told her this wasn't a casual question. Her heart thumped a dull beat in her chest. Surely he wasn't about to—

Sliding his hand in his pants' pocket, he withdrew a ruby ring and held it between his thumb and forefinger. He took hold of her hand. Cleared his throat. "Megan, it's no secret how I feel about you. I've tried to give you the space you said you needed, but I think that was a mistake. It feels as though you're slipping away."

Her gaze was riveted to that ring, glinting red sparks in the waning light. "Tom—"

"Please, let me finish."

Pressing her lips together, she nodded, wishing they could retrace their steps, wishing she'd gone inside with her sisters instead of coming here with him. She was going to hurt him, this kind, loyal man. And she hated herself for it.

"I love you," he murmured softly, his green gaze urgent. Pleading. "I want you to be my wife. I want to spend the rest of my life with you, raise a family together. What do you say, Megan? Will you give us a chance?"

Megan squeezed her eyes tight, desperately searching for the right words, the kindest way to tell him how she felt. There could be no more cowardice. When she felt the whisper of his mouth against hers, she gasped, fell back, wrenched her hand from his.

"Don't do that," she ordered, insides in uproar.

He advanced, looking very determined. "Megan—"

"I'm in love with Lucian," she blurted.

He jerked as if struck. "In *love* with him? You hardly know the man!"

"I know him better than you think."

"Believe it or not, I understand his appeal. I do. He waltzes into town with his fancy clothes and perfect manners. He's the type of man who knows how to make a woman feel like she's important to him. Charm is bred into men like that from birth." Threading impatient fingers through his short, dark hair, he set his jaw. "Do you honestly believe he'll offer to take you back with him?"

Pain seized her. Of course Lucian would never do such a thing. She wasn't what he considered a suitable bride.

Lifting her chin, she said, "I wouldn't go even if he did ask. This is my home. My family is here. My entire life is here."

"Then why?" Lightly grasping her upper arms, Tom

bent close. "Megan, please. If you don't see a future for the two of you, then give us a chance. You *know* me. You know that I'm a man of my word and that you can trust me never to hurt you. We can have a good life together, you and me and the ten kids you're so keen on having. Is he willing to give you that?"

Seeing the promise in her friend's clear green eyes, she felt tears welling up and spilling down her cheeks. This whole situation was impossible! She was in love with a man who didn't want her. And the man who *did* want her…well, her love for him was a comfortable, friendship type of love. She couldn't marry Tom or any other man. Not when her heart belonged to Lucian. Would *always* belong to him.

Thumbing moisture from her cheek, Tom picked up her hand and pressed the ring into it, curling her fingers around it when she opened her mouth to protest.

"You've a lot to sort through. Keep the ring until you've had time to consider everything I've said."

The jewel bit into her palm. "But—"

"Our friendship demands you give my proposal serious thought, don't you think? In fact, I don't want an answer until after he's gone. That way you can look at things with clearheaded perspective."

She wanted to tell him Lucian's whereabouts wouldn't change things. "I'll keep the ring for the time being, but, Tom, I—I'm afraid you're only setting yourself up for further disappointment."

"We'll see." The light had faded to the point she could barely make out his features, the woods surrounding them brimming with shadows. "Come on, it's getting late. You know how Jane worries."

Slipping the ring deep into her pocket, she walked

beside him along the path, the night noises competing with her chaotic thoughts. At the cabin, he bade her a solemn good-night. Sinking down onto the top step, she watched his retreating figure, her entire being weighed down as if a giant boulder sat upon her shoulders. He'd be crushed if he knew what she was thinking. Wishing with all her heart that the ring in her pocket was Lucian's.

Chapter Eighteen

Megan and the girls were sitting down to breakfast when Lucian's valet rapped discreetly on the door. The note he gave her requested her presence for lunch. Just her. Not her sisters. That meant she and Lucian would be alone. She couldn't deny the prospect was a daunting one. Lucian was a perceptive man. Would he notice her preoccupation? She did not want him to know about Tom's proposal. Didn't want anyone to know.

"Please tell Mr. Beaumont that I accept." She smiled tremulously at the somber Mr. Smith.

He dipped his head. "Yes, miss."

She was about to shut the door when she spotted Kate striding intently down the path looking as if she might burst with news.

"Kate? What are you doing here?"

Green eyes sparkling, the petite beauty rushed up and seized her hand. "I couldn't believe it when Josh told me Tom planned to propose! What did you say? Where's the ring?"

"Ring?" Nicole and Jane crowded in behind her. "What ring?"

Disbelief skittered across Jane's face. "Tom asked you to marry him?"

Megan held up a hand. "Settle down, everyone. Kate, Tom told Josh about this? When?"

Brushing past her, Kate advanced into the living area and whirled, her green skirts swaying. "Yesterday. He asked Josh for advice." Her gaze grew sympathetic. "I can tell by your expression that it didn't go well. You refused him, didn't you?"

Nicole sniffed. "Of course she did. Why would she marry plain ole Tom Leighton when she could have Lucian?"

"Tom is not plain," Jane hotly defended. "He'll make a wonderful husband."

Megan caught a flash of pain in her younger sister's eyes. Had she been wrong about the crush on Tanner Norton? Did Jane actually have feelings for Tom? Oh, she hoped not. Not only was he seven years older than Jane, but he saw her as a little sister. *You're forgetting the most important point—he proposed to* you.

Oh, Mama, I wish you were here. You'd know exactly what to say. How to handle this.

She met Kate's inquisitive gaze. "I didn't turn him down, exactly. He insisted I wait to give him an answer."

"Tom must be crushed." Looking pale, Jane flopped into the nearest chair.

"Because you don't love him," Kate surmised. "Is it because of your feelings for Lucian?"

Nicole clasped her hands together in a pleading motion. "Please take me with you to New Orleans when you marry Lucian! I promise to make myself scarce. You won't have to give me a single thought."

"I'm not marrying Lucian or anyone else," Megan

said with a sigh, overwhelmed with the pain she was inflicting on Tom. And possibly Jane.

"Do you have the ring?" Kate asked. "Josh mentioned Tom was going to give you his grandmother's ruby."

"Show it to us," Nicole demanded.

"Fine." They'd only nag her if she didn't relent. Retrieving it from her room, she slipped it on her finger for them to see. While Kate and Nicole oohed and ahhed over it, Jane was noticeably quiet.

"Um, my stomach's feeling a little unsettled," Kate announced suddenly, pressing a hand against her middle. She looked strange. "I haven't eaten yet. Do you mind if I join you?"

Megan led her to the table. "You're family, Kate. You don't have to ask. Sit down while I fix you a cup of tea."

To Megan's relief, the focus switched to Kate, who daintily ate her way through a stack of johnnycakes, a thick slice of ham and two eggs. Far more than she normally ate. After assuring them that she felt much improved, she went home and the girls tackled their chores. For Megan, the morning dragged. Was there a specific reason Lucian had invited only her? They had been over there every day this week. Surely he was sick of her company?

With these questions bouncing about in her head, the walk to his house seemed to stretch interminably. His smile when he opened the door seemed to her a bit forced, his brown-black eyes hollow.

"I'm glad you came." He stepped back to admit her, ushered her down the hall and into the dining room where two china place settings occupied one end of the long, mahogany table. Her gaze touched on the sil-

ver vase filled with fresh-cut pink roses and the silver-
domed platters that were, judging by the rich aroma in
the air, hiding something delicious.

"Isn't this a bit formal for lunch?" She waved a hand
over the table, wondering if he could detect her ner-
vousness. Tom's proposal weighed heavily on her mind.
Despite the fact she and Lucian weren't involved in a
relationship, she felt as if she was harboring a terrible
secret. Like she was betraying Lucian somehow.

Across from her, he paused in scooting the chair
back. "You should pose your question to Mrs. Calhoun.
When I informed her that you would be joining me for
lunch, she sprang into action."

"Well, she did a fine job." She took in his informal
attire: a simple charcoal gray shirt—open at the neck—
and black trousers. "You aren't wearing your sling."

"It gets tiresome." He absently massaged the back
of his neck.

When he indicated the chair he'd pulled out, she
rounded the table. "It strains your neck?"

He smiled, white teeth flashing. "You're very observant today, Miss O'Malley."

"Just today?" she teased, seating herself and straightening her blue skirts.

"Every day." Removing the domes from the platters,
he extended his hand for her plate.

"I can serve myself, you know."

"I don't mind."

With a shrug, she gave him the plate, a little self-
conscious. She'd been here alone with him many times
before, but today something seemed different. The silence of the cavernous house pressed in on her, the

emptiness stifling, the scrape of the serving spoons on china magnified a hundredfold.

Lucian seemed preoccupied, not fully attuned to his surroundings. Odd.

When he'd filled both of their plates and had seated himself around the corner from her, he surprised her by saying grace. The meal wasn't an easy one. Her attempts to draw him out fell flat. When he put his fork down and took a sip of lemonade, she dabbed her mouth with her napkin and, refolding it in her lap, leveled her gaze at him.

"What's bothering you, Lucian?"

Pressing his lips together, he studied the silverware, tapered fingers outlining his knife and fork. "I found something." A muscle jumped in his jaw. He pushed his chair back and stood, removing the plates to the kitchen.

Megan didn't move. Found what?

When he returned to the dining room, he went to the sideboard and picked up a wooden box she hadn't noticed before. He carried it back, set it in front of her, his hand lingering on the lid. She tilted her head back to study his face. "What is this?" she murmured, half dreading his answer.

Pain blazed hot in his eyes. "Letters. Proof Charles was telling the truth."

He slid his hand off, lifted the lid. Seating himself once more, he told her, "You may read them if you'd like."

She gazed at the stack, the elegant script on the envelopes. Lucinda's letters to Charles. Her heart squeezed. What must he be feeling right now?

"Where did you find them?"

"In the study."

She finally raised her eyes to his. "I can't possibly read all of these right now. There must be dozens."

He frowned, leaned forward and picked up the stack. Rifling through it, he slid one out and, examining the date, handed it to her. "Try this one."

Swallowing hard, she slid out the parchment with trembling fingers, unfolding it with great care. Curiosity and dread warred in her breast.

"'Dearest Father,'" she began quietly, "'I received the chess set last week. You must understand why I had to tell Lucian it was a birthday gift from me. He was delighted, of course, but you mustn't send anything else. Gerard walked in as I was opening it, and I had to scramble to hide the packaging. I don't like having to deceive my husband and my son.'" Megan broke off to glance at Lucian, who was sitting statue-still, his expression unreadable. "Do you remember the chess set?"

"I kept it all these years, believing it was a gift from my mother," he responded with a grimace. "It's in my study. Read on. It gets better."

Sucking in a breath, Megan read, "'For now, the best thing for everyone is to keep our contact a secret. Please do not come here. Lucian wouldn't understand. Neither would Gerard.'" Her eyes smarted. Poor Charles. He'd wanted to go to them, but Lucinda had persuaded him not to. She flipped over the envelope. "Is this your address?"

"No." He spoke without emotion. "The address is that of Nannette Devereaux, a close friend of my mother's."

This iron grip on his control worried her. He needed to release his frustration, his grief. All the myriad emotions a discovery such as this must inspire.

Hurting for him and for her dear friend Charles, for their immense loss, she covered his hand with hers. "I'm so very sorry, Lucian. I can't begin to imagine how you must feel. Maybe…by willing this house to you and by adding that stipulation, it was Charles's way of reaching out to you from beyond the grave."

"Perhaps," he agreed stoically. "It's a lot to take in. I've had this fixed view of how things were for so long that I'm having trouble accepting this new reality."

She squeezed his hand. "Give yourself some time."

He glanced down at their joined hands. His gaze shot to hers. "What's this? I haven't noticed you wearing it before."

Megan gasped. Tom's ruby ring! Distracted by Kate's episode, she'd forgotten to take it off. She felt as if she might suffocate. "I—uh—"

Snatching her hand away, she stared at the ring as if it were a snake ready to strike.

Lucian visibly braced himself for her answer.

Her cheeks burned with mortification. "Tom was at the cabin when Jane and I got home last night. H-he asked me to marry him."

"I see." Lucian blinked. "I suppose congratulations are in order. When's the happy day?"

Why was he congratulating her? Did the prospect of her marrying another man not bother him? Did he care so little? Her heart broke a little at the thought. Those kisses… This *thing* between them…meant nothing to him?

"Oh, I haven't given him an answer yet." Slipping off the ring, she put it in her pocket. "He asked me to think about it awhile first. I was only wearing it this morning to show the girls."

"Tom strikes me as a fine man," Lucian said without emotion. "And it's obvious he cares about you."

Stung by his apathetic attitude, Megan lifted her chin. "He's more than fine. He's wonderful. My family adores him."

"Megan," he said, leaning forward, suddenly intense, "don't marry him simply because everyone else thinks you should. Your family won't have to live with him day after day. You will."

The tear in her heart widened, nearly rendering it in two. Lucian did not love her. His words proved it. *What did you think? He'd fall down on his knees and beg you to turn Tom down? To marry him instead? He's never going to do that. You're not his ideal wife, remember?*

The pain almost a physical ache, she shot out of her seat and glared down at him. "Don't you dare lecture me! You're the one determined to marry for duty's sake. To the least objectionable female," she mimicked, "one with all the qualifications for the esteemed Lucian Beaumont."

Feeling out of control, Megan headed for the door before she said something she'd really regret.

"Megan, wait!" He was suddenly behind her, his hand gentle but firm on her arm, halting her exit. He turned her towards him. She bit her lip at his pained expression. "I apologize. I wasn't trying to lecture you. It's just that I—" Grimacing, he made a frustrated sound, thrust his fingers through his hair. "I care about you, Megan. I want you to be happy. I don't want a love match, but you do. I want that for you, that's all."

For an instant, his guard slipped, and she thought she saw something in his eyes that said he wanted it, too. With her. But that was just wishful thinking. Lucian didn't want her love.

"I have to go." *Before I turn into a blubbering idiot.*

"Let me escort you home."

"No."

"Smith, then." Was there a desperate edge to his voice?

She stopped at the front door, her hand on the handle, not daring to look at him. "Don't worry about me. I'll be just fine on my own."

"I've upset you. Please, don't leave like this."

Yes, she was upset. He wasn't. Why would he be? His heart wasn't affected.

He was standing close behind her, close enough to feel his heat. Smell his cologne. It wouldn't take much to lean back against him. Shoving aside the temptation, she shook her head. "I don't want to discuss this anymore tonight." She opened the door. "Good night, Lucian."

And she left without a single glance back, head held high. He couldn't know that inside, she felt like a doomed heroine who'd just lost her hero.

Chapter Nineteen

Lucian gripped the porch rail, willing himself not to dash down the steps after her. She was upset. She didn't need him trailing after her like a forlorn puppy.

Too keyed up to go back inside, he strode to the barn in search of his valet. "Smith!"

"I'm here, sir." He stepped out of the stall, surprise at Lucian's tone quickly masked.

"Saddle D'Artagnan." Lucian worked to calm himself.

"But, sir, your arm…" He trailed off, clearly concerned but recognizing it wasn't his place to question his employer.

"Will be fine," he assured him, going to his horse and leading him out of the stall. "I'm not going far."

When Smith had finished, he asked, "Would you like me to accompany you?"

"No, that won't be necessary." He needed movement, a change of scenery. A chance to sort through his tumultuous thoughts.

He hauled himself into the saddle with his good arm. "*Merci*. If I'm not back in two hours' time, feel free to send out a search party." He arched a brow at the man who was a loyal employee but felt like family.

"Yes, sir." He sighed, resigned.

Lucian led his horse beyond the gardens, waving to Fred kneeling in the beds yanking weeds, and entered the sparse woods behind the Calhouns' cottage. The clouds blocked the sunlight, and the air carried the promise of a summer shower. He'd be wise to stick close to home.

Home. Since when had he started thinking of this place as home?

Since you started to care for Megan, perhaps? She was connected to this place, to his grandfather's house. Her presence was stamped in every room, the porches, the gardens. Impossible to separate the two in his mind.

Transferring the reins to his injured hand, he rubbed his chest to dislodge the pain. Only, it wasn't a physical pain, exactly. The image of Tom's ring on Megan's finger...

He growled low in his throat. What was he supposed to do? Rant and rave and beg her not to marry the man? Megan didn't belong with Tom. She belonged with *him*.

Lucian jerked on the reins, gasping as pain radiated up his forearm. D'Artagnan halted. Swished the flies away with his tail.

Cradling his arm against his belly, his gaze swept the tranquil woods, lush greens and deep browns running together. "I could marry her, you know. Well, I could offer. I'm not certain if she'd accept."

D'Artagnan dipped his head as if to agree.

"We're friends, she and I. I trust her implicitly. Megan is a special lady, different from anyone I've ever known. I care about her. A lot." *Too much.* "I should

be talking to a human being about this, not a horse."
D'Artagnan stamped his foot. "No offense, *mon ami*."

Who was he kidding? Megan craved a grand love to
rival the most prolific romance novels. He didn't have
it in him to give her that. Refused to risk repeating his
father's mistakes. No. His place was in New Orleans.
And she belonged here. With Tom. Or some other man
who could give her what she deserved. A man who
would never hurt her.

So this was what misery felt like.

From now on, she was going to stick to adventures
and mysteries. No more romance. In fact, as soon as she
got home from church she was going to stow them all in
a crate and give them away. Why torture herself reading happy endings when she wasn't going to get one?

"Is anyone sitting here?"

Megan lifted her gaze from her lap. Tom, dressed in
his Sunday best, brown hair shiny from a recent wash,
waited for her permission to sit. She inwardly sighed.
Tried to smile and failed.

"No. Please, join us."

With a wide smile, he sat beside her at the end of
the pew. Leaning forward, he aimed that smile at her
sister, seated on her other side. "Hey there, Janie-girl."

"Hi."

Tom's smile faded. Megan shot Jane a sideways
glance. Her lack of enthusiasm was unusual. Off routine. Whenever Tom teased her, she would give it right
back. Not today.

"Are you feeling all right, Jane?" she murmured.
Megan had been so lost in her own troubles lately that

she hadn't been paying particular attention to anyone around her.

"I'm fine." She lowered her gaze to her lap where her hands were tightly clasped, color surging in her cheeks. Something was definitely bothering her. Was it Tom? Could she possibly harbor feelings for him?

"What about you, Megan?" Tom said softly. "You don't look particularly happy this morning."

"I'm fine."

She felt Jane's perusal. Ugh. This was going to be a long morning.

Glancing over her shoulder, she searched for Lucian.

Tom caught her gaze. Frowned. "He's outside tethering his horse. Should I change pews?"

She blinked. "No. Lucian doesn't— That is, he wouldn't—"

"It's all right. You don't have to explain."

Flustered, Megan turned around, determined not to search him out again.

Lucian entered the church. Took one look at Megan and Tom—sitting together and swapping smiles—and turned and walked right back out, oblivious to the curious stares. He couldn't do this. Couldn't sit by and watch her with another man.

All the way home, he fought for control over his emotions. Giving in to them would accomplish nothing. He had to be rational. To plan. To leave Tennessee with his dignity intact. To leave Megan with good memories. He wouldn't cause a scene, refused to cause trouble for her. He'd meant what he said—more than anything else, he wanted her to be happy.

He found Smith straightaway and instructed him to

start packing his things. They would be leaving early next week. He'd stay long enough to say goodbye to the friends he'd made—Owen and Sarah, the Monroes, Megan's family, Fred and Madge Calhoun—and attend one more story time. He wanted to remember her that way—dressed up in a silly costume and reading to the children—forever *his* Megan.

An hour later, he was in the study trying to decide what to take with him when the doorbell rang.

"Tom?" Lucian didn't attempt to hide his surprise. "Would you like to come in?"

"No, thanks. I can't stay long. I'm headed to Sam and Mary's for lunch." He jerked a thumb over his shoulder.

Stepping out on to the porch, Lucian crossed his arms and waited. He wasn't in the mood for games.

Tom looked uncomfortable but determined. "Look, I saw you before services. I know you skipped out early, and I have to assume you did that because it bothered you to see Megan and me together. She told you about my proposal?"

"What do you want, Leighton?" he ground out. Was the man here to gloat?

"I just wanted to thank you for not challenging my relationship with her. I'm good for her, you know. I can give her what she wants."

"Are you sure about that?" Lucian challenged, not because he believed otherwise, but because the truth stung. Of course Tom would be good for her. That didn't make it any easier to swallow.

His green gaze was clear, confident. "Once you've gone, she'll see that I'm the best man for her."

"If you're asking when I'm leaving, the answer is

next week. Is there anything else? Because I've got an awful lot of packing to do."

He shrugged. "Thanks for your time."

Lucian barely held on to his temper, hands curled into fists as the other man ambled off the porch and across the lawn. The pinch in his forearm penetrated the haze of anger clouding his mind and he unclenched his hands. It was wasted emotion, anyway. The only person he had a right to be mad at was himself.

Despite everything—his parents' doomed marriage, his father's cruel indifference and mother's heartbreak, his and Megan's differences—he'd foolishly allowed himself to fall in love with her.

Apparently he hadn't learned his lessons well enough...if at all.

And now it was killing him to walk away from her.

The doorbell pealed insistently just as he sat at the small kitchen table with a sandwich he'd thrown together. Tossing aside his napkin, he strode through the house. If it was Leighton again...

"Megan."

He soaked in the sight of her, silken curls tumbling about her shoulders in disarray, small hands knotted at her waist. The worry shimmering in her luminous eyes sent a shaft of apprehension through his midsection. "What's happened?"

"It's Sarah." Her lower lip trembled as she spoke, and he closed the distance between them, smoothed his hands down her arms in an attempt to reassure her. Reassurance he didn't feel. His mind conjured up a dozen scenarios...all of them dire.

"What about her?" His heart thudded with dread.

"She's sick, Lucian. Owen said the doctor doesn't know what's wrong with her. She woke up yesterday complaining of a headache and then developed a fever shortly after. They can't get the fever to come down."

Her distress a palpable thing, Lucian set aside his own concern, spoke matter-of-factly. "I'll get the wagon ready and take you over there. Surely there's something that can be done. I have resources. I'll send for another doctor, if necessary. More medicine. Whatever it takes to get her well."

None of that helped your mother, though, did it? He shook off the reminder. This was different. Sarah was young and strong. She'd pull through this. Any other option didn't bear thinking about.

Brow puckered, gaze clinging to his with a hopeful trust that twisted his insides, she nodded. He took her hand and led her through the house so that he could grab his coat. In the barn, she insisted on helping him hitch the team to the wagon.

The ride out to the Livingston farm was passed in taut silence. At one point, he surreptitiously checked her left hand, sharp relief flooding him at the sight of her bare fingers. She wasn't wearing Tom's ring. Was she still considering the matter? Or had she refused him?

It was so very wrong of him to hope she had.

When the cabin came into view, they saw Owen outside talking with another man.

"Who's that?"

"Noah Townsend," Megan replied, tension humming along her slender frame. "He's Owen's neighbor. They have something in common. Noah's wife died a year ago. They didn't have any kids, though, so he's alone."

Sadness laced her words. He glanced at her familiar

profile, love for this woman expanding in his chest until he could barely breathe. A woman of infinite compassion, other people's plights touched her as deeply as if they were her own.

She turned her great big, fathomless gaze on him. "If something happens to Sarah, how will Owen go on? He'll have lost everything..." she said on a ragged whisper.

Lucian set the brake. Curved a hand about her cheek, stroking her soft skin with his thumb. "Nothing is going to happen to her."

"You can't know that."

She was right, of course. He couldn't. But clinging to that hope, refusing to accept any other alternative, kept his control in place. His fears subdued.

"At this point in time, it's best to stay positive."

"You're right."

With great reluctance, he dropped his hand. Climbing down, he came around and assisted her. Together, they approached the men.

Owen's expression, as if he bore the weight of the world on his shoulders, tore into Lucian. He'd worn a similar one last year as his mother lay dying. *Forget about the past.* Revisiting his mother's last days wouldn't help anything.

With an offer to help in any way he could, Noah mounted his horse and trotted off shortly after the introductions were made. Owen thanked them for coming.

"Has there been any change?" Megan asked quietly.

"No." He clearly hadn't slept. His clothes were wrinkled and a day-old beard darkened his jaw. "Come on inside. I don't like to leave her alone for any length of time."

With a hand at the small of her back, Lucian guided Megan inside. The curtains had been drawn closed to block out harsh daylight, and it took a moment for his eyes to adjust. The sight of sweet Sarah lying still and lifeless beneath the quilts quite literally stole his breath away. Blinking fast, he clamped down on his back teeth. *She will be fine,* he told himself. *Just fine.*

Owen paused by the head of the bed, tenderly brushed the hair from her damp forehead. Her little face flushed with fever was the only sign anything was wrong.

Megan slipped her hand into Lucian's, but she centered her gaze on Owen. "Have you been able to get her to take any fluids?" She spoke in a hushed voice.

"A bit. She fights me. Only wants to sleep."

"The medicine Doc left isn't helping?"

He shook his head. "He said to give it to her every few hours. That we'd have to wait and see if it brought her temperature down. He won't say, but I can tell he's worried. He got the same look he had right before Meredith and the baby…" He broke off, covered his mouth with his hand. After a bit, he continued, "He's coming back to check on her before nightfall." The man's grief was a palpable thing.

"I can send for a doctor in Sevierville or Knoxville if you'd like. Money isn't an issue when it comes to getting Sarah the best possible medical care. Just say the word and it's done."

"I appreciate the offer, but I trust Doc. Besides, something like that would take time we don't have." His eyes grew shiny. "And ultimately, it's in the Lord's hands. He loves my daughter even more than I do."

Lucian nodded, although he didn't understand. The

man had recently lost his wife and newborn, was on the verge of losing his daughter and yet his faith in God's love held firm. Lucian's gaze was drawn to Sarah, tiny and vulnerable and precious. So innocent.

Like a powerful ocean current, sorrow tugged at him, threatened to sweep him into uncharted waters. The same sorrow he'd battled as his mother lay dying.

Memories hit him—one after another—the quiet whispers of the servants, the pungent odor of healing herbs, his mother's paper-thin hands as he cradled them in his own, urging her to fight. To get well. And for once he didn't block them. The helplessness had been the worst....

He felt pressure on his hand. "Lucian?" Megan whispered, her troubled gaze searching his face. "The doctor is here. We should wait outside."

He'd somehow missed his arrival. "All right."

Lucian appeared lost in his own world, raw anguish swirling in the brown-black depths. Megan urged him outside. In deep conversation beside the door, Owen and Doc didn't pay them any mind. Her fingers threaded through his, she continued walking until they were well away from the cabin. Unfortunately, she didn't notice the graves until too late. When she attempted to change direction, Lucian resisted, his gaze riveted to the wooden crosses.

Pale beneath his tan, his earlier confidence was gone. Seeing Sarah like that had affected her, as well, but she sensed something more was going on with him.

"What are you thinking about?"

"Death."

"This isn't just about Sarah, is it?"

He took a shuddering breath. "For so long, I've tried not to think about my mother's last days. To avoid thinking about her, period. Seeing that little girl in there…" His voice grew thick with emotion and he couldn't finish.

Her own throat knotting with tears, she placed a palm against his cool cheek. "And it brought it all back?"

His bleak gaze clinging to hers, he nodded.

"When my father died, I was in shock for days. Weeks, even. Slowly but surely, it sank in that he was never coming back. His presence was everywhere. His hat hanging on the coat rack. His shoes by the door. My first reaction was to try to avoid the memories and, in so doing, avoid the pain of his absence. But you know what I eventually realized? That by not talking about him, by refusing to even *think* about him, I was discounting his importance in my life. I was dishonoring the man that he was. And I thought, is this what I want after I'm gone? For my loved ones to pretend I never existed? That I never *mattered?* Of course not.

"Lucian, the memories will get easier to bear. And, although you might not think so now, they will eventually bring you comfort. You must allow yourself to grieve."

Trembling, he pulled her into his arms, hugged her as if he might never let go. She felt him struggling to release his sorrow, knew that it was difficult for some men to cry because they saw it as a weakness. Praying silently, she rubbed his back and simply held him.

Because she loved him, his sorrow made her own heart ache. Her utmost desire was to be there always for him, to comfort him when life got hard and rejoice with him in the good times. But he wasn't prepared to accept her in his life. All she could do was be here for him now.

Later, after he'd gone, she'd deal with the grief. Not hide from it.

When he pulled away, he turned his back, dashing the moisture from his cheeks. "I miss her. But I'm angry at her, too, and that makes me feel incredibly guilty."

"That's to be expected, considering the circumstances."

He faced her once more, his manner subdued. "Understanding why she did it doesn't make it easier to accept. I wish my grandfather had forced the issue. She couldn't have very well turned him away if he'd shown up on our doorstep."

"Look at what happened the first time he tried to force his will upon her. Perhaps Charles was afraid if he did that, he'd lose all connection with her. With you."

His brow knotted with regret, and he jerked a nod.

"You'll work through this. God will help you." She touched his hand and, because she didn't know what else to say, she asked, "Would you like to pray with me for Sarah?"

"Yes, I would." He inhaled, absently rubbing his cast. "But I've never prayed out loud with anyone before." His dark eyes were cautious, unsure, which was completely unlike him.

Taking his hand again, she suggested, "You could pray silently while I pray aloud."

"No," he said with brows lowered. "I'd like to try. After you, of course."

Bowing her head, Megan prayed for Sarah's healing, comfort for Owen and wisdom for the doctor. Lucian's prayer was short and direct. Hearing him petition God, when weeks earlier he'd questioned His love and care, brought tears of joy to her eyes.

"We should probably go." She sniffed, released his hand. "Doc is still in there. I don't want to be in the way."

"I agree."

Megan quickly let Owen know they were leaving. When they reached her place, she insisted she didn't need help getting down. He stayed seated, his gaze tracking her every move. She wished he would jump down from there and take her in his arms and tell her he was wrong. About love. About her.

"Thank you, Megan. For everything."

She nodded, unable to regret any of it. Meeting him. Loving him. "Good night, Lucian."

Looking resigned, he signaled the team to head out. She watched him go, something inside telling her his time here was short. He would leave. Soon. And she would have to find a way to live without him.

Chapter Twenty

"Megan." Tom looked at once surprised and pleased to find her on his doorstep. "Would you like to come in?"

"That's all right," she declined, determined to keep this visit short. "Do you have a moment?"

"Sure." Leaning sideways to grab his hat from a knob inside the door, he settled it on his head and closed the door behind him. Taking her arm, he led her to the single maple tree in the corner of the yard, its leafy bower providing much-needed shade. He tipped the brim up. "Any word on Sarah Livingston?"

"If anything, she's worse. I went there this afternoon to drop off some food for Owen, and she was thrashing about, her fever holding firm." At the memory, Megan's stomach hardened into a tight ball. She'd stayed only long enough to give him the food—and for him to mention that Lucian had stopped by in the early morning.

Frowning, he toed a stick with his boot. "I'm sorry to hear that."

Megan forced her mind to the task at hand. Her spirits were already low. Better get this over with before she lost her nerve.

Reaching into her reticule, she withdrew the ring. Held it out to him. "I want you to take the ring back, Tom."

His green gaze zeroed in on the ring, then lifted to her face in confusion. He made no move to accept it. "I thought you agreed to wait. To take some time—"

"Time isn't going to change my answer. I'm sorry, I—" she broke off, hating the dawning hurt spreading across his kind face. But stretching this out wouldn't make it hurt any less. She squared her shoulders. "I can't marry you."

With a sharp breath, he reluctantly took the ring from her nerveless fingers and tucked it in his pocket. "Has he changed his mind about marrying you, then?" he asked without rancor. Pain-filled eyes met hers.

"No." *This is so hard, God. All of it. Lucian. Tom. Sarah. When will it stop hurting?*

"I don't understand."

"I will marry for love or not at all. Friendship isn't enough for me. Can you understand that?"

"I understand that I love you," he pushed out. "And… you don't love me."

She touched his arm, and he flinched. "Oh, Tom, I love you like a brother. You're a dear friend. I know you don't want to hear that, but it's the truth."

Gaze riveted to the ground, he merely nodded.

"I hope we can still be friends."

"I'll need some space. Time to move past this."

"I understand." Megan felt like weeping. Felt vile for wounding him. "I have to go now, Tom. Nicole and Jane are expecting me home in time for supper."

"Tell them hello for me, will you?"

"I will."

Turning on her heel, she walked quickly through the grass and untethered Mr. Knightley. In the saddle, she chanced a glance at where he stood. Tom waved. Gulping back emotion, she waved and headed down the lane.

At home, Jane was waiting for her in the barn.

"I thought you'd be inside fixing supper." Megan dismounted, shot her a questioning glance.

"You turned him down, didn't you?" Her chest heaved, auburn hair wild about her shoulders. "You hurt him," she accused, eyes blazing.

Megan stilled, stunned by her normally even-keeled sister's outburst. "I gave him back his ring, yes."

A tear slipped down her cheek. She angrily scrubbed it away. "I don't understand how you could do that. Tom is a wonderful man! He deserves someone who will appreciate him."

"Someone like you?" Megan prodded gently.

Her eyes widened. Face crumpled. The tears began to flow in earnest, and Megan's already heavy heart splintered into a dozen pieces. Putting her arms around her sister, she stroked her hair as she cried against her shoulder. "Shh. It's going to be okay."

Oh, Mama, I wish you were here. You'd know exactly what to say to make her feel better.

When Jane pulled away, she rubbed at the moisture on her cheeks. Sniffed. "I'm afraid Tom will never see me as anything more than a pesky little sister."

"Maybe that's because of the age difference," Megan pointed out as delicately as she could. "He's twenty-two. You're fifteen."

"Almost sixteen," she protested. "Besides, lots of girls get married at sixteen."

"I don't know about *lots,* but you're right, there are some girls who do marry young. But I know Mama would prefer you wait a few years. Maybe when you're eighteen."

"But that's two years away," she wailed. "Tom will have found someone else to marry by then!"

"Maybe not. If Tom is the man God has picked out for you, it'll work out."

"And what if he never gets over you?"

Megan closed her eyes and sighed, thinking of her love for Lucian. A love she'd never get over. "I pray that isn't the case," she said fervently.

"I know you love Lucian. Does he…?"

"No."

Jane sighed, took Megan's hands. "I'm sorry. I know how much that hurts."

Megan looked into her sister's face full of sympathy. "You're not angry with me?"

"No, not angry. I admit to being jealous. I—I've wished it was me Tom was pursuing instead of you."

"I'm sorry."

"I still love you." She managed a watery smile.

Megan tenderly brushed Jane's hair behind her shoulder. "I love you, too. I always will, no matter what happens."

"I suppose I should go inside and help Nicole with supper before she scorches it," she said with a grimace.

"Or burns down the cabin," she agreed. "I'll be inside as soon as I get Mr. Knightley squared away."

Megan watched her sister go, wishing she'd seen

the evidence of her feelings much sooner. If she'd been aware, she could've been more sensitive in her handling of the situation.

Crouched in the garden picking tomatoes the next morning, Megan lifted her head at the sound of wagon wheels creaking over hard earth. Wiping the perspiration from her brow, she shaded her eyes with one hand and squinted. Lucian's unmistakable form came into view. Her pulse leaped.

Placing a tomato into the basket beside her feet, she stood and dislodged the dirt from her hands. He spotted her advancing along the row and lifted his hand in greeting. Why was he here?

Bounding to the ground, he came around to greet her, sweeping off his black bowler. He'd left off wearing his sling entirely.

"I was in town just now and noticed Doc heading in the direction of the Livingstons' place. I thought perhaps we should go out there in case there's been a change." His intense gaze swept her dusty dress, the rogue curls escaping the ribbon at her nape. "Owen might have need of some company. Do you have time now?"

"Sure. Give me a moment to take my basket inside and change. Would you like to come in for a glass of lemonade or tea?"

"*Non, merci.* Why don't you go on in and I'll retrieve your basket?"

"You don't have to do that." She glanced at his spotless boots, his formal clothes in shades of blue that made his skin glow with vibrancy.

The barest of smiles tilted his lips. "I don't mind."

"If you say so." She self-consciously brushed at the dirt on her apron. "I'll be right back."

"Take your time, *mon chou.*"

Little pastry. The familiar nickname triggered a smile. As observant as he was, had he noticed her discomfiture? Was the endearment a subtle way of telling her that, despite her untidy appearance, she was still attractive to him?

Right, Megan. Now you're being fanciful.

Inside, she hurriedly explained to her sisters that Lucian was taking her to check on Sarah.

Jane had her hands buried in bread dough. "Tell Owen we're still praying."

Nicole looked up from her sewing. "Do you think she'll pull through this?"

"I hope so." Megan hadn't stopped thinking about the little girl these past three days. She'd tried to stay positive, but doubts had crept in at times. "I'll give you a full report when we return."

Once she'd washed her hands and face, tidied her hair and changed into her apricot-hued dress, she descended the stairs to find Lucian in the living room chatting with Nicole. He'd delivered her basket to Jane in the kitchen. Spying her, he stood, his gaze lighting with appreciation.

"All ready to go?"

Her cheeks warmed. "Yes."

Bidding her sisters goodbye, he held the door for her and joined her on the porch. They walked side by side to the wagon, where she paused to regard him with open scrutiny.

"Owen mentioned you paid them a visit yesterday morning."

"Yes, that's right."

"You went alone."

His brow wrinkled in confusion, he rocked back on his heels. "I did."

Must she spell it out for him? "Why didn't you just follow Doc? Why come and get me?"

Understanding dawned. His mouth twisted. "Because it was so much easier with you."

"Oh." He'd basically confessed to needing her. Satisfaction—futile though it was—spiraled through her. "I see."

She frowned. Since when had she started talking like him?

"Sarah wasn't doing so well when I was there." He gave her a hand up and walked around to the other side, using his uninjured hand to lever himself up. The narrow seat shifted with his weight. He angled his face towards hers, his eyes shadowed by the hat's brim. "How was she when you stopped by?"

"Not good. I didn't stay long." A lump formed in her throat as she recalled Sarah, soaked with sweat and thrashing about in delirium, and Owen, looking slightly desperate.

With a grim nod, he set the wagon in motion.

Father God, please prepare us for what we might encounter. Give us the strength, the words to comfort Owen. Above all, help us to accept Your will in this matter.

Needing a connection with Lucian, Megan wove her hand beneath his arm, fingers curled about his biceps.

He sent her a sidelong glance fraught with concern. He was worried, too.

The horses seemed to be traveling at a slower rate of speed than usual, the lane stretching endlessly before them. When at last they reached the turnoff, Megan tensed.

Doc's wagon was still there. Lucian covered her hand with his own, a comforting weight. "Are you ready?"

"I am."

He helped her down, his hand a constant pressure at the small of her back. A physical reminder of his support. Before he could raise his hand to knock, the door swung open and Owen stood in the doorway. Her breath stalled. Beneath his scruffiness, relief softened his features.

"Owen?"

"She's going to be okay," he said firmly, as if still trying to absorb what he was saying. "Her fever broke this morning just after dawn. Doc's checking her over."

Lucian rubbed her back in a soothing manner. "You're certain she'll be all right?"

Despite his exhaustion, Owen managed to look like a man reborn. "Come on in and see for yourself."

Moving out of the way, he went to stand beside the fireplace, his weight supported by the rough-hewn mantel. Doc's broad shoulders blocked their view. After a moment, he snapped his bag closed and edged to the foot of the bed.

"Miss Megan. Mr. Lucian." Propped up with a mound of pillows, Sarah's weak voice couldn't disguise her delight. While her blond hair was a tangled mess, she was wearing a fresh nightgown. "Did you bring me another present?"

Megan chuckled. Lucian shot her a glance, smiled broadly. Sarah was going to be fine. Just fine.

The majority of Gatlinburg's residents turned out Friday night for story time. Word of his departure had traveled like wildfire through the small town, and here they all were to bid him farewell. A sort of going-away party.

Mrs. Calhoun had outdone herself. In anticipation of the crowd, she decided to set up the refreshments in the dining room. This week she'd engaged in a baking frenzy. Cakes, pies and pastries occupied every flat surface in sight. He'd been sent to Clawson's twice for extra sugar.... No telling what kind of effect all this bounty would have on the kids.

Funny, he believed he was actually going to miss the little creatures.

He would definitely miss Megan's costumes.

He studied her over the rim of his cup. Dressed like a true cowgirl, complete with hip holster and boots with silver spurs, she stood in the archway between the kitchen and dining room. Her pale curls, restrained with a leather strip, glistened in light thrown off by the wall sconces. Cradled against her shoulder was a cherub-faced infant who strongly resembled her mother, a friend of Megan's named Rachel Prescott. The father, Cole Prescott, was playing a game with the infant, tickling her beneath the chin and making her giggle with delight.

Megan caught him staring. Her wistful smile made his gut clench with regret.

A hand clapped him on the back then, and he nearly spilled his drink. Nathan chuckled beside him. "Didn't mean to startle you, Beaumont."

"That's quite all right."

Those unreadable silver eyes studied him. "It's true, then? You're leaving us Monday?"

"I mean to get an early start." He willed his gaze not to stray to Megan. Nathan would surely notice. Had he witnessed her sad smile?

Nathan took a drink of steaming coffee, shifted to let two young men pass by. "Do you plan on coming back for a visit sometime?"

Not likely. How could he when Megan was sure to be happily ensconced in married life? "I don't know."

He nodded, considering, and glanced at Megan across the way. "We all appreciate your kindness in leaving the house in Megan's care. You don't have to worry. She won't violate your trust."

"I know that."

If Nathan noted the hint of melancholy in Lucian's voice, he didn't comment on it. Instead, he carefully surveyed the crush of people, lazily observing, "I'm surprised Tom Leighton didn't show up."

"It wouldn't be hard to miss him in this crowd." He'd been on the lookout for him since the night's beginning, dreading the encounter, seeing him claim Megan as his own.

"I don't think so. If he was here, he'd be at Megan's side." He grew thoughtful. "I stopped by his shop today for a trim. He was tight-lipped, not at all like his usual happy-go-lucky self."

Unable to stop himself, Lucian directed his gaze at Megan once more. Had something happened? Had they quarreled? Or was his absence totally unrelated to her?

The hope surging within him was wholly inappropriate. And petty. Selfish. He desired her happiness. *But not with Tom, right? You want her to be happy with* you.

That was impossible, of course. He knew it, understood it, but that didn't stop his foolish heart from yearning for the unattainable.

Another couple approached Lucian, and Nathan moved off with a quiet farewell. It took supreme effort of will to focus on their words. Megan dominated his thoughts. She was there in his peripheral vision, silently drawing him, making it all but impossible to make sane conversation. Had she decided not to marry the barbershop owner? Or worse…had Tom hurt her? His hands curled into fists. If he had…

The remainder of the night dragged. His guests weren't as eager to leave as he was for them to leave. He craved a few minutes alone with Megan. More than a few, actually. He was well aware that his time with her was growing short, every minute slipping past another minute lost to them.

It was nearing eleven when the last guest slipped out the door, and he returned to the dining room to find her assisting Mrs. Calhoun and three other young ladies he'd hired to help with tonight's festivities. Dirty dishes and cups littered the parlor and library, as well as the dining room. Cleanup would take at least an hour.

Impatient, determined to have her to himself, he stepped in front of her and took the plates from her hands, setting them aside. "Let's go for a stroll in the gardens."

"It's late."

"Fred lit the gas lamps, and the weather is fine."

She worried her lower lip, gestured to the room. "I should help with the cleanup."

"That's what these ladies are getting paid for." He tilted his head at the women watching them with interest as they went about their work. Leaning forward, he lowered his voice. "Wouldn't you like to see the gardens in the moonlight?" This may be their last chance to say a proper goodbye.

Sadness lurked in the liquid depths of her sea-blue eyes. "All right. I'll come with you."

With her hand in the crook of his elbow, he led her outside into the star-studded night. Balmy air, sweetened with the scent of magnolias, enveloped them in a warm cocoon. The fat, pearlescent moon dominated the night sky. Gas lamps situated along the path flickered, points of light in the shadows.

Their footsteps against the stones were muted. "Are you going to see Sarah and Owen one last time before you go?"

"I doubt it. I'm not good at goodbyes." This one he couldn't escape, however difficult. Megan was too special, too dear.

"Isn't that what this is? A goodbye?" She stopped and angled towards him, one pale brow arched in challenge.

"Yes. I can't deny that it is."

Lips compressing, she fell silent. Wouldn't look at him, diverted her gaze to the wildflowers behind him. He was at a loss for words. What could he say that would convey how much she'd come to mean to him that wouldn't also confuse her?

"I heard your mother and sister are coming home at the end of next week," he said as they took up walking again. "I wish I could've made their acquaintance."

"Me, too. I'm certain they both would've taken to you as quickly as the rest of my family." She smiled faintly.

"I'm eager to have my mother home again. Jessica, too. Jane needs her twin now more than ever."

His brows drew together. "Is something going on with Jane?"

Megan stopped again, her hand dropping away. "She fancies herself in love with Tom."

Poor Jane. And Megan. What a terrible fix to find herself in. "I see."

"No, I don't think you do." She lifted her chin. "I returned the ring. I'm not going to marry him."

Lucian stilled, barely breathing as relief and happiness swept through him. She turned him down. She wasn't going to marry Tom, after all.

The question was…what was he going to do about it?

Chapter Twenty-One

Megan watched the play of emotions across Lucian's face. Hope sprouted. He'd said he cared for her.... Was it possible his feelings ran deeper than what he'd conveyed?

"May I ask why?"

"I don't love him." *You're the one I love,* she wanted to shout. "Not the way a woman is supposed to love her husband. A dear friend is all he'll ever be."

Swallowing hard, he edged closer, skimmed his knuckles along her cheekbone. His eyes shone bright as the stars above, illuminating the darkened corners of her heart. "Megan, *mon bien-aime,*" he whispered, his warm breath caressing her jaw.

Capturing his hand, she pressed her cheek into his palm. Being with him like this made her dizzy with joy. "I've heard you say that before. What does it mean?"

He paused. "My beloved."

Megan could only stare up at him. Was that the same as saying he loved her? "Lucian—"

His lips cut her off, his kiss marked with a yearning that matched her own. The hands cradling her face trembled. The trace of desperation in his touch worried her, however.

When he pulled his mouth away and pressed her into his chest, his heart thundered beneath her ear. He couldn't leave. How could she go on without him?

Easing back, she gazed into his dear face, holding nothing back. "Please don't go, Lucian. I love you. Stay here. With me."

He froze. "*Non*. Don't say that."

"Why shouldn't I?" She left the circle of his arms, stung by his response. "It's the truth."

The intense regret marring his expression deflated her hopes. "It won't work."

"Why not? Because you're a polished city fellow and I'm a simple mountain girl?"

"No, of course not. To be honest, I've grown quite fond of your mountains. I consider the people here my friends."

"So it's me you don't want." Turning away, she hugged her arms about her waist, wishing herself far from here. Humiliation warred with hurt. "I thought..."

Lucian stood very close behind her. "Please forgive me. It was never my intention to lead you astray, to hurt you," he answered, self-recrimination straining his husky voice. Settling his hands lightly on her shoulders, he turned her towards him. "The truth is... I—I do want you."

"Wanting someone isn't the same as loving, Lucian."

His gaze burned into hers, and for a second, he allowed her to see the depths of his feelings. But then he threw his hands up in defeat. "What does it matter what I feel, anyway? It won't change anything. It can't."

"Because of your parents? There's no guarantee we'll repeat their mistakes."

"I can't take that risk. Don't you see? This whole thing between you and me," he protested as he motioned between them, "it mirrors my parents' situation. I won't make the same mistakes as my father. I saw what it did to my mother, and I will never do that to you."

He loved her, she was convinced, but he was fighting it. She had to try to convince him to take a chance. "You are not your father. I'm not Lucinda. We're different people, you and me. We can have a different life. You just have to be willing to try."

His shoulders rigid, implacable, he set his jaw. His eyes had lost their brilliance and were now dull. Flat. "I refuse to risk your happiness."

On this point, he was resolute. He hadn't changed, not really, was still the jaded aristocrat determined to follow duty's path.

"Then I guess this is goodbye." It hurt to breathe.

He grimaced. Stood statue-still, hands fisted at his sides. "Yes, I suppose it is."

With one last parting glance, she attempted to memorize his features. Then she turned and walked away, leaving a part of her heart behind.

"I have an announcement to make."

Looking entirely too pleased with himself, Josh sat relaxed in his chair, one arm slung about Kate's shoulders. Conversation ceased. Setting down her fork, Megan swallowed the last bite of pie, her gaze meeting Kate's across the table. A becoming blush stained her cheeks, and her green eyes sparkled.

Josh pulled his wife closer, and the two exchanged secretive smiles. "Kate and I are expecting."

Mary gasped, jumped up to bestow hugs on the happy couple. Sam patted Josh heartily on the back. Nathan shook his hand and offered his congratulations. Nicole and Jane took turns embracing Kate, and then it was Megan's turn.

"I'm so happy for you both." Megan gave Kate's fingers an affectionate squeeze. "How long have you known?"

"We've had our suspicions these last couple of weeks. I've had several dizzy spells."

"And your eating habits have changed drastically." Megan laughed at her friend's sheepish expression.

"It's true. If I keep this up, I'll be as big as a house by the time the baby comes." Her eyes went soft and dreamy. "I wonder if it will be a boy or a girl."

Megan smiled broadly, praying her friend wouldn't detect the prick of jealousy her happiness incited. "Considering Juliana just had a boy, I think you and Josh should have a girl."

"Mary would be thrilled to have a granddaughter."

"You do realize it's out of our hands, right, Goldilocks?" Josh inserted himself in the conversation, his blue eyes dancing with merriment.

In the face of this dear couple's joy, Megan blinked away the moisture gathering in her eyes. She was truly grateful God had blessed them with their heart's desire. Feeling sorry for herself in this moment was not an option.

"I'm not sure I like the sound of Cousin Megan," she said. "Auntie Megan sounds much better, don't you think?"

Josh tweaked one of her curls like he'd done when they were younger. "Whatever you're called, she or he will adore you as much as we do."

"Now you're just trying to make me cry," she protested, swatting his arm.

Nicole spoke up, the wheels in her head clearly turning. "I can go ahead and make up baby clothes in neutral colors and then, if it's a girl, I can add ruffles and overlays."

Surprised pleasure brightened Kate's expression. "That would be wonderful, Nicole. Thank you."

The raven-haired girl shrugged. "Practice makes perfect. I need lots of experience if I plan on having a successful boutique."

Kate and Megan shared a look. Typical. Nicole's purposes served herself first, others second. At least Kate and the baby would benefit.

"Once the baby comes, Jessica and I will bring food over so you can rest," Jane volunteered.

"Thank you, Jane." Kate's smile was gentle.

Megan looked at the couple, once again battling melancholy. Just because her dream wasn't coming true didn't mean she couldn't rejoice with others.

"Yours won't be the only new addition this winter," she added. "Rachel and Cole are expecting. They're due at Christmastime."

Her friend had pulled her aside at Lucian's to relay the good news.

Josh grinned. "Cole told me last night. He could hardly contain himself—he's so eager to support Rachel in any way he can."

"That's understandable," Nathan inserted, "considering he wasn't around for Abby's birth."

Megan nodded her agreement. She had a feeling Cole was going to stick to Rachel's side like glue. He was overly protective of her and Abby, no doubt due to the fact he'd nearly lost his chance with them.

The group dispersed, the men settling in the living room with their coffee while the women cleared the table and washed dishes. Megan was quiet as she worked, lost in her painful world. A world without Lucian.

You knew a happy ending wasn't possible, a voice accused, *yet you fell for him anyway.*

All yesterday, she'd watched the lane, hoping against hope he'd come to her. And this morning at church, she'd waited for him to show. He hadn't.

She wasn't certain how she was going to get through tomorrow. Or the next day. Or the coming weeks.

Her vision blurred. Hastily wiping the table clean of crumbs, Megan slipped out the back door. She doubted she'd be missed. Mary and Kate were washing dishes, engaged in a lively conversation about the baby, Jane listening intently as she dried. Nicole had slunk off somewhere.

With no one around to witness her breakdown, Megan allowed the tears to fall freely, the loss of her dreams a gaping wound in her chest. She stumbled into the barn's concealing shelter. Sinking onto the first hay bale she encountered, she buried her face in her hands.

It feels as though my life is ending, Lord. I've always considered myself an optimistic sort of person, not often given to the doldrums, but right now... I'm lower than I've ever been and I don't know how I'm supposed to cope.

"There you are."

Startled, she looked up to see Nathan coming towards her. The moment he noticed her tears, he lengthened his stride. Compassion tugged at his mouth. Lowering his tall frame onto the hay beside her, he pulled her into a hug.

Josh, Nathan and even Caleb were like brothers to her, fiercely protective and always there to comfort her. Without them, she never would've survived her father's sudden death, the hardships her family had faced afterward—financial as well as the day-to-day running of a farm—and more recently, the absence of her beloved sister Juliana.

After a while, he tilted her chin up, silver gaze assessing. "This is because of Beaumont, isn't it?"

"I love him. And I believe he loves me." When she attempted to wipe the moisture from her cheeks, he produced a handkerchief from his pocket. "But he's too afraid of repeating his parents' mistakes to give us a chance. He doesn't trust in love."

"Would you like for me to talk to him?"

"No! I'm not a little girl anymore, Nathan. I don't need you to fight my battles." She touched his cheek. "Although, I do appreciate the offer."

"I wish I could make things better for you."

"I know." She gazed at him with rueful affection.

"Would an afternoon of target practice help get your mind off things? At least for a little while?" His smile urged her to say yes.

"Yes, I believe it would," she agreed more for his sake than for hers. "I'll go home and get my gun."

He stood and held out his hand. "How about we go together?"

"In other words, you don't want to leave me alone."

He winked. "You got it, Goldilocks."

She took his hand, allowed him to pull her up. "You're a good man, Nathan O'Malley. One day, a very lucky young lady is going to come along and relieve you of your bachelor state."

"I happen to like being a bachelor," he protested. "Mark my words—you won't see me walking the aisle anytime soon."

"The carriage is ready, sir." Smith appeared in the entrance to Charles's study.

Seated at the desk, Lucian glanced out at the predawn darkness. "How bad is the rain?"

"Barely a drizzle, sir. However, it's difficult to tell at this point whether or not the weather will improve. Would you like to wait until after dawn?"

Lightly rubbing his cast in a vain effort to relieve the itching beneath, Lucian sighed. Another delay? Was God trying to tell him something?

"That would probably be best. See to the horses, will you?"

"Yes, sir." He removed himself at once.

The tick of the mantel clock mocked him, each one a strike against his heart. *You're leaving her. You're leaving her.*

He let his head fall back, closed his eyes. Beyond exhausted, he feared this weariness would be difficult to shake. Lack of sleep had little to do with it. This was a soul-deep yearning for the one woman who'd seen through his austere facade to the real man beneath, who'd challenged him, comforted him. Loved him.

He couldn't quite wrap his mind around the fact that she loved him. Her confession had shocked him; her plea for him to stay nearly brought him to his knees. How he'd longed to declare his own feelings…. Revisiting all the reasons his fears were sound had prevented him. After she'd gone, he'd sat in the garden until the wee hours of the morning, replaying their conversation. Arguing with himself. When he'd at last tumbled into bed, he'd dreamed of her, her anguish a tangible thing. He'd awoken in a sweat, trembling with the need to go to her. To fall to his knees and beg her forgiveness.

The past two days and nights of torment had shaken his convictions. If he left, he'd be leaving here half a man.

What am I supposed to do, Lord? By refusing to give us a chance, I'm doing the one thing I've dreaded doing—I'm hurting her. And myself.

Lucian smoothed the worn, faded cover of his mother's Bible. Unable to sleep for thoughts of Megan, he'd come downstairs around four o'clock and settled in with a cup of coffee to read. He'd found himself in the first book of Corinthians, where his mother had underlined an entire chapter about love, of all things. One verse in particular stuck in his mind. *And now these three remain: faith, hope and love. But the greatest of these is love.*

Was he truly prepared to live without it? To never lay eyes on Megan again?

"Sir?" Smith reappeared. "The rain has let up a bit. Shall I ready the carriage now?"

Lucian stood, adrenaline pumping through his veins. "No."

"No?"

"I want you to unload the trunks."

Smith's brow furrowed slightly. "As you wish, sir."

"Wait." He held out a hand. "Don't unload them yet. She may not accept me."

Reaching inside his coat, he retrieved a handkerchief and, laying it on the desk, peeled back the edges to reveal the disassembled bleeding-heart flower. He glanced at his servant, who was watching him with barely concealed concern. "I'm embarking on a mission of a most delicate nature, Smith. Will you help me?"

His eyes flared wide at the request. "Anything you ask, I will do my utmost to oblige."

"I appreciate your loyalty, Smith. First, I'll need a pair of rabbits…"

Megan awoke shortly after dawn to the *splat, splat, splat* of rain against the porch. She lay beneath the quilt for a long time staring out the window at the smoky gray clouds, her heaviness of spirit a perfect reflection of the gloom.

Maybe the weather will delay his departure.

What would that gain? A temporary stay of the inevitable. Better he left as soon as possible. If she were to see him again, who knew what she might do. She suspected something rash and embarrassing and totally unlike her, like begging him to take her with him.

There came a soft knock on the door.

"Come in." Shoving the hair out of her eyes, she scooted up in bed.

Jane entered bearing a small tray, still dressed in her nightclothes and wrapper, her loose auburn hair gleaming in the watery light. "I thought you might like a cup of cocoa." She smiled over at her as she slid the tray on the dresser. "There's a biscuit with strawberry jam, too."

She came and sat on the bed, empathy etched in her

youthful features. "It's a pity about the rain. I'd hoped we could go for a jaunt in the woods or perhaps have a picnic down by the river."

Touched, Megan gave Jane's hand a squeeze. "You're very sweet to try and cheer me up. Perhaps the rain will let up and we can go for a ride later."

Despite her young age, Jane understood the importance of distraction.

"Are you going to be okay?"

No. Not without Lucian. "In time—" She inhaled deeply, trying to dislodge the pain in her heart. "In time, I will learn to live without him." But she'd never stop loving him.

Tears glistened in Jane's sad eyes. "I feel the same way about Tom. He hasn't been to church since…well, you know."

"We can help each other through this." Battling emotions, Megan hugged her.

Sniffling, Jane leaned away. "I should get dressed."

"Me, too. Lottie will be waiting to be milked."

Jane closed the door with a soft click. Megan made herself get out of bed, trudged over to the wardrobe, and, choosing a navy skirt, she paired it with a buttery-yellow blouse. When another knock sounded as she was pulling her blouse over her heard, she thought it was Jane again.

But it was Nicole, standing hesitantly in the doorway, teeth worrying her lower lip. Strange. Nicole wasn't the uncertain type. She typically barreled through situations with single-minded determination.

"I thought…" she began. "Well, would you like for me to do your hair? I have some combs that would look nice with that blouse."

Megan opened her mouth. Closed it. "Uh, yes, I'd like that very much."

A tiny smile lifted her lips. "I'll be right back."

Megan didn't move, struck dumb by her sister's offer. Nicole wasn't sentimental or overly sensitive to others' feelings, which made her offer all the more meaningful. Tears threatened. She quickly blinked them back as Nicole returned with said combs.

Seating herself in the lone wooden chair, Megan folded her hands in her lap. Nicole had a gentle touch, carefully combing through her curls and securing the sides with the sparkly combs. She handed her the mirror.

"What do you think?"

Megan smiled tremulously up at her. "I think you did a marvelous job, sis. Thank you."

Looking wistful, Nicole touched a curl with the tip of her finger. "It's not hard to make you look beautiful. I've always wished my hair was blond, like yours."

Standing, Megan took her hands in hers. "But you have such gorgeous hair," she protested, "as black and silky as a raven's wing. And your unique violet eyes handed down from Grandmother O'Malley are a lovely contrast."

She scrunched up her nose. "This black hair makes me look like a witch."

Megan gasped. "That's ridiculous!"

"That's what the boys at school used to say."

"They were only teasing you," she insisted. "Besides, we both know true beauty resides in the heart."

Nicole looked thoughtful. "But you have to admit that being well-groomed is important."

"Megan, you should come here," Jane called from

the living room. The queer note in her voice brought Megan running. Nicole followed closely behind.

"What is it?"

She stood at the door holding a crate, her expression one of confused wonder. "This was delivered for you."

"So early? Who was it?"

"More importantly, what is it?" Nicole asked.

Peering down into the crate, Megan's breath hitched. There, huddled together in the corner of the crate on a worn blanket, were two small brown rabbits with white fuzzy tails.

"Jimmy Dixon said a stuffy-looking man paid him to deliver these to you." Jane stared at her. "Do you think he was talking about Lucian?"

A hundred butterflies unleashed in her tummy. "I can't think of anyone else it could've been."

Nicole picked one up and cuddled it close to stop its shivering. "I don't understand. Why would he send you rabbits when he can afford to send something much more valuable?"

The bleeding-heart flower. He'd kept the one she'd used to demonstrate the story, so it meant something to him.

She took the other rabbit out and held it close, its frantic heartbeat pulsing against her finger. How darling. "We don't know for certain that it was Lucian who sent them," she said firmly, ignoring the sudden leap of her pulse.

Setting the crate on the floor, Jane took turns petting the animals, whose fur was damp from their journey in the rain. "They are so precious! What will we name them?"

They spent the next half hour debating names and where they were supposed to put them. When they heard boots thump against the porch, they stilled. Looked at each other.

"You get it, Megan," Jane urged, eyes wide.

Handing her rabbit off to Jane, Megan wiped her palms against her skirt and, sucking in a breath, opened the door. It wasn't Lucian. Swallowing her disappointment, she greeted fifteen-year-old Jimmy.

"I have another package for you, Miss Megan." Huddling beneath his slicker, he thrust a rectangular-shaped box at her. Then he dashed back out into the rain before she could question him. Her sisters crowded around the table where she placed the box. She carefully lifted the lid. Inside lay a pair of elegant, beaded ivory satin shoes lined with ivory kid and possessed of shapely heels.

"These are exquisite, Megan, and easily paired with a wedding gown." Nicole returned her rabbit to the crate so that she could admire the shoes.

Jittery with nerves, Megan explained with a growing sense of wonder, "Lucian is following the pattern of the bleeding-heart legend. I told him about it one afternoon when we were walking through the woods. He actually kept the parts of the flower."

"How romantic," Jane said with a sigh.

Megan couldn't speak. What could be his purpose? He'd been resolute in his determination to leave.

When Jimmy arrived the third time, she caught his arm. "Who sent you, Jimmy?"

"The fancy man from New Orleans."

"Mr. Beaumont?"

"Yep, that's the one."

"Can you tell me where he is now?"

He lifted a shoulder. "He left."

Megan stared. It couldn't be. "He left town? Are you certain?"

Unaware of her distress, he nodded matter-of-factly and waited for her to release him. "Th-thank you, Jimmy. You may go."

She turned back to find her sisters looking at her with sympathy.

"I—I don't understand." She spoke through her tears. Was this simply an extravagant way to say goodbye?

Utter devastation washed over her. He was well and truly gone. For good.

Needing immediate escape, she tossed the box on a nearby chair and grabbed her shawl. "I've got to go."

"You'll be soaked through within the space of a minute!" Jane called as she stepped out onto the porch.

"Don't worry," she said over her shoulder, barely able to form words. "I won't be gone long." That wasn't a promise, just a hopeful saying to allay her sister's worries. In truth, she wanted to keep going, to go somewhere new and strange and devoid of memories.

"But—"

Ignoring her, Megan hurried down the steps and raced for the woods, unmindful of the raindrops pelting her. Jane was right. It didn't take long for her to be soaked through, her hair a sodden mass on her shoulders. Entering the lush green woods, she slowed to a fast walk. The onslaught wasn't as steady here, the canopy overhead acting as a makeshift shelter.

She walked and walked for what seemed an eternity. Walked until her feet ached, the insides of her boots rubbing blisters on her toes. Walked until she was shivering. Spying a hollowed-out log, she sank down, huddled beneath her damp shawl and stared about at the woods she suddenly didn't recognize.

Did she care that she might be lost? No.

Did she care that she might have to spend the night out here? Not in the least.

It didn't matter that she'd skipped breakfast and that she didn't have her weapon with her. Nothing mattered, really, except that she was miserable. Soon, very soon, she was going to have to try to find her way back, to be responsible, but for just a little while, she would allow herself to grieve the loss of her one and only love.

"He did what?" Lucian stared at Jane and Nicole in dismay. "Why?"

"Jimmy told her that you left town, and she got upset. She tore off into the woods and hasn't returned," Jane repeated, wringing her hands.

Lucian pushed down his irritation at the lad. He had more important things to worry about…like finding Megan and admitting he'd been wrong. "How long has she been gone?"

"Over an hour." Nicole chewed on a fingernail, something he'd never seen her do.

The girls must be beside themselves with worry. He was beginning to worry, too. Running off in the midst of a rainstorm wasn't like Megan. But she'd been upset. Because of him.

"I'll find her," he promised, unable to accept any other outcome. She knew these woods like the back of her hand, and she was smart and capable. *Lord, help me,* he prayed, believing with all his heart that God cared. That He was listening. *Please lead me to her.*

He'd gone about this all wrong. By sending the gifts, he'd tried to be romantic, something he knew was important to her. He should've come here first thing and simply talked to her.

Roaming the woods, he searched for signs that someone had recently passed through. He called her name, listening for some sort of response besides the constant, dripping rain. When he at last spotted her hunched on a log, wet and pale and miserable, his fears melted away. Relief weakened his knees. *Thank You, God.*

"Megan."

Startled, she whipped her head up. Stark pain twisted her features. Pain *he* had caused her. Muttering in French, Lucian strode over to her, crouching at her knees so that he could look her squarely in the eyes.

"*Je suis désolé, mon chou.* I'm so sorry."

Megan blinked once. Twice. Lucian was really here. He'd found her somehow.

"I thought you left," she whispered. "Jimmy told me you left."

A muscle twitched in his jaw. "He was mistaken."

He looked upset. Dashingly handsome, as well, his wet hair appearing nearly black, slicked back from his forehead. She had to bury her nails in her palms to keep from lifting a hand to his dear, lovely, austere face.

"I went about this all wrong." He sighed and shook his head.

Desperate for answers, aching to launch herself into

his arms, she said, "What's going on, Lucian? Why did you send those gifts?"

"That was my sorry attempt at romance," he said grimacing, then frowned as a shudder racked her body. Standing, he shrugged out of his black slicker and wrapped it about her shoulders, its warmth enveloping her. Then he sat close beside her, angling his body so that he could look her full in the face.

"I'm not a hero, Megan. I'm not a prince or a knight or a musketeer. I'm no Mr. Darcy or Mr. Knightley or any of Jane Austen's other leading men. I'm just a normal man." His obsidian eyes intense, his gaze lovingly caressed her face. "A man who loves you."

Megan didn't dare breathe or move for fear this was just a dream or a figment of her imagination. Surely this wasn't real. Lucian *loved* her?

"You're wrong, you know." She lifted a shaky hand and pressed it against his hard chest, directly over his heart. At the intimate touch, he sucked in a sharp breath. "You *are* a hero. You're a man of such deep feeling, Lucian. You possess a courageous yet tender heart. The people closest to you, the ones you should've been able to count on, betrayed you and yet despite all that, you opened yourself up enough to trust me. To care for Sarah and the other children. You forgave your mother her deception and allowed yourself to grieve her passing, a difficult, painful thing. A strong man is a man who faces his fears head-on. That's what makes a man a hero."

Ever so gently cupping her cheek, he said wonderingly, "I don't deserve your sweet words. None of that would've came about without you, my love."

Giddy with joy, she watched as he reached into his

pocket and produced a flat, velvet box, held it aloft on his outstretched palm. "I have one final gift for you."

Her stomach flip-flopped. "You do?" She looked at the box for long moments before lifting her gaze to his face.

"Aren't you curious what it is?" he prompted with an endearing smile.

Heart pounding, she took the box from him, fingers fumbling on the lid. At last she was able to open it. There, nestled in the velvet folds, lay a key.

"It's the key to Charles's house."

Lifting her chin, he gazed at her with tender devotion. "I would like for it to be *our* house. Yours and mine together. Will you do me the honor of becoming my wife?"

"Oh, Lucian, I—I want that more than anything else, but…what about your resolve to marry for duty?"

Cradling her face in his hands, he declared, "I only determined to marry for duty because I was afraid to be hurt again, afraid of hurting someone like my father hurt my mother. I admit, I'm still afraid. But my love for you is stronger than my fear. With God's help, I can be a good husband to you."

She covered his hands, smiled at him with all the love she felt for him shining on her face. "You are the only husband I want."

His eyes lit with happiness. "So you'll marry me?"

"Yes!" She laughed out loud, joy unlike she'd ever known filling her heart until she thought it might burst. "Most definitely."

He brought his mouth tantalizingly close. "Soon?"

"As soon as possible," she murmured, sliding her hands up to lock behind his neck.

He kissed her then, a dazzling kiss full of promise. He held nothing back, infusing all the love and affection he felt for her into the embrace. Her despair of minutes ago had vanished, replaced with a heady sense of rightness, of completeness, that only being with Lucian could inspire. This was where she belonged. With him. Her love. Her hero.

Epilogue

Three weeks later
July 1881

"My dear, you look radiant."

Megan's mother, Alice, reached up to tuck a pink rose more firmly into her curls, then stepped back to observe the dress for the umpteenth time. Nicole had offered her the ivory silk confection she'd worn to the poetry recital as a wedding present. With its seed pearls adorning the scooped neck, lace overlay about the skirt and gold-and-silver stitching along the hem, it was a perfect choice for a wedding dress. Instead of the sparkly diamond pins she'd worn last time, Megan had decided to wear roses in her curls.

Tears glistened in her mother's eyes.

"Don't cry, Mama," Megan admonished with a smile, "or else I will, too, and the last thing I want is to greet my groom with splotchy skin and puffy eyes."

Alice glanced about the spacious upstairs bedroom. "It was kind of Lucian to offer the house for you and your sisters to get ready."

"Thoughtfulness is just one of his many endearing qualities."

Pausing in her fussing, she cocked her head to study her. "You've always been a happy girl, but now that he's come into your life, you seem…oh, I don't know the right word. Settled, maybe? At peace? Before, there was a restless gleam in your eye. That's gone now."

Megan swallowed back a tide of emotion. It was true. With Lucian in her life, she felt complete. "You do approve, don't you, Mama?"

"From what I've seen and heard, Lucian appears to be a kind and decent man. And it's plain to see he's besotted with you. I believe the two of you are a good match." She shook her head in consternation. "Just once I'd like to witness one of my daughters falling in love. First Juliana meets her true love while on the run from outlaws and comes home already married. And while I'm away attending the birth of my first grandchild, you fall for a stranger. I'm not leaving home again until your sisters are all settled."

Megan's chuckle was interrupted by a succinct knock before the door swung wide to admit Nicole—stunning in blue, her raven curls piled on top of her head in an elegant arrangement—and the twins, lovely in matching shades of seafoam-green that enhanced their auburn tresses.

Her only regret on this, her most special of days, was that Juliana couldn't be here. Evan had been firm in insisting the journey would be too risky for his wife and baby James. Megan understood. Of course her nephew's well-being was paramount. The fact that she and Lucian would be traveling there in just two days' time softened her disappointment. She could hardly wait to hold James and introduce Lucian to her sister and brother-in-law.

Nicole handed Megan her bouquet. "The ceremony starts in fifteen minutes. We need to head over to the church now if you don't want Lucian to think you've changed your mind."

Jessica gave her a quick hug. "Lucian is going to swoon when he sees you, sis. I've never seen you look more beautiful."

"I don't think grooms swoon." Jane frowned at her twin.

They debated and teased all the way to the church. Megan found it difficult to concentrate on their words, her mind on Lucian. Was he as anxious as she was? The minutes were passing in a blur, and she wished she could make time slow, wanted to savor every moment. In just a little while, she would walk out of this church a married woman.

In the alcove, Owen was waiting with a fully recovered Sarah, who'd eagerly agreed to be Megan's flower girl. Adorable in a cream confection created by Nicole, her fine hair had been braided and twisted into a neat circle about her crown. At the sight of Megan in her wedding dress, her eyes widened. Then, seeing Megan's reassuring smile, she smiled back.

The music started, and everyone hustled into place.

Before she knew it, Uncle Sam was taking her arm and guiding her through the inner doors. The faces on either side of the aisle failed to register, her focus all on Lucian, the man of her dreams, elegantly handsome in his black formal attire, his brown hair tousled like always. She smiled then, happy he hadn't attempted to tame it.

He returned her smile, an action that transformed his features and made her heart kick in recognition. She'd become quite familiar with that dazzling smile over the course of the past three weeks. That and his husky laughter. And his gentle touch. They'd spent nearly every day together, taking long walks and plotting their future.

Now she was here, about to pledge herself to him for a lifetime.

He was gazing at her with awe, as if finding it hard to believe she was his, and an eagerness that matched her own. When she at last reached his side, he took her hands in his, his thumbs gently stroking in a soothing gesture. They spoke their vows with reverence, and when Reverend Monroe announced them husband and wife, Lucian grinned, leaned over and kissed her soundly. Their guests laughed and clapped. And then she and her husband were hurrying down the aisle to a chorus of well-wishes.

He paused on the steps to lean close, a happy grin playing about his lips. "There's no changing your mind now, Mrs. Beaumont. You're mine from this day forward."

"As if I'd ever dream of such a thing, Mr. Beaumont." She splayed a hand on his chest. "I'm perfectly happy with my choice."

Chuckling, he kissed her briefly before they were swept up in the crowd as everyone made their way to their house for the reception. Mrs. Calhoun had joined forces with Alice, Aunt Mary, Kate, Jane and Jessica to produce a brunch worthy of royalty with succulent meats, egg dishes, hearty breads, bowls of fresh fruit and an astonishing array of desserts. Fresh-cut flowers, courtesy of Fred, adorned every room, scenting the air with sweet summertime.

By the time the gifts had been opened and all of the guests besides family had departed, Megan was eager for time alone with her new husband. Catching her gaze from across the parlor, he set down his cup and, with a parting word to Josh and Uncle Sam, strode purposefully towards her. His dark gaze was so full of love it made her want to weep. All of his doubts had been swept away, his misgivings given to God, and now his heart was fully hers for safekeeping.

"Care to take a stroll in the gardens, my love?"

Smiling up at him, she slipped her hand in the crook of his arm. "I thought you'd never ask."

Blushing at the knowing looks her family cast their way, she walked with him through the house—she still couldn't quite grasp it was to be her new home—and on to the back porch, where they encountered Nathan leaning against the porch railing, staring moodily out at the gardens.

He turned at their approach. Smiled and clapped Lucian on the back. "In case I forgot to say it, welcome to the family, Beaumont." Then he kissed Megan's cheek. "Congratulations, cousin. I'm glad you found your happy ending."

"Ah, but this isn't an ending." Lucian shared a smile with her. "It's a beginning."

"Right you are," Nathan conceded. "To a happy beginning, then."

Megan touched his arm. "You looked upset a moment ago. Are you all right?"

He looked surprised at the question. "I'm fine." At the quirk of her eyebrow, he continued, "This is your wedding day. Go enjoy some time with your husband."

"I didn't see Sophie today," she persisted. "Wasn't she supposed to come?"

A barely perceptible change came over him, and he fought to hide his frown. "She told me she'd be here. It could be that her grandfather wasn't feeling well. I'm heading over there soon to check on them."

"Please tell her that we missed her."

"I will."

When he'd gone inside, Lucian guided her down the steps and along the stone path they'd traveled countless times. "Who's Sophie?"

"You don't remember Sophie Tanner? My aunt and uncle's neighbor?"

His eyes lit with recognition. "Oh, do you mean the young tomboy? The one with a younger brother about ten years old? I forgot his name."

"William. And you can't blame Sophie for being a bit rough around the edges. She hasn't had a female role model in her life. Her mother died when she was very young, and her father ran off soon after. She was raised by her grandfather."

"I see." He stopped before the rose arbor, lowered himself onto the stone bench and tugged her onto his lap, wrapping his arms loosely about her. "Enough talk about Nathan's friend. I'd much rather focus on my beautiful wife. How much longer before everyone goes home?" he said wryly.

Arms draped about his sturdy shoulders, she laughed and wiggled her eyebrows. "Perhaps we'll just have to hide out here for a while. They'll get the hint eventually."

"Good idea," he whispered before he brought his mouth to hers in a soul-stirring kiss. When he lifted his head, he gazed at her adoringly. "Has anyone ever told you that you're the loveliest, most radiant bride that ever lived?"

"Actually, they have," she teased. "You're just one in a long line of people."

"What?" He reared his head back in mock horror. "That's unacceptable."

Smoothing his collar, she grew serious. "Are you absolutely certain you'll be happy here? You won't miss city living? Your work?"

His smile was patient and gentle, as if this wasn't the twentieth or so time she'd asked this exact question. "My home is where you are, *mon chou*. All that matters is that we're together. Besides, I like it here. I have a new family. New friends who don't give a fig what my last name is or how much I'm worth. As for work, Fred isn't getting any younger. I'm going to enjoy helping him work the land. I've got plans, my dear. First on the list is building your mother and sisters a new barn. Owen still needs help, and Nathan and your uncle can always use an extra hand—"

"Okay, okay." She laughed, convinced he was sincerely eager to dig into rural life. "I can see you've got it all figured out."

"And if we feel the need for a change of pace, we can visit the city anytime."

"I can't wait for you to meet my sister and Evan. They're going to love you. And I can't wait to hold baby James." They planned to stay about a week in Cades Cove before heading down to Louisiana. His father had sent his regrets—not a surprise to Lucian— along with an extravagant gift. She was a bit nervous about meeting him. "How long do you think we'll stay in New Orleans?"

"For however long you'd like. One day. One week. A month. We'll play it by ear." Then he tossed her a roguish grin that made her blood heat. "We can't stay away too long, though, if we're to get a head start on those ten kids you're set on having."

"And what if all ten are girls?"

His expression turned intense, a fiercely protective glint in his eyes. "I'll love each and every one because they'll be a part of me and you, proof of our love and commitment."

Satisfied, she caressed his cheek. "Twins run in my family, you remember. My father and Uncle Sam were twins. And, of course, Jessica and Jane."

Leaning slightly forward, arms secure about her waist, Lucian glanced around the rosebushes at the stately Victorian awash in golden sunlight, his smile brimming with joyful expectation. "Then it's a good thing we have plenty of space." His expression turned thoughtful. "What do you think my grandfather would think about us?"

"Charles would be thrilled, no doubt about it. In fact, I wouldn't be surprised if he'd considered such an out- come. He knew me well enough to know I'd fight to use the house. And I think he came to know a little about you, too, from your mother's letters. He must've suspected you'd want to hold on to the house."

"He may have willed me a house, but he gifted me with so much more." Eyes burning bright, he buried his fingers in her loose curls. "I love you, Megan."

At home in his arms, she moved in close for a kiss. "And I love you."

* * * * *

THE HUSBAND HUNT

"For my thoughts are not your thoughts,
neither are your ways my ways," declares the Lord.
"As the heavens are higher than the earth,
so are my ways than your ways and
my thoughts than your thoughts."
—*Isaiah 55:8–9*

For a beloved aunt, Linda McLemore, whose support and encouragement mean the world to me. Thanks for all the laughs and the prayers. I love you.

This dream would not be possible without my Lord and Savior, Jesus Christ.

John 15:5: "I am the vine, you are the branches. If you remain in me and I in you, you will bear much fruit; apart from me you can do nothing."

Chapter One

Gatlinburg, Tennessee
August 1881

She was trapped. Stuck high above the ground in her place of refuge—a sugar maple with a trunk too wide to get her arms around and century-deep roots—cornered by a skunk, of all things. The varmint had sauntered up and planted itself at the tree's base and showed no intentions of leaving.

Gripping the branch above her head, Sophie leaned forward and commenced trying to reason with him. "Yoo-hoo! How about you move along? I'm sure there are tastier earthworms along the stream bank. You might even catch yourself a frog."

His frantic digging continued. How long was she going to have to wait?

"You're keeping me from my chores, you know." She blew a stray hair out of her eyes. "Will and Granddad will be wanting their supper soon." Beans, fried potatoes and corn bread *again*. Her specialty.

The snap of a twig brought her and the skunk's head up simultaneously.

Her gaze landed on a face as familiar to her as her own, clashing with silver eyes that seemed to perpetually taunt or condemn her. She swallowed a sigh. She'd long ago given up hoping for approval from Nathan O'Malley.

"Hello, Nathan."

One dusky eyebrow quirked. "I see you've made a new friend."

She peered down. The animal's focus had shifted to Nathan, and it was now stamping the ground in warning. "Yeah, well, my friend doesn't seem to like you very much."

He eyed the skunk with caution. Sunlight shifting through the trees glinted in his light brown hair, cut short so he wouldn't have to fool with it, and bathed his classic features in golden light. Features that were branded into her brain. A straight, proud nose flanked by prominent cheekbones. Square jaw. The crease beside his full lips that flashed every time he smiled.

And who could forget those quicksilver eyes? They dominated her daydreams, hovered at the edge of her consciousness as she drifted off to sleep at night. It was downright irritating.

"I really need to get down," she informed him, scooting closer to the trunk. That jittery feeling was back. If she didn't eat soon, she chanced tumbling out of this tree in a dead faint. Wouldn't that impress him.

"Could you try to lure him away?"

He tore his gaze from the irate skunk to stare up at her. "And how do you propose I do that?"

"I don't know." She cast around the forest floor for

inspiration. When none came, she suggested, "If you move away, maybe he'll follow. Toss a stick in the direction of the stream. Maybe he'll get distracted and realize there's more to eat there."

"He's not a dog."

Frowning, he edged sideways. The skunk hissed. Followed.

"It's working!" Sophie swung her body around and stretched her foot down to the knotted branch below.

"Sophie, stop," Nathan ordered. "Wait until he's gone."

She chose to ignore his warning. Unfortunately, her boot slipped. Her grip on the trunk slackened. Scrambling for purchase, she whipped her head around in time to see Nathan surge forward as if to catch her.

The skunk reacted as expected. Tail aloft, he sprayed.

Sophie gasped. Nathan attempted to shield his face with his arms, to sidestep, but he was too slow. Because his focus was on rescuing *her*. Groaning, she shimmied down the trunk and hopped to the ground as the offended animal scampered in the opposite direction.

"Oh, Nathan, I'm so sorry!" She advanced toward him, only to halt in her tracks as noxious fumes assaulted her nose. He smelled like rotten eggs and garlic. Ugh. Wrinkling her nose, she covered the bottom half of her face with one hand. "Did it get in your eyes?"

His lids blinked open, revealing twin chips of forged steel. Uh-oh.

"No."

Wearing a disgusted expression, he carefully wiped the moisture from his face with his shirtsleeves. He looked down and grimaced. "These were my most comfortable trousers."

He didn't have to say it. Those trousers were headed for the burn pile.

Pivoting on his heel, his long strides quickly ate up the distance to the stream. Sophie followed at a reasonable distance, making a point to breathe through her mouth. Oh, this was terrible. Worse than terrible. He would never forgive her.

On the bank, he tugged off his brown leather work boots, tossed them onto the grass and waded into the sluggish water. While the crystal-clear Smoky Mountain stream dissecting her property wasn't deep enough for diving, it was deep enough to submerge oneself in, and that's what he did. When he came up for air, he threaded his fingers through his hair to dislodge the moisture. His white shirt molded to thick, ropy shoulders, chiseled chest and flat stomach carved from countless hours milking cows, mucking out stalls and working the fields. A farmer's physique.

She forced her too-interested gaze elsewhere, forced herself to remember. *Nathan is my neighbor. My childhood friend. He probably doesn't even think of me as a girl.*

And why would he when she didn't have a clue how to act or dress like one?

Brushing bits of dirt from her earth-hued pants, she fiddled with her rolled-up sleeves and mentally shrugged. She may not dress all fancy like other girls her age, but at least her clothes were clean and pressed and, most importantly, comfortable. Farming was backbreaking, sweaty work. It didn't make sense to wear frilly skirts and fine silk blouses that would only get ruined.

Still…she couldn't help but wonder sometimes what

it might be like to wear a dress, to have her hair done up in a sophisticated style. Would Nathan think her beautiful then?

Get your head out of the clouds, Soph.

"We've got canned tomatoes in the springhouse—" she pointed downstream "—I'll go and get them. Surely that will get the smell out."

"Forget it." Not sparing a glance her direction, he sloshed up and onto the bank. "I'll take a vinegar bath at home."

Twisting her hands together, she took halting steps forward. She wanted to go closer, but she was standing downwind and the odor was overpowering. "How long are you going to be mad at me?"

Pausing in tugging his boots on, he shot her a hard glance and retorted, "For as long as it takes the smell to wear off."

"But—"

"No." He cut her off with a jerk of his hand. "Honestly, Sophie, when are you going to learn to curb your impulses? Think before you act? One of these days you're going to land yourself in a real heap of trouble and I may not be around to help. Quite frankly, I'm getting kind of tired playing rescuer."

Nathan reached his parents' cabin and was climbing the back porch steps just as Caleb emerged. One whiff had his younger brother backing up and raising his arm to cover his nose.

"What happened to you?"

"Sophie Tanner happened, that's what," he muttered, still aggravated with the headstrong tomboy. If she'd only listened to him and stayed put a few more minutes,

he wouldn't smell like a rotten bucket of pig scraps. He
unbuttoned his shirt. "Do me a favor. Grab the vinegar from the cabinet. And ask Pa if he'll help you milk
the cows. I doubt they'll let me near them reeking of
polecat."

"What has Sophie done now?"

Explaining what happened as he undressed, he
chucked his shirt, pants and socks into a heap to be
burned later. Caleb's resulting laughter didn't bother
Nathan. His brother laughed so rarely these days that
he relished the sound of it, no matter that it was at his
expense.

Clad in nothing but his knee-length cotton drawers,
he prompted, "The sooner I get that vinegar, the better. Hurry up."

"I wish I could've seen your expression when that ole
polecat doused you. And Sophie… I imagine she was fit
to be tied." Brown eyes full of mirth, he was still chuckling and shaking his head as he disappeared inside.

Half sitting on the porch rail, Nathan recalled Sophie's last expression all too clearly. Her eyes wide
and beseeching, her face pale, even distraught, as he
stomped off.

He pinched the bridge of his nose to dispel the blos-
soming ache behind his forehead.

You didn't handle that very well, did you, O'Malley?

Caleb reappeared, a black handkerchief concealing
the lower half of his face. The wicked scar near his eye
lent him a sinister air.

"You look like a bank robber."

"I won't say what you look like." Caleb held out the
vinegar bottle. "Why the hangdog expression? Oh, wait.

Let me guess. You gave Sophie a piece of your mind, and now you're feeling guilty."

Grabbing the bottle, Nathan pushed upright and descended the steps. The grass pricked the sensitive soles of his feet. "She's too impulsive."

Following a couple of paces behind, Caleb remarked, "She's been that way since we were kids. Remember that time she took a flying leap off Flinthead Falls and nearly drowned?"

"Don't remind me." His stomach hardened into a tight knot just thinking about it. She'd been fourteen to his nineteen, a beautiful wild thing oblivious to danger, bursting with life and optimism that infused the air around her with sparkling energy. He'd rescued her as he'd done many times before. Lectured her, too. Now eighteen, she'd settled down since then, but he knew that untamable streak yet lingered, poised to make an appearance at any moment.

Caleb waited outside while Nathan retrieved the copper tub from the toolshed.

"And remember that time you and Danny Mabry were entrenched in a tug-of-war and Sophie distracted you? Hollered your name?" He chuckled. "You fell flat on your face in the mud."

Nathan pursed his lips. Talk about being embarrassed. A girl he'd fancied had been watching that tug-of-war and his goal had been to impress her with his strength and skill. She'd taken one look at his mud-caked face and shared a hearty laugh with her friends. That was before he'd decided females were too much trouble to fool with.

Lifting the other end of the tub, Caleb helped him carry it to the porch.

"Oh, and do you remember—"

"I have the same memories as you, Caleb." He cut him off, uninterested in rehashing all the scrapes and fixes Sophie Tanner had gotten herself—and him—into. "I just want to get this smell off."

"Fine." He helped maneuver the tub and straightened, yanking the handkerchief down around his neck, his uncharacteristic good humor gone. "Tell Pa I'm going to get a head start on the milking."

Watching him stalk across the yard, Nathan regretted his abrupt words. The accident that had scarred Caleb and nearly killed his best friend almost two years ago had transformed the lighthearted prankster into a surly loner. He hardly recognized his own brother and it had nothing to do with his altered face.

Please, God, heal his hidden hurts. Help us to love him unconditionally and to be patient. He missed the old Caleb. He wondered if he'd ever glimpse that man again.

Three days and several vinegar baths later, his family no longer cringed when he entered a room. Poor Kate hadn't come around since that first day. His brother Josh's wife was expecting their first child, and her delicate condition magnified her sense of smell, which meant simply breathing the air around him had made her nauseous.

They were seated around the table Thursday night enjoying Ma's pecan pie when a soft knock sounded on the kitchen door. Pa went to answer it. When Nathan heard Sophie's quiet voice, he gulped the remainder of his coffee and, excusing himself, went to greet her.

Hearing his approach, Pa bid her goodbye and returned to the table.

Sophie's gaze collided with his, remorse churning in the blue depths. The final pieces of irritation dissolved and he wished he had gone to see her before this.

"Hey, Soph." He gripped the smooth wooden door and rested his weight against it. "Ma made pecan pie for dessert. Care to join us?"

Not much of a cook herself, she usually took him up on such offers.

She hesitated, fingers toying with the end of her neatly woven braid, honey-blond hair gleaming like spun gold in the sunlight. Spun gold? Where had that fanciful thought come from? He was not a fanciful man. He was a sensible man. A practical man who dealt with day-to-day reality. He wasn't a reader like Josh or his cousins, so his mind wasn't filled with poetry and romance. Must be the effects of the skunk stench.

"No, thanks. Do you have a minute?"

"Sure." Joining her on the porch, he pulled the door closed behind him and went to lean against the railing, arms folded over his chest.

Sophie faced him squarely, hands tucked in her pants' pockets and shoulders back in a familiar stance that said she had something to prove. "I came to apologize for the other day."

The apology didn't come as a surprise. One thing about his neighbor—she was quick to own up to mistakes. "Forget about it."

"I hope the smell didn't disrupt things too much."

Disrupt? As in having to steer clear of the barn while his brother and father assumed his share of the chores?

As in having to take his meals on the front porch so as not to make everyone gag at the supper table?

"Nah, not really." He smiled to erase her lingering regret.

Bending at the waist, she sniffed the air around him. Shot him a hopeful smile. "You smell fine to me. Does this mean we can be friends again?"

He gave her braid a playful tug. "We'll always be friends. You know that."

But his words didn't have the desired effect. Her smile vanished as quickly as it had appeared, long lashes sweeping down. "I don't expect you to rescue me, you know."

Straightening, Nathan settled his hands on her shoulders. "Sophie, look at me." When she lifted her face to his, he said, "I shouldn't have said that. I was angry, and I spoke without thinking. You know you can always count on me, don't you?"

She slowly nodded. He was struck by her diminutive stature, her slender build and the delicacy so often overlooked because of her tomboyish appearance and the air of capability she exuded that had carried her through the many hardships life had thrown her way. But now, gazing into her face, he was reminded that she was no longer the rough-and-tumble little imp trailing behind him and his brothers, insistent on joining in their fun.

The muted light of the summer evening washed her fair skin with a pink tinge of health, her cheeks and bee-stung lips the color of delicate rosebuds. The collared button-down shirt she had on was blue like the sky overhead. The bright hue made her eyes glow like the blue sapphire ring Emmett Clawson had taken in on trade a couple of weeks ago and that now occupied a premier spot in the jewelry case for everyone to admire.

With a start, he realized he was staring and Sophie was watching him with an uncharacteristic guardedness. He released her at once. *What's gotten into you, O'Malley?*

Clearing his clogged throat, he pivoted away to grip the railing, slowly and methodically cataloging the rows upon rows of cornstalks swaying in the breeze, the stately apple orchard marching along the fields in front of Josh and Kate's cabin and the forested mountains ringing the valley.

Okay, so Sophie was all grown up now. So what? That didn't mean he was free to think of her in terms other than neighbor and friend. Disaster lay down that path....

If, and that was a *big* if, he ever decided to marry, Sophia Lorraine Tanner would not be up for consideration. Not ever.

She was trouble, pure and simple. Too impulsive. Too headstrong. Too much. No, if he did decide to find himself a wife, he'd search for someone sensible, cautious and levelheaded. Someone like him.

Chapter Two

Sophie wrapped a hand around the wooden post for support and attempted to appear nonchalant about the effects of Nathan's touch. His nearness. It wasn't as if such touches were rare. They were friends, had been friends as far back as she could remember, and while her handsome neighbor had strict ideas about what constituted appropriate behavior, he was an affectionate man. Compassionate, too. Dependable and trustworthy.

Nathan was everything her wayward pa wasn't. He would never dream of doing something as despicable as abandoning his pregnant wife and child for another woman.

"How's Tobias?" he asked.

Sophie tracked a pair of dragonflies flitting on the wind, their iridescent wings a mix of blue and silvery green. The worry she'd battled since her granddad had taken ill three weeks ago eroded her peace of mind. "Still the same. Weak. The medicine Doc Owens gave him doesn't seem to be helping the cough. I try to encourage him to eat, but he doesn't have much of an appetite."

"I'll ask Ma to make him some of her chicken noodle soup."

Feeling his gaze on her, she turned her head and found strength and a promise of support in the silver depths. "Surely he won't be able to resist that." Her attempt at a smile fell flat. "He won't get well on my cooking alone."

Her heart stuttered in her chest. What if he didn't get better? What would she do without the only real father figure she'd ever had? Her grandfather had practically raised her and her little brother, Will, after her pa left and her ma passed away.

"I don't like that look on your face," he gently reproved. "Don't let your mind go there. We're all praying for Tobias's recovery." A grin transformed his serious face. "Besides, you know as well as I do what a tough old codger he is. Stubborn, too. Though not nearly as stubborn as his granddaughter."

That earned him a punch in the arm. "If anyone is stubborn around here, it's you, Nathan O'Malley."

Chuckling, he rubbed his arm as if it had really hurt. "I won't deny it." Jerking his head, he said, "Come on, I'll walk you home and look in on him. See if I can't convince him to eat something."

Following him down the worn steps and into the lush grass, she moved to walk beside him, keenly aware of his height, the restrained power in his hardened body and the self-assuredness with which he carried himself. He smelled of summer, of line-dried clothes and freshly cut hay. And maybe a little of pecans and corn syrup, which made her regret refusing a piece of Mary's pie.

As they passed the dairy barn, she noticed the cows

weren't crowded around the entrance and all seemed quiet. "You already did the milking?"

"Supper was a tad late getting on the table, so I did it beforehand."

"On my way here, I spotted Caleb heading for the high country." She tossed him a sideways glance. "How long is he going to be gone this time?"

Shrugging, he blew out a breath. "I suppose that depends on how long it takes him to snag a bear."

She dodged a fat bumblebee that zoomed into her path. "When are you going to stop coddling him, Nathan? He has a responsibility to you and the rest of your family."

"In his mind, he is fulfilling his responsibilities. By stocking the smokehouse with all the meat he brings home, he's helping to feed the family. Not to mention the trade value of the hides and furs."

Passing into the dense forest where the air was sweet and cool, the lowering sun's rays filtered through the towering oaks, maples and various other trees, casting sidelong lines of light that made odd patterns on their clothing.

"I understand the accident changed him...and not only on the outside." It had been a painful thing to witness the almost night-and-day change in his personality nearly two years ago. She missed the fun-loving, mischievous Caleb and feared her childhood playmate was gone for good. "I just don't think it's fair that he goes off whenever he feels like it and leaves you behind to do all the work."

"It's frustrating. And sometimes I get resentful." His gaze volleyed between the root-studded ground and her. "To be honest, I haven't a clue how to talk to my own brother."

The admission clearly hadn't come easily. Nathan wasn't a complainer. When Caleb had first started taking off for days at a time, Nathan had simply picked up the slack, milking all the cows himself twice a day, feeding and watering them, caring for the sick and expectant, mucking out their stalls, delivering the milk and cheese Mary made to the mercantile. And when he wasn't doing all that, he was working in the alfalfa, hay and cornfields. His older brother had pitched in to help, but now with his furniture business taking off and Kate expecting for the first time, Josh had little time to spare.

"Why not tell him the truth? That you need him here?"

When his brow creased in contemplation, she reached out and touched the bare forearm exposed by his rolled-up sleeve. The smooth, fine hairs covering the sun-kissed skin tickled her fingertips. She snatched her hand away.

"What?" He threw her a questioning glance.

Clearing her throat, she said almost defensively, "Nothing. Look, I'm concerned about you, that's all. You work too hard."

"I can say the same about you."

Their gazes met and clung. Sophie basked in the warmth of his rare and fleeting admiration. Then he grabbed her hand and tugged her sideways, saving her from smacking face-first into a tree. He chuckled low in his chest. Feeling foolish, she concentrated on the path beneath her heavy black boots.

In the branches far above their heads, birds twittered, hooted and warbled in a melodious tune that echoed through the understory. She loved this place, the vast forest both awe-inspiring and peaceful, expansive yet somehow intimate; a testament to God's power and creativity. A gift of both beauty and practicality.

She loved her home. Had no itch like some people her age to venture out of these East Tennessee mountains and experience city life. *Imagine the gawking stares a tomboy like you would get in the city!* The folks of Gatlinburg knew her and accepted her for what and who she was: a simple farm girl just trying to survive, to keep the farm afloat, to be both mother and father to her brother and caretaker of her beloved granddad. She had no grand dreams for her own future, no big expectations. Better to take each day as it came.

The trees thinned, allowing more light to spill into the meadows as they neared her family's property. Much smaller than the O'Malley farm, the Tanner spread consisted of a single-pen cabin in the midst of a small clearing, a cantilever barn whose top-heavy structure resembled a wooden mushroom, a very tall, very skinny chicken coop and a springhouse straddling the cold, rushing waters of the stream winding through the trees. A small garden beside the cabin provided just enough vegetables for the three of them. Compared to Nathan's place, her farm looked worn around the edges, a bit forlorn, the buildings sagging and bare. Even if she had the resources to fix everything that needed attention, there wasn't enough time in the day. Still, she loved this land that she poured so much of her heart and soul into.

"Hey, Nathan!" Crouched in the water, Will let the large rock he was looking under resettle in the silt and hurried up the bank. He snatched up his pail and crossed the grass in his bare feet, unmindful of his mud-splashed overalls.

"Hey, buddy." Always patient with her ten-year-old brother, Nathan greeted him with a ready smile. "What you got there?"

"I caught five crawdads. Wanna see?" He held up the pail, enthusiasm shining in his blue eyes handed down from their mother, the same hue as her own. A streak of dirt was smeared across his forehead and flecks of it clung to his brown hair.

Nathan peered at the miniature lobsterlike creatures and made an approving grunt. "Looks like you got some big ones."

"Will, where are your shoes?" Sophie frowned. "What happens if you step on a bee or cut your foot on a rock?"

He rolled his eyes. "I won't."

"You don't know that."

"You worry too much." He laughed off her concern. "I'm going to see if I can catch some more. See ya, Nathan."

The last year had wrought many changes in her brother and not all of them bad. He'd shot up two inches, his face had thinned out and he was *always* hungry. A bright kid in possession of a tender heart, his boyish enthusiasm had calmed and smiles had to be coaxed out of him. More and more it seemed as if he was pulling away from her in an effort to gain his independence. The brother she'd practically raised herself was growing up, and she didn't know how she felt about that.

"An ounce of prevention is worth a pound of cure," she called to his retreating back.

Nathan angled toward her and lifted a sardonic eyebrow. "Prevention, huh? I wonder if you thought about that right before you plunged off the falls? Or when you befriended that stray wolf that everyone warned you was probably rabid? Oh, and what about the time Jimmy Newman dared you to cross the fallen log high above Abram's Creek with your eyes closed?" He scowled. "Thought for sure my heart was going to give out that time."

Sophie resisted the urge to squirm. Why couldn't he conveniently forget her past shenanigans like a true gentleman? "If you'll remember, I made it across just fine." She brushed past him and headed for the cabin. "And that was a dog, not a wolf," she corrected, tossing the words over her shoulder.

"And what about the falls?" His challenging tone stopped her.

She turned around. "What about it?"

He prowled toward her, residual anger churning in his stormy eyes, reminding her of that long-ago summer day and the frothy, forceful water that had sucked her under, stealing her breath until she'd thought her lungs might burst. And then strong arms had wrapped around her waist, pulling her to safety. How well she recalled him frantically calling her name. His hands cradling her with a tenderness she hadn't known since she was a little girl, since before her mother died. How amazing…how sweetly wonderful it had felt to be held in his arms!

It was in that moment that she'd realized she was in love with Nathan O'Malley. And, as his concern had morphed into a familiar lecture, she had known he would never love her back.

His features were set in an obstinate expression. "You nearly died, Sophie."

"That was four years ago. Why are you so angry all of a sudden?"

"I'm not angry, exactly." He paused, a tiny crease between his brows as he mulled over his next words. "I just want you to take your own advice. Think before you act. Exercise caution."

In other words, think like he did. Frustration over her own shortcomings and the futility of trying to please him sharpened her voice. "Is this about the skunk? Because I'm not sure what else you expect me to say—"

"No, it's not that." He dropped his hands to his sides. "Let's just drop it, okay? I'm going inside."

This time, it was he who brushed past her. Why did she suddenly feel as if she'd been dismissed?

The inside of the Tanners' cabin looked much the same as it had when he was a young boy. Plain. Austere. The small glass windows were clean but bare. No pictures adorned the thick log walls. There was only one rug, faded and worn and situated close to the stone fireplace opposite the cast-iron stove. A simple square table with four chairs, a brown sofa that had obviously seen better days and two rocking chairs were the only furnishings. Tobias slept in the single bedroom beside the kitchen while Sophie and Will shared the loft space overhead.

What the place lacked was a feminine touch.

As he passed the fireplace, his gaze lit on a small tintype of Sophie and Will's parents, Lester and Jeanine Tanner. He barely remembered Sophie's mother. Not surprising considering he'd been thirteen when she died giving birth to Will. A quiet woman, she'd hovered in the background like a shadow as if to blend in. Perhaps to avoid attracting her husband's attention?

Unfortunately, Nathan remembered Lester Tanner all too well. The man was hateful, lazy and in possession of an explosive temper that all the local kids feared and tried their best to avoid. The family was well rid of him.

He couldn't help but wonder if Sophie might have turned out differently had she had a mother's tender hand to guide her instead of being thrust into the role of caretaker at eight years old.

He tapped lightly on the door standing ajar. "Tobias?"

A breathy voice beckoned him in. He moved deeper into the shadows where a single kerosene lamp on the bedside table cast the elderly man's face in sharp relief. Nathan sucked in a startled breath, alarmed at Tobias's frailty and the changes wrought in the one week since he'd last seen his neighbor. Knowing Tobias wouldn't appreciate his pity, he carefully schooled his features.

Easing into the straight-backed chair beside the bed, he folded his hands in his lap. "How are you today?"

"Not so good." The cloudy blue eyes staring back at him were filled with resignation.

"I'm sorry to hear that. Your granddaughter tells me you don't have much of an appetite. How about I bring some soup tomorrow?"

Bringing one gnarled hand up to cover a cough, the gray-headed man shook his head, panted to catch his breath. "I appreciate the offer, son, but not even Mary's cooking sounds good these days."

Nathan swallowed against sudden sorrow. He sensed Sophie's grandfather had given up.

"I'm glad you're here. Need to talk to you about Sophie and Will." Sadness tugged at Tobias's craggy face. "I'm worried more about my granddaughter than I am about the boy. Can I count on you to watch out for her after I'm gone? She may act tough but inside she's as sensitive as her mother." His chest rattled as he pulled in more air. "She needs someone to take care of her for a change."

"My family and I will always be here for them. But you're strong, sir. I have faith you can beat this."

"No, son, I'm ready to meet my Lord and Savior face-to-face. And I long to see my sweet Anne and Jeanine again. It's time."

Throat working to contain the tide of emotion, Nathan surged to his feet and stepped over to the window. Beyond the warped glass, Sophie unpinned laundry from the line and placed it in the basket at her feet. The sight of her pensive expression made his heart weigh like a stone in his chest. Losing Tobias, the closest thing to a parent she'd ever known, would devastate her. How in the world was he supposed to help her deal with that?

Chapter Three

Sophie bolted upright in bed. What was that awful racket?

Her hens' hysterical squawking shattered the quiet. Her heart sank. At this time of night, it could only mean one thing—predator.

Blinking the sleep from her eyes, she shoved the quilt aside and sank her tired feet into her boots without bothering to lace them. In the bed opposite hers, only the top of Will's head was visible above his blanket. Thankful his slumber hadn't been disturbed, she made her way to the ladder in the inky darkness, rushed to light the lamp on the table below.

"Sophie?" Somehow her grandfather's breathless voice reached her above the din.

"I'm here." She wished he'd been able to sleep through this as easily as Will. He desperately needed his rest if he was going to recover. "I'm going outside to investigate."

"Watch yourself, ya hear?"

A grim frown touched her mouth at his labored effort to speak. "Don't worry, I'll be careful."

White cotton nightgown swishing around her ankles, she lifted her trusty Winchester from its place above the mantel and headed into the sticky night.

The barn loomed large in the semidarkness, the brittle structure and surrounding trees washed with weak moonlight. Adrenaline pumping, she rounded the corner of the cabin and stopped dead at the sight that greeted her. Her fingers went slack on the gun handle.

Her too-tall henhouse was no more. It had been tipped over and smashed into a hundred bits and pieces by an enormous black bear that was even now pawing one of her hens with the intent to devour it. Those who had managed to escape the beast's jaws were running around in endless circles.

"What have you done to my chickens?" Outrage choked any fear she might have had. They *needed* those birds and the precious eggs they produced.

Hefting the rifle up, she found the trigger and aimed for the air directly above his head. She should kill him. Considering his size, the meat would likely sustain them for a month or more. Not to mention the hide sure would make a nice rug for the living room.

But she wouldn't. Killing animals for food was a part of mountain life, and she had no issue with that— as long as the animal was a pig or chicken or fish. But bears, well, they fascinated her. Had ever since she was a little girl and she'd happened upon a mama and her three cubs fishing in a stream farther up in the mountains. The cubs had been so cute and playful, the mama tough yet tender and fiercely protective, that Sophie had hidden in the bushes and watched, barely breathing, until they'd moved on.

Focus, Sophie. Anchoring the butt against her shoulder, she fired off a single shot.

A limp hen caught between his teeth, the bear lifted his head and shifted his opaque black eyes to her. Her lungs strained for air. *Don't make me shoot you.* He took a step in her direction. Again, she aimed above his head. Fired a second time.

When the lumbering beast casually turned and disappeared into the forest, Sophie released the air in a relieved whoosh and lowered the gun, muscles as limp as soggy corn bread. She surveyed the damage, dreading the job that awaited her come daylight. Weariness settled deep in her bones. They couldn't afford to purchase lumber for a new henhouse. How was she supposed to find time to chop down trees, strip and saw them into planks when so many other chores awaited her?

Anxiety nipped at her heels as she coaxed the addled hens into the barn for the night. What she really wanted to do was park herself at Granddad's bedside until she was absolutely certain he was on the mend. A frisson of stark, cold despair worked its way through her body; the possibility of losing him looming like a menacing shadow. How sad that she simply couldn't spare the time. Not if the animals were to be fed, the vegetable garden tended, the laundry mended and washed, and food placed on the table.

Feeling sorry for yourself won't get you anywhere, Sophia Lorraine.

Traversing the tomblike yard, words of defeat slipped from her lips. "Lord Jesus, sometimes I just don't know how I can go on like this."

Sometimes she wondered what it might be like to have a strong man around to help shoulder the burdens.

A partner. A helpmate. Someone like Nathan—strong and valiant and willing and able to meet any challenge. A man who could be both tough and tender. Sort of like that mama bear, she thought as she replaced the Winchester on its hooks.

But while her heart pined for him, in his eyes she was nothing more than an irritating brat. A down-on-her-luck neighbor he was forced to tolerate and occasionally rescue.

"Everything all right?" Tobias called.

Entering his room, she crossed to the narrow bed, straightened the quilts and took his hand between hers, tenderness welling in her chest at the feel of his feeble, knotted fingers.

"Everything's fine. You should go back to sleep."

"I worry about you." His eyes gleamed in the darkness. "This farm is too much for one young girl to manage."

She stroked his hand, determined to put his fears to rest. To ignore her own reservations. "I'm not a little girl anymore, you know," she gently reminded him. "I may not look like much but I can work as hard as any man."

"I'm not doubting your abilities, Sophie, but I want more for you and Will. I—" his chest expanded "—don't want you to struggle—" and deflated "—alone. Maybe it's time you settled down."

Her brows shot up, stunned at this first mention of marriage. "Why would I want to get hitched? Besides, I'm not alone. I've got you."

When he didn't respond, she leaned down and kissed his wrinkled forehead, smoothed his wispy gray hair. "I think we'll leave this conversation for when we're both rested and thinking straight. Good night."

"'Night." He sighed.

Pausing to grip the doorframe, she turned back, compelled to speak words rarely spoken between them. Not because they didn't care but because emotional expressions just wasn't their way. "I love you, Granddad."

"I love you, too." Pride and affection thrummed in his voice.

Once again in her bed, with no one around to witness her emotional display, she allowed the tears to fall, slipping silently onto her pillow. Fear, cold and black and relentless, threatened to crush her. The what-ifs, the endless responsibilities, nearly overwhelmed her.

Having a man around full-time would help. But was a husband really the answer? Her father's temper, his disdain for her mother and contempt for Sophie made her reluctant to hand over her life to just any man.

Their future was too important to gamble on.

Wiping the moisture from her forehead with her sleeve, Sophie tried once again to lift what used to be the henhouse's right sidewall. It refused to budge. A gloved hand appeared out of nowhere and covered her own. She jerked back and in the process scraped her palm on the jagged wood.

"Nathan!" She stared as he heaved the wall up as if it weighed nothing, shoulders and biceps straining his white-and-blue pin-striped shirt, and lowered it out of the way onto the grass. "What are you doing here?"

Pink and purple fingers of dawn gradually chased away black sky, lightening the wide expanse above to a pale blue. He should be at home milking his cows, not standing here in front of her with his hair damp and his cheeks smooth and touchable from a recent shave, his beautiful eyes gazing at her with resolute intentions.

"I ran into Will downstream and he mentioned what happened." His gaze swept the scattered feathers and eggshells, the bucket filled with carcasses and the splintered wood on the ground before zeroing in on her face. "Are you all right?"

"I'm fine." She shrugged off his concern. "I managed to scare him off with two shots."

"You could've killed him."

"You know how I feel about bears."

Stepping over the mess, he stopped in front of her, his chest filling her vision as he took the hand she'd been clutching against her midsection in his. He gently unfurled her fingers and lifted her palm up for a better view. Her stupid heart actually fluttered. Wouldn't he be amused if he knew how he affected her? Amused or horrified, one of the two.

His lips turned down. "This is a pretty bad scrape." Pulling a red handkerchief from his pants' pocket, he wound it around her palm and tucked the ends under. "Why aren't you wearing gloves?"

She wouldn't tell him that they were too far gone to provide any sort of protection and she didn't have the means to buy a new pair. Better he think her foolish than pity her.

She slipped her hand from his grasp. "You're right, I should have put them on."

A flicker of understanding warned her that he suspected the truth, but he didn't voice it. Instead he tugged off his own gloves and handed them to her.

"I can't take yours."

"Josh will be here soon. I have another pair in the

wagon." He began to pick up the broken boards and pitch them in a pile.

"Why is Josh coming?" She gingerly pushed her fingers into the large deerskin gloves, the lingering heat from his hands a caress against her skin.

"He's bringing the lumber we need to rebuild your henhouse."

"He's *what?*"

Nathan tossed another board and arched a brow at her. "Now don't get all huffy on me. We have plenty to spare."

"You know I can't pay you."

"Don't expect payment." Shrugging, he turned his attention back to his task.

Torn, she fiddled with the end of her thick braid. "I don't want to sound ungrateful—"

"Then just say 'thank you' and let us help you." He was using his extra-patient voice, the one he used to coax her into seeing his side of things.

Frowning, she bent to gather crushed eggshells. For as long as she could remember, the O'Malleys had been there for her family, stepping in to help whenever they had a problem or a need to be met. And while she was extremely thankful for their generosity, it was difficult to always be on the receiving end.

As the jingle of harnesses spilled across the meadows, they both straightened and turned toward the lane. "There he is now." Nathan dusted his hands on his pants and started forward to meet his brother.

Trailing behind him, she spotted Will perched on the seat beside Josh. As if sensing her unspoken question, Nathan tossed an explanation over his shoulder.

"Will wanted to help load the wood. I didn't think you'd mind."

"No, of course not."

When the team halted, Will jumped down and joined Nathan at the back. Josh waved and smiled a greeting. "Hey, Sophie."

"Morning, Josh."

The eldest son of Sam and Mary O'Malley, Josh was a more laid-back, more outgoing version of Nathan. Only two years apart, they shared similar features. Both were tall, tanned and gorgeous. Josh's hair was a touch lighter than Nathan's, his eyes blue instead of silver and he sported a trim mustache and goatee that lent him a distinguished air.

He never looked at her with disapproval. But then, she'd never yearned for Josh's approval like she did Nathan's.

"How's Kate getting along?" she asked.

His smile widened, eyes shining with a deep contentment that made Sophie a little jealous. Okay, more than a little. What she wouldn't give to inspire such emotions in Nathan!

"She's feeling a lot better these days—as long as she steers clear of my brother." He shot Nathan a teasing look, laughing when he scowled in response.

Suppressing a grimace, she gestured toward the wagon. "You're a good neighbor."

"And here I thought we were friends." He winked.

"You know what I meant." She smirked, following him to the rear of the wagon.

When they had finished unloading the lumber, Josh turned to her. "Sorry I can't stay and help, but I've got to deliver a dining set before lunch."

"I understand you've got a lot to do. It's no problem."

He hooked a thumb toward the cabin. "Before I go, I'd like to say hello to Tobias if he's awake."

"Yes, please do," she said, smiling through her worry. "He'd like that."

As Josh let himself in the cabin, Nathan and Will joined her beneath the wide-limbed oak tree. Even though the sun had a long way yet to climb, the air was thick with humidity and the promise of scorching heat.

"I don't want beans again for supper," her brother informed her, sweat glistening on his face, "so I'm going fishing. Will you fry up my catch?"

While they could use his help with the henhouse, beans for the third night in a row didn't appeal to Sophie, either. Maybe fried fish would tempt Granddad to eat. "Sure thing." She squelched the urge to smooth his hair. A few years ago, he wouldn't have minded. Things were different now, though.

She watched as he ambled off to the barn to fetch his fishing pole.

"Are you ready to get started?" Nathan prompted.

She shifted her gaze to his face, shadowed by his Stetson's black brim. "Not yet."

"Uh-oh, I've seen that look before. What's on your mind?"

"If you want to help me, you have to allow me to give you something in return."

Something mysterious slipped through his eyes, something she'd never seen before—a mini-explosion of heat and want immediately contained, hidden from view as if it had never been. Her heart thudded in her hollowed-out chest. What—

"Sausages," he blurted.

"Huh?"

His entire body stiff, he turned and walked away, jerking up the ends of four long planks and dragging them toward the spot where they would rebuild.

"Everyone knows you make the best-tasting sausages around. If you insist on paying me, I'll take some of those."

Sophie stayed where she was, not a little confused by his reaction to a simple statement. "Okay. Sausages it is. If you're sure that's what you want."

He dropped the planks and shot her an enigmatic look. "I'm positive that's all I want from you."

She went to help him, certain she was missing something and feeling her mother's absence more keenly than ever.

Chapter Four

Three hours later, Nathan hammered the last nail into place on the new roof. Despite his fatigue, the thin film of sweat coating his skin and the hunger pangs in his belly, satisfaction brought a smile to his face. He stepped back to admire his and Sophie's handiwork.

This henhouse was shorter and wider than the original…and all but impossible to tip over. A small ladder led up to the hatch above the man-size door, allowing the chickens to come and go as they pleased during the day.

"What do you think, Soph?" He glanced over to where she was replacing her tools in the box.

She shot him a tired smile over her shoulder. "I think this one will outlast you and me both." When she stretched out her hand to snag her hammer lying in the grass, he noticed her fingers shaking.

Chucking his own hammer on the ground, he crossed to the elm tree and the basket of food he'd put there. "Can you help me with something?"

Straightening, she flipped her golden braid behind her shoulder and joined him without a word, taking the ends of the red, white and blue pinwheel quilt he held out to her and helping him spread it on the ground.

"Now what?" She looked to him for direction.

"Have a seat." He knelt on the quilt and withdrew the smoked ham and cheese sandwiches, jar of pickled beets and container of coleslaw.

Eyeing the bounty, she gestured behind her. "I should put my tools in the barn and go check on Granddad."

"You checked on him fifteen minutes ago." He lifted two mason jars full of sweet tea and propped them against the trunk. "How about you eat something first? I packed enough for both of us. Will, too. I'm sure he'll come 'round when he's hungry."

She wavered.

Nathan produced a cloth-covered plate. "Aren't you curious what's under here?" he teased.

When Sophie sank down on the quilt, the hunger finally showing on her face, he couldn't suppress a grin.

"Oatmeal cookies?" she asked hopefully.

"Nope."

Tapping her chin, she mused, "Peach turnovers?"

"Uh-uh."

She threw up her hands. "Tell me already."

He lifted the white cloth to reveal thick slices of apple crumb cake.

"Mind if I have my dessert first?" She grinned mischievously and swiped a slice, humming with pleasure as she sank her teeth into the spicy-sweet cake.

Nathan couldn't tear his gaze away. Her eyes were closed, and he noticed for the first time how her thick lashes lay like fans against her cheeks, how her neat brows arched with an intriguing, sassy tilt above her lids. A breeze stirred the wisps of hair framing her oval face.

She opened her eyes then, caught him staring and flushed. Shrugged self-consciously. "I forgot to eat breakfast."

He pointed to where stray crumbs clung to her lips. "You, ah, have some, ah…"

Averting her gaze, she brushed them away. He turned his attention to his sandwich, his thoughts flitting around like lightning bugs trapped in a jar. Why all of a sudden was he noticing these things about her? Why was he acutely aware of her appearance when he hadn't been before? Whatever had caused the change, he didn't like it. Not one bit. Not only was this preoccupation inconvenient, it had the potential to embarrass them both.

Halfway through his meal, he put two and two together. If Sophie went too long between meals she got jittery and light-headed. And it had been right around suppertime when he had come upon her and that skunk.

He lowered his sandwich to his lap. "Sophie?"

"What?"

"The other day when the skunk had you cornered, why didn't you tell me you were feeling puny?"

She swallowed her last bite of cake and looked at him in surprise. "You didn't give me a chance."

Of course he didn't. He'd been livid. "I'm sorry."

She hitched a shoulder. "I could've waited a little longer. Moved a little slower."

"No." He shook his head. "Your well-being comes first, no matter what."

Remembering how he'd scolded her, he grimaced, regret tightening his stomach.

It was a pattern, he realized. Back when they were kids and she'd first insisted on tagging along with him and his brothers, he alone had seemed to mind her presence. Josh had treated her with the same teasing affection as he did their cousins, and Caleb, impressed with her adventurous spirit, had been thrilled to have her around. Not Nathan. More often than not, the two of them had been at odds. While he was cautious and tended to think before he acted, she was impetuous and spontaneous and didn't always anticipate the consequences of her actions.

Which led to disagreements. And him lecturing her like an overbearing older brother.

She's not a little girl anymore, O'Malley. She's a mature young woman in charge of her own life and capable of making her own decisions. No doubt she doesn't appreciate your know-it-all behavior.

Perhaps it was time to step back and give her some space. This friendship of theirs was morphing into something unrecognizable, with strange new facets he wasn't quite comfortable with.

Sophie didn't know what to say. Or think. Nathan was an intelligent man. Perceptive, too. A quality that served him well in dealing with his five female cousins. That he'd noticed her need just now—the shakes had set in with a vengeance right about the time she'd begun sorting her tools—and understood that her haste the other day had stemmed from the same issue didn't surprise her.

Hasn't he always watched out for you? Even when he was tempted to throttle you.

It was true. Nathan's protective instincts were legendary. Not only had she heard the O'Malley girls complain about his overprotective ways, she herself had been on the receiving end of his lectures countless times—lengthy discourses about safety and the wisdom of taking proper precautions—and, she recalled with a shudder, his ire when he thought she'd acted recklessly. To give him credit, many times she *had* deserved his set-downs.

What she couldn't figure out was why he was acting strangely today. There was a distracted air about him, a confounded light in his eyes that aroused her curiosity.

As she finished her sandwich, the salty ham and cheese between soft white bread chasing away her hunger pangs, he helped himself to the cake.

She dabbed her mouth with her napkin before broaching the subject that had been bothering her ever since she'd interrupted the conversation between him and her granddad last evening.

"What were you and Granddad talking about when I came into his room? The two of you looked awfully serious."

Nathan's bleak expression had troubled her long into the night.

Now he schooled his features into a careful blandness that scared her. If he was trying to avoid hurting her, then she was right to worry.

"Nothing special." His fingers tightened on the jar balanced on his thigh. "I tried to tempt him with Ma's cooking but he insisted he wasn't hungry. He doesn't seem to have much energy."

An understatement. "Doc Owens has been tight-lipped, as usual, but I can tell by his manner that he's concerned."

"When is he supposed to come and check on him again?"

"In a couple of days, unless he gets worse and I need him before then...." *Please, Lord, don't let that be the case.* "Are you sure that's all you talked about? He didn't say anything strange?"

Nathan lifted the jar to his mouth. "Like what?"

"Like asking you to marry me."

He choked. Sputtered. *"Marry you?"* His brows shot to his hairline, and he jammed his thumb into his chest. "Me? And you?"

Humiliation burned in her cheeks. Shoving to her feet, she glared down at him with clenched fists. "Is the prospect of marrying me so distasteful, then? You think no man in this town would want me?"

"No! That's not it!" He quickly stood, his eyes dark and searching. "You just shocked me is all. D-did Tobias suggest it to you?"

"No."

The relief skittering across his face pierced her heart. Sent her confidence tumbling. Unable to look at him, she observed a ladybug clinging to a swaying stalk at her feet. "He did suggest I start thinking of settling down. That I need a man around to take care of me," she scoffed. "Imagine!"

She'd been taking care of herself since she was eight. Why did Granddad think she needed help?

Weren't you thinking the same thing just last night? an unwelcome voice reminded.

"He's your grandfather. Of course he wants to see you settled and happy." Nathan looked particularly *un*-settled, a line forming between his brows as he looked past her to the cabin.

"A husband can't guarantee me that." Her own mother's misery was proof.

He shifted his gaze back to hers. "Tobias wants to make certain your future is taken care of."

"You make it sound as if he's not going to be around for it," she accused.

"Sophie—" He moved to close the distance between them, but the sympathy wreathing his mouth sent her a step back, away from him.

"Don't." She held up a staying hand. She couldn't handle his compassion right this moment, couldn't bring herself to face what was happening to her grandfather. Not if she didn't want the tears welling up to spill over. Losing control of her emotions in front of this man wasn't something she was willing to do.

Will's whistling saved her.

Nathan twisted around, silent as her brother approached with a proud smile, pail swinging from one hand and his pole in the other. "I caught four rainbow trout," he told them, lifting the pail for them to inspect.

"Nice catch," Nathan admitted, but his somber gaze was on Sophie.

"I'll take those inside for you," she quickly volunteered, taking the pail from his willing hand. Tilting her head to indicate the quilt spread out behind them, she said, "Nathan brought us lunch. Help yourself."

Will's eyes lit up. "Miss Mary's the best cook around." Setting his pole out of the way, he plopped down and began rifling through the basket.

Before Nathan could speak, she rushed ahead. "Thank you for everything today. I should go in and change. I have errands in town this afternoon."

He nodded slowly. "I have chores waiting, too. I'll keep Will company while he eats, then head out."

"See you later, then?"

"Later."

The promise in his deep baritone let her know not only would he be seeing her, but sooner or later they would finish this conversation.

The bell above the mercantile door jingled. Sophie didn't look up from the two thread spools she was trying to choose between. Because her brother spent much of his time on his knees in the creek, it seemed like every other week there was another tear for her to mend.

Light footfalls and feminine giggles drifted closer. She frowned. Recognizing the voices, she peered over her shoulder and spotted April Littleton and her two closest friends, sisters Lila and Norma Jean Oglesby. The same age as Sophie, the trio was extremely popular with Gatlinburg's single male population. And why shouldn't they be? Besides being beautiful and stylish in their pastel dresses and beribboned curls, they were accomplished flirts, able to monopolize a man's attention with very little effort.

Next to them, Sophie felt ordinary. Gauche.

April caught her staring. Brown eyes narrowing, she made no attempts to hide her disdain.

"Hello, Sophie." Her nose pinched as if the air around her suddenly reeked.

An only child born to her parents late in life, April had been coddled and adored from the moment of her birth, and the results were a spoiled, self-absorbed young woman. Her parents weren't well-off, just simple farm folk like many of the families in this mountain town, but they scrimped and saved to be able to outfit her as if she was a city debutante.

"Hi, Sophie." Lila offered her a tentative smile. The older sister, Norma Jean, remained silent. Both were slender, blonde and blue-eyed with fair skin.

"Hello." She quickly replaced one of the spools without making a conscious color choice. No reason to linger for what would prove to be an unpleasant encounter.

April's jealousy fueled her dislike of Sophie. Not of her appearance, of course. April didn't consider her competition. It was Sophie's friendship with Nathan that she envied. Even if Lila hadn't let that little nugget slip, it was obvious the dark beauty wanted him for herself, and it killed her that Sophie shared any sort of connection with him.

"We were discussing our outfits for the church social tomorrow night," April said with mock innocence. "What are you going to wear, Sophie?"

Clutching the thread, she pivoted to face them. Shrugged as if she didn't care. "I haven't given it much thought."

April raked her from head to toe and shot a knowing glance at Norma Jean. "Of course you haven't."

"Tell her about your new dress," Lila encouraged her friend, her round face devoid of malice. Sophie sometimes wondered why Lila would waste her time with a girl like April. The seventeen-year-old appeared to have a good heart.

April's eyes shone with confidence as she ran her hands over her glossy brown ringlets. "It's buttercup-yellow…"

She went on to describe the dress in excruciating detail. Sophie tuned her out, biding her time until she could escape. She had no interest in scalloped hems and pearl buttons.

The mention of Nathan's name snapped her out of her reverie.

"What was that about Nathan?"

"I'm making Nathan's favorite for the social. Apple pie."

Sophie bit her lip. That wasn't his favorite—it was rhubarb.

"What are you bringing?" Norma Jean smirked. "Sausages?"

The girls' laughter stirred her temper. For once, Sophie wanted to prove she was as capable as any other girl. "Actually, I'm baking a pie, too," she blurted.

The laughter died off as all three stared at her in amazement.

A delicate wrinkle formed between Lila's brows. "I didn't know you baked."

"Everyone knows she doesn't," Norma Jean muttered in a too-loud aside.

April, however, grinned in expectant pleasure. "Well, I, for one, am looking forward to tasting your pie. What kind is it?"

"Rhubarb."

"Oh, how…interesting. I'll look for it tomorrow night. Let's go, girls. I want to find just the right color hair ribbon to match my dress."

Sophie hesitated, watching as they gravitated toward the fabrics whispering feverishly together, before hurrying to the counter to pay for her purchase.

Outside, walking along Main Street, she was oblivious to the sun's ruthless heat, the stench of horse manure and the nods of greeting aimed her way.

What had she gotten herself into?

She didn't know how to bake! After her ma passed, Granddad had taught her the basics: how to fry bacon and eggs, how to make flapjacks and corn bread. Stews and soups. Roast chicken. And, of course, beans. That was the extent of her kitchen skills. Not once had she attempted to bake a cake, let alone a pie.

What had she been thinking? Despite her trepidation, she couldn't back out. She refused to give April the satisfaction.

Determination lengthening her steps, she reached the cabin in less than the usual time. Sophie had found a collection of recipes in her ma's cedar chest a while back. Surely there was something in there she could use.

As she cut across the yard, her gaze went to the new henhouse. She stopped short. There, strutting around in the dirt, were approximately five new chickens. Dark Brahmas, a hearty breed revered for their gentle disposition. She pushed the door open and entered the dark interior of the cabin.

"Will?" She set her small package on the table. "Granddad?"

"In here."

"Hey, there." Sinking gently down on the edge of Tobias's bed, she held his hand. Propped against a mountain of pillows, his skin had a sallow cast. "Can I get you anything? Would you like for me to open the curtains? It's a bit stuffy in here." And dreary, she thought, compared to the bright summer day outside.

His dry, cracked lips shifted into a grimace as he shook his head.

"I noticed some unfamiliar chickens outside. Do you know anything about that?"

"Nathan," he wheezed. "He brought us two dozen eggs, too."

To replace the ones they'd lost. She squeezed her eyes tight, deeply touched by the gesture.

"You all right?"

She inhaled a fortifying breath and eased off the bed. "How does a cup of chamomile tea sound?"

"No need to trouble yourself—"

"It's no trouble at all. I'll make some for both of us. We'll sit together and drink our tea and visit." The endless farm demands could wait a little while longer.

In the kitchen, she filled the scuffed tin teakettle with water from the bucket and set it on the stovetop, then added kindling to the firebox. As she readied two mugs, her mind refused to budge from Nathan.

Why did he have to go out of his way to be thoughtful? It would make things easier if he were hateful. Or selfish. Maybe then she wouldn't yearn for his high regard. Maybe then she wouldn't entertain foolish, impossible dreams. Maybe, just maybe, she would see him as no one special, an ordinary guy who didn't matter to her at all.

Chapter Five

At one end of the dairy barn lit by kerosene lamps hanging from post hooks, Nathan stood in front of the waist-high wooden shelves replacing lids on the crocks of milk he'd just filled. In the stalls stretching out behind him on either side of the center aisle, his cows were happily munching hay.

In the corner where they kept a bin of clean water, he washed and dried his hands, the familiar scents of cowhide, hay and fresh milk filling his lungs. Satisfaction pulsed through him. He relished his work, the straightforward nature of it and the solitude. He liked that he could plant a seed of corn and watch it grow tall, witness a calf enter this world and help it thrive. Farming was in his blood, passed down from his father and grandfather and great-grandfather. If he could do this for the rest of his life, he'd be a happy man. No need for a wife or kids. Well, kids might be nice. A wife he wasn't so sure about.

Mentally rehashing that awful turn in his and Sophie's conversation yesterday, he grimaced. He hadn't meant to hurt her feelings. It was just that the notion of a union between the two of them was so absurd as to be laughable. He and Sophie were like oil and water, dry forest and lightning. They just didn't mix. Not romantically, anyway.

The barn door creaked and he turned, expecting to see his pa. But there, framed in the predawn darkness, stood Sophie, a cloth-covered bucket in her arms.

"Hey. Is everything all right?" Laying the cloth on the shelf, he went to her, hoping against hope this early morning visit and the shadows beneath her eyes didn't mean what he thought it might.

One slender shoulder lifted. "I couldn't sleep, so I thought I might as well bring over the sausages I promised you."

Nathan exhaled. He accepted the bucket she held out, tucking it against his middle while he did a careful study of her. Aside from the troubled light in her eyes, she looked much the same as usual. Her long hair had been freshly brushed and plaited, the sleek, honeyed strands pulled back from her face, emphasizing her cheekbones and the gentle curve of her jaw.

"Thanks for these." He cocked his head. "Walk with me to the springhouse?"

"Yeah." Noticing the crocks, she walked over and slipped her hands around one. "How many are you storing?"

"Just two this time. I'm taking one to Ma and the rest will go to Clawson's. That's heavy," he said when she started to lift it. "Why don't you take the sausages and I'll get the milk?"

Before Tobias got sick, a suggestion like that would've gotten him an earful. Sophie didn't take kindly to insinuations that she was weak or incapable.

The fact that she didn't protest was proof of her pre-occupation.

Using the moon's light to guide them, they walked the dirt path to the stream and the stone springhouse that housed perishables. Trickling water intruded upon the hushed stillness of the fields and forest. Beside him, Sophie was silent.

I don't know what to say to ease her anxiety, God. I don't like seeing her like this. Please show me how to help her. How to reassure her.

Stooping beneath the low doorframe, he carefully placed the containers inside and pulled the door closed, letting the latch fall into place. When he straightened, he noticed her staring at the moonlight-kissed stones scattered in the streambed. Her lost expression tugged at his heart and made him want to wrap his arms around her and shelter her from heartache.

She'd been dealt too many blows in her life. If Tobias didn't make it, would she break? The idea terrified him. Sophie was one of the strongest people he knew. He couldn't imagine her any other way.

He stood close but didn't hug her. Instead he reached out to graze the back of her hand and somehow found his fingers threading through hers. Her head came up, blue eyes flashing to his, dark and questioning. She didn't pull away, though, and he decided it would be awkward to disengage now. Besides, her skin was cold, the bones fragile. Let his heat warm her.

Friends could hold hands and not have it mean anything, couldn't they?

"What you did yesterday…" she said, her voice muted. "The henhouse, the chickens and eggs… It means a lot to me. To all of us. Thank you."

"I did it because I wanted to, not because I felt I had to," he pointed out. "I like helping you."

As long as he was able, he'd eagerly meet any and all of the Tanners' needs. Growing up, he'd witnessed his parents' generosity toward others, giving selflessly of their time, energy and possessions. It was a lesson he'd taken to heart.

"I know."

She surprised him by laying a hand against his chest. Her touch seared through the material, scorching his skin. His heart jerked.

"You're a good man, Nathan. The best." Then, as if deciding she'd said too much, she pulled free of his hold. "I should go."

"Wait." Sophie didn't often dole out praise, so it meant a lot coming from her. He just couldn't figure out why she'd sounded so resigned. So solemn. "Are you going to the social tonight?"

She grimaced. "I am. Mrs. Beecham cornered me last week and insisted on sitting with Granddad so that Will and I could go. There's no arguing with that woman."

"It'll be good for you to get out and socialize."

She looked dubious. "If you say so."

"Think of all the delicious food you'll have to choose from."

Her mouth lifted in a pretty, albeit fleeting, smile. "Since I don't dance, the food is the biggest draw for me, you know. And speaking of food, I have to get back before Granddad or Will wake to find me gone. They'll be wanting their breakfast. I need to get to it."

"See you later, then."

Nodding, she gave a little wave and walked away,

head bent and long braid bouncing against her back. He watched until the trees swallowed her up, thinking it might not be a bad idea to find himself a date for tonight. Nothing serious. Just harmless fun.

Because whatever it was sensitizing him to Sophie— loneliness, although he didn't exactly *feel* lonely, the unrecognized need for female companionship, perhaps—had to be snuffed out before he did something stupid.

"You don't expect me to eat a slice of that pie, do you?" Will bounced on his toes, eager to make his escape.

Sophie slid it onto the dessert table in between a towering stack cake and a buttermilk pie. "It doesn't look half bad." She eyed her creation critically.

While the crust wasn't perfectly round and smooth, it did have an appealing golden hue like the other pies on the table. And the rhubarb filling had filled the cabin with a sweet, pleasant aroma. She'd followed her ma's recipe carefully. Surely it would be edible. Maybe even good.

"I don't understand why you decided to make one, anyway," Will said doubtfully. "You don't bake."

She couldn't understand it, either. Oh, yeah. April and her insults. And a desire to prove to those girls— and Nathan, too—that they were wrong about her. That she was more than just a rough-around-the-edges, act-before-she-thought-it-through tomboy.

"There's a first time for everything," she told him with false confidence.

"Hey, Will." Redheaded, freckled Charlie Layton

halted midstride and motioned him over. "We're get-tin' ready to race. Want to join us?"

"Sure thing!" With a muttered farewell, he ran to join Charlie. The two friends jogged off in the direction of the trees edging the church property where a group of about twenty boys their age had gathered.

The social was already in full swing, many of the men clustered alongside the white clapboard church, no doubt comparing farming techniques or debating quicker, more improved trade routes with the larger towns of Maryville and Sevierville, while the women relaxed on quilts, chatting and laughing and tending to fussy infants. Children darted in and out of the mix, chasing each other in friendly games of tag. Courting couples strolled arm in arm in the distance, keen on a little privacy.

At six o'clock, the heat of the day lingered despite the puffed cotton clouds suspended in the cerulean sky. Not even a hint of a breeze stirred the air. Sophie's neck was damp beneath her braid, and she pictured her ma's honey-blond hair arranged in a sleek, efficient bun, a throwback to her childhood in a strict Knoxville or-phanage. If Jeanine had lived, would she have taught Sophie how to arrange her hair the same way? She'd tried her hand at it, of course, but with disastrous re-sults.

"Sophie?"

Kenny Thacker weaved through the tables to reach her.

"Hi, Kenny." She smiled at the skinny, pleasant young man who, because of their last names and the teacher's penchant for alphabetical seating, had occu-pied the seat beside her throughout school.

"The guys are arm wrestling out at the old stump." He gestured behind the church. "They sent me to ask if you're up to joining us."

She really shouldn't. However, she did get a kick out of showing up guys like her pa who thought girls were weaker and dumber than them.

"I think Preston wants a rematch. He can't accept that he was beaten by a girl." He grinned broadly.

Sophie debated. She sure wouldn't mind besting that arrogant Preston Williams a second time.

"Well, I—"

"Oh, hey, Nathan." Kenny nodded in greeting.

Turning her head, her wide gaze landed on her too-handsome-for-words neighbor. Wearing a charcoal-gray shirt that molded to his corded shoulders and broad chest, the deep color made his silver eyes glow and shorn hair gleam a richer brown. Black trousers emphasized his long, lean legs, and he wore a sharp-looking pair of black leather lace-up boots. Quiet confidence radiated from his stance, his square shoulders and straight spine, his determined jaw and the unspoken message in his expression that he could handle any challenge that came his way.

Nathan wasn't the showy type. Nor was he a man who liked to be the center of attention. His appeal was his complete unawareness of his attractiveness, his obliviousness to the single young ladies' admiring glances.

Sophie hadn't heard his approach, but apparently he'd been there long enough to hear Kenny's question because his cool gaze was watching her closely, waiting for her response.

What will it be? his eyes seemed to challenge. *Will you do the proper thing, or will you give in to impulse and act the hoyden?*

Because she knew that no matter what she did she could not ultimately win his approval, Sophie was tempted to do it simply to irk him.

"I'm ready now, Nathan." Pauline Johnson approached with a goofy grin and a buoyant light in her eyes. The tall, curvaceous blonde, stunning in teal, sidled close to Nathan. "Oh, hello, Sophie. Kenny."

Sophie opened her mouth but couldn't find her voice. Her heart beat out a dull tattoo. They were clearly here together. On a date. When was the last time Nathan had squired a girl around? He wasn't interested in pursuing a relationship. Wasn't that what he always said whenever his brothers gave him a hard time about being single?

Seeing Pauline curl her hand around his forearm, Sophie felt physically ill.

"Just a minute." He barely allowed the blonde a glance, still obviously intent on Sophie's response to Kenny's summons.

Sophie glanced once more at the pie. It mocked her now. The foolish piece of her heart that refused to listen to reason, that still clung to the hope that one day he'd see her as an accomplished and attractive young woman worthy of his regard, withered and died.

Jerking her chin up, she determined he would never guess how deeply he'd wounded her. "Hello, Pauline," she said, forcing a brightness to her voice. *Please let it ring true.* "You're looking lovely this evening."

Her grin widened, cobalt eyes shining with humble gratitude. "You're kind to say so." She gestured over her shoulder to where the O'Malleys were gathering. "Will you be joining us?"

Us. As in Pauline and Nathan and his family.

"I'm afraid not." Not now, anyway. Her throat thickened with despair. *Admit it, you're jealous.* Ugh! The kicker was that she actually liked Pauline. The same age as Nathan, Pauline was not only beautiful but considerate, friendly, and one of the best sopranos in Gatlinburg. Folks loved it when she sang specials at church.

Smart, sensible and accomplished. Unlike Sophie, Pauline was perfect for Nathan.

The knowledge cut deep.

"I actually have other plans." To Kenny, she said, "Tell Preston I accept his challenge."

His eyes lit up. "Nice."

"Sophie—" Nathan growled.

Holding up a hand, she shot a pointed glance in Pauline's direction. "You should tend to your guest. Enjoy the picnic, Pauline."

Head high, she pivoted on her heel and called out to Kenny, "Wait up. I'll walk with you."

She left him standing there, bristling with disapproval. But she refused to let it sway her decision. Worrying about Nathan O'Malley's opinion of her was a complete waste of time.

Nathan wanted nothing more than to go after her. The young lady at his side prevented that. *Probably just as well. You're not Sophie Tanner's keeper. Distance, remember?*

"Nathan?"

Ripping his gaze from the duo's retreating forms, he plastered a placating smile on his face. "Let's go join my family, shall we? Or we can sit with yours, if you'd rather."

It would spare him Josh and Kate's curiosity. The happily wedded couple had recently started hinting it was time he think about settling down. And, since this was the first time in months—possibly years—he'd escorted a girl anywhere, they were right to have questions.

Maybe that's why Sophie had seemed so shocked to see him with Pauline. Her face had gone as white as the clouds above—

"I'd prefer to visit with your family." The pretty blonde beamed at him, fingers clutching his sleeve a little too possessively. *Just your imagination.*

A long-time acquaintance, he'd chosen Pauline Johnson because she wasn't the type of girl to read too much into a single outing. Nor was she so romantically minded she'd be miffed at his last-minute invitation.

Leading her past the long tables sagging beneath the weight of the food, he guided her to a prime spot on a gentle knoll beneath the protective branches of a sweet gum. Josh was propped up against the trunk, lazily observing the crowd. Keen interest sparked in his expression the moment he spotted them.

Ma elbowed Pa in the ribs, nodding and smiling as if he'd given her a surprise gift. Great. He had a sinking suspicion this wasn't going to be as fun as he'd imagined.

"Pauline, how nice to see you." Ma gestured to an empty patchwork quilt next to theirs. "Have a seat."

He waited until she was seated, her crisp skirts arranged around her, to lower himself a good twenty-four inches away. Not because he was afraid of his reaction to her—he'd established with immense relief that she didn't affect him in any way, good or bad—but because he wanted no illusions to form in her mind or anyone else's.

Her cloying perfume wafted from her sleek blond mane and tickled his nose. He sneezed.

"God bless you."

"Thanks," he muttered, inconveniently recalling Sophie's natural, pleasing scent.

"How is your sister and her new husband getting along?" Mary asked. "Do they like living in Sevierville?"

Pauline's mouth formed a moue. "Laura's homesick. Ma wishes they'd move back here, especially before they start a family." She relaxed back on her hands, extended so that her fingertips nearly grazed his thigh. Was that on purpose? He shifted slightly to the right.

A scowl curled his lips. Maybe this wasn't such a good idea. After all, Sophie still dominated his thoughts and hadn't that been the point of this exercise? Distraction?

Mary nodded. "I can understand. I feel so blessed Josh and Kate settled here. I'll get to spend a lot of time doting on my first grandchild."

The conversation turned to babies. Nathan tried to stay focused, he really did, but an irritating little voice demanded to be heard. What if Sophie got herself into a fix? Those guys could play rough sometimes. What if she got hurt?

A cloud of aggravation lodged in his chest, expanding until he couldn't ignore it a second longer. He jumped to his feet, earning him the attention of everyone present. "I, ah, have to check on something. I'll hurry back."

His date's look of confusion, his ma's barely hidden consternation and Josh's amusement stayed with him as he traversed the field. He was going to regret this. He just knew it.

Chapter Six

Adrenaline fueled by deep distress gave Sophie the upper edge. The sight of Nathan and Pauline looking cozy branded into her brain, she bested David Thomas. And John Beadle. And Preston Williams.

Granted, David was fifteen and spindly. And John was too much of a gentleman to put forth much effort into beating her. Cocky Preston, on the other hand, had been a true challenge. If not for her heated reaction to Nathan's surprise date, she very well could've lost.

Grumbling his displeasure, Preston shoved his way through the spectators.

"Who's next, fellas?" Sophie taunted, feeling dangerous. In this moment, she didn't care one whit about being a lady or what anyone else thought of her. Nor did she heed the burning sensation in her forearm and biceps. She needed an outlet for the restless energy thrumming through her, the weighty disappointment clamping down on her lungs.

"Don't you think you've proved your point?"

Nathan. Why was she surprised? The underlying steel in his cool voice warned her she was on shaky ground, but she wasn't in the mood to heed it. Spinning, she clasped her hands behind her back and arched a challenging brow. "What point would that be?"

Boots planted wide, hands fisted at his sides, a muscle twitched in his rock-hard jaw. "Do you really wanna discuss this here?"

All around them, young men ceased their talking to stare.

"You started it." She jutted her chin at a stubborn angle.

"And I'll finish it." His nostrils flared. "Just not in front of an audience."

Snickers and whistles spread through the small gathering.

When he reached for her arm, she jerked away, feeling slightly panicked. What if he got her alone and her true feelings spilled out? She didn't trust her mental muzzle right now. "Wait, don't you wanna give it a go? Or are you afraid you might lose to a girl?"

Though his eyes glittered silver fire, his tone was gentle. "I wouldn't want to ever hurt you, Sophie."

She caught her breath. *You already have. You just don't realize it.*

"Later, guys." Striding past him, she walked in the opposite direction of the crowd, stopping beside a grouping of young Bradford pears. "So tell me, what was so important you felt it necessary to abandon your date?"

Folding his arms across his substantial chest, he glared at her. "Would you believe I was actually worried about you?"

When he caught sight of her surprise, he laughed derisively. "I know. Silly, huh? After all, you know exactly what you're doing, right? You can take care of yourself."

"Of course. In case you've forgotten, I've been doing that since I was a kid. I don't need looking after, Nathan. I'm not one of your cousins, nor am I your little sister."

"Oh, believe me, I'm quite aware of that fact." He ran a frustrated hand through his short hair.

Nathan and sarcasm didn't normally go hand in hand. What had him so steamed? This wasn't the first time she'd engaged in behavior he deemed unfitting for a young lady.

Annoyance stiffened her shoulders. "Why do you have such a problem with me arm wrestling? Last I heard, it wasn't illegal."

His eyes narrowed. "Sophie—" Exasperation shifted quickly into resignation, and he gave a quick, hard shake of his head. "No. I told myself I wasn't going to lecture you anymore. You're an adult capable of making your own decisions."

"That's right, I am," she huffed. "And just because you don't happen to agree with my decisions doesn't mean they're wrong."

"While I agree we have different opinions about things, you can't argue the fact that you're flaunting clear-cut societal rules. Look around you—" he waved an impatient hand "—do you see any other young women arm wrestling? Engaging in spitting contests or tug-of-war games? *Wrestling* with grown men?"

Sophie lowered her gaze to the grass beneath her boot soles. She'd done all he'd said and more at one time or another. Not only did she enjoy a little friendly competition, she felt more comfortable around the guys. They didn't judge her based on her appearance. Nor did they expect her to discuss the latest fashions and recipes or know how to quilt and then make fun of her when she didn't.

"You don't understand. You never have."

"There you are." Josh rounded the tree closest to them, his astute gaze bouncing between them. "Nathan, Pauline is wondering what happened to her escort."

His expression shuttered. "I'm coming."

Kate appeared a couple of steps behind, stylish in a forest-green outfit that made her skin appear dewy fresh. Today, her chocolate-brown mane had been tamed in a simple twist. "Sophie, how are you?"

"Just swell."

"Nathan let me sample one of your sausages at lunch," she said, her smile encompassing the two of them, "and it hit the spot. Your recipe is delicious. I have to have it."

"Only one?" Josh winked at his wife. "Are you sure about that?"

Her cheeks pinked. "Well, maybe two. Or three. I wasn't able to eat much breakfast, so I had to make up for the lack."

Of their own accord, Sophie's eyes slid to Kate's midsection. Was that a slight bump? The dark material made it difficult to tell. When the happy couple announced last month that they were expecting, Sophie had wondered for the first time what it might be like to have a baby of her own. The prospect simultaneously intrigued and frightened the daylights out of her.

"The bacon didn't sit well with her," Josh explained.

"Maybe the baby doesn't like bacon," Sophie ventured, then blushed furiously when Nathan returned his attention to her. *What an absurd thing to say. Muzzle, remember?*

But Kate just laughed in delight and linked her arm through Sophie's. "I think you may be right, dear Sophie. Why don't you come sit with us? There's ample space."

"I wouldn't want to intrude." Just what she'd envisioned for today—observing Nathan's courting efforts up close.

"Nonsense." Kate waved off her resistance "You're practically family."

With a sinking stomach, Sophie allowed herself to be led to where the O'Malleys had gathered. As Pauline watched their approach, a tiny crease appeared between her fine brows. Of course, she had a right to wonder what had taken Nathan from her side. Her greeting smile held a hint of bravery, however, and she pulled him into the conversation with his parents with ease.

Sophie held back. Where to sit?

Kate pointed to Nathan's blanket. "There's space there, Sophie. We've loaded up extra plates of food, so help yourself."

Reluctantly she lowered herself on his other side, as close to the edge as possible without actually sitting on the grass. Although he was concentrating on Pauline's words, tension bracketed his mouth. Unlike all the times before when she'd joined the O'Malleys, she now felt like an intruder. An interloper. Oh, this was a nightmare! But she couldn't very well be rude and abandon Kate after she'd gone out of her way to include her, could she?

Grabbing a plate without taking stock of its contents, she ate quickly, not really tasting any one flavor. It could have been liver and onions, for all she noticed. Conversation swirled around her. Nathan shot her a couple of furtive glances, but he didn't speak directly to her. As if she wasn't worth talking to. That hurt.

They were just finishing up their meal when a shadow fell across their legs. Sophie lifted her head and promptly dropped her fork.

April Littleton, looking sweetly feminine in the flowing yellow dress she'd described in the mercantile yesterday, bore a plate between her hands as if it held the Queen of England's crown. The spiteful gleam in her eyes put Sophie on guard.

"Hello, Sophie." Her smile smacked of gloating superiority. "Nathan." She completely ignored Pauline.

"Hi, April." Nathan set aside his empty plate. "How have you been?"

"I've been a busy woman of late, I must admit. I made this dress especially for tonight. What do you think?"

"I, ah…" Clearly not expecting such a question, he scrounged for an appropriate response. Shot Sophie a help-me look, which she ignored. What could she do but wait April out? "It's very nice."

April batted her lashes, cherry-red lips widening into a wolf-in-sheep's-clothing smile. "Why, you're kind to say so. This isn't all I've been busy making, though. This here is a special family recipe—my great-grandmother Bertha's delicious cinnamon-apple pie. I heard apple was your favorite, so I brought you a slice."

She extended the plate toward him, which he accepted with a slight nod.

"That's thoughtful of you, April. Thank you."

Of course he would be polite. He wouldn't embarrass

her by correcting her. It smarted that he had no such reservations when it came to Sophie.

She stared at the plate, feeling slightly queasy. The slice closest to her was the apple. But what was the other one? Was it too much to hope it wasn't what she suspected it was?

She craned her neck to get a glimpse.

"I also brought you a piece of Sophie's pie," April tacked on with an innocent air. "I haven't tried it yet, but I sure am eager to see what it tastes like, aren't you?"

Chapter Seven

Something told him this already dismal outing was about to get worse. Much worse.

Beside him, Sophie fidgeted with nerves, tugging on the sleeves of her brown shirt, fiddling with the collar. And April's too-cheerful demeanor rang false. By now, Pauline and his family were watching the exchange with interest.

Shooting Sophie a quizzical glance, he kept his voice low. "I didn't realize you'd made a pie."

"It was a spur-of-the-moment decision."

One she regretted, judging by the way she was gnawing on her bottom lip, dread stalking her eyes. The pulse at the base of her slender throat jumped.

"What are you waiting for?" April's silken voice prompted.

"Right."

Dreading this almost as much as Sophie, he sank his fork into the fluffy layers of crust and soft apples and lifted it to his mouth. April hadn't exaggerated. The blend of sweet fruit and spices melted on his tongue.

"I can understand why your family has held on to this recipe. It's wonderful."

Pauline leaned forward. "I like apple, too. I wish you'd brought me one, April."

A flicker of annoyance dimmed her gloating pleasure, and she shot the blonde a look that suggested she get her own. "Now the rhubarb."

Sophie inhaled sharply, but he didn't look at her. Couldn't.

Best to get this over with as quickly as possible. The pie didn't look half bad, he mused as he forked a bite. Maybe Sophie would surprise them all.

Then again, maybe not.

The crust tasted doughy as if undercooked, and the rhubarb filling was so tart it made his jaw ache. He fought a grimace as he forced himself to chew quickly and swallow the offensive bite, blinking at the tears smarting his eyes.

"Drink," he choked out.

Kate slapped her tea jar into his outstretched hand and he drank long and deep. He thanked her and she nodded, a line of concern between her brows.

"It doesn't appear you enjoyed that very much." Arms crossed, April wore a smug expression.

Without warning, Sophie leaned close and, snagging the fork from his hand, scooped up a piece for herself. He watched her chew once, her eyes growing big, lashes blinking furiously as she choked. Behind him, his ma made a commiserating sound.

"I don't understand." Sophie shook her head in consternation, her thick, shimmering braid sliding over her shoulder. "I followed Ma's recipe very carefully. I did exactly what it said—"

When she clapped her hand over her mouth, he prompted, "What?"

"There was a smudge." She spoke without removing her hand, muffling her words. "A water stain, actually, right where she'd written the amount of sugar. So I guessed."

April's lip curled. "Don't you know baking is a science? You can't guess at it or else you'll have a disaster on your hands." Whirling around in a swish of skirts, she marched in the direction of the dessert table, waving her hands to get the attention of those within hearing distance. "Do not eat Sophie Tanner's rhubarb pie, folks! Not if you want to avoid a terrible stomachache." Scanning the table, she located the pie and deposited it into the nearest waste bin. People stopped and stared. When Nathan caught the triumphant smirk she shot over her shoulder in their direction, his blood burned white-hot.

There was movement beside him, the air stirring and with it the familiar scent of Sophie—dandelions and sunshine and innocence. He pulled back from his anger long enough to see her hurrying away.

"I'll go talk to her." Kate started to get up.

"No, I'll do it." He waved her off before getting to his feet. "But first, I'm going to have a word with Miss Littleton."

"Nathan, wait." Josh pushed up from the tree and laid a hand on his shoulder. "What's it going to look like if you go marching over there and yell at her? Look around, brother. Everyone's watching. I think it would be best if you focus on Sophie right now."

"She didn't deserve to be humiliated like that," he grumbled.

"No, she didn't," Josh agreed, questions swirling in his blue eyes as he studied him. "It's not like you to lose it. What's going on?"

"Nothing."

At least, nothing he could confess. Josh was right. Of the three brothers, he was the calm, controlled one. The quiet one. Some would even say shy.

But for weeks now he'd been wrestling with confusing reactions to a girl he'd always viewed as a pal, an unexpected and unwelcome awareness of her that frustrated him to no end. And his ability to contain that frustration was becoming less and less sure.

Josh squeezed his shoulder. "Whatever it is, you know you can talk to me anytime."

"I know." Slowly, he unclenched his hands. Took a calming breath. "I'd better go find her."

He took a single step, then remembered. With an inward wince, he turned back. "I'm sorry, Pauline, but I have to—"

With a tentative smile, she waved him on. "Go. Your friend needs you right now."

"Thanks for being understanding."

Feeling slightly guilty for neglecting his date, he started off in search of Sophie, wondering why his life had suddenly become messy. He didn't do messy. He preferred things clear-cut. Straightforward. No surprises.

The problem was that Sophie was synonymous with unpredictability. She blurred his thinking. Knocked him off-kilter. He didn't like that.

He used to be able to ignore it or to simply brush her off, but…they weren't kids anymore. Things had changed without him wanting or expecting them to.

And if he was going to reclaim any sense of normalcy, of balance, he was going to have to put some distance between them.

Right after he made certain she was okay.

He hadn't gone far when he spotted her boots swinging from a limb.

Of course she'd be up in a tree. It was her favorite place to go when she craved space. Too bad he wasn't going to give it to her. Not yet.

A fleeting glance was her only acknowledgment of his presence. Her features were tight as she stared straight ahead. No tears for Sophie.

Since they weren't within eyesight of the church, he grabbed hold of a low-slung branch and proceeded to climb up, settling on a thick limb opposite her. How long had it been since he'd done this? Years?

"I'm not in the mood for a lecture, Nathan. If that's why you're here, you can just climb back down and leave me in peace."

A green, leafy curtain blocked the outside world. His left boot wedged against the trunk and one hand balanced on the branch supporting him, he shook his head. "I'm not here to lecture you. I'm done with that."

Disbelief skittered across her face. He didn't blame her for doubting him. He'd made reprimanding her into a profession. "Besides, you didn't do anything wrong."

She frowned. "Didn't I? My pride is the reason I was just humiliated in front of the entire town. I let April's superior attitude get to me." A fuzzy black-and-orange caterpillar crawled over her hand, and she touched a gentle finger to it. "I was trying to prove a point. I proved one, all right."

Nathan hated the defeat in her voice. "It takes guts to try something new."

She was silent a long time, her attention on the caterpillar in her cupped hands. Her legs slowed their swinging. "Do you remember when we used to play in the treetops? You, me and Caleb?"

"How could I forget?" They'd made up all sorts of adventures for themselves.

Her lips twisted in a wistful sort of smile. "I liked playing pirates most of all. Caleb was the big, bad pirate, I was the damsel in distress and you…" Her eyes speared his as her words trailed off.

"I was always the hero, swooping in to rescue you," he finished for her, lost in her sapphire eyes full of memories and mystery.

"Yes." Lowering her gaze, she released the caterpillar onto the branch to go on his merry way. "Sometimes I miss those days."

Resisting the pull she had over him, he spoke gruffly. "Things change. *We've* changed. Don't you think it's time you stopped climbing trees, Sophie? Stop living in the past? Put our childhood behind us?"

For a split second he glimpsed the hurt his words—said and unsaid—inflicted. Then she jerked her chin up and glared at him.

"No, I don't. I like climbing trees, and I don't see any reason to stop. I'll probably still be doing it when I'm old and gray. With any luck, you won't be around to scold me."

And with that, she hurried down and stormed off. Left him there feeling like an idiot.

* * *

Today was a new day.

Sitting in a church pew with his family listening to the reverend's opening remarks, Nathan was confident he'd made the right decision. Lounging in that tree long after she'd gone, he'd determined that what he and Sophie needed was some space. As he'd reminded her last night, they weren't kids anymore. Maybe that was their error—assuming things could stay the same. He feared if they continued in this manner, one of them—more than likely *him*—was bound to say or to do something so damaging, so incredibly hurtful, their friendship wouldn't survive. He would hate that.

He had to be careful to make his distance seem natural, though. The very last thing he wanted was to hurt her. He would curtail his visits, and if she questioned him he could blame it on his heavy workload. She was busy, too. This would work.

No sooner had the thought firmed in his mind than the rear doors banged open. The reverend faltered, and the congregation turned as one to see who was behind the interruption. When he first saw her, disapproval pulsed through him. Not only was Sophie late, she'd made an entrance no one could ignore.

But then her panicked expression registered, and as she rushed to whisper in Doc's ear, Nathan grabbed his Bible and, pushing to his feet, hurried down the aisle toward her, his decision forgotten, uncaring what anyone else thought.

Something was wrong with Tobias.

As much as Nathan's immediate reaction of censure chafed, Sophie dismissed it. The disturbance couldn't be helped. Granddad was fading fast, and she didn't care if she had to interrupt the President of the United States himself if it meant getting help.

Gray hair flittering in the breeze, Doc ushered her outside and down the church steps. "Are you able to ride your horse or would you prefer to ride in my buggy?"

She knew she looked affright, her hair pulled back in a disheveled ponytail and her breathing coming in ragged puffs. "I'll take my horse."

With a curt nod, the middle-aged doctor settled his hat on his head and strode for his buggy parked near the church entrance.

"I'm coming with you."

Sophie jumped at the sound of Nathan's gravelly voice right behind her. She spun around, ready to tell him not to bother, only to falter at the disquiet darkening his silver eyes to gunmetal gray. He was offering her support. Something she desperately needed right now, even if she was irritated with him.

Admit it, you don't want to be alone if this truly is the end.

She cleared her throat, barely holding the tears at bay. "Fine."

Dropping his Stetson on his head, he strode to his horse and, securing his Bible in the saddlebag, mounted up. They rode hard and fast through town and along the country lane leading to her place, arriving right behind the doctor. Will, who'd stayed behind, burst through the door, his small face pinched with fright.

Sliding to the ground, she dropped the reins and grasped his shoulders. "Will?"

"I'm scared, sis," he whispered, burrowing his face in her middle.

Her chest constricting, she wrapped her arms around his thin frame and held him close. The flimsy piece of string restraining her hair had broken free during the jolting ride and now her hair spilled over her shoulders, shielding her face. Good. Nathan wouldn't be able to see how close she was to losing it, the grief and fear surely written across her features.

He stood very close to them, almost touching, the strength emanating from his tall frame surrounding them like a tangible force. When she lifted her head, she risked a glance his direction, afraid he'd see through all her flimsy defenses and realize she wasn't as strong as she pretended to be. That she was, in fact, weak. Vulnerable. Fragile.

However, his eyes were closed and his lips moving. With a start, she realized he was praying. For her and Will and Granddad. While she knew Nathan's faith was solid and very important to him, he was a private man. She'd heard him pray a handful of times over a meal but this was personal. This was him petitioning God for her sake.

Her heart swelled, her love for this man burrowing so deep that she suspected she'd never be able to uproot it.

Movement in the doorway caught her attention.

"He's asking for you."

The finality in Doc's voice washed over her like a bucket of icy water and, despite the midmorning heat, goose bumps raced along her skin and she shuddered. With an arm around Will, she forced her feet to move, to lead them both inside.

Memories of another death slammed into her. It was as if she was eight again, fear and dread clawing in her chest as she walked into this very room to say goodbye to her ma. To place a kiss against her cool, color-less cheek. Granddad had been right there to hold her, to comfort her.

Why God? Why must I say goodbye? I'm not ready!

They hesitated in the entrance. Will trembled be-neath her arm, and she hugged him closer, attempting to instill comfort with her touch.

Tobias's eyes fluttered open and he lifted a finger. "Come…closer, children."

Needing to be near him, Sophie eased down on the bed and took his withered hand in hers, clinging with as much pressure as she dared. Will stationed himself beside the bedside table, eyes huge in his face, hands clamped behind his back.

In the back of her mind, she registered Sam and Mary's voices mingling with those of Doc Owens and Nathan's in the living room.

"I love you both." Tobias dragged his gaze from Will's face to hers. His tired eyes exuded calm assur-ance. Acceptance. "And I'm proud of you."

"I love you, too, Granddad," Will murmured, snif-fling.

Tears blurred her vision. Stroking his hand, she leaned down and kissed his sunken cheek. "You know how much I love you. How much I need you. Please, don't leave us." Her voice cracked.

God, help me. I can't do this.

"You'll be fine," he rasped, "just fine. The Lord's calling me home, Sophie." He was quiet a long moment, his lids sliding shut. "I wanna see my Anne."

Will stood solemnly staring down at him. Sophie held on to Tobias's hand, her fingers stroking back and forth. The hushed voices in the other room filtered in but she couldn't make out the conversation. Tobias's jagged breathing sounded harsh in the stillness.

They remained that way for a long while. Half an hour, at least. Maybe longer. Sophie spent the time praying, her gaze trained on her granddad's face, memorizing the beloved features. Without warning, his chest stopped rising. His fingers went slack.

"Granddad?" She rested her head on his chest, but there was no heartbeat. "No. No!"

Tears coursed unchecked down her face. She couldn't breathe. The edge of her vision faded to black. Where was that heart-wrenching wailing coming from?

And then, suddenly, strong arms were lifting her up, cradling her. Murmuring softly, Nathan carried her away. She wasn't aware of where he was taking her. Eyes shut, she buried her face in his chest and let the tears flow. There was no hiding from him now. And right this minute, it no longer mattered.

Her granddad was gone, and she was all alone in the world.

Chapter Eight

Sophie gradually became aware of Nathan's slowed footsteps, of him lowering them both onto a fallen log out of the direct sunlight. The stream was nearby. She couldn't see it, but she heard the steady rush of water above her heart thwacking against her rib cage.

He held her securely, his arms looped around her waist and his chest solid and warm beneath her cheek.

"I'm sorry, Sophie," he whispered, his lips brushing the curve of her ear. "So sorry."

Sniffling, she lifted her head to gaze up at him, belatedly realizing her hands were still clasped behind his neck. She didn't remove them because she was caught by the sorrow mirrored in his eyes like dense fog cloaking the forest floor.

Granddad had been fond of Nathan, and she knew Nathan had reciprocated the feelings. He was hurting, too.

When a fresh wave of grief washed over her, she didn't try to mask her emotions. Here and now, in the shelter of his embrace, she felt free to be transparent.

"What are Will and I going to do without him?" She sounded raw and broken. "We don't have anyone left."

His brows pulled together. Gently smoothing her hair away from her face, he wiped the moisture from her cheeks with a tenderness that stunned her. "You have me. And my parents. My entire family." His gruff vow lent her an odd sense of comfort. "Whatever you need, we'll be here for you."

Watching Sophie's expressive features, Nathan floundered at the hopelessness brimming in her sad eyes. A fierce swell of protectiveness coursed through him and, more than anything, he wished he could shield her from this hurt.

He smoothed the long golden hair tumbling down her back, his fingers threading through the silken strands. Once again, the smell of dandelions filled his senses, and he had the insane urge to bury his face in the mass. With her hair unbound, her cheeks dewy and eyelashes damp from tears, she was purity and beauty and enticing vulnerability.

This was Sophie Tanner without her barriers, open and accessible to him. A rare and precious gift…a moment he'd cherish for the rest of his days, despite the fact their futures lay down different paths.

She must've seen the shift in his expression, the clanging shut of an emotional doorway, for she stiffened in his arms. Her gaze skittering away, she released his neck and popped up, turning her back on him. "I'm sorry for getting your shirt all wet."

Regret intertwined with relief. Had he so easily forgotten the decision he'd made to gain perspective where she was concerned?

He stood and dislodged the bits of dirt from his pant legs. "It'll dry soon enough."

"I should go back." She straightened her spine and pivoted back. Sunlight sifted through the leaves to make patterns on her navy shirt and set her hair to shimmering like a golden halo. "Will needs me."

"He's with my parents right now. Are you sure you don't want to stay here awhile longer?" He didn't think seeing Tobias again so soon would help. Better to wait until Doc prepared him for burial.

Her lower lip trembled even as a tiny flame of resolve flickered in her eyes. "I have to be strong for him, Nathan. I remember how I felt after Ma died, and I don't want him to worry about anything."

The reappearance of the I-can-do-it-all-by-myself Sophie sparked irrational anger low in his gut. When she made to walk past him, he sidestepped to block her path.

"And what about you?" he blurted, hating that once again she was left to bear the weight of responsibility. "Who's going to be strong for you?"

"Y-you've already offered to help," she stammered, "but if you've changed your mind…"

"I'm not talking about the farm, Sophie." He gentled his voice. "I'm asking who are you going to allow close enough to share your worries? Your fears? Your dreams? Who are *you* going to depend on?"

She looked as if he'd struck her. "Are you offering to be that person, Nathan?"

He froze. All the reasons why that would be an unwise choice, the risk such an undertaking would pose to their friendship, robbing him of coherent thought.

Her expression shuttered. "I didn't think so."

Pushing past him, she jogged along the bank. He watched her go, feeling like an unfeeling cad for upsetting her when all he'd really wanted was to lessen her pain.

The funeral passed in a blur. A sea of black-clad mourners shed quiet tears, conversed in hushed voices, faces drawn. Somehow Sophie made it through without breaking down as she was tempted to do, the entreaty "Help me, Lord Jesus" an unending refrain in her head. The knowledge that many of these people were praying for her and Will brought her a measure of peace. Still, the ache lodged in her chest refused to budge. Her gruff yet tenderhearted granddad was gone for good.

Try to keep it together a couple more hours, Sophia Lorraine. The folks mingling outside her cabin, eating the bounty Mary and a number of neighbor ladies had supplied, wouldn't stay forever.

Despite the crowd and their sincere sympathy, Sophie felt adrift. Alone. Not to mention strangely conspicuous in a frothy black concoction—Kate's thoughtfulness knew no bounds—that Sophie was certain made her resemble a harried crow. While the bodice and waist fit okay, the skirt was three inches too short and her clunky work boots peeked out from beneath the lace-trimmed hem. She wasn't sure if the furtive glances sent her way were on account of her loss or the unusual sight of her in a dress.

Pausing on the small square stoop, she searched for Will. Last night—their first without Granddad—had been rough. She'd held him as he'd cried himself to sleep long after his usual bedtime, soothing him when he woke calling for Granddad. She picked at the lacy wrist cuffs. How was he coping with all this?

Her gaze snagged on Nathan. Tall and dashing in an all-black suit that lent him city-flair, he stood with Josh and Kate, as well as barbershop owner Tom Leighton and Gatlinburg's sheriff, Shane Timmons. He'd hovered nearby ever since yesterday afternoon—she hadn't allowed herself to relive what had transpired between them—grim and withdrawn and looking like he'd lost his best friend.

Pauline was here, too, but it didn't appear as if they were together. Not if her frequent, pining glances in his direction were anything to go by. She really was quite beautiful. Her sleek blond hair shined bright and golden beneath the black veiled hat angled on her head, her black shirtwaist and skirt making her appear even taller and more statuesque than usual. Kindness, pure and unadulterated, radiated from her being.

Pauline Johnson wouldn't be caught dead arm wrestling with a bunch of rowdy men.

Sophie felt as if a dull knife had carved out her insides. This was the type of girl Nathan would admire, one he'd be willing to give up his bachelorhood for. One he deserved.

How long had Nathan harbored an interest in her? she wondered. Her midsection cramped. Was he— Had he decided to get married? And if so, how soon? How would she survive? It was one thing to accept he would never desire her, but to actually witness him pledging his life to another woman…to see them as husband and wife…starting a family…

Nathan shifted his weight and glanced her way, a ripple of regret crossing his face as his gaze intersected hers. Regret for what? Tobias? Their closeness yesterday? Their charged exchange?

The arrival of an unfamiliar carriage diverted her attention.

Nathan immediately separated himself from the group and strode over. "You expecting company?"

"No."

Conversation fell away as the driver halted the team, jumped down and, swinging open the door, assisted a fashionable lady down the carriage steps.

A well-cut plum ensemble fit her top-heavy figure like a glove and atop her brown curls a riot of black feathers bounced and bobbed with every tilt of her head. An uglier headpiece Sophie had never witnessed. As the newcomer peered haughtily around, the cucumber-thin nose, high cheekbones and pursed mouth nudged Sophie's memories and she gasped.

"Aunt Cordelia!"

"Your father's sister?"

"I had no idea she was coming." What had it been, four or five years since she'd visited?

Shaking herself out of her stupor, Sophie descended the steps and approached, aware that Nathan had stayed behind and foolishly wishing he had accompanied her. Cordelia was an intimidating woman. At least, she had seemed so to Sophie when she was younger.

Cordelia studied her with cool appraisal. "Sophia?"

"Hello, Aunt," she greeted cautiously, noting the fine lines radiating from her pinched upper lip and the streaks of silver webbed through her dark hair. "I didn't realize you were planning a visit. I'm afraid you've come—" *Too late.* Clearing her throat, she plunged ahead, "Granddad is gone. H-he passed away yesterday afternoon."

Cordelia's only response was a further compression of her lips, until they practically disappeared from her face. No surprise there. Sophie hadn't expected an overt display of emotion. After all, Cordelia had left Gatlinburg shortly after her eighteenth birthday and hadn't kept in close contact with her father or brother. Nor had she seemed to care about her orphaned niece and nephew. Sophie recalled her aunt's visit shortly after her ma's passing, how stern and forbidding she'd been, like a beady-eyed bat in her black mourning clothes. She hadn't held Will even once.

Where Sophie's pa had been all fiery temper, Cordelia was as cold as ice.

Twisting slightly, Cordelia addressed the driver awaiting her instructions beside the team. "Wait here for me. I won't be long." Returning her steel-blue gaze to Sophie, she stated, "You and I have some things to discuss. Shall we do it here in front of the entire town or in private?"

Things? What things? A sense of foreboding tightened her midsection. "We can go inside."

Ignoring folks' expressions of recognition, Cordelia swept across the yard with single-minded purpose. Sophie followed a few paces behind, shaking her head at Nathan's uplifted brow asking, Do you want me to come with you? Since she didn't know what to expect, she'd rather he didn't witness this.

Thankfully, the handful of people in the living room cleared out as they entered.

"Would you care for a cup of coffee?" Sophie's quick retreat to the kitchen was hampered by her skirts. The stiff collar scratched the sensitive skin along her collarbone, and the bodice was given to twisting so that she was continually straightening it. What she wouldn't give for her comfortable pants right about now.

"I've reached my quota for the day. We stopped for lunch at the little café on Main Street before coming here. Not a horrible place," Cordelia allowed, lowering herself onto the worn sofa. Posture ramrod-straight, she let her sharp gaze roam over the cabin's interior, no doubt finding it lacking.

Too bad, Sophie thought. It was *her* home, and she liked it just fine.

Sophie went to sit on the opposite end of the sofa, hands folded in her lap.

"How was your trip?" She attempted politeness.

"Incredibly long." She sniffed. "Dusty and with enough bumps I no doubt will be covered in bruises by the morrow."

"That bad, huh?"

Cordelia angled toward her. "Where is Will?"

The question threw her. "I—I'm not exactly sure. He's probably with his friends down by the stream."

One pencil-thin brow lifted. "You should keep better tabs on the boy, Sophia. He should not be allowed to roam freely and do whatever he likes."

"He's ten," she said in defense. "Plenty old enough to be out of my sight."

"That may be the case here in the wilds, but not in civilized society."

The wilds where she herself grew up? Sophie bit off a retort.

"Will has a good head on his shoulders. I trust him not to make foolhardy decisions."

"You will understand why such a reassurance coming from you does not impress me. Do you think I'm unaware of your impulsive, unladylike behavior, Sophia Lorraine Tanner?" Her nostrils flared in distaste. "I may not reside here, but Father kept me abreast of all your exploits."

Her fingers curled into fists. Where was she going with this?

"Father wrote to me several weeks ago when he first became ill. He was concerned about your future. If something were to happen to him, he asked if I would be willing to do my duty by the two of you."

Sophie stilled. "What exactly does that mean?"

"I've come to take you and Will back to Knoxville to live with me," she stated with finality, as if they had no say in their future. She flicked a dismissive glance around. "From the looks of things, it shouldn't take long to pack."

"Will and I aren't going anywhere." Defiance laced with a tiny frisson of anxiety burned her throat. How dare she? "This is our home."

Just then, the door banged open and thudded off the log wall behind it. She and Cordelia quickly rose to their feet.

"It wasn't my fault, Sophie! Robbie pushed me first." A rumpled, sopping wet Will skidded to a stop in front of her, his mouth falling open when he spied their aunt.

Nathan entered behind him, wearing an apologetic expression. "I tried to stop him from interrupting your chat, but he slipped past me."

Why, oh why, did her brother have to pick today of all days to get into trouble? She braced her hands on her hips. "What happened?"

"We got into an argument. He said something bad about Pa." Gaze downcast, he scuffed the floor with his shoe. "It made me really mad, so I said something about his pa. He pushed me."

"They both ended up in the water." Hands on his hips, the sides of his suit jacket dislodged to show off his impressive physique, Nathan let his gaze slide between the two women.

"See what happens when you allow a child too much freedom?" Cordelia huffed. "Perhaps I was wrong in leaving Father to raise you. Things will have to change once we've returned to the city." She glared at Will. "Fighting will not be tolerated, young man. And you, Sophia, will learn to comport yourself like a lady. I daresay once we've smoothed out your rough edges, it won't take us long to find you a suitable husband."

Will tugged on Sophie's sleeve. "What is she talking about?"

Nathan dropped his hands and scowled. "What's going on, Sophie?"

She opened her mouth to speak, but Cordelia answered for her.

"Simple. Sophia and Will are moving to Knoxville."

Chapter Nine

"I won't go!" Will backed toward the door, a trail of water in his wake. "You can't make me!"

"Will—" Sophie reached out to him, but he dashed through the open door before she could utter another word. Aching for her brother, she rounded on the other woman. "How dare you waltz in here today of all days and upset him further? If you knew anything about raising children, you'd know not to dump news like that on an unsuspecting child." She didn't realize she was trembling until Nathan, standing behind her, settled comforting hands on her shoulders in silent support, lightly kneading her rigid muscles. "And let's get something straight right here and now—this is our home. We have no intention of ever leaving it. You've wasted your time."

A fine film of frost glossed Cordelia's blue eyes. "I disagree." She tilted her head at a condescending angle, the obnoxious black feathers bobbing above one brow. "This has given me an opportunity to see my father was right in contacting me. You've reached the age of maturity, which means I can't force you to come with me. However, Will has many more formative years ahead of him, and it's perfectly clear he needs discipline and guidance that you are either unwilling or unable to provide. Stay here if you wish, Sophia, but Will is coming with me."

"He's *my* brother!" Outrage pulsing through her veins, Sophie jammed a thumb against her chest. "I've been taking care of him since he was a baby. You can't take him away from me."

Cordelia didn't flinch in the face of her outburst. "Think about it. What judge is going to award guardianship to you instead of me? I'm comfortably settled in a fine house with the funds to see to his every need. He'll go to a well-appointed school with boys his own age where he'll learn proper manners as well as how to curb the cursed Tanner wild streak."

Sophie's stomach dropped to her toes. Cordelia was right. No judge would ever choose her—an eighteen-year-old struggling to make ends meet—over someone like her aunt. Cordelia's husband, Lawrence Jackson, had been a state representative and the two of them had been well-connected, well-liked fixtures in Knoxville society. Upon his death three years earlier, he'd left a small fortune to his wife.

Sophie couldn't compete with that.

Behind her, Nathan shifted, bringing his enveloping heat closer. His chest brushed against her back. His fingers stopped their kneading, but he didn't relinquish his hold on her. Sophie relished the sense of solidarity the connection gave her.

"Now is not the time for such a weighty discussion." He leveled his words at her aunt. "We're all attempting to deal with Tobias's death. Emotions are running high, and we're exhausted. I think it would be best if we postpone it until a later time."

"Who are you?" Cordelia looked stunned he would interfere.

"I'm Nathan O'Malley, Sophie's neighbor and good friend." He leaned forward and extended one hand, which she reluctantly shook. "My family and I watch out for her and Will."

The older woman studied him, apparently heeding the undercurrent of warning in his voice.

"Fine. Since Gatlinburg still doesn't have a hotel to speak of, I'm going to let a room from the Lamberts. I will give you until tomorrow afternoon to think on what I've said, but I won't postpone my return much longer than that, so be prepared to give me your decision. You can come with us or remain here alone. It's up to you."

The door snapped shut and, for a moment, neither spoke. Then Sophie spun in his arms, clutched at his shirtfront. "Nathan, what am I going to do?" She stared up at him, willing him to make this nightmare disappear. "I can't lose him. I can't."

Losing Granddad had carved deep fissures in her lonely heart. Losing Will would break it clean in two. What kind of life could she have here without him?

He covered her hands with his own. "You're not going to lose him."

"How can you be so sure?"

"Will belongs with you." His noble features radiated a confidence she didn't share. "Once everyone's had a good rest and a chance to clear their heads, we'll talk to her. I'm certain we can make her see reason."

Panic spiraled upward. "And what if we can't? What if—"

"Sophie." He ducked down so that they were eye

level, his gaze blazing into hers. "I'm not going to let her take Will, I promise."

There was a rap on the door. Josh poked his head in. "Most everyone is heading home."

Releasing her, Nathan swiveled to face his brother.

Josh walked in, nervously fingering his goatee, his gaze bouncing between them. "Is everything all right?"

"I don't mind if you tell him," she told Nathan, suddenly needing to find Will, to hold him tight. "I'm going to go talk to my brother."

She was on the stoop when Nathan called out, "It will be okay, Soph."

Glancing back over her shoulder at him, so grave with purpose, she nodded. But deep down, she wasn't sure she believed him.

Sophie found Will perched on a flat rock, chin resting on his knees pulled up to his chest, staring morosely at the water coursing past. His damp hair spilled onto his forehead, nearly obscuring his eyes. So sad. And lonely. Her heart twisted with regret.

God, why is this happening? Why did You take Granddad? We needed him, Father. And now Aunt Cordelia is threatening to tear us apart.

Jumping up at her approach, he jutted his chin in a familiar display of stubbornness. "I won't go with her. You can't make me. I'll run away if you try." Beneath the defiance lurked a desperation that matched her own.

Run away? "Will, I don't want you to go anywhere without me," she exclaimed. "No matter what happens, you and I will be together. I promise you that." A promise she would move heaven and earth to keep.

"But Aunt Cordelia said…" He faltered, clearly confused.

"We've agreed to table the discussion until later. She's tired from traveling and we…well, we've had a rough few days."

He dropped his arms to his sides. "I don't want to leave my friends or the O'Malleys. You're going to make sure we stay here, aren't you?"

Staying together? Definitely. Staying *here?* She wasn't so sure about that.

A seed of an idea sprouted in her mind.

"Sophie?"

She brushed the hair out of his eyes. "Leave everything to me, okay? You don't have to worry about a thing."

At the sight of his younger brother perched on a stool milking Bessie, Nathan stopped short and balanced a hand against the wooden stall post.

"When did you get home?"

Caleb hitched a shoulder without turning around or halting the rhythmic movement of his hands. "Not long ago. Where is everybody?"

"You'd know the answer to that if you stuck around any length of time," he snapped, not in the mood to coddle him. Sophie's problems weighed heavily on his mind. He'd waited around until everyone had left, thinking she'd return with Will. She hadn't. And with suppertime fast approaching, he'd had to come home to tend his cows.

Caleb shot a dark look over his shoulder.

Nathan huffed a weary breath. "Tobias passed away yesterday afternoon. The funeral was today."

Caleb's hands stilled. Shifting slightly, he pulled his lips into a frown. "How is Sophie?"

Nathan pushed off the post. "Again, something you'd know if you'd been around." Irate now, he stalked to the corner and washed his hands, filled a pail with clean water and settled himself in the stall opposite Caleb's. After washing Star's utters, he attempted to lose the tension cramping his back and shoulders. He didn't want it transferring to the cow.

"Nathan?" Caleb growled.

"How do you think she's doing? She just lost her grandfather." And to add insult to injury, she was dealing with a tyrannical aunt bent on wreaking havoc.

"What's gotten into you?" his brother demanded.

Jolting to his feet, he ignored the tipped stool and Star moving restlessly behind him. "I'm tired of shouldering your share of the weight around here. Of seeing Ma's disappointment when you don't show for yet another supper and Pa's unease when you don't come home for days on end. Josh and Kate are expecting a baby. You're going to be an uncle for the first time." He glared at Caleb, who was standing with boots braced apart in the straw, fists clenched and knuckles white. "What if something happened while you were gone and we had no way to reach you? How would you feel if you came home and discovered one of us had been hurt or worse?"

He blanched. "That's why I stay away," Caleb stormed. "To protect you all from my carelessness. To prevent any more accidents."

Nathan stared. Accidents. He was referring to the accident that had scarred him and nearly cost his best friend his life. And the more recent one last fall. The wagon he'd been driving had overturned during a thunderstorm, and their ma had suffered a broken leg. Apparently he still blamed himself.

"You honestly think you can protect us, keep us safe, by keeping your distance? You're not God, Caleb."

"*I* did this." He sneered, jabbing a finger to the jagged lines near his eye. "Because I was irresponsible and cocky. Adam almost died because of me."

"But he didn't. And you didn't. Because God deemed it so. He's the one who has the ultimate say in our lives."

He shook his head, his shaggy black hair scraping his shirt collar. "You don't get it."

Crossing the center aisle into the stall, he stuck his face near Caleb's. "No, *you* don't get it. Sophie needs me right now, and I aim to be there for her. In order to do that, I need for you to stick around and help out around here. Got it?"

His younger brother's heavy lids flared at this uncharacteristic display, the loss of control. "Fine. I'll stick close to home until things settle down."

It wasn't exactly the response he'd been looking for, but it was enough. For now.

"Good."

Shoving his hands through his hair, he returned to his stool and sat down hard.

Focus, O'Malley. Sophie and Will need you to be cool and levelheaded. Calm. Controlled. Acting rashly will not solve this mess.

He'd promised to make things right. Disappointing her was not an option.

As soon as the cows were milked, Nathan returned to Sophie's to check on her. He couldn't stop thinking about the moment Tobias died. Her gut-wrenching cries. The sorrow draining the light right out of her. He couldn't forget how he hadn't hesitated, hadn't even blinked before going to her, taking her in his arms and comforting her and the overwhelming protectiveness he'd felt. Still felt.

It was what was propelling him back there.

Sophie and Will were alone in that cabin, surrounded by painful reminders and facing an uncertain future. He owed it to her—as her friend and neighbor—to help in any way possible.

Dismounting Chance, he let the reins drop to the ground. The cabin door stood slightly ajar, and through the opening he witnessed a blur of movement. He placed a flat palm on the wood and eased it back.

"Sophie?"

Looking harried, she whirled from her spot in the kitchen, her eyes a touch wild. Like a deer sensing a predator.

"Wh-what are you doing here?"

He took in the half-packed saddlebag open on the sofa and the dislodged dishes on the shelf above the stove. His gut clenched.

Removing his hat, he advanced into the room and lobbed it onto the scarred tabletop. Settling his hands on his hips, he surveyed her men's apparel. The odd-fitting black dress had been exchanged for her usual attire—dark pants, dark shirt and boots.

"Going somewhere?"

Hand trembling, she smoothed errant wisps away from her face.

Crooking his finger, he gently lifted her chin so

that she had to look him in the eyes. "Hey, you can be straight with me."

She swallowed hard. "We're leaving town."

It was as he'd suspected. Frustrated with the situation and her utter lack of forethought, he let his hand fall to his side. "You're running away."

Her eyes pleaded with him to understand her point of view. "It's the only option. I won't let her take Will. And we're not going to Knoxville. Neither of us would be happy living with her."

He blew out a breath. *Be calm. Remember her loss, the panic that's clouding her thinking.* "Where will you go? Where will you live? It takes money to start over."

And they both knew she didn't have those kinds of resources.

Disquiet pulled her pale brows together. He pressed his case. "You don't want to end up lost in these mountains without shelter or food or protection. That wouldn't be doing what's best for Will."

She wrung her hands. "What do you expect me to do? Sit back and let her ruin our lives?"

"Of course not," he soothed, that protective instinct surging to the surface, obscuring the dawning horror the idea of her and her brother traipsing unprotected through the countryside spawned. Taking her shoulders, he guided her to sit in one of the hard-backed chairs situated around the table and then set the water to boil.

He sat across from her. "What we need is a solid plan of action. A practical solution that will allow you to stay while satisfying your aunt at the same time."

Doubt tugged her mouth into a frown. "Like what?"

He fisted his hands to prevent them from reaching over and covering hers, small and tight with tension.

Gone was her usual confidence, the sparkle of determination in her big eyes. Tobias's death and her aunt's threats had stolen her inner fire. She appeared as fragile as fine china, easily breakable, with shadows beneath her eyes and her skin ashen.

"I don't know yet," he admitted. "But I'm certain if we take our time and examine the situation from all angles, we can come up with something foolproof."

"Staying here is risky."

"Riskier than running off?"

Although it didn't seem possible, she went paler.

Leaning forward, he gave in to the urge to touch her, taking her hands in his and stroking the petal-soft skin with his thumbs. "Give me some time to come up with a plan. At least until tomorrow morning."

"What happens if I don't like your plan? What then?"

"Then we'll come up with a new one. One you can live with."

She sagged in her seat, clearly unconvinced.

"I'm going to make you some tea," he said, going to the stove, "and then I'm going to go home and think this through." Kettle aloft, he turned and looked at her, tempted to camp out on her doorstep. "Can I trust you to stay here?"

Slowly, begrudgingly, she nodded. "I'll be here."

"Good."

He knew then he'd do just about anything to drive that stark fear from her eyes, to rekindle her inner flame, to make her smile again.

Chapter Ten

He'd failed her. All through the night, he'd tossed and turned, prayed and plotted and…nothing. Not one single good idea. No solid plan of action. Not even a hint of one. A situation that had him doubting himself and, if he were honest, just a little depressed. He was supposed to come through for her. He had the rescuer bit down pat, didn't he?

That he'd failed in this, her most desperate time of need, troubled him deep down in his soul.

He wasn't ready to wave the white flag of surrender, however. Hope yet lingered. What they needed was more time. Somehow he had to convince Cordelia to give them an extra day or two. Then he'd gather his family members and, together, they'd come up with an answer to Sophie's problem.

His knock was quickly answered by Will, who didn't grin or welcome him with his typical eagerness. "Hey, Nathan."

"Hey." Moving past him, he summoned a smile for the kid. "Catch any more crawdads recently?"

"Nope."

Nathan sought out Sophie, who was standing by the kitchen table appearing much more collected this morning, her hair neat and smooth and a hint of color in her cheeks. Her expression, however, was somber as she watched her brother. Picking up a plate laden with glazed round cakes, she offered, "How about you join us for some tea cakes and milk, Will? Mrs. Greene brought them from the café."

"Maybe later." He frowned and grabbed his hat off the wall hook. "I'll be in the barn for a while."

After he'd gone, Sophie lowered the plate. Sighing, she extended her hand to the chair opposite. "Have a seat. Can I get you milk? Coffee?"

"Coffee, please."

Lowering himself into the chair, he hooked his hat on the back and pushed a hand through his hair, watching as she filled the kettle and stoked the oven fire, her braid swinging side to side with each twist and turn. She really was a dainty thing. No doubt he could span her waist with his hands. She wasn't skinny, though. Sturdy and well-made with feminine curves in all the right places.

Stop right there, O'Malley.

Forcing his gaze elsewhere, he wondered why he couldn't be fascinated by Pauline's appearance. Or some other acceptable young lady. Why was his mind turning traitor of late? Such a waste of energy.

Sophie Tanner was his polar opposite. If he was what was considered a rule-follower, then she was a rule-bender. He saw the world in black and white; she, a riotous rainbow of color. He preferred the sidelines and she naturally attracted attention wherever she went.

While he tended to proceed with caution, she rushed headlong into situations without thinking them through.

It was enough to drive him mad.

By the time she placed two steaming mugs of rich-bodied coffee on the table, he had his thoughts back on track. Sophie smoothed a white cloth napkin in her lap and offered him first pick of the tea cakes. "I hope that studied frown means you've come up with a plan."

He sipped the hot brew, wishing he didn't have to disappoint her. "Not exactly."

Her fingers worried the mug's handle. "What does that mean?"

"We need more time."

Storm clouds brewed in her eyes. "You don't have a plan, do you?"

With deep regret, he shook his head. Her reaction was what he'd expected. A growing sense of despondency twisted her features. Her posture dipped.

"What am I going to do?" she whispered through colorless lips.

"We'll think of something." *Lord, let it be so.*

"But what?" Pushing away from the table, she began to pace. "Cordelia doesn't exactly strike me as the patient type. What if she refuses to wait?"

"We'll involve the sheriff. She can't kidnap your brother. These things take time."

"She's wealthy, Nathan. Wealth equals power. I don't doubt she could take him anytime she likes and get away with it. Like she said, she holds all the cards. A lifetime of care is nothing compared to what she can give him."

"Do you think she's the type to forcibly remove him?"

"I honestly don't know."

The sorrow haunting her expression tore at him. "Come and sit down, Soph. Let's figure this out together."

Surprisingly, she sat without argument. Deflated. Defeated.

He pushed the plate toward her. "Eat. The sugar will do you good."

Again, she did as he suggested, nibbling on the round cake, seemingly a million miles away.

"Let's review the facts. Surely if we think this through and look at all the angles, we'll come up with a solution. Two heads are better than one, right?"

"I suppose so."

"Your aunt's main concern is that Will isn't getting the guidance she thinks he needs. How can we convince her otherwise?"

"Discipline. You forgot discipline." Her eyes flashed defiantly.

"Okay. Guidance and discipline. Besides from a guardian, namely you, where would a ten-year-old boy get those things?"

"His schoolteacher?"

He nodded. "And the reverend."

"We could ask them to speak with her." She brightened, brushing crumbs from her lap. "They could assure her what a good kid he is."

"Will that be enough?"

"There's Mr. Moore, the mercantile owner. And your father."

All good suggestions. Would their assurances sway Cordelia's opinion?

"I think," he said slowly, finger tracing the indentions in the wood, "that having a permanent male influence in his life would be the best way to reassure her that Will was receiving steady, hands-on supervision."

He didn't mind accepting the responsibility. He and Will already spent a lot of time together. Though it would mean a tighter schedule, he could fit in at least an hour a day with the boy. Or perhaps Will could spend afternoons at his place, helping out around the farm, learning from Nathan, a stand-in father figure.

The more he thought about it, the better it sounded. They'd both benefit. He relaxed against the chair back. At last, a solution.

"You're brilliant!" Sophie suddenly exclaimed, an ecstatic smile chasing away her gloom like sunshine after a rainstorm.

His brows met over his nose. He hadn't shared his conclusions with her. "I am?"

"Why did I ever doubt you?" Shoving upright, she bounded around the table and planted a kiss right on his cheek. "A husband is exactly what I need!"

"A *what?*"

She playfully batted his shoulder. "Don't go acting all humble. You're right, if I marry, she won't have any objections to him staying with me. And even if she did pursue legal action, a judge would be far less likely to take Will away from two loving guardians. Oh, thank you, Nathan. I could kiss you right now!"

He absently rubbed his tingling cheek. "You already did."

"Oh, right." Soft pink color surged. She resumed her pacing, and he could practically see the wheels turning.

Her leap of logic left him reeling. Husband? For Sophie? That wasn't what he'd meant at all. The thought of her as someone's wife…well, he just couldn't fathom it.

"Ah, Sophie—"

"I'm not exactly marriage material, though. The men around here see me as a pal. A buddy, not a potential wife."

Sidetracked, bothered by this negative view of herself, he responded, "The only reason those men don't have romantic inclinations toward you is because of the way you dress. If you were to fix yourself up and maybe wear a dress once in a while, I guarantee they'd have their eyes opened real fast."

She chewed on her lower lip. "You really think so?" she murmured doubtfully.

He could've kicked himself. *You're supposed to be discouraging her from this ridiculous notion of marriage, not stoking the fire.*

"I don't own any dresses, but your cousin Nicole is an excellent seamstress. Maybe she would agree to make some for me in exchange for my services. I could do her chores for a week or maybe she likes sausages?"

"Sophie, wait. I didn't mean—"

"I know!" She halted midstride. "We'll make a list of eligible bachelors. A list of decent, upstanding men whom I wouldn't mind marrying and who might not be averse to marrying me." Scanning the kitchen, she said, "Now where did I stash my pen and paper?" She snapped her fingers. "Right. Upstairs. I'll be right back."

Nathan's tongue stuck to the roof of his mouth. Nonplussed, he watched her disappear up the ladder. How could an innocent suggestion blow up in his face? His plan was so much easier. A mentor for Will. And yet here she was making a list—an actual list—of potential husbands.

Typical Sophie. Seize on an idea and run with it without giving it proper consideration. Woe to the unsuspecting males in this town!

When she sat across from him and began her list, he braced his forearms on the edge of the table and clasped his hands. "You misunderstood me."

His quiet yet forceful words brought her head up, forehead bunched in confusion.

"I wasn't suggesting you marry. I was actually thinking of taking Will under my wing. You know, spend more time with him here and at my place, teaching him things."

"Oh." Her lips puckered. "I thought… My mistake." Her gaze bounced around the room before finally zeroing in on him once more. Her chin came up. "A husband is a good idea, though. Better than your idea. Spending an extra hour or two with Will isn't going to be enough."

"That may be so, but are you certain this is the right choice? This is a life-long commitment you're talking about. Marriage isn't something to be taken lightly."

"Don't look at me like that."

"Like what?"

"Like I'm an irrational child." Hurt flashed in her eyes. "I realize the seriousness of the situation. Otherwise, I wouldn't be considering hitching myself to some random man. But after Granddad… Let's just say I'm willing to do almost anything to keep my family intact."

"I don't want you to do something you'll regret. This is big, Soph. Huge. One of the most important decisions you'll ever make." He didn't want to cause her pain, but he had to make her see reason. "You don't want to end up like your ma, do you?"

She jerked as if slapped. "I will never end up like her. You want to know why?" Slamming her palm flat on the table, she leaned forward, sapphire eyes smoldering. "I'm not afraid to stick up for myself. And for my loved ones. I would never, ever, allow any man to treat me like my pa did her."

Sighing, he nodded. "I believe you." *But will you be happy?*

Frowning, not entirely satisfied, she returned to her list and began to tick off the candidates. A restless, unsettled feeling lodged in his chest. Every man she named was a man he knew, and it was strange to imagine Sophie with any one of them. He felt as if he was perched on the back of a bucking bull, moments away from being tossed to the ground and trampled.

"What about Tom Leighton?"

"My guess is he's not ready," he muttered. "He proposed to Megan last month, and she turned him down, remember?"

She didn't look up. "Right."

"I have to go." He finished off his coffee, unwilling to help her with this wild scheme. While he may have inadvertently pointed her to this conclusion, he couldn't sit there and assist in a husband hunt.

That got her attention. "Now?"

Scooting his chair back, he smashed his hat onto his head. "I have to get out to the cornfields."

"Will you come back this afternoon? I'd feel better if you were here to help me explain this to Cordelia."

"Yeah. Sure."

"I have a good feeling about this plan." She smiled

tentatively. "I know it isn't exactly what you'd envisioned, but I'm confident it will work."

Inexplicably cranky, he edged toward the door, eager for escape. "Right. I hope so."

"I'll be working on the list." She waved a hand over the paper. "Hopefully, I'll have it ready by the time you get back, and you can share your opinion on my choices."

"Fine. Bye."

Seizing the reins, he practically vaulted into the saddle, startling Chance. "Sorry about that, boy," he murmured, patting the horse's flank. "Let's get out of here before I lose my mind."

Looking refreshed and elegant in an ice-blue outfit, Cordelia sat stiffly in a rocking chair, hands curled around a matching reticule in her lap. She glanced from Sophie to Nathan, seated together on the sofa opposite. "You're getting married?" she repeated. "I hadn't realized the two of you were courting."

Nathan stiffened. The grave expression he'd arrived with darkened into something forbidding.

"You misunderstand, Mrs. Jackson. Sophie and I are friends. We don't see each other in a romantic light."

Hearing him voice his feelings in such a final, offhanded manner was like a dagger plunging deep into Sophie's heart. He didn't want her. Would never consider putting his name on her list.

When Cordelia's penetrating gaze rested on Sophie, she schooled her features. No one could know her secret.

"Who, then, are you planning to marry, young lady?"

Nathan answered for her. "There are many single,

eligible men in this town. Sophie is considering her options."

Turning her head, Sophie studied his granitelike profile. Was that a hint of censure in his voice? His silver gaze flashed to hers and then away, but not before she glimpsed…what? Disappointment? In her?

"Let me get this straight." The grooves in Cordelia's forehead deepened. "You aren't currently being courted by anyone. Instead, you're compiling a list of men you'd like to marry?"

"A husband hunt," Nathan muttered with a slight shake of his head.

Sophie attempted to rein in her irritation. Whose side was he on, anyway?

Resisting the urge to toy with her braid, she pressed her hands together and addressed her aunt with what she hoped was calm assurance. "Will and I belong together. Here, in our home. I'm willing to do whatever it takes to make that happen. If that means I must find myself a husband, so be it."

Admiration flickered, but was quickly squelched. "I admit I don't know quite what to make of your scheme." Rising gracefully, crisp skirts rustling against the coffee table, Cordelia crossed to the window and stared out at the sun-washed yard.

Gaudy blue feathers spilling from her hat shivered over her forehead. What was she thinking? Did this place hold any good memories for her? Granddad had told Sophie that her pa, Lester, had taken pleasure in tormenting his younger sister.

"I believe the right male influence would do you both good," she said at last. Pivoting, she clasped her gloved hands at her waist. "However, the pool of potential husbands here must surely be limited to lonely, uneducated farmers or widowers with babies who want you for a substitute mother. In Knoxville, you can have your pick of men who would set you up in high style. Lawyers. Doctors. Business owners. With a good education, Will could go far in life. Why won't you at least consider it?"

Cordelia's frank curiosity, the absence of dictatorial attitude, caught her by surprise. For the first time since her aunt's arrival twenty-four hours ago, Sophie thought beyond her current predicament and wondered what was driving the other woman. Why would she bother with them? Was it simply to exercise her authority or something else altogether?

Twisting slightly in her seat, she met her aunt's steady appraisal. "I do appreciate your willingness to aid us, Aunt, but this is the only home we've ever known. We don't need prestigious schools or clothes or well-to-do friends to make us happy. Simple pleasures are enough for us. This is the life we want."

"I think you're being stubborn," she retorted, staring down her nose. "And foolish."

"I'm being honest."

Nathan unfolded his tall frame, his tanned hands curved at his sides and his turbulent gaze trained on her as he addressed her aunt. "Sophie doesn't have a shallow bone in her body. She knows what's truly important in life, things like family and friendship and a personal relationship with God. I've never met a more hardworking, tenderhearted person. Tobias was very proud of the young woman she's become. I know because he told me shortly before he died."

Sophie's breath caught in her chest, her heart melting like butter in a frying pan at the unexpected praise.

She closed her eyes to ward off tears. *Oh, Granddad. I wish you were here. I wish I could hug you one more time. Tell you I love you.*

Cordelia's boots clicked against the floorboards.

Opening her eyes, Sophie saw the older woman motioning for Nathan to resume his seat. "Sit down, young man. There's no need to get feisty."

Her expression assessing, she studied them in a way that made Sophie uncomfortable. What was going on behind that eaglelike gaze?

When she had their attention once more, Cordelia said, "Have you given any thought to how long it will take to find a suitable husband? You should know I'm not willing to stay here indefinitely. We need a time limit. Three weeks should be plenty."

"Three weeks?" Sophie gaped.

"That's unreasonable." Nathan ran a weary hand down his face.

"I'll give you a month, no more. Though what I'm going to find to fill the time, I've no idea." Cordelia hefted a sigh and rolled her eyes.

"One month." She was expected to find a husband that quickly? Panic roiled through her stomach. What if none of the men on her list agreed to marry her?

"If you haven't managed to snag a husband by then, Sophia Tanner, your brother will be returning to Knoxville with me. Do you understand?"

"Unfortunately, I understand quite clearly."

She understood too well that she no longer had any control over her own life. A week ago, her biggest problems had been convincing Will to wear shoes outdoors and building a new henhouse. Now she was being forced to find a husband—not the husband she'd dared to let herself dream about but someone else altogether.

And while she could take another man's name and pledge to honor him the rest of her life, how in the world was she going to convince her heart to stop loving Nathan?

Chapter Eleven

Nathan didn't normally attend singles' shindigs. Without parental supervision, the girls were bolder than usual—a situation that didn't bother most guys in the slightest—and the games were silly. All too often the losers were expected to pay a forfeit. Something embarrassing such as reciting a poem or singing a solo. Not his style.

He wasn't in the market for a wife, nor was he the type to enjoy a shallow flirtation, so why bother coming? He'd have more fun camped out on his front porch whittling or playing checkers with his pa.

And yet here he was, stationed beside the fireplace in his cousin Megan's parlor sipping stout make-your-eyes-water lemonade and trying to avoid Amberly Catron's flirtatious gaze.

The moment he'd stepped through the door, she'd rushed up and invited him to walk the gardens with her; an invitation he'd declined with as much finesse as he could muster. A romantic, moonlit stroll through isolated gardens with a girl who had obvious designs on him would not be in his best interest, he was certain.

He shifted his stance to glance at Sophie, taking perverse pleasure in the way her lips pursed after a sip of lemonade. It was only fair she suffer along with him. "I can't believe I let you talk me into this."

She leaned in close, bringing with her the fresh, appealing scent that put him in mind of spring meadows in full bloom. "I need your input on my list of choices because you know these men better than I do. I trust your judgment."

Light from the chandelier candles above highlighted the golden streaks in her sleek blond hair. The memory of holding her in his arms resurfaced, reminding him of how wonderful it had felt to hold her. With her glorious hair framing her face, her delicate beauty had stunned him into speechlessness.

"After all—" her brow puckered "—I'll have to live with the man for the rest of my life."

Nathan tore his gaze from her to glare down at his boots. *Forget what happened. She was in need of comfort and you gave her that. You're here to help her choose a husband.*

Firming his resolve, he observed the game participants with her list in mind. Seated in front of a white sheet suspended from the ceiling, a man attempted to guess the identity of each person's shadow as they passed behind it. Landon Greene.

"Take Landon off the list." A hefty dose of charm and wit hid what Nathan knew to be a bullying, mean-spirited heart.

Sophie's curious gaze fell on the arrogant blond. "Why? He's well-liked. Funny. And from all accounts, a hard worker. His family's farm is productive and the animals are well cared for."

Reluctant to go into details, he speared her with a look. "I thought you said you trusted me."

Her brows lifted. "I do, but—"

"I'm here to help you, aren't I? How about Frank Walters?" He indicated the short, nondescript man trying to blend into the wallpaper. Although reserved, he was an intelligent, prudent man. And Nathan was confident he would treat Sophie well. If he was expected to play a part in this mad scheme, he would make certain she chose wisely.

She wrinkled her nose. "I don't know."

"You put him on the list, didn't you?"

Running a finger inside the collar of her forest-green shirt, she hedged, "Now that I think about it, I can't really picture myself with him. He's nice and all, but he's not exactly the type to inspire romantic notions."

Romantic notions? "Since when do you care about that?"

Sophie and romance didn't belong in the same sentence. She wasn't anything like his cousins, who fussed over their hair and clothes and sighed over popular romance heroes. His friend didn't concern herself with such things.

She averted her face to set her unfinished lemonade on a side table. Slipping her hands into her pants' pockets, she observed the room's occupants.

"You know what I mean," she remarked with studied carelessness. "There are some people you can see yourself with in a romantic relationship, while others simply don't appeal to you in that way."

"I suppose."

She angled toward him. "Does Pauline appeal to you in that way?"

The question stumped him, as did the husky note of vulnerability in her voice. "Pauline and I are friends," he grumbled with finality. He was not about to discuss this with her.

"Only friends? You don't have more serious intentions?" Her sapphire orbs glittered with an odd light. "Because as far as I can tell, she's perfect for you."

Why such a statement should irk him, he had no idea. A dull throb set up behind his eyes. "We're here to focus on your love life, not mine."

The gathering erupted into high-pitched whistles and clapping. April emerged from behind the sheet looking like a cat with a bowl of cream. Landon, who must've finally guessed correctly, surged out of his seat and received a fair share of hearty claps on the back.

"What forfeit shall he pay?" someone demanded.

Wearing a smug smile, Landon raised his hands to curtail the suggestions. "Since I'm the one who made the right guess, I should name the forfeit." Holding out his arm, he wiggled his eyebrows. "How about a stroll in the gardens, Miss Littleton?"

"I'd love to." Eyelashes fluttering, she placed her hand on his arm and, together, the pair made their way to the exit amid suggestive laughter.

Nathan scowled. Surely Sophie didn't think Landon romantic?

Sophie tracked Landon and April's progress until they disappeared into the hallway, his blond-haired perfection set off by her dark hair and olive skin. They looked entirely too chummy for her peace of mind. Perhaps Nathan was right to ask—make that demand—that she remove the gentleman's name from her list. There was a self-important air about him, a look in his gorgeous eyes that led her to believe he was very aware of his attributes and how he affected women.

Still, it annoyed her that Nathan refused to explain himself, instead expected her to follow his directions without question.

Spying his identical twin cousins, Jessica and Jane, in the arched doorway, she decided to let it slide for the time being.

Nearly sixteen, the girls were lovely in both appearance and manner, their auburn hair similar to oldest sister Juliana's and blue eyes the same shape and hue as Megan's, the second eldest. Sophie and the girls were somewhat close in age, and the twins had occupied the seats in front of her and Kenny at school. They'd been unfailingly kind to her. Since completing her final term a year ago this past spring, she'd missed visiting with them. Oh, she saw them at church every weekend and occasionally at Nathan's place, but it wasn't the same.

Jessica, the more outgoing and spontaneous of the two, spotted them and waved, her heart-shaped face radiating her excitement. She nudged her sister and nodded in their direction. Jane's reaction was more reserved but no less sincere, her smile widening in genuine pleasure.

"The twins are here," she told Nathan, who was staring into his drink as if it held the answers to all his problems.

His brows lowered. "Aren't they a little young for this sort of thing?"

"Their birthday is in two weeks," she pointed out. "Besides, it appears your aunt Alice approved or they wouldn't have come."

As they made their way across the polished wood floor, their upswept curls shone coppery in the candle-light. Jessica wore a scoop-necked, sea-blue shirtwaist with cap sleeves and dainty silk bows adorning the skirt's hemline. Jane had chosen a more simple look—a holly-green, short-sleeved dress with a single row of pearl buttons on the bodice. The O'Malley girls were always dressed to impress due to middle sister Nicole's talent with a needle and thread.

Sophie became ultra-aware of her appearance, feeling drab and unattractive in her black pants and un-adorned button-down shirt, the unsophisticated style of her hair and her lack of polish. How could she hope to snag any man's attention? Even if she was able to choose an acceptable candidate, what was the likelihood the man in question would be interested? Serious doubts wormed their way into her mind, doubts that she could pull this off, that she could keep Will with her.

She must have made some sort of noise, because Nathan's warm fingers grazed her elbow. "Soph?" His intent gaze probed hers.

"I'm fine." She drummed up a smile for her friends. "Hey, girls, I wasn't expecting to see you here."

Jessica gave her a quick hug. "We convinced Mama to let us come with Nicole." She motioned over her shoulder to their raven-haired sister staring moodily around, elegant in all black and easily the most beautiful girl in attendance. Her sourpuss attitude marred her features, however.

Jane took Sophie's hands in hers, expressive eyes brimming with compassion. "How are you holding up?"

Sophie fought the sorrow that reared up, the empty hole her granddad's passing had created threatening to swallow her whole. "I'm okay." That wasn't the case, of course, but she wasn't about to risk a meltdown here in front of everyone.

Nathan frowned.

She looked away, unable to bear his concern.

"Have you heard from Megan recently?" Sophie's voice was thick as she sought to change the subject. "How are she and Lucian enjoying their wedding trip?"

"We received a letter just the other day," Jane said, smiling gently, "and she wrote that they are enjoying their time in New Orleans so much that they are extending their stay another week."

"I'm glad. It's generous of them to allow us to use their house while they're away."

The stately yellow Victorian had belonged to Lucian Beaumont's late grandfather, Charles Newman, who, along with Megan, had opened it up for the community's use. Every Friday afternoon, Megan hosted story time for the local children. And once a month people met here for poetry night, musical recitals and plays. Fred and Madge Calhoun were in charge of the property until the couple returned home.

"Time for Blind Man's Bluff." Tanner Norton waved a bunch of white strips above his head. "Who's in?"

"I thought only one person played the role of the blind man," Jessica commented.

Sophie rolled her eyes. "Tanner is forever changing up the rules. Says it makes things more interesting."

As he passed out the blindfolds, the twins voiced their interest. "Let's play."

While Sophie didn't normally mind joining in the games—they were harmless fun—tonight she had an agenda. "I don't think so."

Jessica linked her arm through Sophie's. "You have to play! This is our first time at a single's party and we want to have fun."

Oh, what harm could one game do? "All right."

"Wonderful. Tanner, over here!" Extending her hand, Jessica caught his attention and snagged three strips, handing one to her sister and one to Sophie.

Jane looked at Nathan. "You're playing, too, right?"

Leaning against the wall, arms folded across his chest, corded forearms visible beneath the rolled-up sleeves, he surveyed the proceedings with indifference. "No, thanks," he drawled. "You girls go ahead. I'll watch."

"You aren't intimidated by an innocent little game, are you?" Sophie couldn't help prodding him, irritated when he refused to loosen up and try new things.

He turned those intense silver eyes on her and she felt their searing heat to the tips of her toes. Boy, was he in a mood tonight. A mood that had started, if she recalled correctly, the day she'd come up with the marriage idea. What she wouldn't give to get inside that complicated brain of his to see for herself what he was thinking!

"Intimidated? No. Bored out of my mind is more like it."

Tanner stood in the center of the room and made a slow circle. "Everyone split up and put on your blindfolds."

The twins moved away to stand beside the refreshment table before putting theirs on. With a shrug, Sophie tied the cloth around her eyes. Folded into layers, the material completely masked her vision.

"You all know the drill," Tanner said. "When you bump into someone, try to guess their identity. The first one to guess correctly gets to remove their blindfold. The other person must move on and continue playing. The last person left wearing their blindfold is the loser.

"Ready? Hold up. Nathan, I'm the only one who gets to be without a blindfold as I'm the overseer. You either play the game or leave the room."

Quiet filled the space. Then Sophie felt the air stirring as he passed her, his spicy aftershave teasing her nose. His boots thudded on the hardwood floor as he left. Disappointment rattled through her. Why couldn't he at least give it a try? He deserved a little fun now and then. A little laughter.

Tanner gave the signal to start and immediately the quiet gave way to muted laughter. Putting her hands out in front of her, she trudged along so that she wouldn't trip and crash into someone or something.

The first person she encountered was definitely a female, one who smelled of vanilla and cinnamon and whose hair was coarse and straight. But who was it? As she moved around the room, she realized she was at a disadvantage because of her braided hair.

The chuckles and conversation increased in volume as more and more people unmasked. Sophie got the sinking feeling that she was the last one in the game. Then male hands curved around her upper arms and her mind went blank.

Unlike the other guys who'd guessed her identity, this one's touch was confident and sure. She got a sense of his towering height, the muscular bulk of his torso blocking the light and the slow-burning heat his body emitted. Slowly, his hands moved upward, lightly skimming her shoulders until they encountered her neck. The slide of his work-roughened fingers against her

sensitive skin discharged sparks along her nerve endings from shoulders to fingertips. Her ears tingled. Her
stomach flip-flopped.

Only one man's nearness had ever affected her this
way.

She whipped off her mask without a word, forcing
his hands to drop. "I thought you weren't playing," she
accused.

The sight of Nathan in the blindfold, his lean face
partially obscured and the muscle jumping in his square
jaw screaming his discomfiture, squeezed her heart. He
looked miserable. And…vulnerable. He really did hate
to be the center of attention.

Glancing around, she noticed everyone else had their
blindfolds off. They were all staring. At them.

"Uh, Nathan, you can take it off now."

He did. And then he noticed their audience. Dull red
crept up his neck.

Tanner pointed. "Nathan's the loser. What forfeit
shall he pay, folks?"

Nathan stood stone-still, fingers curled into fists,
waiting for the verdict like a man condemned.

Sophie hurt for her friend. She'd been wrong. This
wasn't his idea of fun. She didn't mind the attention;
she was used to it. But Nathan *despised* it. *Please don't
let it be a poem. Or worse, a song.*

"A kiss!"

"Yeah, make him kiss Sophie!"

Horror filled her as Nathan jerked as if slapped. He
kept his gaze glued to the floor, refusing to look at her.

"Good call," Tanner agreed with a laugh. "You heard
them, O'Malley. Get to it."

Finally he lifted his head and looked at her. His eyes

blazing an apology, his mouth pulled into a grimace as he stepped close. He looked ill.

No, no, no. This couldn't be happening. As many times as she'd dreamed about this moment, she'd give anything if she could rewind time and insist on sitting this one out. Nathan didn't want to kiss her. He *dreaded* it.

She stood immobile, afraid to blink, afraid to breathe as he dipped his head. What would it be like? His sculpted, generous mouth neared hers. The crowd faded to the edge of her vision, the furniture faded to black and it was just her and Nathan, breaths mingling, her heartbeat loud in her ears.

At the last second his mouth veered away and landed on her cheek. Warm and fleeting, like the brush of a butterfly's wings. And then gone.

Someone gasped.

"I don't blame him," she heard an unidentified male mutter. "I wouldn't wanna kiss a tomboy like her, either."

You're not gonna cry. You can't. Not here, not now. Not in front of him. He can't know....

She blinked rapidly. Struggled to drag air into her lungs. To remain upright. Humiliation rushed through her like a raging river, crashing over her again and again until she thought she might drown in it. All the taunts, the dismissive glances and the gossip couldn't compare to what Nathan had just done.

Chapter Twelve

What had he done?

The devastation darkening her eyes to storm-tossed blue kicked him in the sternum. He'd embarrassed her. Hurt her. All because he didn't trust his ability to hold himself aloof.

Admit it, you're scared you might actually like *kissing Sophie. What then?*

Amused titters pierced his self-recrimination. Anger pounded at his temples, anger at the insensitive clods who dared laugh and make unkind remarks in her presence and at himself for inciting their reactions in the first place.

So do something about it.

Soaking in Sophie's pallor, the trembling of her lower lip and the moisture clinging to her eyelashes, he made the decision. There was only one way to make this right.

Reaching up, he framed her face with his hands. Hmm. He'd been up close and personal with her countless times—usually in the heat of an argument—but it had never occurred to him that her skin would have the texture of a rose petal.

Her gaze shot to his. Confusion furrowed her forehead. Her bee-stung lips parted in surprise, snagging his attention.

As the reality of what he was about to do sank in, his heart bucked in anticipation.

He tipped his head. Settled his mouth against hers. He felt a shudder course through her, vaguely registering when she gripped his waist for balance. The room spun. He felt dizzy and out of control, yet somehow grounded at the same time, Sophie acting as his magnet, preventing him from flying apart. Her softness, her sweet sigh of surrender awakened unfamiliar emotions. The need to protect her was nothing new, but there was something else here he didn't recognize, something needy and wishful, something he was too much of a coward to analyze.

This is Sophie, remember? Too young and too headstrong. All wrong for you.

With great reluctance, he lifted his head and dropped his hands. For the first time in his life, he was grateful to be the center of attention. Because if not for their audience, he would have taken the embrace to a whole new level and that would have been a mistake. One of massive proportions.

He watched as Sophie touched her fingers to her mouth, wonder and longing mingling on her face. Then hot color surged in her cheeks. "I—I have to go." Pivoting on her heel, she rushed from the room. The front door slammed. Conversation erupted....

Nathan stood rooted to the spot, attempting to process her reaction. The twins appeared in front of him, mirror images of wide-eyed concern.

Jessica touched his arm. "Nathan, what was that? You and Sophie looked—"

"Don't say it," he warned. He didn't want to know. He could pretty well imagine, and it was as much of a shock to him as it must be to those who knew him. Knew *them*.

"She seemed really upset." Jane gave him a steady stare. "Aren't you going to go after her?"

He jerked a nod. "Don't be out too late, okay?"

Ignoring the stares as he passed by, he grabbed his hat from the entrance hallway table and let himself out, all the while scouring his brain for something to say that wouldn't make him sound like an idiot. But what? "I'm sorry I was such a jerk?" or "That kiss knocked me for a loop. Can we try it again?"

He groaned. "You're an adult, O'Malley," he muttered to himself, "how about you act like one instead of a hormonal teen?"

Main Street was deserted at this time of night, the shops were closed and a single light was shining in the jail's window. As he neared the Little Pigeon River, the balmy air stirred with the scent of churning water, the sound as familiar to his ears as his cows bawling or the hush of a scythe cutting through tall grass.

When his boot contacted with the wide wooden bridge spanning the river, a shadowed form poised near the railing turned. Smothered a gasp. A flash of pale hair as she took off divulged her identity.

"Sophie, wait!"

She wasn't running from him, exactly, but going fast enough to spike his heart rate. He caught up to her in the lane. With endless forest on either side, it was impossible to make out her expression. Neither of them had thought to bring a lamp, but then, they knew these parts like the backs of their hands.

"Soph, stop." He seized her wrist. "We need to talk."

"What do you want?" The distress roughening her voice gave him pause.

"Look, I'm sorry about what happened back there. It wasn't my intention to embarrass you." Not being able to see her, to read her body language, frustrated him. She was a formless outline, as insubstantial as the shadows cloaking them.

She jerked out of his grasp. "What did you think would happen after that pity kiss?"

"What?"

"Don't tell me you would've kissed Pauline Johnson on the cheek! Or April Littleton. Or any of those other girls!"

He closed his eyes. "I was trying to be a gentleman."

"No, Nathan. You're forgetting I saw your face right before—" The defeat in her voice had him imagining he could see the fight drain out of her. "You were rushing to my rescue yet again. That kiss was designed to silence the barbs. I'm just sorry doing your perceived duty was so abhorrent to you."

Abhorrent, ha! If she only knew. "Hold on a second." He moved in, his boots bumping hers. "Why does it matter so much *why* I kissed you?"

She inhaled sharply. "Y-you're right, it doesn't matter." Her boots shuffled in the dirt, her braid whacking his chest as she turned to go. "This conversation is over."

"We're not finished here, Soph."

"Oh, yes, we are."

She stalked off. There was nothing he could do to

stop her—short of physically restraining her—and while he was tempted, it would only make her madder and less inclined to talk. It went against the grain to leave things unresolved, but at this point he didn't have a choice. Better to give her a chance to calm down.

Once they'd both regained proper perspective, they could put this event behind them and go back to the way things used to be.

Somehow Sophie summoned the wherewithal to smile and pretend all was right in her world in front of Sam and Mary O'Malley. While she waited for her brother to gather his things, she answered their questions about the party with surprising equanimity. If they noticed her fidgeting or her frequent glances out the window, they didn't let on.

The older couple were dear, special people, including her in their family gatherings as if she were one of them, going out of their way to lend a hand whenever she had a need. Leaving them behind would rip a hole in her heart similar to the one her granddad's passing had carved. It would hurt Will, too.

Which is why you have to put Nathan out of your mind and concentrate on finding yourself a husband.

She managed to hustle Will out of there before Nathan arrived, listening with half an ear during their walk home as he told her about his evening.

Only when absolutely certain he was asleep did she allow her composure to slip. Sinking onto the couch, she curled up on her side, yanked the quilt over her face and let the hot tears of self-recrimination fall.

You are a first-class fool, Sophia Lorraine. He will

never want you for more than a friend. He will never love you.

The memory of his kiss taunted her. The anger he'd clearly felt at being forced into that position had melded into awful resolve, those unusual eyes of his glittering and hard as he bent his head to hers. So his careful handling of her had come as a complete shock. The gentleness in his hands, the soft pressure of his mouth… Sophie's world had gone topsy-turvy and she'd had to grab on to him to keep from falling.

Oh, Father, how am I supposed to marry another man when Nathan possesses my heart?

Helplessness and frustration swamped her. *Why are You allowing all this to happen, God? Why did You take Granddad away? Why aren't You doing something to stop Cordelia? It's in Your power to intervene…. Why don't You?*

She lay there until there were no more tears left to cry, until she was too spent and weak to get up and change into her nightclothes. Lids heavy, head aching, she closed her eyes and had nearly drifted off to sleep when a verse from *Proverbs* she'd memorized as a child came to mind.

Trust in the Lord with all your heart, and lean not on your own understanding; in all your ways acknowledge Him, and He will make your paths straight.

Sophie understood that God was in control, and that He had a plan for her life. Sometimes, though, it was hard to trust. Hard not to try to take matters into her own hands. Hard to wait.

Help me, Father. I don't know what to do or which way to turn.

Slipping into a fitful sleep, she tossed and turned until the wee hours of the morning before finally settling down. Persistent knocking some time later jolted her upright. Shoving her mussed hair out of her eyes, she gasped when she noticed midmorning sunlight streaming through the window.

Will sat calmly at the kitchen table, eating his breakfast.

Throwing off the covers, she demanded, "Why didn't you wake me? And what are you eating?" She'd fixed his breakfast every morning since the day he was born. The boy didn't know how to cook.

Sipping his milk, he held up a cinnamon roll. "Miss Mary sent these home with me last night." His chin rose. "And I'm not a little kid anymore. I can get my own breakfast."

She quickly folded the quilt into a neat square. "But the chores—"

"I already fed the chickens and gathered the eggs. I can help out around here, Sophie. Together, we can keep the farm going."

This from her ten-year-old brother? "I know you're worried—"

Another rap on the door startled her. "Please don't let that be Aunt Cordelia," she muttered. Finding Sophie still abed at this hour and Will fending for himself would underscore Cordelia's concern. Give her ammunition to use if this went to court.

"Just a minute!" she called, smoothing her hair and straightening her wrinkled shirt as best she could before opening the door.

"Nicole?" Nathan's eighteen-year-old cousin rarely darkened her doorstep. Anxiety sharpened her voice. "Is something wrong?"

Assessing violet eyes scanned Sophie from head to toe, bow-shaped mouth pulling into a grimace at the sight of her disheveled state. "There's no emergency, if that's what you mean. I'm here to offer my services."

Still groggy, Sophie was having trouble connecting her thoughts. "I, uh—" She moved aside. "Why don't you come inside? I was about to fix myself some coffee. Would you like some?"

Giving a quick shake of her head, the movement setting her raven ringlets to quivering, Nicole entered the cabin. "No, thanks. I don't drink coffee or tea. It stains your teeth."

"Oh." Come to think of it, Nicole's teeth *were* white enough to blind a person. "How about some milk?"

"I'm not thirsty." Her gaze landing on Will, she nodded uncertainly. "Good morning."

"Mornin', Miss Nicole," he said, wiping his mouth on his sleeve. Hopping up from the table, he told Sophie, "I'm going to muck out the stalls now."

Sophie stopped him with a hand on his shoulder. "What did I tell you about using your napkin? And I'll clean out the stalls."

Shrugging off her hand, he backed away, his features earnest. "I want to help."

She slid a glance at their guest, who was busy inspecting the cabin. Now wasn't the time to have this conversation.

"Okay."

Grinning as if she'd given him a gift, he lifted his faded tan hat off the hook and slipped outside.

Sophie tossed kindling in the firebox and prodded the pile with a short poker, praying her brother wasn't bound for disappointment. He cherished this place as much as she did, and if she couldn't find a way for them to stay…

With the kettle on to boil, she went to join Nicole. "Please, have a seat."

"I can't stay long. I promised Ma I'd make this visit quick. Today is laundry day." She sighed long-sufferingly.

Even dressed in casual clothes—a deep purple paisley skirt and coordinating blouse—she managed to look sophisticated. Maybe it was the elaborate hairstyle; some sort of fancy ponytail with shiny curls cascading down. More likely, it was the innate confidence oozing from her pores. Nicole was a natural beauty, and graceful to boot.

Sophie had been a little in awe of the other girl since childhood. It wasn't that Nicole had ever been hateful or unkind—she hadn't joined in with the other girls' taunts—but she'd never gone out of her way to befriend Sophie, either. Seemed to her, Nicole held herself apart from everyone else.

"So what can I do for you?"

"Actually, it's what *I* can do for *you*. You see, I overheard my cousins talking last night about your predicament. I can help you."

"My predicament?"

Her black brows winged up. "Your plan to snag a husband?"

Sophie's breath left her lungs in a whoosh. How could Nathan do that to her? It wasn't his place to tell anyone. The last thing she wanted was for the whole town to know that poor Sophie Tanner was desperate for a husband.

"That's not something I'd like to get out."

Swinging her reticule from her wrist, she began to walk a circle around Sophie. "Oh, don't worry. My lips are sealed."

Sophie's brows collided. What in the world? "Um, Nicole?"

Her gaze carefully scanning as she completed the circle, she frowned and tut-tutted and sighed. "Let's be frank, shall we? You're going to need a complete over-haul. Luckily for you, I'm gifted in that area. I can sup-ply you with a new wardrobe. Show you how to dress, how to style your hair." Excitement lightened her eyes. "I have a nearly completed dress that I believe will fit you. I just need to take your measurements."

Sophie watched, nonplussed, as Nicole pulled open her reticule and retrieved a cloth tape measure.

"I don't understand. Why would you want to help me? I can't possibly afford to pay you for your labor or the materials. Unless you want me to do chores for you?" Even if she agreed to this, how would she find the time?

Tape measure held aloft, Nicole smiled widely, trans-forming her countenance into something almost... sweet.

"All I want in return is credit for your transforma-tion. Showing up for Sunday morning services together should do the trick, I think. If I'm ever going to achieve my dream of owning a boutique in the city, I'll need more revenue. When people see the new you, my hope is that the dress orders will come pouring in." Tugging

Sophie's braid, she confided, "Besides, I've wanted to get my hands on you for years!"

"But the cost of the materials—"

"You're forgetting I have a wealthy new brother-in-law. One who is very generous to his poor relations."

As Nicole took her measurements and hastily scribbled them on a scrap of paper, all the while chatting about color palettes and accessories and hairstyles, Sophie's mind whirled with the implications. What would she look like when Nicole was finished? What would people think? If she were honest with herself, the only person's opinion that truly mattered was Nathan's, and at this point, she didn't think changing her hair and wearing a skirt would impact him in the slightest.

Chapter Thirteen

Sitting on a hard pew waiting for Reverend Munroe to take his place in the pulpit, Nathan resolved not to think of *the incident* for at least the next twenty-four hours. What had happened at that party had haunted him nearly every minute since. Waking or sleeping, the memory of their embrace refused to leave him be.

Help me focus on the goal here, Lord. To find Sophie a suitable husband and appease her aunt.

Across the aisle, Landon Greene slanted him a smirk; a silent reference to the very thing Nathan was trying to avoid thinking about. Although Landon had been escorting April through the gardens at the time, he'd certainly heard about it. Juicy gossip like that didn't stay contained for very long in this small town.

Beside him, Caleb's uneasiness was showing. Bent forward, elbows resting on his knees, he glared at the knotty pine floorboards as if they were responsible for him being there. He'd surprised them all when he'd arrived at the breakfast table dressed for services. Nathan couldn't recall the last time his younger brother had bothered to come. On the other end of the pew, their ma wore an expression of pure pleasure. Pa just looked anxious.

The rear doors opened and Nathan heard footsteps as late arrivals passed through the alcove and rounded the corner into the high-ceilinged space where the congregation gathered. Then a gasp echoed off the walls, unrest reverberating through the gathering.

Caleb twisted around, then elbowed him in the ribs, his hooded gaze entreating. *You have to see this.*

Nathan complied. At first his mind didn't register what his eyes were seeing. He recognized Nicole, of course, and the smug set of her features. But the lovely, elegant young woman beside her? It took a minute to place her. And when the truth finally penetrated, his jaw hit the floor.

She was… She was… He floundered for a fitting description. *Every man's dream.*

His lungs tightened. His childhood friend, the rumpled and at times downright dowdy tomboy, had transformed into a sweet, beautiful, poised lady. The cute caterpillar into a graceful butterfly.

Sophie was downright stunning. Mouth-drying, eye-popping, toes-curling-in-his-boots stunning.

Gone were the dark colors, the ill-fitting shirts and pants and clunky boots. In their place, a luxurious two-toned creation that hugged her slender frame and showcased her feminine curves, trim waist and the slight flare of her hips. The golden flower-print jacket with high, stiff collar and triangular opening at the throat spilled over her waist in gentle folds, and beneath it peeked a ruffled matte-rose skirt that skimmed the tops of cream-colored kid boots.

Running his gaze back up, he zeroed in on her

honeyed hair, which had been swept to the side and smoothed into a sophisticated bun at the base of her neck, tendrils caressing delicate ears adorned with earbobs—earbobs!—and sleeker-looking cheekbones. Shimmering hair framing her face softened her features, made her sapphire eyes appear even larger, her pink mouth lush and beckoning.

This vision couldn't be his friend. Surely not.

The single men in the crowd wore matching expressions of awe.

Nathan snapped his mouth shut. Did he look as conked-on-the-head as they did?

The logical part of his brain assured him this was a good thing. She wanted a husband, didn't she? She'd worried she wouldn't be able to secure a gentleman's interest, hadn't she? Well, looking like this, all elegant and poised and like a brightly wrapped package, there would be no shortage of eager candidates.

Regardless of his reservations, Sophie was determined to pursue her current path. And there wasn't a doubt in his mind she'd be successful.

Sophie resisted the urge to flee.

Nicole had insisted on arriving right before services to achieve maximum effect. Judging from the seamstress's smug pleasure and the congregation's reaction, they'd achieved it.

Being the singular focus of a crowd this size proved unnerving.

This is what you wanted, though. A chance to change others' perception of you. Remember Nicole's instructions—shoulders back, head up, no reaching for the braid that is no longer there. Exude confidence.

Easier said than done.

Starting down the aisle—Nicole had insisted in that irritating way of hers that Sophie join her and her sisters in the second row—she mentally cataloged the varying expressions.

Many of the young women smiled encouragingly, obviously pleased for her, while others appeared jealous. Jealous. Of *her.* She could hardly fathom it.

Seated between her parents, April Littleton's initial slack-jawed disbelief changed to thin-lipped fuming. Sophie bit the inside of her cheek to stop a satisfied smile from forming. *Pride goes before destruction,* she scolded herself. *A haughty spirit before a fall.*

Kenny Thacker's reaction had her smothering a giggle. He and Preston Williams and all the other guys who viewed her as a buddy gaped as if she'd grown a set of horns. Landon, on the other hand, eyed her with awe-tinged appreciation. And a hefty dose of speculation. He wasn't the only one, either.

She sobered. Did this mean her husband hunt might be successful, after all?

They were nearing the O'Malley sisters' row when her gaze encountered Nathan's. At the curious mix of emotions on his face—wonder, admiration, wariness, regret—she faltered. Why regret?

Nicole linked her arm with Sophie's and unobtrusively guided her forward to sit, unfortunately, directly in front of Nathan and his brother.

It was a long, excruciating service.

Sophie sensed the attention directed toward her from the general congregation, but it was Nathan's gaze burning into her scalp that made her want to squirm. Aware of his every shift in the pew, every scuff of his boots against the floorboards, every huff and sigh, the reverend's words flew in one ear and out the other. *Forgive me, Lord, I simply cannot concentrate today.*

When Reverend Munroe at long last uttered the closing prayer, she'd barely made it into the aisle when the people descended to exclaim over her dress and her hair, much to Nicole's delight. The compliments boosted Sophie's confidence. For the first time in her life, she felt beautiful. Accepted. It was…nice.

Pauline's sincere compliments and quick hug sparked feelings of guilt. The woman was unfailingly kind. She didn't deserve Sophie's jealousy. It wasn't Pauline's fault she represented everything Sophie could never be, everything Nathan admired.

As the ladies dispersed and the men crowded around, she watched the tall blonde smile uncertainly at Nathan and utter a brief greeting before proceeding up the aisle.

He stood slightly apart, his expression stony, clearly uncomfortable and on edge, alert to possible danger. Ever her protector.

Cordelia parted the men with a single, superior arched brow. Her inscrutable demeanor made it difficult to ascertain whether or not she approved of Sophie's new look.

"I have to admit I'm surprised, Sophia. You look the part of the proper young lady. Was this your plan all along? To stun the men into offering for your hand?"

Sophie stiffened. Embarrassment rooted her to the spot.

Beside her, Kenny acted scandalized. "First you've gone and changed your looks, and now you're angling for a husband? I thought you weren't like the other girls. What will I do without my fishing buddy?"

Smirking, Preston bunched his biceps. "At least now we know who's the local arm wrestling champ." The guys chuckled.

"I can still beat you, Preston Williams, dress or no dress," she retorted.

Cordelia frowned at that.

Landon Greene chose that moment to insert himself between Kenny and Preston. Taking Sophie's hand, his lips grazed her knuckles.

Her aunt's frown deepened.

"I had no idea that beneath the tomboy exterior existed a beauty more lovely than the rose, more stunning than the sunset, brighter than the biggest star," he breathed, blue eyes twinkling with mischief, earning good-natured groans and plenty of eye-rolls.

Sophie didn't have a chance to respond, because Nathan was suddenly there, his lean body hovering close. Staking his claim? But no. That was ridiculous.

"I think it's time to leave, gentlemen." His tone brooked no argument. "The lady's dinner is long overdue."

"As is mine," the reverend, who was always the last to leave, chimed in good-naturedly from the back of the church.

Eyes narrowing at Nathan, Landon reluctantly let her go. He dipped his head in her direction. "I'll see you soon, sweet Sophie."

Nathan opened his mouth to speak, but was cut off by the twins, who flanked her on either side. "Come with us to Aunt Mary's. We want to hear all the details."

Sophie found herself swept along by her eager friends, leaving Nathan to wallow in his self-imposed temper.

"Did you see the crowd that descended on Sophie after the service?" Seated on one end of Sam and Mary's sofa, Nicole looked up from the swath of material in her lap, needle hovering midair. "The men hovered like hungry bees. If not for Nathan's interference, I doubt they would've let us leave." Satisfaction brightened her expression.

Beside the massive stone fireplace, chessboard spread out between Nathan and herself, Sophie risked a glance at him. Perched on the chair across from her, elbows on his knees, he pondered his next move. Chess was their game. They were both good…and competitive, which meant the games would sometimes last for hours. As far as who was a better chess player, that hadn't been determined yet. She and Nathan were equally matched.

He must have sensed her regard, for his enigmatic gaze lifted, zeroed in on her. That intense focus heated the surface of her skin, brought every nerve to prickly awareness, on edge and yearning for his touch. What was he thinking?

All the way home, all through dinner, he hadn't uttered a word about her appearance. Not a single one. If she were honest, she'd admit his lack of reaction stung.

"I would say her transformation is a complete success." Nicole practically purred.

"You outdid yourself with that dress, Nicole." Kate lowered her copy of the *New York Times* sent to her by her parents. She smiled at her cousin-in-law. "The detail work is exquisite, the material choice inspired. Sophie, you look as if you stepped off the pages of *Harper's Bazaar.*"

An heiress born and raised in the highest society circles in New York City, Kate knew fashion. Sophie shrugged. "Nicole is very talented."

"True," Kate agreed, "but it is you modeling her creation. You've never looked more beautiful."

"I agree." Josh sat very close to his wife, an arm slung casually around her shoulders. He crossed his legs at the ankles. "What do you think, Nathan?"

Cheeks burning, Sophie couldn't bring herself to look at him, watching instead his large hands, how they clenched and the knuckles went white. "I would say she hasn't changed all that much."

"Excuse me?" Nicole glared at him.

"How can you say that?" Mary, who'd just entered the room and was setting a plate of cookies on the coffee table, sounded personally affronted.

Sophie inwardly cringed. Of course. She'd known, hadn't she, that a new look wouldn't alter the way he viewed her.

Caleb surged up from his crouched position near the fireplace. "Time to get your eyes checked, brother," he muttered on his way out of the room.

"She hasn't changed," Nathan drawled softly in the gathering silence, "because she's always been beautiful, inside and out."

Startled, Sophie's gaze shot to his face. Surely she hadn't heard right? And yet there, in the softening of his mouth, the flicker of a smile, she witnessed appreciation and approval. A giddy sort of joy infused her insides, warming her from the inside out.

Indicating the board, where he had no legal moves left, he said, "Stalemate."

She stared. Very rarely did they call a draw. The game's outcome was clear, however. Neither one of them was a clear winner.

Excusing himself, he left without another word.

"That was downright poetic." Josh winked at Sophie.

"I thought it was sweet." Kate sighed dreamily.

When Mary eyed Sophie with open speculation, she tried not to squirm.

Josh hopped up and assumed the seat his brother had vacated. "Finally, I get a chance to play Sophie."

Smiling gratefully, she replaced the carved wooden pieces. It appeared rescuing females was an O'Malley family trait. The game with Josh didn't last all that long. He didn't play often, so his skills were rusty, and she quickly bested him.

He grinned, long fingers stroking his goatee. "I see I need some more practice if I'm ever going to beat you."

"Thanks for the game, Josh." Standing, she glanced out the windows. Will had been there earlier, romping in the grass with the family's new puppy. "And thanks for the meal, Mary. Will and I need to be getting home."

"Anytime, dear."

Bidding everyone a good afternoon, she went outside. Will was nowhere in sight. After scanning the fields and outbuildings, she decided to check the barn. Sometimes he played in there if kittens were in residence.

Skirts lifted several inches off the ground, she entered the dusky interior and peered down the center aisle. "Will? Are you in here?"

A dark form separated itself from the shadows, feeble light from the entrance falling on a familiar charcoal-gray shirt. "He's not here."

So this is where Nathan had disappeared to. She advanced down the aisle, her pulse picking up speed. This was their first moment alone since that awful row in the lane. "Have you seen him? My aunt is paying us a visit later this afternoon. She expects him to be there."

"No." He met her halfway. Folding his arms across his chest, he studied her with hooded eyes. His short brown hair was rumpled from one too many finger-combings. "Your aunt seemed to approve of your new look."

"Yes, well, I wish she hadn't mentioned the marriage thing."

His dark gaze roaming down the length of her felt like a caress. "How does it feel? Being all gussied up?"

Suppressing a shiver of want, she pressed a hand to the exposed flesh at the base of her neck. "Strange. Stiff. However, unlike the dress Kate lent me for the funeral, this one fits me like a glove. Nicole knows what she's doing. I daresay I'll get used to dressing like this eventually."

"So no more braids?"

She smiled at the teasing hint in his husky voice. "Did I mention she came after me with scissors?"

His arms fell to his sides. "She *cut* your hair?"

Sophie smoothed a light hand over the side-sweep. Of all the changes his cousin had wrought, she liked her hair the best. The moment she'd spied her image in the looking glass, she'd been transported back in time to when her ma had still been alive. With her hair arranged like this, she resembled her.

"She whacked a good six inches off. I don't mind, though." She shrugged. "It's easier to take care of."

"Six inches," he repeated, frowning.

Why was he acting as if it was a crime? As if her personal decisions affected him?

"You'll be happy to know I took your advice." She forced a brightness into her attitude she didn't feel. Side-stepping him, she moved to the stall where his horse, Chance, stood observing them with soft brown eyes.

"Oh, yeah? What advice is that?"

She stroked her fingers along his powerful neck, addressing the animal instead of the man. "I accepted an invitation from Frank Walters. He's taking Will and me on a picnic tomorrow afternoon."

Silence.

Sophie twisted around, wincing as her skirts caught on the wooden slats near her feet. She was going to have to be more careful. More aware of her movements if she didn't want to destroy Nicole's handiwork. "Aren't you going to say something?"

Heaving a sigh, he kneaded his neck with impatient fingers. "I'm not so sure you should've listened to me. Frank's a good man, but he's a bit passive for the likes of you."

"Are you insinuating I'm pushy?" She bristled. She wouldn't mention the outing hadn't been Frank's idea. When they had happened upon him outside the church that morning, Nicole had cunningly maneuvered him into it.

"You're a woman who knows her own mind." He joined her at the stall, his arm brushing her shoulder. His body heat radiated outward, tugging at her. He was too handsome for words; his generous mouth wielding tempting memories. His gaze probed hers. "What you need, Soph, is a strong man. A partner, not a pushover."

Are you volunteering? she almost blurted. Sliding her gaze away, she murmured, "I don't have time to be choosy."

"I don't like this."

"And you think I do?" she challenged.

"Can a man like Frank truly make you happy?"

No. No one except you will ever do.

She buried her fingers in Chance's black mane. "If it weren't for Cordelia's meddling, I wouldn't be contemplating marriage at all. I hate being forced into this, but ·I'll do anything to keep Will with me. That will have to be enough."

"I hope for both your sakes that it is."

Frank Walters was a nice guy. Shy, but nice.

A year older than Nathan, he was six years her senior. And while they'd grown up in the same small town, they hadn't exchanged more than a dozen words. Sharing a meal with him was proving to be an awkward experience.

"This pie is delicious," she told him between bites.

"My mother is an accomplished cook," he said soberly. "I sampled your rhubarb pie before April discarded it. Mother would be happy to teach you how—" He broke off abruptly, looking pained. "I didn't mean... That is, if you wanted her to."

She set her empty plate beside the picnic basket.

"That might be nice." Inwardly, she grimaced. Bonnie Walters wore a perpetual expression of disdain. Nothing seemed to please her. Poor Frank. Perhaps he was searching for a reason to leave the home he shared with her?

Perspiration dampened the hair at her temples. The overhead shade did little to dispel the stifling August heat. Sophie adjusted her full peach skirt to make sure it covered her ankles, still finding it awkward to move and sit like a lady. When Frank had arrived at the cabin, he'd complimented her, saying the pastel hue made her skin luminous. Then his face had burned scarlet. Poor Frank.

He wasn't one of those men who stood out in a crowd. Of average height, he had a pleasant face and wiry build, brown hair that tended to curl if he went too long between haircuts and warm brown eyes. He dressed like every other farmer in Gatlinburg, his clothes neat and pressed.

So he's a decent guy. What will it be like to live with him? To prepare his meals and mend his clothes? To have children with him?

Sophie sucked in a sharp breath. For the first time since she hit upon the marriage idea, it hit her full-force what she was getting herself into. She looked at Frank. *Really* looked at him. At his mouth that would kiss hers, his hands that would hold hers. As his wife, she'd be expected to show him affection.

Sweat beaded her upper lip. The buttermilk pie churned in her stomach. She squeezed her eyes tight and focused on pulling grass-scented air into her nostrils.

Impulsive. Irrational. As usual, she'd seized on the solution to her problem without thinking it through.

She'd been desperate for one. No doubt if Nathan had suggested joining the traveling circus, she would've packed their bags and hit the trail.

I can't do this—

"Watch out!"

A ball bounced precariously close to their log cabin–patterned quilt and the food and drinks spread out across it. Will, face streaked with sweat and grass stains on his pant knees, darted over. "Sorry about that."

Frank retrieved the ball from where it had rolled to a stop and tossed it to her brother. "No problem."

As Will returned to the clover-dusted field rolling into the distance, Sophie reminded herself why she was here. *You* can *do this. You have to. For Will's sake.*

First order of business? Get to know him.

"So, Frank, what do you like to do in your spare time?"

"Not much of that, as you know." He frowned, running his thumbs along his suspenders. "The farm takes up most of my time and energy."

"Yes, but surely there're moments when you're not working," she persisted. "What do you do then?"

He thought for a moment. "Normally at the end of the day, I read the newspaper while Mother knits."

Sounded…boring. Or restful, depending on which way you looked at it. *Look for the positive, Soph.*

"Do you like music?"

At the barn dances held throughout the community during spring and summer months, Frank mingled with the older men. He didn't dance. Sophie didn't, either, and not because she didn't enjoy music. She did. But instead of risking being abandoned on the sidelines—

who'd want to dance with the resident tomboy, anyway?—she insisted she was too self-conscious to dance.

"I learned how to play the banjo as a boy, but Mother doesn't like noise."

Irritation swelled at Bonnie Walters's selfishness. It was Frank's house, too. "Couldn't you practice in the barn?" She smiled her encouragement. "I'm sure the animals wouldn't mind."

Frank looked at her in surprise. "The thought hadn't occurred to me." He scratched his head. "I suppose I could do that. My pa was the one who taught me. He was a fine banjo player." The note of wistfulness in his voice touched a chord deep inside.

He must miss his pa like she missed her ma and granddad.

Roy Walters died many years ago when they were still kids. From what she remembered, he'd been as jolly as his wife was taciturn. Poor Frank. Was there any lightheartedness, any fun, in his life anymore? Or had Bonnie snuffed it all out?

"I have an idea. Why don't you come over for supper one night this week and bring your banjo? You can play for us."

His brows shot up. "You're serious?"

"Yes, of course." His barely suppressed excitement softened her heart to the consistency of warm molasses. Such a simple thing, this request, and yet it brought him to life like never before. "Please say you'll come."

A rare smile brightened his features. "I'd like that very much. Thank you, Sophie."

Suddenly unable to speak, she nodded her reply. The way he was looking at her, as if she personally had a hand in hanging the moon and stars…well, no one had ever looked at her like that before. And it felt…wonderful.

If only Nathan—

No. Sophie resolutely shoved thoughts of him aside. She was going to have to come to terms with the fact that Nathan wouldn't be playing a starring role in her life. Someone else would fill that role. Someone like Frank Walters.

Chapter Fourteen

The following morning Sophie was on her hands and knees in the dirt, tugging weeds from between her pepper plants, when Philip Dennison rode onto her property. Strange. While she considered him a friend, he didn't make a habit of coming 'round.

Standing, she dislodged the dirt from her pants and, wiping the sweat from her brow, strolled to the end of the row. When the red-haired young man dismounted, he tucked his thumbs in his waistband and openly inspected the cabin and surrounding land.

"Mornin', Philip. Want to come inside for some lemonade?"

Finally his gaze got around to her. "No, thanks. I just came by to ask if you and Will wanna have lunch at our place on Sunday."

This was a first. Philip's parents didn't approve of her. They assumed she took after her pa. That she'd inherited his wild streak and one day she'd inevitably follow in his footsteps. "Uh, sure, I suppose we could do that."

"Great." His hazel eyes took in her appearance, and

his lips compressed. "You're planning on wearing a dress, right? I mean, you aren't going to go back to dressing like a boy, are you?"

"I plan on wearing dresses to church—" she jutted her chin "—but that doesn't mean I'm going to get all fancied up just to dig in the dirt."

His face reddened, masking the smattering of freckles on his fair skin. "Don't get mad, Sophie. You know my ma. The only reason she asked was because she thinks you've turned over a new leaf."

"So this was her idea, not yours?"

"Actually, it was Pa's." Twisting his upper body, he again surveyed the outbuildings and fields. "You've done a remarkable job keeping up the farm."

Sophie gritted her teeth as annoyance flared. She was beginning to put two and two together and she didn't like the emerging picture. Still, she'd already accepted.

"Thanks." Jerking a thumb over her shoulder, she said, "I guess I should get back to work. Lots to do."

"I'll leave you to it, then." Tugging on the brim of his hat, he mounted up and waved. "See ya Sunday."

She stood at the edge of her small vegetable garden and watched him ride away, a disturbing thought weaving through her mind. Now that Tobias was gone, how many farmers viewed her land as up for grabs? And how many of them were willing to use her to get it?

"What's got you so distracted you didn't hear me coming?"

At the deep rumble of Nathan's voice near her ear, she yelped. Spun around, a hand to her chest. "You frightened me!"

"Sorry." He kicked up a shoulder, one brow quirked. "What were you thinking about?"

"Philip Dennison stopped by to invite me to Sunday lunch."

The good humor in his eyes evaporated like mist. His expression closed, shutting her out. "Is that so? I guess Nicole worked her magic, huh?"

She jammed her hands on her hips, disguising her hurt with anger. "Why is it so difficult for you to believe a man might be interested in me?"

His mask slipped, exposing sincere contrition. "I didn't mean it that way." Burying his fingers in his choppy hair, he took out his frustration on a stick, kicking it away with his boot. "I wish we could go back to how things used to be. Before this crazy husband-catching scheme."

"I didn't ask for any of this, you know," she snapped. "Perhaps you should take up your objections with Cordelia."

The pounding hooves of an approaching rider deepened his scowl. "What is *he* doing here?"

Pivoting, Sophie recognized the horse first. "Why is Landon paying me a visit?"

"That's what I'd like to know."

Nathan positioned himself in front of her as if to intercept her visitor. What was with him? There weren't too many people in this town he couldn't tolerate, so what had Landon done to get himself on that short list?

Moving to stand beside him, she nudged his shoulder. His sharp-edged gaze slid to her.

"You don't really think I need protection from him, do you?"

"He's not for you, Soph," he said cryptically.

"Why—" But she was interrupted by Landon's cheerful greeting as his boots hit the ground.

"Sweet Sophie. How are you this fine day?" His grin was known to have a devastating effect on the general female population of Gatlinburg. And, she had to admit, the man was a looker. Blond hair, blue eyes, golden skin. Tall and strong as an ox. Charm oozing from his pores.

His gaze, when it flicked to Nathan, didn't alter one way or another. If anything, his grin grew wider. "O'Malley."

"What do you want, Greene?"

Landon's brows lifted. "I came to speak with Sophie, if that's all right with you," he drawled.

Sophie studied the two men. Nathan's dislike radiated off him in waves. Landon, on the other hand, attempted to conceal his. It was there beneath the surface, though.

"What can I do for you?" Reaching for the end of her braid out of habit, her fingers instead met the loose strands of her ponytail.

He tipped the brim of his caramel-colored hat up. "I came to ask if you'd accompany me to the singing this Saturday night."

Nathan's sharp inhale told her exactly what he thought of the invitation. He didn't want her to accept. Except, Landon was on her list. He was an upstanding member of the town, came from a good family who, unlike the Dennisons, treated her with respect. He wasn't known to indulge in alcohol. He was a faithful church attender. And even if he did possess a flirtatious nature, she couldn't afford to say no.

"I'd like that."

His eyes lit up. With triumph? Rubbing his hands together, he nodded. "That's great."

"She can't go with you."

Sophie's jaw dropped. Anger licked along her veins. Swiping her ponytail behind her shoulder, she demanded, "Nathan, what—"

"Have you forgotten you agreed to go with me?" he challenged, his expression warning her to play along.

Of all the high-handed— "Yes, I believe I have. I'm racking my brain, and I simply can't remember you asking me."

Landon spoke up, intruding on their silent battle of wills. "That's a shame. I'd hoped to walk in with you on my arm and make all the other guys jealous."

That diverted her attention. She stared at him, absolutely certain no man had ever entertained a similar notion about her before.

"Since you've disappointed my hopes," he went on in light recrimination, "will you agree to go on a horseback ride with me Sunday afternoon?"

"Yes," she rushed to say before Nathan claimed to have plans with her then, too. "I'm having lunch with the Dennisons, but I'm sure that won't take long. How about we say two o'clock?"

"I'm looking forward to it."

An inexplicable gleam in the blue depths niggled at her, but she attributed it to her imagination. Landon Greene may be a bit of a rogue, but he was in no way dangerous.

When he'd left, she rounded on Nathan. "How dare you interfere!" She threw up her hands. "Have you forgotten that if I don't find a husband, my aunt is going to take Will away from me?" She'd already lost her beloved granddad. She couldn't lose her brother, too. Fear bubbling over, she shoved him, surprise forcing him back a step. "I don't have time for games."

Seizing her hands, he held them flush against his chest, ducking his head down so they were on eye level. Secrets swirled in the silver depths. "This isn't a game. You need to steer clear of him."

Being this close to him, his touch warm and sure, transported Sophie back to the party and the earth-shaking kiss. A kiss he wouldn't be repeating. She steeled herself against the yearnings coursing through her.

"Again the dire warning without explanation? I'm just supposed to trust you, is that it?"

His gaze slipped to her mouth. Snapped back up. "Yes."

"That's funny, because I seriously doubt you'd take my word about anything. You'd demand to know my reasons."

A muscle jerked in his rigid jaw. "You're right, I would. But in this situation, I can't go into details."

"Can't? Or won't?"

He released her then, and she fought a sense of abandonment.

Putting space between them, he rested his hands on lean hips, squinting in the bright sunlight. "You don't have to go with me if you don't want to. Just don't go with him. And please, cancel that ride."

"I'm not going with you on principle." Oh, how it hurt to refuse such an opportunity. *Better a little hurt now than a heaping helping later.*

"Who will you go with then?"

"Who says I have to have an escort? Men will be more apt to approach me if I'm alone, anyway."

"Right." Frowning, he tugged his hat down, casting his features in shadow. "I've got to go."

Not knowing what to say, Sophie watched him leave. It wasn't until he'd disappeared into the forest that she realized she didn't know why he'd come in the first place.

Ascending the stairs of the grand Victorian home Saturday evening, Sophie felt her heart quiver like a frightened rabbit's. She would rather be anywhere else but here, alone and dressed to impress, where everyone would watch and know her purpose. Thanks to her aunt's slip, the news of her quest would be buzzing around town.

In the entryway, she peeked in the oval mirror above the slim mahogany table and smoothed an errant strand to the side. Still wasn't easy to achieve this hairstyle, but she was getting the hang of it.

Guests milled around in the green-and-blue parlor on her left. The program was set to begin in an hour. Sixty minutes to scope out the place, and perhaps engage an eligible gentleman in conversation. She stuck out her tongue at her reflection. Had she really been reduced to this? A desperate female on the prowl?

Navigating the wallpapered hallways to the spacious dining room, she offered a harried-looking Madge Calhoun her assistance.

The plump, gray-headed lady waved her off. "No, child. Help yourself to a glass of ginger water and a cake. Enjoy yourself."

Choosing a pink-tinted glass, she wandered over to the wall of windows and soaked in the beauty of the flower gardens.

"Sweet Sophie." Landon appeared out of nowhere, his footsteps masked by the plush rugs. "You are especially lovely tonight." His blue eyes, warm with appreciation, scanned her outfit.

Sipping the tangy liquid, she returned his smile. "Thank you. So are you." She touched the yellow daisy tucked in his button hole. "That's a nice look."

Waggling his eyebrows, he leaned forward conspiratorially. "Makes me appear more sensitive in the ladies' eyes. Romantic."

"Ah." Well, at least he was honest.

Glancing over his shoulder, he said, "Where is your escort?"

Her smile faltered. "Nathan and I— That is, I told him I would rather come alone."

A peculiar gleam lit his eyes. "That's good news." Cocking his head, he held his arm aloft. "Would you care to accompany me to the gardens?"

It wasn't the best idea. While he was charming and handsome, something about the man set her on edge.

"I don't know—"

At the edge of her vision, she caught movement. Nathan stepped across the threshold, irresistible in a gray-and-white pin-striped shirt and black trousers, rich brown hair shiny in the candlelight. Tan and fit and lean.

But what was he doing here? He didn't attend these functions any more than she did. At least she had a reason. What was his?

Beside her, Landon stiffened. Nathan's slow survey of the room's occupants eventually jarred to a halt with them. Shock followed quickly by annoyance showed on his face. His lips pursed. He was going to come over here. Of course he was.

Feeling weak and susceptible where he was concerned, Sophie seized Landon's hand. "On second thought, I think a stroll is exactly what I need right now."

Surprise flashed. "As you wish, my lady." His satisfied near-sneer didn't bother her as much as it should have.

Hustling her out the door, Landon guided her down the back porch steps and along the winding stone path. Before long, they were deep in the lush gardens, hidden from view of the yellow two-story. Disconcerted and breathless from their hasty retreat, Sophie inhaled the fragrant, slightly sweet scent emitted by the rainbow of pastel blooms. The water fountain trickled in the distance.

That was a close call. Nathan had stayed away for days; an unwelcome reprieve albeit a necessary one. When he'd held her captive the other day, her hands imprisoned against him, his dear face hovering near, she'd been tempted to throw caution to the wind and kiss him, her irritation a minor thing compared to her need for him. The man of her heart.

Sinking onto a wide stone bench beneath a rose arbor, she arranged her skirts and clasped her hands in her lap. The setting sun warmed her skin as she observed two black-and-orange butterflies flitting above the blossoms.

You have to move past this, Sophie.

Her companion sat beside her, his thigh brushing hers; a bit too close for comfort. But there wasn't room on the bench to scoot away. Nathan's insinuations came to the forefront of her mind.

"That night you lost the shadow game, what exactly did you and April do out here?"

He tilted his head back and laughed heartily, the strong column of his throat a golden brown above his black suit coat. His blond hair, so light a color it was difficult to describe, glowed in the waning light. He smelled clean and soapy.

Setting an arm around her shoulders, he said, "Such candor! You are a refreshing female, Sophie Tanner." When he leaned in close as if to kiss her, she pushed hard on his chest and jumped up.

"I asked you to tell me what you did, not show me!"

Tugging on his sleeves, his mouth tightened in displeasure for a fraction of a second, so fast she wasn't sure she'd seen it at all. When he lifted his head, he once again wore a relaxed, unaffected grin. "No need to get riled, sweet Sophie. It was an innocent mistake."

"You and I aren't courting. I don't know about you, but I don't give affection freely."

He unfolded his tall frame. Approached. Quirked an insolent brow. "You kissed Nathan."

She stiffened, unhappy with the reminder. "That was a game." Studying him, she said, "Why don't you and Nathan like each other?"

"That's not an interesting topic. You, on the other hand, intrigue me." He crowded her, touched a finger to her earbob. "Pretty."

Stomach tightening, she backed up a step. "I'm ready to return to the house now."

Tipping his head, he offered her his arm. "As you wish, my lady."

She would not be sitting with Landon Greene tonight. Time to move on to the next available contender.

* * *

Nathan paced the wide porch wrapping around the house, debating whether or not to go after her. Most of the guests were already seated in the parlor, awaiting the recital set to start in fifteen minutes.

He scanned the trees and shrubs and flower beds. Surely Landon wouldn't try anything at such a public event.

Remember the last time you attempted to rescue her? She was fine. Perfectly capable of handling herself.

Still, his lungs deflated with relief when he caught sight of her and her escort emerging from the verdant vista. He studied her expressive face. No fear there. Irritation, maybe.

Goodness, but she was a sight. He couldn't help this stunned reaction every time he saw her looking more like a wealthy socialite than his childhood playmate. Her fitted jacket of aquamarine was trimmed in chocolate brown and caramel, the same hue as her voluminous skirts, and atop her coiled locks perched a petite, round, flower-bedecked straw hat. Stylish and breezily beautiful, she put the radiant blooms spread out around her to shame.

Landon spotted him first. The corners of his eyes tightened, his mouth turned down in dislike. Nathan challenged him with a glare and a silent threat—*hurt Sophie, deal with me.*

She didn't notice his presence until they had reached the top of the stairs. Lashes flaring, color bloomed in her apple cheeks. She surreptitiously edged closer to him and away from Landon. What exactly did that mean?

"I enjoyed our time together." Landon half bowed to her. Ignoring Nathan, he went inside.

"Your aunt sent me to find you," he told her, offering his arm. "I'm to take you to her as soon as possible." Cordelia had phrased it exactly that way, too.

"I'm pretty sure I can find my own way."

"You would cause me to suffer her wrath?" he lightly challenged.

"Oh, all right." Blowing out a breath, she adjusted her jacket hem and fussed with her skirts, smoothed her hair and fumbled with her earbobs. If he didn't know any better, he'd think she was avoiding physical contact with him. That wasn't Sophie's way. It didn't used to be, anyway. Things were changing with breakneck speed. Who knew what was normal anymore?

When she at last tucked her gloved hand in the crook of his elbow, the pressure against his arm was faint, barely detectable, and yet her touch made him feel strong and capable and willing to protect her at all cost.

Was this how Josh felt about Kate? Eager to go to battle for her?

The notion was most unsettling.

Sophie didn't need him to do battle for her. What she couldn't handle on her own, her future husband would take care of.

Holding the door for her, he asked, "How was your outing with Frank?"

"Wonderful." She kept her gaze straight ahead.

"Truly?"

Lifting luminous eyes to him, she adopted an earnest air. "He may be shy, but Frank's a good-hearted man. Decent. Too hardworking, perhaps. He deserves a little fun in his life."

And what of her? What did she deserve?

"I'm certain you can give him that."

She looked surprised, which in turn surprised him. Wasn't she aware of all she had to offer?

He knew then what Sophie deserved. Love. She'd given so much of herself to everyone around her. She'd sacrificed her childhood to care for Will. She'd bestowed her heart and compassion upon Tobias, had poured time, attention and hard labor into the family farm. She deserved to be taken care of, to be pampered, even.

As her friend, it was his duty to make certain the man she chose would treat her accordingly.

Chapter Fifteen

Much to Sophie's dismay, Nathan not only delivered her to her aunt's side, he joined them. Sandwiched between the two of them, she couldn't concentrate on the beautiful music or the words being sung. Could only focus on the keen awareness of his person so close to hers—his strong, tanned hands holding the program listing the evening's performers, neatly clipped fingernails, light blue veins beneath tanned skin, a stray nick on his knuckles. Occasionally, his black-clad knee bumped hers and she didn't mind it at all. That she would be so affected by her lifelong friend and neighbor was beyond fathoming.

Why did she have to feel this way for him? The one man who would never return those feelings?

The program dragged on interminably in her mind, stuck in a mad place between pleasure and pain. Afterward, her attempts at escape were thwarted. Cordelia commanded them to wait on her on the rear porch, giving no reason for her wishes.

"What was your favorite song?" he asked now, his back supported by a white column, his hip nestled against the railing that wrapped around the back of the house. Moonlight washed the gardens in pastel glory, the faint tinkling of the water fountain blending with cicadas' familiar hum. Distant laughter rippled through the night.

The air caressed her skin, teased the hair brushing her nape. "'Rose of Killarney' because of its haunting melody. What about you?"

"My favorite, 'What a Friend We Have in Jesus.'"

His smile burned itself into her consciousness. He didn't smile enough, she thought suddenly. Who would bring fun to Nathan's life? In her opinion, he needed a little shake-up.

"I like that one, too. Mr. Hostettler has a nice voice."

"If you're satisfied with this performance," a commanding voice intruded, "you should hear my church choir. Now there's real talent."

Nathan straightened and Sophie pushed away from the railing as Cordelia strolled into the pale light spilling through the windows, gray-threaded hair piled high and topped with yet another feathered concoction passing as a hat. Adorned in head-to-toe black, she wore her usual expression—mouth pinched in perpetual criticism, astute gaze missing nothing.

"I thought the singers were remarkable." Sophie met her aunt's stare with one of her own. The more time she spent in the older woman's company, the less intimidated she became.

"Hmm." She regarded them with narrowed eyes. "I will concede the cook—Mrs. Calhoun, I believe her name was—did a passable job with the hors d'oeuvres."

"It's Madge Calhoun. She and her husband, Fred, manage the property for Charles Newman's grandson,

Lucian. Surely you remember them, Aunt? They've lived here many years."

Hands clasped behind her back, Cordelia glared imperiously down her nose. "When I left, I did my utmost to forget everything about this town, including the residents."

Sophie glanced at Nathan, whose classic features were arranged in thoughtful consideration. Was he wondering—as she was—what life must have been like for her aunt? Based on her own experience, Sophie could only guess how the townspeople had treated the sister of Lester Tanner.

She touched her aunt's arm. "They must've been very cruel for you to want to do that."

Shock softened Cordelia's features. Then she snapped her mouth shut and reassumed control, sniffing as if such a sentiment was far-fetched. "I don't know what you're talking about, Sophia Tanner."

"It couldn't have been easy," she continued quietly. "Pa wasn't exactly well-liked, was he? I saw how horribly he treated my mother. And—" her heart squeezed with regret "—I also saw how he controlled and manipulated Granddad. If Granddad didn't stand up for Ma, I'm guessing he didn't do that for you, either." She loved Tobias with all her heart, but that didn't mean she was blind to his faults. "Lester must have made your life miserable."

Cordelia blinked fast. In the dim light, Sophie could see tears glistening. Her heart softened. She didn't really know her aunt at all, did she?

Cordelia addressed Nathan. "Would you mind giving us a moment alone?"

"I'll be inside." He shot Sophie a meaningful glance. He'd be nearby in case she needed him. Typical.

When they were alone, her aunt joined her at the railing, all business once again. The faint scent of verbena wafted over, the delicate perfume an unexpected choice for the tough-as-nails lady. "How is your hunt for a husband going?"

A sigh escaped. "Slow."

"You mustn't dillydally, Sophia. You need to use the momentum created by your transformation to snag one before the men's interest wanes."

"This decision will affect the rest of our lives. I won't rush it." Sophie sucked in a calming breath. "Surely you want what's best for us?"

"You don't have to marry at all." Cordelia watched her closely. "You can come and live with me. Will would receive a good education, and you can get involved with the many social organizations available to young women. When you're ready to marry, you can have your pick of suitable men."

Sophie stilled at the note of entreaty in her voice. What had happened to her simply doing her duty? Could it be possible Cordelia *wanted* them there with her? If that were so, why would she be pushing Sophie to marry?

"We're happy here. We don't want to leave."

"In the city, you won't have to toil from dawn to dusk each and every day. We have indoor plumbing. The shops offer all sorts of merchandise. Why, we can get you a whole new wardrobe. My cook was once employed by a ritzy French couple, and she turns out the most delectable dishes you've ever tasted. How can you turn that down?"

"It does sound wonderful," Sophie admitted with a slight smile, "especially the indoor plumbing. But those things aren't important to me. You're right, life here can be difficult and demanding. But this is our home. Our heritage. While we appreciate your offer, this is where we want to be."

Compressing her lips, Cordelia turned her attention to the gardens, illuminated with flickering gas lamps. Hand in hand, a couple slowly wound their way along the stone path, heads close together as they swapped secrets. Her aunt's solitary station in life was impressed upon her then. Cordelia lived alone. Ate the majority of her meals alone. Sophie could picture her in an enormous dining room, seated at the head of a ridiculously long dining table, the chairs all empty. How depressing.

"Do you have a lot of friends, Aunt?" she blurted.

"Of course I do," she retorted sharply, glowering. "Why would you ask such a question?"

"No reason." Prickly, wasn't she?

"Speaking of friends, I'm certain they're becoming concerned over my prolonged absence. In case you haven't noticed, I've put my entire life on hold for you. The clock is ticking, Sophia. You have three weeks remaining. I won't wait a minute longer."

Engaged in a predictable conversation about farming, Nathan excused himself when he spotted Cordelia in the entryway preparing to leave. He beat her hand to the doorknob, earning an imperious look when he held the door for her. And when he followed her outside, she turned before descending the steps.

"You wished to speak with me?" she demanded.

"I'd like to talk to you about Sophie." *Lord, help me*

keep a cool head. "What you're doing to her is wrong and unnecessary. It's unfair to them both."

"I'm not surprised you feel that way. You didn't have to utter a word for me to ascertain your opinion on the subject." She cocked her head, her forceful gaze reminding him of a certain intimidating schoolteacher he'd had as a boy. He held his ground. "Why unnecessary? Surely you admit a farm is too much for a young girl to handle on her own."

"It is." At her satisfied expression, he held up a hand. "But Sophie doesn't have to do it on her own. She's part of the family, and we take care of our own."

"You're very passionate about my niece's well-being. Why don't you marry her if you're so concerned?"

"Sophie and I would make each other miserable, believe me," he scoffed. "We're friends. That's all we'll ever be."

She looked thoughtful. "Are you so sure about that? Sometimes the best marriages start out as friendships."

"It's not going to happen."

"Well, then, I suppose you have two choices. Help her choose wisely or convince her to leave Gatlinburg."

Tipping her head, she bid him good-night. Left him there to stew over her parting advice, neither choice an appealing one. Either way, he would lose his friend.

"I enjoyed our ride, Sophie."

Strolling beside her in the shaded lane, Landon flashed a satisfied smile. He'd removed his hat and hooked it on the saddle horn, unaware the rumpled look lent him a boyish appeal, his short blond hair slightly damp at the temples and sticking up in spots.

Their horses plodding behind them, she said with some surprise, "I did, too."

After those few, awkward moments with him last evening, she'd been slightly apprehensive about spending the afternoon with him. As if to make up for his slipups, he'd turned on the charm, soothing the agitation aroused by her uncomfortable lunch at the Dennisons' home.

Philip was getting scratched off her list. He was nice and all, but she wasn't about to subject herself or Will to his parents' barely concealed dislike.

"Come out to the farm one day this week. Let me show you around for a bit and then you can have supper with us."

Another awkward family meal? Landon's parents were nice people. Perhaps it wouldn't be too bad. Besides, if she was seriously considering him, she'd have to spend time with them. Test the waters.

"Hey." He snagged her hand a little too forcefully, compelling her and her horse to come up short. She opened her mouth to protest, stalling when he lifted a finger and smoothed the line between her brows. "It's not a marriage proposal." He chuckled. "Just a simple dinner invitation. No need to fret over it."

She tugged her hand free and backed up a step. "I accept."

"Good."

"Soph? You all right?"

Spinning on her heel, she realized they were at the turnoff to her cabin. Nathan, a string of fish dangling from the pole balanced on his shoulder, stood watching them with narrowed eyes and a scowl shouting his displeasure.

"Of course she is." Landon stiffened, his good humor slipping away. "Are you insinuating I'm not a gentleman, O'Malley?"

Nathan's gaze never wavered from hers. "Soph?"

What was with these two? "I'm perfectly capable of taking care of myself."

Nathan thought the top of his head was going to blow off.

Her perturbed tone warned him to back off. Fat chance. The instant Landon touched her, fury had licked through his veins like flames in a pile of dry leaves, threatening to burn up every last shred of self-control. If the brute so much as left a finger imprint on her skin—

"Nathan."

Her cool fingers wrapped around his wrist, applying slight pressure. Glancing down, he attempted to blink away the red haze.

"He's leaving," she said, dark gaze shooting daggers.

Retreating horses' hooves finally registered. Sophie was safe for the time being, but men like Landon Greene didn't reveal their true natures in the beginning. No, they bided their time, lowering your guard until you were caught in their web of deception. Nathan knew from experience. He and Landon had been friends once, a long time ago.

Releasing him, she lifted a hand to flip her braid behind her shoulder only to realize there was no braid. She huffed in frustration. "Why are you here?"

"I'm spending time with your brother." He shifted

the pole higher on his shoulder. "Do you have a problem with that?"

"You know I don't."

"Then why the attitude? Oh, wait, I know." He snapped his fingers. "You're irritated because I caught you in a lie."

She gasped. "What lie? I never said I would cancel my ride with him!"

"You let me assume. Same thing."

"That's not true." But her gaze slid sideways and she bit her lip, sure signs she wasn't being entirely forthcoming. He stamped out the urge to shake some sense into her.

"I thought you agreed to trust me on this. Behind the slick smiles, Landon Greene is a brute and a bully. His ultimate goal is to gain control over you."

"Why are you saying this? Are you jealous of him or something?"

A snort of derisive laughter escaped. "You're joking, right?"

"There have to be reasons for your allegations." She jutted her chin. "I'd like to know what they are."

He didn't blame her. What did he expect from the headstrong miss, anyway? To simply take him at his word? That wasn't her nature. His either, truth be told. Still, he couldn't bring himself to talk about the past. Too humiliating.

"I know what he's really like, Sophie. You only see what he wants you to see. He's doing his best to impress you. To gain your trust." When she continued to look at him with disbelief, he gritted his teeth. "If you set everything I've said aside and focus on his behavior toward women, would you agree he's a flirt?"

"I will give you that, yes."

"What do you think he and April were doing in Lucian's garden? Naming constellations?"

Her cheeks pinked. "I said I agreed, didn't I?"

"And you don't have a problem with that?"

Brushing past him, she shot him a look over her shoulder. "He's not married, nor is he in a committed relationship. Being a flirt doesn't make him an adulterer."

Fingers digging into the rough-hewn pole, he strode after her. "I would think after what your pa did that you'd want a man you could trust wholeheartedly. No reservations."

Sophie stopped so suddenly he nearly plowed into her.

"What—"

"Don't do that." She spoke quietly. "I know you don't like Landon, but don't bring Lester into this."

He'd spoken without thinking. Knew how sensitive she was about the subject. "Soph—" He gently squeezed her upper arm. She flinched. Retreated again.

"Wait." Hurrying ahead, he cut her off, disregarding her withering glare. "I'm sorry. I didn't mean to bring up painful memories. What do you say we call a truce for one night?" He summoned a smile. "I've got these fish that need frying and a little friend who's probably wondering where I am."

Shifting her gaze to the forest and the descending dusk, she nodded. "And who's probably hungry, too." With a sigh, she thrust out her hand. "Fine. Truce."

Nathan wrapped his free hand around hers, unable to resist stroking the soft skin with his thumb. "Fine," he rasped, struck by an impossible yearning to ease her closer, to caress her nape, her face.

What would it be like to kiss her without an audience? an irrational voice prompted. *Enough.*

This was nothing but age-old physical attraction. He wasn't blind to the changes in his friend. Of course he would notice and be appreciative. That didn't mean he could give in to it.

With reluctance, he released her. Cleared his throat. "One more thing. You know how you feel about discussing Lester? That's how I feel about divulging my history with Landon. Can you understand that?"

Her brows pulled together, her blue eyes churning with speculation. "Something happened between you two. Something bad."

An understatement. "Yes."

"Okay."

"Okay?" She wasn't going to press him?

Her stomach rumbled, and she grinned. Surprised him by linking her arm with his and tugging. "Will's not the only one who's starving around here. Let's get going."

Lecturing himself all the way, he allowed her to lead him to her cabin.

Will did not attempt to hide his enthusiasm. He whooped and hollered and did a quick jig.

Chuckling, Nathan ruffled the boy's hair. Will was bright, sensitive at times, eager to please. As they crouched side by side at the stream, skinning and gutting the fish, it struck him that Sophie's marriage would change things. He and Will wouldn't have as much time to spend together. Her new husband would take the boy fishing and hunting, teach him the ways of farming.

He frowned. He didn't even know if they'd stick around. Maybe they'd go live on her husband's homestead.

Preoccupied, his knife slipped, slicing deep into his finger. He smothered an oath. Dropping the knife, he jerked his hand back before the blood dripped all over the fish.

"I'll get Sophie!" Will bolted toward the cabin before he could stop him.

Fumbling for the handkerchief in his pocket, he covered the wound and yanked the material taut. He hoped it wasn't deep enough to warrant stitches. Needles were for fabric, not human skin. He shivered.

What's the matter? a voice from the past taunted. *Not tough enough to handle the sight of blood?*

Forehead growing damp, he shoved away the memories. He heard the door slam open, and then Sophie was skidding to a stop in front of him, face white but otherwise calm. Will tripped along behind her.

"What happened?"

"It's nothing. A small cut, is all."

She focused on his hand, held steady against his belly. "Let me see."

As she peeled back the material, he trained his gaze on her hair. No need to risk making himself sick.

"It's still bleeding," she said matter-of-factly, replacing the blood-soaked handkerchief. "You're going to need stitches. Do you want me to do it or would you rather I take you into town to see Doc Owens?"

"Neither."

She pressed a hand against his lower back. "Come on, big guy," she cajoled. "Let's go get this over with.

I'm known for my speed and precision. You won't even have a scar."

When she had him seated at her table, she flitted around the room gathering supplies. He watched her to keep his mind off the throbbing pain and the looming prospect of more.

"It's better if you don't watch," she warned as she gently cleansed the site.

"I wasn't planning on it," he drawled, closing his eyes and homing in on her delicate scent, the whisper of her skirts and the slight pressure of her leg against his thigh as she worked.

When she inserted the needle, a rogue groan escaped. He locked his jaw and held his breath. To her credit, Sophie didn't pause. She worked quickly and efficiently and had him sewed up in a flash.

His finger ached something fierce, but at least the worst part was over. But then he made the mistake of looking at it, the misshapen, angry-looking flesh. Images from long ago rose up to taunt him. And his stomach revolted. Lunging for the door, he made it to the side yard before casting up his accounts.

Walking back inside, he felt shaky and weak. And foolish.

Sophie watched him with large, compassion-filled eyes. "Are you okay?"

Sinking onto the sofa, he grimaced. "You'd think I'd be able to handle a little blood. I am a farmer, after all. For some weird reason, I can handle animal blood a sight better than human."

She brought him a peppermint stick. When she smoothed his hair with a tender hand, Nathan's heart kicked against his ribs. With that simple touch, she was letting him know she cared, that she was worried and hated to see him in pain. Gratitude and longing flooded his chest, confusing him. This wasn't longing for her specifically...was it?

Were Josh and his sister-in-law right? Was it time he settled down, found himself a wife? Someone suitable. Someone like Pauline?

"Everybody has different tolerance levels. Just because you're a tad squeamish doesn't make you weak." Easing down beside him, affection shone brightly in the sapphire depths of her eyes.

He swallowed hard. Battled against a sudden, crazy need to hold her. "I hope I didn't ruin supper."

Cocking her head, she said, "Why don't I make fish stew instead? That might be easier on your stomach. I've already got the potatoes peeled, and it won't take any time at all to chop up an onion and carrot."

"That sounds good." He broke the candy into two sections and popped one in his mouth.

She held up her hands. "I'm not making any promises."

His stomach slowly settling, he chuckled. "As long as you don't try to feed me any pie."

A grin transformed her mouth. "Don't worry, my pie-making days are behind me."

Nathan was amazed at her calm demeanor, her take-charge attitude in the face of calamity and the tenderness in her treatment of him. He'd underestimated her, focused always on the things that drove him crazy instead of her strengths—her nurturing nature, her courage and indomitable strength, her loyalty and capacity for love.

Without thinking, he leaned close and cupped her

jaw. She stilled, her gaze twining with his, sweet breath fanning across his mouth.

"You're going to make some lucky man a fine wife, Sophie Tanner," he murmured, his heart a jumble of confused emotions. Then, because it was all he would allow himself, he pressed his lips to her cheek. "My prayer is that you choose one worthy of you."

Chapter Sixteen

Weddings were the pits. Not only did Nathan have to wear a suit—a three-piece getup that hemmed him in and made his neck stiff—but he also had to sit in said suit for what seemed like hours while the preacher waxed poetic about everlasting love and commitment, the married women crying sentimental tears and single misses plotting how to land a groom of their very own.

For the life of him, he could not imagine himself up there, standing in front of God and the townsfolk, and pledging to honor and cherish his chosen bride. Those rogue thoughts he'd had at Sophie's must have been the result of blood loss.

Today he'd made an exception to his no-wedding rule. Sophie was here somewhere and, despite his warnings, he wasn't convinced she'd stay away from Landon.

Propped against the base of an elm, arms folded and one foot hooked over the other, he scanned the milling crowd. The reception for newlyweds Dan and Louise Kyker was in full swing. Guests chatted together in groups, eating wedding cake and sipping lemonade, the younger couples dancing to lively fiddle music while the older generation reclined on chairs set up on the lawn. Kids darted around, a few trying to sneak second helpings of cake.

April and her friends strolled past. When she spotted him in the shade, she waved, her smile both saucy and provocative. He nodded a response but didn't return her smile, hoping it would deter her. He wasn't in the mood for her games. Thankfully, she moved on.

Surveying the crowd again, he became impatient when he didn't see Sophie. Where was she? He pushed away from the tree. Looked as though he was going to have to join the merriment if he wanted to find her.

"Nathan!"

A small, warm female launched herself against him, arms wrapping tightly around his neck.

"I'm so happy to see you!" she exclaimed, her words muffled.

White-blond curls tickled his chin. He grinned. "Megan."

Aware now that it was his cousin accosting him, he wrapped his arms around her middle and lifted her off the ground. It had been at least six weeks since he'd seen her last. Married in July, she and her new husband had visited her eldest sister, Juliana, in Cades Cove before traveling down to New Orleans to spend time in Lucian's hometown. Relieved she was finally home, safe and sound, he set her down and away from him to get a good look at her.

Aside from the new, stylish clothes and added sparkle in her baby blues, she looked pretty much the same. He tugged on a curl. "How is married life treatin' ya, Goldilocks?"

Glancing over her shoulder at Lucian, who was deep in conversation with Aunt Alice and the twins, she turned back and flashed him a smile that hinted of secrets. "Fantastic. You should really consider trying it out for yourself."

He ran a finger beneath his collar. The late-afternoon heat lingered in the air. "I told you before, I'm not in the market for a wife."

"Someday the right girl will come along and change your mind." Megan sounded confident. She squinted at the dancers. "Am I seeing things? That can't be Sophie Tanner. Does she have a cousin we didn't know about?"

Nathan followed her line of sight to where the musicians played beside the barn. There, standing apart from the dancers, was Sophie—breathtaking in a scoop-necked, two-piece lacy creation of pastel pink, cream and light blue. Frank was right beside her. Nathan had to admit they looked good together, Frank's dark coloring complementing Sophie's fair beauty.

"No cousin. Sophie, uh, underwent a transformation a few weeks back. Your sister is the one responsible."

One pale brow winged up. "Nicole? Why would she—" She tapped her mouth. "Oh. Of course. It all comes back to her determination to get out of town. She's quite put out with me that I didn't take her with us to New Orleans." She studied Frank and Sophie. "While I wouldn't have paired them together, I must admit they make a handsome couple. Perhaps theirs will be the next wedding we attend."

His heart squeezed uncomfortably. "Perhaps."

Her smile faltered. "You don't look happy. Why—" She broke off, squealing as Lucian snuck up behind her and slid his arms around her waist. "You shouldn't sneak up on me," she chided playfully.

Shooting a grin at Nathan, Lucian bent his head and whispered in her ear. Something that made her blush.

Feeling like an intruder, Nathan averted his gaze, automatically seeking out Sophie. The sun's rays shimmered in her upswept hair, the slight breeze teasing stray tendrils that framed her face. She looked as though she really wanted to dance.

"Hi, Nathan." Pauline strolled in his direction, her brother Dex with her.

"Afternoon, O'Malley."

"Dex." He shook the other man's hand. Pauline hung back, her smile a touch uncertain. Nathan nodded and smiled encouragingly. Apparently he'd wrongly attributed her with a practical outlook. Guessing from her manner, she must have construed his prior invitation to mean more than it had. He hated that he'd raised false hopes. "You're looking well, Pauline."

Dumb thing to say, O'Malley.

Her dark eyes sparkled anew. "Would you care to dance?" she asked hopefully.

Sensing Dex's steady stare, Nathan extended his arm. "I'd love to."

Joining the other dancers midsong, he spotted his cousin Jane dancing with Tom Leighton. The barbershop owner appeared to be cajoling her out of a bad mood. Unusual for sweet-tempered Jane. He hoped she kept Tom too busy to notice Megan and Lucian's arrival. Seeing the happy couple would surely be hard on the rejected suitor.

Pauline squeezed his hand, pulling his attention back

to her. "Megan is practically glowing with happiness. Married life suits her."

He smiled. "I wasn't confident in her choice at first, but I've since realized Lucian is the right man for her."

Executing a turn, his gaze connected with Sophie's. The haunting sadness in her eyes socked him in the gut. What could have caused such wrenching emotion? Quickly, she averted her face to address Frank.

His partner followed his line of sight. "I heard about Sophie's husband hunt."

"Who hasn't?" he grunted, still staring at the couple.

"Who do you think she'll end up with?" she persisted.

Shrugging, he looked at her with what he hoped was a bland expression. "That's anybody's guess."

Pauline tilted her head to the side, regarding him with frank appraisal. "Some people think you might volunteer for the job."

"Me?" He accidentally stomped on her toe. "Isn't it obvious the two of us wouldn't suit? Besides, I'm not interested in marriage right now. From what I've seen, falling in love is a painful, angst-ridden process that doesn't always end well."

"It doesn't have to be that way." She stared at him in consternation.

"Even so, I'm not interested," he said firmly. "Not now. Maybe not ever."

The music died away and he couldn't be more grateful. She'd bristled, her manner suggesting he'd announced his disgust for small children and pets.

Preston came to his rescue, tapping his shoulder and

inviting her to dance the next song, oblivious to her clear upset.

Clearing the group, he saw that his path would take him past Sophie and Frank. Recalling her earlier expression of longing, he couldn't deny her a chance to dance at least once this day.

"Would you like to dance?"

Her eyes widened at his abrupt request. With a quick glance at Frank, she nodded and accepted his outstretched hand. The music segued into a slow, pensive number and she faltered. "I'm not good at this."

Settling an arm around her waist, he pulled her as close as he dared. "Let me lead you."

Lost in her trusting eyes, reveling in the feel of her small hand upon his shoulder, Nathan guided them both in a simple dance. Their first. For the entirety of the song, he would forget about the rumors going 'round about them, forget about everything except chasing away her sadness.

"How is it that you and I have never danced together?"

"I—I don't know." Her fingers tightened on his sleeve. She sounded slightly breathless. From the dance? Or something else entirely?

"Well—" he grinned as he maneuvered her in a tight circle that made her lips part in surprise "—you're a great partner."

"Thank you, Nathan," she said quietly, looking as though he'd handed her the moon with that one compliment.

That's because she's used to lectures from you, not praise.

He frowned.

"Is something wrong?" she asked. "Did I crush your toes?"

He pulled her closer, a move that earned him a raised eyebrow from the older gentleman sweeping past with his wife. Ignoring him, Nathan gazed down at her. "No. You did nothing wrong. My mind wandered, is all."

"How's your finger?"

He unconsciously flexed it, the bandage straining. "Still a little sore but healing nicely thanks to you."

She smiled. "I'm glad I could help."

For the remainder of the song, he focused on the moment, the surprisingly pleasant way she fit against him. When it ended, he found himself foolishly wishing for more time. "Can I get you a glass of lemonade?"

"I'd like that."

But when they separated themselves from the dancers, Frank was there with two drinks in his hand. He offered one to Sophie. With an apologetic look at Nathan, she accepted it and thanked her date. Her *date*. Right. The two of them were here together, which meant it was his cue to get lost.

At least he could boast success in one area—she looked happier than she had a few minutes ago.

"Well, I guess I'll see you both later. Thanks for the dance, Soph."

And he walked away, leaving her to her hunt.

Sophie longed to call him back. To dance with him again. Held in Nathan's strong, warm embrace, she'd felt as though she were floating in the clouds, a peaceful place far removed from her tumultuous world. His molten silver gaze had thrilled her. Made her believe, for the space of a song, that she was special to him. More than a friend.

But that was wishful thinking. And so far from reality as to be laughable.

Willing her gaze away from his retreating back, Sophie turned to Frank. "I don't see your mother anywhere. Did she stay home?"

"She's sitting over there."

Sophie glimpsed Bonnie's short brown curls. Craning her neck, she was able to get a fuller view of the woman seated alone. "She doesn't look like she's having much fun."

Frank sighed. "Ma doesn't like crowds."

"Or music."

He gave a wry smile. "Or much of anything, to be honest. She's the exact opposite of my pa. I'm not sure how they ever ended up together."

She sipped the tart drink. "She's missing out, especially with regard to your playing. Will and I enjoyed it immensely."

He flushed, clearly unused to praise. "I had a good time the other night."

"So did I," she said, meaning it. Frank was quickly becoming a friend.

She nodded her head to indicate the musicians. "You should be up there playing."

"I don't think so."

When she laid a hand on his arm, his dark brows lifted an inch. "Don't let your ma hold you back, Frank. Do what makes you happy. Life is short."

Her granddad's face flashed in her mind, and she blinked back moisture. She missed him every moment of every day. Sometimes she'd curl up on his bed simply to try to feel closer to him, dreading the day his familiar scent faded from his pillow.

"I think I'll go and get a piece of cake."

"I can get it for you—" Frank offered.

"That's all right." She waved him off. "I'll be back in a moment."

Heart hurting, Sophie weaved through the throng to the refreshment table. This wasn't the time or place to give in to her grief. Not truly hungry, she chose a plate with the smallest piece, not noticing the female trio standing nearby.

"Aw, isn't it sweet, girls?" April drawled. "Sophie's trying to imitate a lady."

She bit the inside of her cheek to keep from retorting.

"I—I think you look beautiful, Sophie," Lila offered softly.

Turning to face them, she managed a tight smile for the younger girl. "Thanks, Lila."

April rolled her eyes. "Beautiful? She looks like a little girl trying to pull off her mother's clothing. Oh, wait. Your ma isn't around anymore. Neither is your low-life pa."

Lila gasped. "April!"

Her sister, Norma Jean, looked uncomfortable, her gaze volleying between them.

Sophie's temper flared. Setting her plate down, she turned to leave before things got ugly.

But April wasn't finished. "My ma says your brother will turn out exactly like Lester—a lying, cheating, amoral philanderer."

"Leave my brother out of this," she said through clenched teeth, fingers tightening on the glass in her hand. "Say all you like about me. I'm a big girl. I can handle it. But Will hasn't done a thing to deserve your insults. He's innocent."

"I can say whatever I like. Don't think that because you've put on a dress and changed your hair and turned all the men's heads that you're better than me. Inside, you're still a dumb, dirty hick," she jeered. "And your brother is Tanner filth."

Cold fury swept through Sophie, too fast to stop her reaction. Lifting her glass, she dumped the contents over April's head.

The dark-headed girl sputtered and wailed.

Sophie was only vaguely aware of the gathering circle of spectators, her sole focus on shutting April up.

"How dare you!" April raged. Her hand shot out and grabbed a glass, then tossed the liquid on Sophie's bodice.

The sticky wetness seeped through the material. Oooh! Grabbing a fistful of cake, she smashed it in April's snooty face. "Now that's an improvement," she murmured.

Sophie's satisfaction was short-lived. A hand clamped down on her arm. "That's quite enough."

Glancing up into Nathan's stern face, her stomach plummeted. Her anger evaporated. Humiliation burned in her cheeks.

He ushered her away from the murmuring crowd, waiting until they were hidden behind a copse of trees to drop her arm as if it burned him. "How could you, Sophie?"

The disappointment in his eyes, which only moments ago had been friendly and full of caring, made her want to disappear. He wore a path in the grass, frustration oozing from his stiff frame.

"I'm sorry."

He stopped short and tossed her a look of exasperation. "It's not me you should be apologizing to. Did you see Louise's face? This is her wedding day, possibly the biggest day of her life, and you made a mockery of it."

She bit her lip, willing herself to hold it together until he'd gone. "You're right," she rasped. "I'll get cleaned up and apologize."

"I think you've done enough for one day," he said without emotion, unwilling at that point to even look at her.

Her shoulders drooped. He was right. She'd acted like a child, causing a scene at such an important event. She deserved his censure.

"I'll just go, then."

"Soph?"

"Yes?"

Emotion burned in his eyes. "Promise me you'll try and curb your impulsive streak. After you're married, I won't be around to bail you out of trouble. To be honest, that worries me."

"After I'm married, I won't be your responsibility anymore," she choked out, then spun and fled, hot tears dripping down her cheeks.

A vortex of emotions swirling out of control in his chest, Nathan stalked to Josh's side. He felt like punching something. Beside the table, Georgette Littleton attempted to console her daughter as she wiped frosting from her forehead. People cast curious glances his way, as if he could explain what had happened.

"Is it time to leave yet?" he growled, silently vowing to make his excuses the next time a wedding invitation arrived.

Concern wreathed Josh's face. "You gave her a hard time, didn't you?"

Guilt penetrated his ire and pricked his conscience. "She deserved it."

"Are you sure about that?"

"What did you expect me to do?" he snapped. "Applaud her creativity? 'Gee, Sophie, the cake was a nice touch. Good aim.'"

"You aren't her judge and jury, Nathan." His older brother's piercing glower could still make him squirm even after all these years. "I made that same mistake with Kate and almost lost her. You know, you two have been at daggers drawn ever since we were kids. I don't think Sophie instigated it, either. She was merely reacting to your condescending behavior. You're the only one who had a problem with her. Have you ever stopped to wonder why that is?"

"I don't have to wonder," he snapped, beginning to feel like a parrot. "Sophie and I are as different as night and day, that's why."

Josh cocked a sardonic brow. "You have love of God and family in common. You're both hard workers. Both love the outdoors."

"So what? There are a lot of people with those same values. Doesn't really make things easier between us." When he made to leave, his brother clamped a hand on his shoulder.

"I heard the entire exchange. April said some rather cruel things about Lester and Will."

His gaze locked with Josh's. The grim truth in the blue depths soured his stomach. When it came to her little brother, Sophie was as protective as a momma bear with her cub, a trait he'd always admired.

With a frustrated groan, he dragged a hand down his face. "I've been a real idiot, haven't I?"

Josh winked. "Nothing a little groveling won't cure."

Chapter Seventeen

Nathan hated that he'd jumped to conclusions. Hated that he'd hurt her.

You're not her judge and jury, Nathan. Josh's statement continued to cut at him. His brother was right. Who did he think he was? And why had he erected barriers between them all those years ago? Continually searched for reasons to push her away?

Too much of a coward to delve too deeply for answers to those questions, relief swept through him when he entered the meadow near her cabin and saw her boots dangling from her favorite tree.

When a stick snapped beneath his boot, she didn't turn her head to look at him. She sat very still, spine straight and hands braced against the thick branch supporting her, floral-print skirts billowed around her with a hint of ruffled pantaloons beneath the hem.

He halted at the tree base. "I need to talk to you. Will you come down?"

"No."

"Please?"

"I can't," she breathed. "I'm stuck."

Huh? "What do you mean?"

"My hair's caught in the branches," she confessed, frowning. "I wasn't paying attention and sat farther out than I normally do."

Shrugging out of his suit jacket, he draped it over a low-lying limb. "I'm coming up."

She was quiet as he climbed and, maneuvering himself onto the branch, scooted close, her frothy skirts overlapping his black trousers. "Good thing this is sturdy." He patted the rough wood that barely gave beneath his added weight.

"I'm glad you came," she said somberly, "otherwise, I might've been here awhile. I've tried to untangle it but ended up making it worse."

At the sight of the tear tracks on her cheeks, the dewy moisture clinging to her eyelashes, he cringed. He was an ogre. Heaving a sigh, he leaned slightly back to inspect the problem. There were a number of branches snagged in the hair loops and pink ribbons.

"It doesn't look bad. I'll be as gentle as I can."

She nodded, then winced.

"Careful, now." Angling closer, he worked to disengage the ribbons first, then her hair, which was like fine silk whispering through his fingertips. Being this near to her, inhaling her scent and registering the changes in her breathing, heightened his senses. Awareness turned his blood to sludge and his thoughts had trouble connecting. He risked a glance at her profile. Where her cheeks had been colorless before, they were now flushed a soft pink. Her pulse beat frantically in the dip of her throat.

Focus, O'Malley.

Fingers fumbling, he somehow managed to free her. "There." His voice croaked. "All finished."

Sophie lifted a hand to her hair, grateful to be free. "Thank you."

She started when Nathan laid his palm gently against her cheek, his thumb brushing the wetness away. Remorse darkened his eyes.

"I'm sorry I scolded you," he whispered. "I'm a terrible friend. Please forgive me?"

Leaning into his hand, she whispered back, "You were right to lecture me."

His brows pulled together. "I should've asked what happened before reading you the riot act. I was wrong."

"I should've kept my temper in check."

His expression turned fiercely tender. "You have a right to defend yourself and your family. I would've done the same in your situation."

Obviously he'd found out what April had said. "I can't see you dumping lemonade on anyone."

Lifting a shoulder, his mouth softened. "Maybe not. I can think of a few people who deserve cake in the face, though."

"You wouldn't do any of those things. You have heaps more self-control than I have."

His hand slipped to her nape, a warm, wonderful weight, the work-roughened skin sending delightful shivers along her shoulders. Her scalp tingled.

His face hovered near hers, their noses nearly touching. "I've given you a hard time all these years, not once telling you how much I actually like you." His husky drawl enveloped her, cutting off the birds and squirrels, buzzing insects and trickling water. All that existed was this man. "You possess many fine qualities, Soph. I admire your fire and determination. Your courage. The way you put others' needs before your own." His beautiful eyes shimmered, inviting her in for the first time.

Sophie's heart whirled and dipped in a dizzying dance. "You do? L-like me, I mean?"

"I do." His gaze dropped to her mouth. "Very much."

He was going to kiss her. Not because of some silly game. Because he wanted to.

His fingers tightened a fraction. *"Soph."*

Dipping his head, his lips brushed hers, gentle and warm and soft. Exploring. Caressing.

Feeling bold, Sophie delved a hand into his hair and poured all her pent-up emotions into her response. Surely he could sense the depth of her feelings for him!

When he framed her face with his other hand, together their balance shifted and Sophie experienced a falling sensation. Nathan broke off their kiss and, chuckling low, grasped her waist with one hand and an overhead branch with the other.

His lazy smile made her heart sing. "I guess I forgot where we were there for a minute."

"Me, too," she said, suddenly shy. What did this mean?

"Sophie?"

At the sound of Will's voice, Nathan's gaze shifted to the ground and his expression shuttered closed. There, a few steps behind her brother, was Josh, watching them with keen interest. And Frank.

She'd forgotten all about him! Had he witnessed their embrace?

No matter what, you could never, ever, forget Nathan.

"I'll go first," Nathan said stiffly, "then I'll help you down."

Her joy deflated, she accepted his help. Was he regretting his actions? Once on the ground, she attempted to smooth her disheveled coiffure.

"Why did you leave early, Sophie?" Will asked, brow crinkled. "Frank was looking all over for you."

Dare she hope her brother hadn't heard of her lapse in judgment and, more importantly, the slurs April had cast on their family? "I, uh, needed some time to myself."

"I was worried." Frank approached, shooting a curious glance at a frowning Nathan, who didn't budge from her side. "I saw what happened with April."

His utter lack of condemnation didn't surprise her. He'd inherited his generous spirit from his father.

"I apologize for abandoning you."

"What matters is that you're all right."

Sophie couldn't think of a single thing to say. Oh, what an awkward coil this was! Frank was utterly clueless about what had just transpired between her and Nathan. And Nathan—what must he be thinking? She couldn't bring herself to look at him.

"Thank you for bringing him home," she finally managed to say. "You, too, Josh."

"No problem." When his lips twitched in amusement, indicating he was aware of her predicament, her cheeks flamed in mortification. This was worse than any food fight.

Hands deep in his pockets, Will rubbed at the ground with his shoe. "I told Josh I'm old enough to see myself home, but he insisted."

Josh laughed. Sophie grimaced. "He did that as a favor to me. Please use your manners and thank him."

"Thank you," he murmured. "Can I go change now?"

"Yes, you may. And don't forget to hang your clothes up," she called after him.

He didn't look back, just waved a hand over his head.

Risking a glance at Nathan, she caught him shaking his head at his brother, who was wearing a knowing smirk. What was that all about?

"I've got to get back to Kate," Josh told her. "Are you coming, Nathan?"

Please stay, she silently pleaded. *Stay and explain what that kiss meant to you. Tell me I can call off this ridiculous scheme because* you *want to marry me.*

But that wasn't possible with her date looking on, was it?

"Yeah, I'm coming." Looking grim, he retrieved his suit jacket and slung it over his shoulder. When he'd joined his brother and the duo turned to leave, she raised a hand.

"Nathan, wait."

He halted and looked over his shoulder at her, grim and closed off.

"Frank, would you mind waiting for me at the cabin?"

"Sure."

Josh tugged on his hat brim. "See you later, Sophie."

"I'll catch up with you in a minute," Nathan called after him, facing her with trepidation.

That didn't bode well.

Summoning her courage, she went to him, stared deep into the silver recesses of his eyes and came away frustrated by the lack of answers. "What just happened here?"

"I lost my head," he said woodenly. "I apologize."

An apology wasn't going to cut it. "This wasn't a

forfeit," she told him. "There was no one around to see. Why'd you do it?"

Nostrils flaring, he buried his fingers in his hair. "What are you angling for? A proposal? It was just a kiss, Sophie. It meant nothing."

She fell back a step. Nothing? "That didn't feel like nothing." Not to her. To her, it had meant *everything*.

"Look, you're all grown up now, and you're—" he waved a hand up and down "—you're wearing dresses and fixing your hair differently. It was bound to happen sooner or later. Attraction. That's all this is. Plain and simple attraction. Now that we've got it out of our systems, things can go back to normal."

"Attraction." She nodded, her throat knotting with unshed tears. "Sounds reasonable."

Only, what she felt for him was far from reasonable. And it wasn't simple at all.

"Yeah, well…" He angled his thumb over his shoulder. "I should go. Frank is waiting for you."

"I don't want to keep him waiting." Her voice sounded completely calm. Surprising, considering her insides were quivering with suppressed emotion.

This is it, Sophia Lorraine. It's time to give up this childhood dream. Time to move past your feelings and plan for a different future. One without Nathan O'Malley. Because loving him will get you nothing but heartache.

Following the Sunday meal, Nathan escaped to his sanctuary. Normally he enjoyed the conversation and camaraderie of his extended family, but not today. Not after yesterday's fight with Sophie. That kiss. And their less-than-ideal parting.

He was a total wreck. He'd lashed out at her in anger. Only, she wasn't the one he was mad at. He was angry at himself, for being weak and careless, for acting on impulse—the very thing he disliked in her.

Pulling on a pair of deerskin gloves to protect his injured finger, he found the pitchfork in the corner and began the tedious task of ridding the straw of rubbish. The physical exertion did little to clear his mind.

"Here you are." Caleb waltzed in through the double doors standing ajar, the habitual scowl curling his mouth. "We need to talk."

Nathan forked a pile of straw. "I'm busy."

Resting an arm on the stall's edge, Caleb challenged him with a glare. "Too busy to tell me what Sophie's doing with Landon Greene?"

He straightened, hand tightening on the handle. "Did you see them together?"

"After services. As soon as Will left with Cordelia, Sophie and Landon rode off."

"Maybe she was going to the Greenes' for dinner." Icy dread pulsed through his veins.

Caleb shook his head. "Uh-uh. They were headed in the opposite direction." Brown eyes impaled his. "Why didn't you warn her?"

"I did," he snapped, despising the sense of helplessness coursing through him. If Sophie was in trouble, there'd be nothing he could do about it. "She wouldn't listen."

Caleb pushed off from the stall, jammed his hands into his pockets. "Have you told her everything?"

"No."

"I think you should."

"You're right." Propping the pitchfork against the wall, he snagged his hat. "I just hope it's not too late."

Striding into the aisle, he fetched Chance's saddle.

"Where are you going?"

"To her place to wait. If she isn't back by night-fall, I'll head over to the Greenes'. Find out where they went."

"Want me to come with you?"

Smoothing the blanket over his horse's back, Nathan tossed him a grateful look. "Thanks for the offer, but I've got to handle this on my own."

"Sophie's family." Caleb stroked Chance's neck while Nathan worked to saddle him. "If he lays so much as a finger on her, he'll have the wrath of the O'Malley clan raining down on him."

Vaulting into the saddle, Nathan smiled grimly down at his younger brother. "I'm glad you're here."

His resulting expression warned him it wasn't for long. As soon as Nathan said the word, Caleb would be gone again.

"Be safe" was his response.

As Chance picked his way along the familiar forest trail toward the Tanner homestead, Nathan prayed. For Sophie's safety. For his peace of mind. And for forgiveness. For if not for his pride, she wouldn't be courting the enemy right about now.

"I could never tire of this view," Sophie sighed. A break in the trees allowed them a glimpse of mountain ridges stretching into the far distance. The air was fresh and slightly cooler at this elevation. Behind them, their horses grazed. "It's stunning. A true testament to God's glory."

Landon, shoulder pressed against hers, turned his head to regard her with blatant appreciation. "I could never tire of it, either," he said softly, clearly referring to her, not the mountains.

She chose to ignore the insinuation. Up until this point, Landon had been his entertaining self, and the afternoon had passed rather pleasantly. When he'd approached her after church and asked if she'd like to accompany him on another picnic, she'd hesitated. Nathan didn't like the man. Nor did he trust him. Sophie's curiosity had prompted her to agree. She was dying to learn what had transpired between the two men.

"Tell me something…" He ran a finger down her cheek. "Where is my name on your list? I hope I'm near the top."

Sophie's jaw dropped. "How do you know about that?"

"Gossip is kind of like poison ivy. One slipup and it spreads without you even realizing it. Until the itchin' sets in, that is." His grin seemed a touch mean-spirited.

Head spinning with the revelation, she smacked at a mosquito humming near her neck. "Who was it? Nicole?" she demanded with rising irritation. The younger girl had vowed to keep her secret, and Sophie had trusted her. Wasn't it enough that folks knew about her need to marry without them knowing about her suitable husband list?

"Patrick heard it from his sister, Carrie, who helps out the Lamberts. She overheard your aunt telling Mrs. Lambert."

Aunt Cordelia! "I don't understand. Why would she do that?"

"That's beside the point." He waved away her concerns with an arrogant smirk. "Let's talk about the list some more. So, am I number one?"

"I'm not discussing this with you."

"Give me a name, then. A man needs to know who he's up against."

"Nathan."

Beneath his hat brim, his face hardened, eyes glittering with dislike. She'd tossed out the name to irk him, and perhaps to goad him into revealing something of the past.

"Is that right?" Velvet voice cloaked in menace, he edged closer, his hulking body looming over her. "I've been wondering something. What is the exact nature of your and O'Malley's relationship?"

Though adrenaline raced through her body, priming her for flight, Sophie held her ground. "What do you mean?"

"I know you two are friends, but it seems to me he's awfully protective of you. Some would even say possessive." His gaze raked her with awful suggestion. "Are you lovers?"

She gaped at him. "How dare you! Nathan and I have done nothing to be ashamed of."

His large hands snapped around her rib cage. "You've gone beyond the bounds of friendship, though. I can see the truth in your eyes."

Their complete and utter isolation hit her then, stole the air from her lungs. Maybe this outing hadn't been her smartest move, after all.

Alarmed now, she braced her hands on his biceps. "He warned me about you."

Thrown off guard, one blond brow quirked. "Did he, now? What did he accuse me of?"

"Nothing specific." She met his gaze unflinchingly, unwilling to let him see her fear. "I inferred that you used to be friends. Nathan isn't a vindictive person, nor is he so shallow as to sever a friendship over a minor dispute. Whatever you did must've been pretty bad."

"We were never friends. I tolerated him." His lip curled. "The reason he hates me is because I know he's a fraud. A weak excuse of a man."

Outrage seared her insides. "You're the fraud, Landon. You pretend to be the perfect gentleman when deep down you're really a conniving snake." Pushing against him with all her might, she demanded, "Let me go."

He was bigger and stronger than her, and her attempt to break free failed miserably.

Landon sighed long-sufferingly. "There's no one around to hear if you protest, *sweet* Sophie. Don't fret, all I want is a kiss. You need to see for yourself what a real man is like."

His mouth came down hard on hers. Sophie froze. He was really doing this. *Forcing* himself on her. Taking her lack of resistance as compliance, Landon crushed her to his chest and tilted her head back at an awkward angle.

Defiance bubbled up, bursting forth in a cry of protest. Her heel came down hard on his toe. He ripped his mouth away. Muttered a stinging oath. Her knee contacted high on his inner thigh, and his hold slackened.

But before she could scramble out of his reach, his fingers fisted on her dress. She reared back. The sound of material ripping frightened her as nothing ever had before. Drawing on strength she hadn't known she possessed, she elbowed him in the nose. A cracking noise met her ears. Blood gushed down his face, a face she'd once thought of as boyishly good-looking. Now that she was privy to his true nature, he just looked ugly.

"I'll make you pay for this!" he growled.

Hurrying toward her horse, she mounted clumsily, urging him to flee while she was still half in the saddle. He obeyed. The shakes overtook her halfway down the mountain, but there were no tears, only anger. At Landon for his boorish behavior. And at herself, for not heeding Nathan's warnings.

Chapter Eighteen

When she rode into the yard, Nathan was sitting on her front stoop looking mad enough to spit nails.

She wasn't prepared to face him. Not when she was so very vulnerable and desperate for his arms around her, for his reassurances that everything was going to be all right.

Dismounting on wobbly legs, she paused to bury her forehead in her horse's flank and to pray for strength. *Baby steps, Sophie. Letting go of him is going to take time. Lots of it.*

"I suppose you're here to check up on me," she muttered without glancing his way, taking the reins and starting past the cabin in the direction of the barn. Her unbound hair acted as a curtain, masking his view. "Who told you?"

"My brother." His boots scuffed the grass as he strode after her.

Inside the barn, he intercepted her efforts to heft the saddle off, gently nudging her aside. Sophie kept her head bent, taking her time locating the brush amid the assorted tools and tack in an effort to delay the confrontation.

"Look, I didn't come here to argue with you." Lowering the saddle to the ground, he spoke to her back. "I wanted to make sure you're okay."

"I'm fine." Picking up the brush, she gripped it tightly. *Please leave before I throw myself in your arms.*

"Funny. You don't sound fine." He stepped closer, his nearness welcome and unthreatening. Not like Landon's. "Are you sure everything's okay?"

How was it that Nathan was perceptive of her moods and yet blind to her feelings for him? She sighed. No sense hiding this. She was fairly certain she'd broken Landon's nose. News like that would travel fast.

Slowly, she faced him. The concern wreathing his handsome features dropped away the instant he spotted her ripped sleeve. Horror widened his eyes. "What happened? What did he do to you?"

"Nathan—"

Looking ill, he skimmed his thumb across her lower lip. She jerked. "Your lip is bleeding."

She touched her mouth, only now aware of the dull soreness. Landon must have inadvertently bit her when she'd stomped on his foot. She shuddered. "You were right. He's not a nice man."

"Tell me what happened, Sophie," he urged, panic edging his voice.

"He kissed me. That's all."

It was just a kiss, Sophie. Nathan's harsh words taunted her. *It meant nothing.* Funny, his rejection had wounded her more deeply than Landon's attack.

"He hurt you." A terrible anger turned his face to

cold marble, frightening her. "He's going to pay for that."

Nathan wasn't a violent man, but threaten someone close to him and he became the noble avenger. What if he confronted Landon and got himself into trouble? What if he got hurt?

She pressed a hand against his hard stomach, determined to calm him. "I'm perfectly fine, Nathan. Honest." She scraped up a shaky smile. "I didn't need a rescuer this time. I rescued myself. Aren't you proud of me?"

She'd meant it as a joke. He stared at her, more somber than the day his favorite bloodhound died. "I'm very proud of you, Soph. Fighting back took a lot of courage."

He carefully skimmed her hair behind her shoulders, his tenderness inviting her to lay her head on his capable chest and cry it out. But she couldn't. Not if she was to extinguish the love burning like the North Star in her heart and soul.

"It's my actions I'm ashamed of. I should've told you everything from the beginning." Pivoting, he sank onto the wooden chest shoved up against the wall and buried his face in his hands. "If not for my pride, you wouldn't have been in harm's way."

Setting the brush on the shelf, she went to sit beside him. "What happened today was not your fault. By ignoring your warnings, I put myself into an unpredictable situation. Fortunately, nothing serious happened."

Shifting so that the barn wall supported him, hands resting on his thighs, he shot her a look filled with regret. "He hurt you."

"He hurt you, too, didn't he?" she countered softly. "What exactly did Landon do? I want to know."

A muscle jumped in his tight jaw. "You may find this hard to believe, but he and I were once friends."

Gatlinburg's most popular and quiet, shy Nathan? Yeah, it was a stretch.

"Imagine my surprise when he started paying attention to me. Here was this kid who had everything going for him—a nice, well-established family, good marks in school and more friends than he knew what to do with—and he wanted to hang out with *me*. I thought maybe, by associating with him, some of his good traits would rub off on me." He scowled in self-recrimination. "I quickly learned Landon was a fake. His ego demanded constant feeding and, more than anything, he needed to be in control. He must've seen me as a weak mark."

"Don't say that. There's nothing weak about you, Nathan O'Malley."

Nathan surged to his feet and commenced pacing, his towering presence shrinking the small structure.

"At first, we did normal things. Fishing. Swimming. Then one day, we were up in the barn loft playing with his new kittens, and he dared me to throw one over the side."

Sophie gasped, dreading his next words. That poor, helpless animal.

"I refused, of course, but he grabbed the one from my lap and tossed it over, laughing hysterically as I cried over its limp body."

Knowing Nathan's depth of respect for animals, she could only imagine his anguish. "That must've been a nightmare."

Still pacing, he ruffled his already tousled hair.

"I was so upset I didn't speak to him for days. You

can imagine how well that went over. At first, he was livid. Then he changed tactics, apologizing and promising never to do it again."

"And you believed him."

"I did. The cycle kept repeating itself. Stretched on for months. The final straw came in late July, a few days before my eleventh birthday. Landon and I were out at old man Miller's swimming hole, horsing around, when he lured me up into a tree. He dared me to jump off into the water. It was high, and I didn't want to do it. When I tried to get down, he pushed me." Grimacing, he held up his right hand. "Broke two fingers. One of the bones pierced the skin. Now you know why I can't stand the sight of blood. It was a gruesome injury. Doc had to perform surgery. Ma was beside herself with worry."

Nauseous, Sophie forced herself to stay seated instead of going to him. "I recall asking you about the scars. You were evasive."

"I didn't share what happened with anyone outside my immediate family. I swore my brothers to secrecy."

"Josh didn't want to pound Landon?"

"Oh, yeah, he did, but Pa warned him against it."

"Surely other people have discovered his true nature," she said, amazed she hadn't seen through Landon's act before now.

"He has countless acquaintances and no true friends. He doesn't let anyone close. Control is his obsession. He's been very careful not to reveal himself. That's why he can't stand me, because I know who he really is." His expression turned stormy. "Your connection to me is the reason I think he lost it today."

Sophie nodded, her hair swinging forward. "He

questioned my relationship with you." She clamped her hands tightly together. "H-he accused us of…"

He muttered something unintelligible. "I'm going over there."

"No!" She whipped her head up. "There's no need. He won't be bothering me again…. I broke his nose."

His brows collided with his hairline as his jaw dropped. "I can't believe you did that." Dismay flitted across his face, followed by grudging admiration. "Wait. Yes, I can. You're the gutsiest girl I know."

She deflected the praise, intentionally dredging up his flippant disregard of what had been the sweetest moments of her life. *Just a kiss, Sophie. Attraction. That's all this is.* During the long, arduous ride down the mountain, she'd had ample time to think. To stew over her problems. And she'd had a revelation. If she were to have any chance at all of moving forward, of having a fulfilled and content life, she had to oust him from her heart. The easiest way to do that? Embrace a different future than the one she'd envisioned. Embark on a new life with a new husband. She'd create a new and different family for her and Will.

"I've made a decision."

"A decision about what?" Distracted, he was still thinking of Landon, of the attack.

"My hunt is over. I've decided to marry Frank," she said with as much dignity as she could considering she was sitting there with her dress ripped and hair falling down around her face. "If he'll have me."

He went very still. "This is awful sudden, isn't it?"

"As you are aware, time is not on my side."

Looking pained, he slipped his hands into his pockets. "Are you certain?"

Pushing to her feet, she stepped around him. Pressed her hands to her chest where, beneath flesh and bone, her heart cracked and bled drops of regret. "He'll make a fine husband. We've become friends." Through the opening, a cloud passed over the sun, blocking its radiance.

Tension-filled silence stretched between them. "If you're sure that's what you want, I'll support your decision."

"Thank you. I appreciate that." Why did this have to hurt so much? "Now, if you don't mind, I need to go inside and change before I pick up Will from the Lamberts'."

"Of course. I'll go." In the doorway, he turned back and propped a hand against the frame. "But first I want to apologize for my hasty words yesterday. I was harsh. That was uncalled for. I was angry at myself, not you. I'm the one who instigated the kiss—"

"Stop." Holding up a hand, she struggled to maintain her composure. "There's no need to rehash the details. I'm hoping to become engaged very soon and once that happens, I won't spare another thought on what was an unfortunate mistake."

Liar, an inner voice accused. *You'll never, ever, forget it.*

Nathan flinched a little, then nodded. "Right. Well, that's my signal to leave. Bye, Sophie."

Watching him stride away, she felt utterly bereft and, as usual, alone.

Her parting words, stinging like a thousand fire ant bites, stayed with him all the way home.

What did you expect after your sorry behavior? You deserved worse and you know it.

Sophie had made her choice, had she? He tried to be happy for her and felt petty when he couldn't. Her and Frank? He found it difficult to believe they'd be happy together. Frank was too passive. And everyone knew he didn't take a single step without his mother's permission.

Beneath the dissatisfaction burned a desire to exact retribution on that scum Landon Greene. Something had to be done. Look at what had happened because of his continued silence.

Reining in Chance at the barn entrance, Nathan hollered for Caleb. His brother appeared after a minute—sweaty, bits of straw sticking to his pant legs, hands propped on his hips, impatience marking his expression. One look at Nathan and he started forward. "What happened?"

"Sophie finally showed up at her place with a busted lip and her dress ripped." At the alarm skittering through Caleb's brown eyes, Nathan held up a hand. "She's fine. She handled Landon."

Caleb's mouth firmed. "Now it's our turn," he said, pivoting on his heel. "I'll just be a minute."

Nathan foolishly allowed his mind to wander to Sophie's encounter, imagining Landon's hands on her, forcing himself on her, and the real possibility that things could have gotten much, much worse. If not for her bravery and quick thinking…

White-hot rage simmered in his veins. His horse shifted nervously beneath him, no doubt detecting Nathan's wrath, and he smoothed a hand along his powerful neck. "It's okay, boy."

As he waited for Caleb to saddle Rebel, he prayed and asked God for guidance, wisdom and self-control. As much as he longed to plant his fist in Landon's face, it wouldn't accomplish a thing, would only spur the bully to further action.

His brother led his horse out of the barn and mounted up. As they were about to ride out, Josh emerged from the orchard and waved them down, insisting on joining them when he heard what they were planning.

The ride out to the Greenes' place was accomplished in tense silence. Nathan was glad of his brothers' support—this confrontation had been brewing for years—however, the last thing he wanted was for one of them to suffer injury. While neither of them went out seeking violence, the pistols in their holsters said they meant business.

It being Sunday afternoon, a time most families in these parts spent relaxing and visiting with neighbors, they found Jedediah Greene rocking on his porch. At the sight of them entering his yard, he lowered his pipe and came to the top of the steps.

"Howdy, gentlemen." Scanning their serious expressions, his bushy brows met over his nose. "What can I do for you?"

"We need to talk to you and your son," Nathan said. Jedediah was a reasonable man. Maybe exposing Landon's true nature to his family would be the wisest course.

He waved the still-smoking pipe. "Come on in. I think he's in his bedroom."

Dismounting, they left their mounts in the yard and preceded the short, balding man inside. Wanda Greene, who'd been reading at the table, quickly masked her surprise at the sight of three armed men entering her home. Glancing at her husband, she hurriedly stood and offered them coffee, which they refused.

"Landon," Jedediah called, "you've got company." As he chose a chair beside the fireplace, he indicated the leather sofa. "Please, have a seat." He watched them with open curiosity. It wasn't every day the O'Malley brothers paid a formal visit.

Nathan hadn't been here since he was a kid. It was still neat and tidy, the furnishings plain yet sturdily built, pictures on the walls. A home to be proud of.

Landon strolled into the living area, stopping short at the sight of them, immediately on the defensive. "What do you want?" Hands fisting, he glared at his father. "What's going on here?"

"Calm down, son," Jedediah ordered, clearly confused and embarrassed. "Why would you have a problem with the O'Malleys paying us a visit?"

Lips thinning, he didn't answer. At the sight of the bandage covering his nose, the bruising beneath his eyes, Nathan battled the urge to do further damage.

"You'll have to excuse his bad mood." The older man shifted uncomfortably in his seat. "He's in a lot of pain because of his broken nose."

"Did he mention how that happened?" Nathan queried, leveling a challenging look at Landon.

Sensing an undercurrent of antagonism, Jedediah's gaze bounced between the two men. "Ah, yes… he wasn't watching where he was going and ran smack into a tree."

"And you believe that pitiful story?" Caleb snorted.

Nathan nudged his knee against Caleb's. With a quelling look, Josh spoke with quiet authority.

"That's not how it happened."

Having recovered from his initial shock, Landon regained control of himself. "How dare you come into my home and accuse me of being a liar. Father, I won't stand for this. They're here simply to stir up trouble. I want all of you out. Now." His voice radiated insult and disbelief. What a performance.

"I've known these men all my life. Why would they want to cause trouble for you?"

Startled at not having his father's immediate support, he affected an affronted scowl. "They're jealous of my popularity. My success."

Jedediah's dawning disappointment permeated the room. "How did you break your nose, Landon?" he demanded. "The truth, this time."

"I told you the truth."

Impatient, Nathan surged to his feet. "Earlier today, Landon led Sophie Tanner to an isolated place and accosted her. She resisted and, in doing so, injured him."

Hovering near the pie safe, Wanda's hand flew to her mouth, eyes wide with horror. "My baby wouldn't do such a despicable thing!"

Jedediah's complexion darkened, a muscle jumping in his cheek as he shoved out of the chair. "Sit down, son."

"You believe him over me?"

"I can have the young lady in question brought over here to clear up the matter, if you'd like."

His eyes narrowed. "I'm not a kid anymore. I don't have to listen to this."

Jedediah halted his retreat with a rebuke. "As long as you live under my roof, you'll respect your mother and me. Sit down."

Tossing Nathan a look of pure hatred, Landon did as he was told. As the details unfolded, and Nathan proceeded to relate all that had transpired years earlier, Landon schooled his features to careless impassivity. He wasn't the least bit sorry. And that niggled at Nathan.

Would he leave them alone? Or would he bide his time, waiting for a chance to get even?

Resting his hand on the Colt .45 at his waist, he leaned in, hovering over his enemy. "If you value your life, you'll stay away from Sophie. Don't approach her. Don't look at her. Don't even say her name." The sight of her torn dress flashed through his mind, and his fingers tightened on the gun handle. "Erase her from your mind."

Caleb edged to his side. "If you don't heed Nathan's warning, you won't have just one O'Malley to worry about. Got it?"

Landon looked first at Josh, whose forbidding expression eliminated the need for words, then at Caleb and Nathan. His lip curled. "You think I care about that—"

"Be very careful, Greene," Nathan growled. "My restraint has its limits."

Jedediah scooted closer. "I think you've made your point, gentlemen."

Silence, thick with tension, stretched through the room. Josh made the first move. Nodding, he touched Nathan's arm. "Time to take our leave."

Caleb pointed a finger at Landon. "I'll be watching you."

Outside, Nathan and his brothers mounted up.

Josh stroked his goatee. "That needed to be done.

However, I'm not sure we didn't throw grease on the fire."

Caleb's gloves tightened on the reins. "He's a slick one. I say we warn Sophie to be on her guard." He looked at Nathan. "He despises you. And since you and she are close…"

His gut clenched with dread. "Yeah, I already put two and two together. I'll talk to her." *And pray she'll listen.*

Chapter Nineteen

A quarter of a mile past Main Street, Wayne and Amelia Lambert resided in a plain but roomy white clapboard house situated on a lovely plot of land dotted with weeping willows and crepe myrtles. When their youngest child had married and relocated to Maryville five years ago, the couple decided to open their home to paying visitors.

So far, Cordelia hadn't voiced any complaints about her accommodations. On the contrary, she'd praised Amelia's cooking—simple though it was—as well as her proficient management of her household. And though Amelia was about ten years older than Cordelia, the two women appeared to be striking up a friendship, a development that surprised Sophie. Her aunt's prickly demeanor made it difficult for people to get close.

Walking down the worn path, Sophie spotted the two women on the wide, welcoming front porch, leisurely sipping tea on the porch swing. When they noticed her, Amelia waved. Cordelia didn't smile, exactly, but her expression bordered on pleasant. That is, until Sophie came near enough for her to see her damaged lip.

"Amelia," her aunt began, "I believe my niece and I have some things to discuss. Would you mind giving us a moment?"

Leave it to Cordelia to boss someone in their own house. Amelia didn't seem to mind, however. A smile creasing her plump face, silver hair swept back in a simple bun, she came and patted Sophie's hand. "Will is inside playing checkers with Wayne. As soon as you're finished, come inside and have a drink and a snack."

"I will. Thank you, Mrs. Lambert."

When she had disappeared through the glass-paned door, Cordelia indicated the empty space beside her with an incline of her head. "Come and sit, Sophia." Bare-headed and dressed in a casual gray skirt and white blouse, she didn't cut quite as imposing a figure as usual.

Sophie sank onto the swing, setting it to rocking, exhaustion seeping into her bones. She hadn't slept well the night before—tossing and turning amid disturbing dreams of losing Will—and after the trying meal at the Dennisons', the altercation with Landon and the horrible scene with Nathan, she was drained. Depleted of energy. Defeat sat like a heavy railroad tie across her shoulders, and hope for a brighter future was nothing more than a distant memory.

Balancing her glass on the white porch railing, Cordelia angled slightly to study her. "Do you care to tell me how you acquired that busted lip, young lady?"

Sophie ran a finger along the crease in her blue pants. After Nathan had left, she'd changed into her most comfortable pair, and brushing out her hair, plaited it as she used to. Just for today, she'd needed to feel like her old self.

"Do you know who Landon Greene is?"

One brow arched. "He's the young upstart who blathered on and on the day you bowled everyone over with your new look."

"That's him." Gaze lowered to her lap, Sophie related the afternoon's events.

"He should be whipped!" Cordelia exclaimed with more emotion than she'd hitherto displayed, furiously fanning herself, bright flags of color in her cheeks. "However, I will say that you handled yourself quite well. Your unconventional upbringing aided you in this instance. A broken nose is the least he deserves."

Having expected a dressing-down for her unladylike actions, Sophie could only stare at the rare praise. "I thought you'd be angry."

"For defending yourself? No." Her pearl-handled fan paused midair. "In the city, you would've had a chaperone, of course." She sighed. "As for that dreadful scene at the wedding last evening, I hear you were defending your brother's honor. While I don't condone your actions, I at least understand the reasons behind them." Her lips turned down. "Growing up, I sometimes liked to pretend that Lester wasn't my brother. In my daydreams, I imagined a very different sibling, someone who would protect me and play with me." She shook away the thoughts. "But dreaming didn't get me anywhere. It took leaving this place to change my situation."

This was the first time her aunt had willingly opened up about her childhood. "I suppose him taking off was actually a good thing for Will and me."

Cordelia relaxed back against the bench and lowered

the fan to her lap. "Yes, I believe it was. In the short time I've been here, I've seen how much you care for Will."

A lump formed in her throat. "I love him very much. Sometimes I feel more like his mother than his sister." When her aunt remained silent, Sophie cautiously ventured, "Are you certain you won't change your mind about my need to marry? Now that you've seen the depth of my devotion?"

Her chin set at a stubborn angle. "Since you refuse to come and live with me, I want to see you settled before I leave. It's what your granddad would've wanted."

"What about love?" Sophie countered hotly, resentment knotting in her chest. Not that she'd ever find love—her heart would forever belong to Nathan. Her aunt shouldn't have any say whatsoever in where or how Sophie lived, but the prospect of having to fight for custody choked off further argument.

Please, God, help me not to harbor anger toward this woman who's more like a stranger than family.

"Love?" Cordelia huffed a dry laugh. "Love is a foolish emotion, my dear. I'm certain your poor ma fancied herself in love with Lester when she married him, and where did that get her?

"Lawrence and I married because of the many advantages we each brought to the union. We coexisted quite peacefully for twenty-five years without the burden of romantic entanglements."

She patted Sophie's knee. "Forget romance, my dear. Find yourself a sensible man, someone you respect and trust. That's far more important."

Sophie watched a blue jay flit to the railing and perch there for a time as she admired its brilliant color and interesting face. Clouds had rolled in during her walk over, and now thunder sounded in the distance even as raindrops splattered on the steps.

Cordelia rescued her glass from the sudden onslaught and stood. "It looks like you and Will will be joining us for supper."

Sophie stopped at the steps and peeked up at the blackening sky. "I didn't think to bring an umbrella."

"Come on, Amelia always makes extra food."

Cordelia held the door open, waiting to be obeyed, as usual.

Sophie preceded her inside the house, spirits turbulent and gloomy like the storm whipping up outside. Tomorrow she would go and see Frank. She would make the sensible choice.

The rain didn't let up until the following morning. Thick, white mist clung to the treetops, an incessant drip-drip-drip echoing through the understory. Beyond their front stoop, puddles filled the yard.

Sophie didn't relish the prospect of venturing out—a minute or two in that and they'd be a muddy mess—but something told her that if she didn't pay Frank a visit today, she would chicken out.

Will gave her an earful of complaints. "Why can't we wait until tomorrow?" he grumbled for the third time as he stuffed his head through the slicker. "What's so important?"

Umbrella held aloft, Sophie's boot tapped the floor impatiently. "As I've already told you, Frank and I have important business to discuss." Fingers on the latch, she swung the door wide. Her hand flew to her throat.

"Nathan!" Clad in a drenched slicker, black hat tugged so low it nearly obscured his eyes, his hand was lifted to knock.

With a little squeal, Will fisted Nathan's sleeve. "Can you stay with me?" he pleaded. "I don't wanna go to Frank's. I wanna stay here."

Shifting the basket to his other arm, Nathan's guarded gaze shot to hers. "I didn't realize you were going out. Ma asked me to deliver a couple of loaves of sourdough bread and some cheese."

"That's very kind of her," she managed to say, stepping back to make room for him to enter. Conscious of the water sluicing onto her floor, he didn't venture far into the room, staying near the row of hooks holding their coats, scarves and hats. If he noticed her braided hair and the pants peeking out from beneath her slicker, he didn't let on. A girl should be dressed up when she went fishing for a marriage proposal, but the weather combined with her mood had eclipsed that notion.

Feeling sorry for ourselves, are we, Sophie?

Accepting the cloth-covered bundle, she carried it to the table, oblivious to the mouth-watering aromas wafting upward.

"Can't you stay and play checkers with me while Sophie conducts business with Frank? I promise to let you win at least once," Will wheedled. "Please?"

Her back to the room, Sophie winced. Business with Frank. That sounded so…so impersonal.

"I don't know," Nathan hedged. "Your sister may want you to accompany her."

Sadness washed over her. After her marriage, both

her and Will's relationship with Nathan would change. He wouldn't be dropping in whenever the mood hit, wouldn't be delivering food or lending a helping hand around the farm or taking Will fishing. If he agreed to marry her, Frank would be assuming the role of both husband and father.

Spinning around, she forced a too-bright smile. "Actually, Nathan, I'd appreciate it if you could hang around. I'm certain I won't be gone long, and Will would love to spend time with you. That is, if you don't have pressing matters to attend to."

His gaze narrowed and she feared he could see through to her soul. He gave a curt nod in her direction before aiming a tight smile at his buddy.

"I'd like that."

"Terrific!"

As Will shrugged out of his rain gear and tugged off his boots, Sophie hurried to the door, anxious to make her escape. But she paused in the doorway, arrested by Nathan's sober expression, watching as he hung his hat up and, retrieving his handkerchief, mopped the rain-water from his neck. What she wouldn't give to rewind time, to go back to when life was simple.

"I'd like a word with you before you leave."

Avoiding his gaze, she picked up her umbrella. "What about?"

"Not here." Moving close enough for her to catch a whiff of his spicy aftershave, he reached around her to tug open the door. His rock-hard chest bumped her shoulder. "Sorry." To Will, he said, "I'll be outside with your sister for a few minutes."

"Okay. I'll set up the checkers."

The stoop wasn't large. Huddled beneath the overhang with him, the rain boxing them in lent the situation disturbing intimacy. Her obvious reasons for going to see Frank hung in the air, an invisible yet tangible barrier.

Water droplets clung to his sleek hair, sparkling in the light penetrating the window glass. "After leaving here yesterday, my brothers and I paid Landon and his family a visit."

"You did what?" She raked his person for obvious signs of injury. Seeing none, she threw up her hands. "Why? I thought you weren't going to confront him."

"I never said that. You *assumed*." Folding his arms, he raised a mocking brow, a silent reminder of their argument over her first outing with Landon.

"What happened?"

Anger darkened his eyes to smoky gray, a reflection of the dreary day. "He denied everything, of course."

"And his parents? Did they believe you?"

"Jedediah accepted our account of what happened more easily than I'd anticipated. I think he's seen signs along the way that all wasn't right with Landon. Wanda had a harder time coming to terms with it."

Sophie thought of April. "I think it's easy for some parents to blind themselves to their children's faults to the point of it being unhealthy."

"Sophie, we think he still may be a threat to you. I want you to promise me you'll stay alert to your surroundings. Don't go anywhere near him."

"Why would he bother me again? Especially after what I did to him. He knows I can take care of myself."

Genuine concern passed over his features. "Exposing him was the right thing to do, but you didn't see his utter lack of remorse. He simply doesn't care if he hurts others, including his own family. The outright hatred in his eyes when he looked at me… I'm afraid he'll try to exact revenge by targeting you."

Wrapping her arms around her waist, she suppressed a shiver. What Landon couldn't know was that she really wasn't all that important to Nathan. He'd incorrectly assigned a relationship that simply didn't exist.

"Promise me, Soph," he said quietly, rigid steel punctuating his words.

"I promise."

When he continued to stare at her, she rolled her eyes. "I have absolutely zero desire to be around that man. You have no reason to worry." She opened her umbrella. "Look, I have to go. Thanks for watching Will for me."

Looking unconvinced, he merely nodded.

What more could she say? She left him standing there, acutely aware that she was headed for a future she hadn't asked for and certainly didn't want.

The journey to the Walters' place wasn't nearly long enough. The modest spread a mile east of town was smaller even than hers. Neat as a pin, the dogtrot-style cabin tucked into a narrow cove. Riding into the yard, Sophie dismounted next to the two-pen barn. Faint music filtered from the right side of the structure.

Frank.

Praying for courage, she eased open the door and entered the cozy lamp-lit space, the smell of damp hay and livestock heavy in the air. Against the opposite wall, Frank sat on a low stool usually reserved for milking, strumming his banjo. The lively tune defied the dreary weather outside.

Catching movement, he lifted his head and his fingers stilled on the strings. "Hi, Sophie." Standing, he rested his instrument on the stool and gave her a smile riddled with questions. "You caught me playing hooky."

Sweeping off her hat, she glanced around to avoid looking him in the eyes. "Not much you can do with all this rain." She gestured to the banjo. "That was a pretty song. What is it?"

He tugged on his earlobe, hesitating to answer. "It's, uh, one I made up."

Sophie looked at him then. "You're very talented, Frank. You should share that gift with others."

Color darkened his cheeks, but his brown eyes held hers. "Thank you, Sophie. Your encouragement means a lot. To be honest, I composed it with you in mind."

Surprise flashed through her. "Really? I don't know what to say." Shifting her weight from one foot to the other, nervous energy had her slapping her hat against her leg, spattering raindrops everywhere. "I… I'm flattered. No one's ever written a song about me."

His gaze following her jerky movements, he held out his hand. "Want me to take your hat and coat? Mother's taking a nap. Her arthritis always flares up with the rain. We can visit in here for a while, though."

"No, thank you. I have to get back to Will."

He dropped his hand, clearly disappointed.

Get it over with, Sophie. Either he'll have you or he won't.

"You are aware of my need to marry?"

Frank's brows inched up at her bluntness. "I heard your aunt mention it, yes." A calico cat emerged from the shadowed corner and wound its way between his boots, long tail curling around his calf. "Hey, Pumpkin," he greeted softly, bending to pick it up and hold it against his chest. Stroking the sleek fur, he said, "I suppose you've come to tell me you've chosen Landon. I don't blame you. I understand that our association will have to end, but I admit I'll miss our conversations. If it weren't for you, my banjo would still be in the cabinet collecting dust."

So not all news got around. No doubt Landon wouldn't want folks to know the real cause for his broken nose and had fabricated a story.

Reaching out to pet the purring cat, their fingers collided. "I'm not marrying Landon."

"You're not?" Confusion, then hope, swirled in the brown depths of his eyes. "I thought… Well, the assumption was—" He broke off with a grimace. "I'm glad you're not marrying him. There's something about him I don't trust."

"I feel the same way."

Purpose stole over his features. Setting Pumpkin on the floor, he grasped Sophie's hands, his pleasant face arranged in serious lines.

"Sophie, I know our friendship is still new, and I'm probably not who you envisioned for a husband, but would you consider marrying me? In the short time we've spent together, I've come to care for you. What do you say?"

"Yes." Her acceptance whooshed out. Bittersweet tears glittered in her eyes. *At least you didn't have to do the proposing,* she consoled herself.

"Yes?" he repeated incredulously. "You'll marry me?"

Unable to speak, she nodded. With a blinding grin, Frank bussed her cheek. "Come on, let's go tell Mother." He tugged her toward the doors. "This is news worth waking her up for."

Chapter Twenty

Whether Bonnie Walters was irritated because of her abbreviated nap or because of Frank's announcement, Sophie couldn't tell. Brown curls askew, mouth pinched in annoyance, she perched stiffly on the edge of her straight-backed chair situated beside the fireplace.

"I was afraid of this." She threw an accusing glare at her son. "Are you sure about her, Frankie?"

Seated next to Sophie on the ancient golden-hued sofa, his arm stretched out behind her, his jaw firmed. "I wouldn't have asked her if I wasn't certain, Mother."

"Humph." Bonnie's brown gaze snapped to her. "If you plan to join this family, I expect you to act and dress like a young lady at all times. Hoydenish behavior will not be tolerated."

Sophie squeezed her hands tightly together. *Father, help me to be polite to this woman, my future mother-in-law.* Too many decisions had been taken out of her hands. She wasn't going to bend on this matter.

"With all due respect, Mrs. Walters, it's my choice how I dress. While I intend to wear dresses for church and other outings, I will wear pants for everyday chores."

"Frankie?" Her irate tone silently induced him to do something.

"Sophie is entirely capable of making her own decisions, Mother." He flashed Sophie a shy smile. "She can wear whatever she wants."

Her respect for him went up a notch. The fact that he'd stood up for her on this small issue gave her hope he'd do the same on more important ones.

"You and your brother will live here, of course," Bonnie announced matter-of-factly. "I need Frankie. I can't keep up the farm at my advanced age."

Whoa. Live here? With Bonnie? She turned to Frank. "What about my place?"

He smoothed a hand over his jaw. "Is it important that you keep it? There's always the option of selling it."

"I don't want to sell it. It's been in my family for generations."

He looked stumped. "I suppose we could bring the livestock over here. I'd need to build an addition to the barn, though."

Sophie battled rising panic. Leave her childhood home? The memories, both faint and fresh, that bound her to her lost loved ones?

"What about my furniture? All our things?" This cabin had only two rooms. "Where will my brother sleep?"

"Don't be materialistic, girl," Bonnie chided. "What we can't use, we can sell or donate."

Removing his arm from the sofa back, Frank shifted uncomfortably. "Mother, do you think you can be a little less harsh? Sophie's things are important to her."

Getting to her feet, Bonnie threw her hands up. "Is this how it's gonna be? Now that you've got yourself a bride, you're gonna talk to me as if I'm a child? Boss me in my own home?"

With a sigh, Frank stood and went to her. "Mother, please...let's not argue. I realize you've been given a shock, but we're going to have to make some compromises. Sophie and Will are going to be family. This is a good thing."

A marriage announcement wasn't supposed to come as a shock, but a pleasant surprise. Sophie stared at a portrait of the mountains, heart heavy for Frank. He clearly loved his mother, difficult though she was, and did his utmost to please her. Trouble was, Bonnie wasn't inclined to be appeased. Today or any other day.

What kind of life could they have here?

The older woman shrugged him off and, making a beeline for the stove, began banging pots around.

Frank motioned for Sophie to join him on the small covered porch. The rain was starting up again, this time a light drizzle.

"I'm sorry about that. Mother doesn't like change."

Strolling to the far railing, she peered out at the wet grass, watching as a greenish-brown frog hopped along the cabin's foundation. "Are you sure us moving here is going to work, Frank? You never did say where Will would sleep. And my things...where will we put them?"

"We have time to figure it all out. I'll build an extra shed if I have to." He stopped beside her. "And don't worry about Mother. It'll just take some time for her to get used to the idea."

She glanced at his somber, studious profile, the dark hair brushing his forehead, and wondered if she'd ever grow to love him. Would he ever grow to love her? Or would his mother's negativity poison their relationship before it even had a chance?

At least you and Will will be together.

"My aunt is impatient to see me settled," she said, forcing the words through wooden lips. "She would like for me to wed before she returns to Knoxville."

"Oh? When is that?"

"Two weeks."

"Oh." He digested that information. "That moves things up a bit. I don't need an elaborate ceremony, though. Do you?"

This wasn't the wedding of her dreams, so… "No."

"How about next Saturday?"

"Fine."

If he noticed her lack of excitement, he didn't comment. "We don't have to sort all the details out yet. Plenty of time for that. I'll go talk to the preacher right now." He gave her an awkward hug. "In less than two weeks' time, we'll be husband and wife. How about that?"

"Yes." She faltered, patting his back. "How about that?"

Her future yawned in front of her, as bleak and lonely as the gray, cloudy day pressing upon them.

Dawn chased the clouds from the sky Wednesday morning as the sun peeped over the mountain peaks, showering buttery rays onto the valley floor. At last, a clear day. Nathan had had enough of foul weather.

Because of his sizable deliveries, Caleb had agreed to ride along. He sat wordlessly on the bouncing seat, soberly taking in the passing scenery, scowl deepening

the closer they got to town. Nathan knew his younger
brother was getting antsy, that he yearned to retreat to
the high country and his precious solitude.

If Sophie's business with Frank had been successful,
Caleb would soon get his wish. When she'd returned to
her cabin Monday afternoon, she'd been close-lipped.
He hadn't had the nerve to force the issue.

He guided the team across the still-damp bridge leading into town. This early in the morning, Main Street
was quiet, a couple of horses tied to hitching posts on
either side and the boardwalks empty. At the last store,
Nathan urged the team left, circling around to the back
of the buildings so that he and Caleb could make use of
the mercantile's rear entrance.

Another wagon waited there. Nathan eased his team
to a stop behind it, set the brake and climbed down,
slimy mud squishing beneath his boots. He and Caleb
had their arms full of crocks and were ascending the
stairs when the mercantile's wooden door swung open
and out stepped a pretty, dark-haired girl whose clothing had obviously seen better days. Her gaze collided
with Nathan's, then careened to Caleb's. Her nostrils
flared in dislike.

"Good morning, Rebecca," Nathan greeted with a
friendly smile. *Please let her keep her peace, Lord.
There's no chance my brother will stick around for long
if he can't escape the past.*

Rebecca and Caleb used to be friends. Before the accident that had left Adam, her former beau and Caleb's
best friend, in a wheelchair.

With a scowl that matched Caleb's in ferocity, she
nudged the sagging bill of her faded bonnet out of her

eyes. "It was a good morning until *he* came along and ruined it."

Behind him, Caleb's hiss stirred the air. As they reached the landing, Rebecca scooted away as if to avoid sharing the same space, clutching an empty chicken cage to her chest. Despite her poor attitude and his plentiful flock, Nathan resolved to purchase a chicken or two of hers. With both parents recently deceased and a younger sister to care for, Rebecca Thurston needed all the assistance she could get.

Maybe he'd give the animals to Sophie.

Dismissing the thought, he toed open the door and held it ajar with his shoulder. But Caleb had stopped to address the girl.

"How've you been, Becca?" he asked quietly.

"Don't pretend to care, Caleb O'Malley." Glaring, she jerked her chin up and edged around him to the top stair. "I don't buy it, and neither does anyone else in this town."

Caleb's jaw tightened, but he didn't defend himself. He wouldn't. Not when he placed the blame for what happened squarely upon himself. "H-have you heard from Adam?" He practically scraped the words out. "Do you know how he's doing?"

She sucked in an audible breath. "That's none of your business."

When she turned to go, Caleb reached out and touched her sleeve. "Please, Becca," he softly intoned, "I need to know."

Head bent, her jaw worked. "I haven't heard from him since he left town over a year ago." Bitterness laced her words. "My letters went unanswered."

Nathan's heart went out to her. Adam's decision to

break off their engagement had spread like wildfire through the town, stunning everyone. Adam and Rebecca had been childhood sweethearts, and after his accident, she'd remained faithfully by his side. His leaving must have felt like a betrayal.

"I'm sorry." Caleb's face turned to stone.

"Right," she huffed in disbelief. "Like I believe that. Why don't you do the rest of us a favor and stay away?" Whirling, she hurried down to her wagon, threadbare skirts swirling an inch above the muddy ground.

"Don't listen to her," Nathan urged. "She's just upset."

Anguish, quickly extinguished, sparked in his brown eyes as he passed by. "I don't wanna discuss it."

"Not talking about it for two years hasn't helped matters," Nathan pointed out as the door thudded closed behind them.

No response. Typical. Like the rest of their family members, Caleb had inherited the O'Malley stubborn streak.

Passing the private quarters and the floor-to-ceiling shelves of supplies, they entered the store, pausing at the long counter where Emmett Moore assisted a customer.

The store owner stood at the scale weighing out sugar, curly hair sticking out in tufts. Nodding a greeting, he said, "Set those down on the counter, boys. David will be in shortly. The rest I'd like stored in the springhouse. The cheese, too. Ruthanne will get you the key."

"I'll get it," Caleb offered, slipping away.

Wandering over to the jewelry case, Nathan's gaze immediately homed in on the sparkling sapphire ring amid the brooches and earbobs. It was the same brilliant hue as Sophie's eyes. The simple setting, a classic circular design in white gold, would suit her perfectly.

Somehow he doubted Frank was the type of man to buy a woman a ring like that. Pity.

The bell above the door jangled. April Littleton's mother, Georgette, walked in with list in hand. Striding to the counter, her warm welcome did not include him. Apparently she held him personally responsible for Sophie's "attack" on her dear daughter.

Her fingers clutched the paper, wrinkling it beyond repair. "I hear your little friend snagged herself a fiancé." Her eyes flared with annoyance.

"Who's engaged?" Emmett's ears perked up.

Ruthanne zipped out of the office behind them, spectacles perched on the end of her nose. "Someone's getting married?" She gazed expectantly at Georgette.

"Sophie Tanner, that's who." She sniffed.

Nathan gripped the counter's edge, tuning out the resulting conversation.

She'd really done it. She'd gone and engaged herself to Frank.

The questions pelting Georgette sounded fuzzy to his ears, the words distorted.

A hand seized his elbow. "Come on, brother." Caleb propelled him back the way they'd come. "Let's go finish unloading."

Out in the fresh air and sunlight, Caleb released him. "What's with you, Nate?" He squinted at him. "I thought you were gonna pass out or something."

He forced himself to focus on the here and now. "I'm fine."

Descending the stairs, he hefted a crate of cheese from the wagon bed. Caleb went ahead to the springhouse, located beside the river at the base of a slight embankment, and bent to unlock it. Over his shoulder, he called, "It has something to do with Sophie, doesn't it? I always wondered about you two. After all, they say where there's smoke, there's fire. And there's a ton of smoke, not to mention sparks, when you and she get together. Always has been."

Nathan gritted his teeth. "Let's just get this stuff put up and go home. I've got a list of chores a mile long waiting on me."

Straightening, Caleb reached for the crate with a knowing smirk. "Now who doesn't wanna talk about it?"

Ignoring him, Nathan trudged up the slippery incline. Not even the sun warming his back and drying out the earth was enough to cheer him. The image of that ring refused to let go.

They worked in silence until all the crocks were stored and the key returned to Ruthanne. When Caleb met him at the foot of the stairs, he crossed his arms and looked him straight in the eyes. "Once Sophie weds, am I free to leave?"

He'd known this was coming. He just hadn't expected it so soon. "That's your choice," he snapped, brushing past him to climb into the wagon.

Heaving a sigh, Caleb walked around to his side and dropped down onto the seat. Swaying with the forward motion of the team, he tugged his hat brim low, a habit he'd formed after the accident. "If you still need me, I'll stick around awhile longer."

Pulling around the buildings, Nathan scanned the street and, seeing nothing, edged onto Main Street. Customers were beginning to fill the boardwalks. Spying

Josh unlocking the furniture store, he lifted a hand in greeting.

"Having you around these past few weeks has been great. Not only is my workload lighter, but I can see the difference your continued presence has made in Ma and Pa."

"Thanks for the guilt trip," Caleb muttered, hands fisting on his thighs.

The horses' hooves clattered over the bridge. Nathan shot him a sideways glance. "I'm not going to sugarcoat the facts, Caleb. You're a part of this family, and we need you."

Caleb kept his silence, turning his head to scan the forest on his side.

As much as they needed him, Nathan understood what drove him. Seeing Rebecca again couldn't have been easy.

"Look, we can manage without you," he conceded, relenting. "We've done it before, and we can do it again. But I'd like you to promise me something."

He twisted his head to look at him. "What's that?"

"Promise me you'll deal with this. After all, you can't run forever."

Exiting the church, Nathan waited near the stairs, determined to speak with Sophie. He hadn't seen her all week. Although he'd toyed with the notion of going to see her, he'd ultimately decided against it, surmising she was probably busy planning her wedding. Watching her during the service today, however, sandwiched between Frank and his domineering mother, he couldn't deny she looked miserable. As miserable as he felt.

Those in attendance now making their way to their

wagons tossed him curious glances. Moving deeper into the shadows cast by a live oak planted at the building's corner, he attempted to uncoil his taut upper back muscles, to relax his shoulders. He didn't want to argue with her. This would be a pleasant how-are-you-doing conversation.

Gaze on the doorway, he saw Cordelia and Sophie emerge first, followed by Will, Frank and Bonnie. At the top of the stairs, Sophie happened to glance his way, full lips parting in surprise. Dressed in a butter-yellow creation that highlighted the blond streaks in her hair, she was a vision of loveliness.

When their party reached the ground, he lifted his hand and called to her. With a quick word to Cordelia, she separated herself and joined him beneath the tree. Frank tipped his hat before moving on. Bonnie looked disapproving. He ignored them, training his focus on Sophie.

The scent of dandelions filled his nostrils, and he breathed deeply, wanting to contain the delicate fragrance for future reference. He pressed damp palms against his trousers. "Hello."

"Hi." Fidgeting with the pearl buttons on her bodice, she exuded a guardedness that irked him. His childhood friend was one of the most open, transparent women he knew. Was this what he could expect from now on?

"Do you want to come over for lunch?" he blurted, hoping for some time alone with her. He missed his friend. "Ma baked peach pie."

"I can't." Her face was a blank mask. "Will and I are having lunch at the Lamberts'."

"Oh." Frustration speared him. "Have you been spending more time with your aunt, then?"

"Yes." Her gaze moved to some distant point beyond his shoulder. "I've come to realize she's not a mean-spirited person. Just incredibly lonely with a penchant for bossing people around. I believe she's learning that in order to have friends, she has to first be a friend."

Nathan wanted to shake her. "I find it difficult to fathom how easily you've accepted her role in your current situation."

Mr. and Mrs. Conner strolled past, openly gawking.

Taking hold of her hand, he tugged her around the corner, away from prying eyes.

"She's my aunt," she stated defensively. "She's the only family we have left. I can hardly cut her out of my life."

Folding his arms across his chest, he demanded, "When were you planning on telling me of your engagement?"

A storm surged in her eyes, unnamed emotions swirling, clashing with his. "I told you of my plans that night in the barn."

At last, proof she was alive inside that indifferent shell. Softening his tone, he touched her sleeve. "You don't look happy about it. Is Frank's ma treating you fairly?"

She tried to shrug off the question. "Bonnie's in shock right now. I'm sure she'll eventually grow accustomed to the fact she has to share her only son."

Nathan could see the hurt simmering beneath the surface, the unhappiness she was trying so desperately to hide from him. This wasn't a future worthy of her. He couldn't stand by and do nothing. He had to fix this.

"Marry me," he blurted.

Sophie's head snapped up. The color leached from

her face. Groping for the wall behind her, she sagged against it. "W-what did you just say?"

He wasn't at all sure where that proposal had come from, but an odd sense of rightness swept away the shock reverberating through him. They were friends. He could do this for her. "Think about it, Soph. You're already an unofficial member of our family. If you marry me, you won't have to worry about a thing."

Wary, disbelieving, she studied his face. "I thought you said we wouldn't suit."

"We've managed to stay friends all these years," he pointed out. "I think we could make it work, don't you?" Intent on helping her, he took her hands in his. "When I found out you were with Landon, and I couldn't get to you, didn't know whether or not you were okay, the fear and worry nearly crushed me. As my wife, you'll be safe. Protected."

Wincing, she tugged her hands free. "That's just it, Nathan, I don't need protecting. As much as you refuse to see it, I can take care of myself. I appreciate the offer, but I can't marry you."

Why was she being so stubborn? Couldn't she see she'd be miserable with Frank? "Maybe you should take some time to think about it."

Pushing away from the wall, she set her shoulders and looked him square in the eyes. "I won't allow you to sacrifice your happiness. Not for my sake."

"My happiness isn't at issue here. Since I've never been keen on the idea of marriage, it doesn't really matter who—" He clamped his lips tight at the dawning horror on her face.

"Go on, finish it. It doesn't matter who you marry."

"That didn't come out right," he mumbled. *Way to go, O'Malley.*

"No, I think your meaning is crystal clear."

When she turned to go, he clutched her wrist. "Wait, Sophie—"

"You know what your problem is?" She pivoted back, eyes glittering. "When it comes to me, you have this warped sense of duty. You've made it your life's mission to protect me, Nathan, if not from others then from myself."

"What's wrong with that?"

Her mouth fell open. "What's wrong with that? If I married you, you'd quickly grow to resent me! I'd become a burden."

Sophie? A burden? "No. That's impossible."

Her mouth pursed in disagreement.

"Besides, how are Frank's reasons for marrying you any better than mine?"

Her luminous gaze speared his. "Frank admires me. He wants to marry me because he believes I'll be a good wife to him. Can you say the same?"

The direct question leveled him. Worry and an overabundance of protective instinct where she was concerned had prompted his spontaneous proposal. Not attraction, despite the fact Sophie had but to look at him to heat his blood to dangerous levels. Not admiration, although he couldn't deny she possessed many admirable traits. Certainly not love...

"Is there any other reason you'd want to marry me, Nathan?" she softly prompted, her vulnerable expression a dagger in the heart, especially considering what he was about to do.

"I—" Regret weighing him down, he gave a slow shake of his head. "No. There isn't."

Her face crumpled. "Then there's nothing left to say."

"I'm sorry—"

"Please." She held out a hand to ward him off. "I can't—"

"Sophie?" Frank appeared around the corner, brow furrowing in concern when he spotted her. His gaze volleyed back and forth. "Sorry to interrupt, but your aunt sent me to tell you she's impatient for her lunch."

"T-thank you, Frank." Indifferent acceptance wreathed her pale features. However, twin flags of bright color in her cheeks revealed her disquiet. "I'll walk with you."

Without a single glance Nathan's way, she went to join her intended.

Watching Frank take her arm in quiet consideration, Nathan felt as if something precious was slipping through his fingers. And he had no one to blame but himself.

Chapter Twenty-One

So she'd rejected his proposal. It wasn't as if she'd broken his heart or anything. There were no feelings involved here. He'd offered to help based on their long-standing friendship. Turned out she hadn't wanted his help.

So why was he so disappointed?

Shaking off the traitorous thought, he rounded the bend leading to Megan's house. Needing to clear his head, he'd excused himself immediately after lunch and gone for a walk. And here he was on his cousin's doorstep. May as well announce his presence. He could do with a distraction. Besides, he hadn't seen much of the newlyweds since their return.

Madge Calhoun answered the doorbell's summons. "Come on in." She waved him inside the spacious entryway and offered to take his hat. "They're in the garden parlor. Go on back and I'll bring you some coffee."

She bustled in the opposite direction before he could thank her. Glancing in the oval mirror above the hall table, he attempted to smooth his hair that, come to think of it, was in desperate need of a trim. He shook his head at his reflection. Normally he kept on top of these things. That's what happened when a man allowed himself to become preoccupied by a woman and her problems.

With a sigh, he made his way past the gleaming stairway swirling toward the lofty ceiling and along a floral-papered hall to the back of the house. "The garden parlor," she'd called it. A person had too many rooms when they took to naming them, he thought wryly.

He was happy for Megan, though. If anyone deserved love and happily-ever-after, it was his big-hearted cousin. Nathan had had his doubts about the wealthy New Orleans gentleman at first, but he'd seen with his own eyes how much Lucian treasured her.

Stepping over the threshold, boots sinking into the plush sage-and-cream rug, his gaze landed on Megan, seated together with her husband on the sofa, a pile of cloth napkins in her lap. Momentarily forgotten, from the looks of it. Lucian cradled her close to his chest, gazing deeply into her eyes, mirroring sappy expressions on their faces.

He should go. The floorboard creaked as he took a retreating step, preventing his escape.

Megan's blond head and Lucian's dark brown one snapped up.

"Nathan!" Her face lit with pleasure. Setting the napkins aside, she navigated around the mahogany coffee table and approached with hands outstretched. "I'm so glad you're here."

In her flowing pink dress, curls held back with a matching ribbon, she looked beautiful and refreshed, her eyes shining with contentment.

Lucian stood. To his credit, he didn't appear perturbed at the interruption. Reaching his wife's side, he shook Nathan's hand. Grinned wryly. "We're supposed to be decorating for this afternoon's bridal shower, but I'm afraid we got sidetracked."

His breath hitched. "Bridal shower?"

"For Sophie." She smiled happily, white-blond curls quivering. "Maybe you can help us," she suggested, waving a hand around the airy, botanical-inspired room. "We'll need chairs brought in from the library, and of course, Fred will need help carrying in the flower vases. I've got to finish folding these napkins—"

Mrs. Calhoun arrived then with cups of steaming coffee spread out on a large tray. "I've brought cream and sugar," she said, sliding it onto the low table. Smoothing her apron, she addressed Megan. "Would you like cookies or slices of apple pie to go with it?"

"Oh, no, thank you. We'll be indulging in plenty of sweets when our guests arrive."

With a nod, the older woman left.

"Come sit down, Nathan." Resuming her seat, Megan motioned for him to take the chair closest to her. "Have some coffee while you tell me everything that's been going on with you these past weeks."

Reluctantly he lowered himself into the sumptuously cushioned chair and took the cup and saucer she held out. He sipped the slightly spicy brew.

"Do you like it?" She watched him expectantly. "It contains chicory. We brought a barrel of it from New Orleans."

Leaning back against the cushions, Lucian smiled indulgently at her, then tossed Nathan a lifeline. "It's not for everyone. If you don't like it, we can get you the regular stuff."

He lowered the cup to his lap. "It has an interesting flavor."

"It took me a while to get used to," she admitted, "but now I prefer it."

"Good thing we can order a supply whenever you wish, *mon chou,*" Lucian murmured.

"Now if we could only teach Mrs. Calhoun how to make beignets." She sighed wistfully. "You would adore them, Nathan. Little fried bits of doughy heaven."

Recognizing an opportunity to forestall further questions about himself, he suggested, "Tell me about your trip. What did you like most about Lucian's home?"

The ploy worked. Megan answered his questions in full detail, and when she'd exhausted that subject, Nathan inquired after her older sister, Juliana.

Immediately following their July nuptials, Lucian and Megan had traveled to Cades Cove to see Juliana, Evan and their new baby before making their way down to Louisiana. Watching Megan's excitement as she described the infant, Nathan could see how eager she was to start her own family.

When the mantel clock chimed the three o'clock hour, Megan's hand flew to her mouth. "I lost all track of time! We only have an hour before the guests arrive."

"There's plenty of time." Lucian began clearing the cups. "I'll go and get the chairs while you finish those napkins."

"I'll help you," Nathan told him, pushing to his feet. Since he was responsible for Megan's distraction, he would do his part, making certain he left before the bride-to-be arrived.

That's how he must think of her. The bride-to-be. Frank's fiancée.

Not Sophie or Soph. Not the girl next door. Not his lifelong friend.

Just a girl who was about to walk the aisle to marry someone else.

This was proving to be the longest day of her life.

What should have been a fun-filled afternoon with friends and family, eating too-sweet cake and opening gifts, was turning out to be a sore test of Sophie's acting abilities. Seated in the middle of Megan's lovely parlor, all the prettily dressed ladies circled around oohing and aahing over each and every gift, her smile was pasted on, her enthusiasm forced. She was playing the part of the enthusiastic bride, and, from the looks of things, was executing her part rather well.

Her aunt, however, was not fooled. Sophie sensed it in the way the older woman watched her, a subtle knowing in her astute gaze. Spending time with Cordelia this past week had wrought a change in Sophie's heart, a softening toward the other woman, a deep well of compassion that could have only been accomplished by God. Knowing the resentment and anger she'd harbored didn't please Him, she'd asked Him to alter her attitude, and He had.

Cordelia was abrasive at times, and irritatingly demanding, but she'd suffered a lot of heartache in her life, much of it at the hands of Sophie's pa. Unable to have children, all she'd had was her husband. And now that he was gone, she was all alone. Sophie was certain loneliness had prompted her ultimatum. Cordelia had no doubt assumed Sophie and Will would choose to live with her, and when they didn't, pride prevented her from backing down. Pride and old-fashioned thinking. Her aunt just couldn't accept that Sophie could hack it on her own.

Focus on the positive, Sophia Lorraine. You get to keep Will. You get to stay here, in the mountains you adore and the town that knows you.

Positive. Right. If only Nathan hadn't proposed. If only she hadn't glimpsed, for sweet, precious seconds, a lifetime with her one true love. Those seconds were enough to bring her to her knees. How perilously close she'd come to accepting. The only thing capable of stopping her was the utter lack of true emotion on his face. If she'd seen even a glimmer of longing or affection or admiration, she'd have done it. Instead he'd been logical and calm and perfectly reasonable. This was Nathan assuming his knight-on-a-white-horse persona. This was him helping out a friend in need without a thought to what price he'd be paying.

She'd have made him miserable. Maybe not in a week or a month or even a year. But eventually, he'd have regretted marrying her. And that would've killed her.

Jane had been tasked with handing out the gifts, while Jessica kept a list for thank-you notes. Auburn ponytail swinging, Jane placed a present, a square box tied up with wide yellow ribbon, on her lap. "This is the last one." She winked. "It's from your aunt."

A hushed silence settled over the room as she untied the ribbon and lifted the lid. Staring down at the snowy-white, ribbon-and-lace-adorned nightgown and housecoat, Sophie's heart pounded with dread. Her cheeks flamed. Wedding night attire.

"What is it, Sophie?" someone asked after a minute.

"Uh…" With trembling fingers, she lifted the garments, holding them up for everyone to see.

"How beautiful!" Ruthanne Moore breathed, hands pressed to her thick throat.

Beside Cordelia, Bonnie's face turned a horrific puce color. "Scandalous," she whispered.

Adrift in her misery, Sophie didn't register the male voices entering the room until it was too late.

"Lucian," Megan scolded teasingly from her place near the table, "no males allowed in here."

Sophie didn't hear his response. Heartbeat thundering in her ears, all she could see was Nathan. Still dressed in his church clothes, charcoal-gray suit pants, black vest and white button-down shirt that enhanced his tanned good looks, he stood rooted to the spot inside the doorway, his gaze on the nightgown in her hands. Hastily, she lowered it back into the box and handed it off to Jane.

His features hardened into a frozen, forbidding mask, his mouth a hard slash of discontentment. Without a word, he pivoted out of the room.

Icy pain burst inside her chest, unfurling outward like ripples on a lake's surface, scalding every nerve, sinew and muscle and bone tissue it came in contact with. She was dying, wasn't she? Every part of her screamed for relief. *I can't do this.*

"P-please, e-excuse me," she stammered, rushing from the room. Let them say what they wanted. Escape was her only focus.

Locating the door that led to the gardens behind the house, she burst through it, stumbled down the steps and half ran for the trees. The stone paths wound along riotous, rainbow-hued flower gardens. Hidden beneath a rose arbor was a stone bench. Shudders racked her body as she collapsed onto it, but no tears came.

How she wished her ma was here to hold her. Or Granddad. Someone to lean on, someone to comfort her but also to remind her of what was at stake if she didn't follow through with this wedding. Circumstances had forced her to be strong all her life. She couldn't afford for weakness to triumph now.

After a while, the sun's warmth chased away her inward chill, and she sat there limp and defeated, unmindful of the beauty surrounding her.

"Here you are, Sophia dear." Cordelia appeared in front of her, her towering height blocking the sun's rays. "Are you all right?"

"I apologize for running out on everyone, but I couldn't stay." Gaze downcast, she plucked at the ruffles marching across her skirt.

"Do you mind if I join you?"

Sophie scooted over to make room. *Please, Lord, I can't take a lecture right now.*

Cordelia sat and meticulously arranged her lavender skirts before folding her white-gloved hands primly in her lap. "What a lovely garden," she observed with approval. "Not as expansive or elaborate as my own, but still quite nice."

Raising her head, Sophie cast a sidelong look at her aunt. She didn't appear perturbed in the slightest.

"You must come and visit sometime," she continued, still glancing around in interest. "There's one room in particular I think you'd fancy. The rose room, all done up in soft mauves and pinks and greens with an enormous canopy overtop the bed. It has one of the finest views of the property."

"It sounds beautiful." For the first time, a visit to Knoxville appealed to her. A visit on *her* terms.

"It's yours whenever and however long you'd like." To her surprise, Cordelia smiled. It sat a bit awkwardly on her face, as if the muscles weren't accustomed to such an action.

"Thank you, Aunt. Perhaps after the wedding…"

The smile faded and was replaced with a concerned pucker. She tipped her head, pastel feathers bobbing wildly. "I gather your current mood has something to do with Nathan, since it was his untimely arrival that drove you from the party. Have you and he had a spat?"

"Not exactly." Bowing her head, she recalled that agonizing interlude outside the church hours earlier, the hurt he'd inflicted with his brutal honesty. "He asked me to marry him," she moaned.

"Did he now? You regret refusing him, I take it," her aunt observed dryly.

"I had to. He was doing what he does best—rescuing me." She gave a vehement head shake. "I couldn't let him do it."

"Is that what you told him?"

"Yes."

"You love him."

Sophie met her aunt's direct gaze. "Yes."

"Hmm." Her expression turned thoughtful. "What about Frank? What do you feel for him?"

Guilt made her wince. How could she honor Frank when her heart belonged to Nathan? "He's a sweet man. I care for him as a friend."

"I see." Her pencil-thin brows met in the middle. "I confess to never having been in love. I admired and respected my husband. He was intelligent. Kind. We shared many similar opinions. We had a good life together."

Covering Cordelia's clasped hands with one of her own, Sophie said, "After what you went through with Pa, it must've been extremely difficult to trust. To open up your heart and let someone in."

Her steel-blue eyes widened and, for a moment, Sophie braced herself for a sharp rebuff. Then she nodded resignedly. "You're right. I'm not like you, Sophia. As much as Lester's abandonment must have confused and hurt you, I'm glad he left. You and Will were better off without him."

Sorrow pierced her heart. "I miss my ma. My memories of her have faded over the years…. I had so little time with her. As for Granddad, I feel his absence every moment of the day."

Lifting a finger to wipe a tear from her cheek, Cordelia said, "Don't fret, my dear. You don't want to return to your guests looking like a drowned cat." Then she tacked on an admission with an expression bordering on tender. "My time here hasn't been as horrible as I'd feared it would be. Spending time with you, especially, has made it all worthwhile. I'm proud of you, Sophia."

The unexpected praise brought forth more tears. Fishing a handkerchief out of her reticule, Cordelia awkwardly patted her knee. "Come now, let's stroll for a few minutes and let the fresh air calm you."

"What excuse will I give for my disappearing act?" Sophie sniffed.

Cordelia shrugged. "Let them assume it was pre-wedding jitters."

"Bonnie will be livid."

Strolling side by side along the path, Cordelia said archly, "That woman is a menace. I believe I gave you the wrong gift, my dear. I should've purchased your future mother-in-law an extended vacation in the Orient."

He couldn't sleep. Every time he closed his eyes, the image of Sophie displaying that feminine garment—a personal gift he'd had no business seeing—mocked him.

He was glad the day was over. It had been a rotten one. First, the disturbing sight of Landon with his parents in the service, smoldering with antagonism and making no attempt to preserve his happy-go-lucky facade. Then afterward, that heart-wrenching scene with Sophie. And finally, the intrusion on her bridal shower.

If only his mind would settle and let him slip into slumber's blessed oblivion. The desk clock ticking, the occasional creak and groan of the cabin and Caleb's soft snoring across the hall were magnified in his ears.

After a couple of hours of tossing and turning and fluffing his pillow in the futile hope it would get softer, Nathan gave up.

Lighting the bedside lamp, he scooted up in bed and spent the next hour reading his Bible. He checked the clock again. It was four in the morning, an hour and a half earlier than his usual wake-up time, and pitch black outside. But he was wide awake. May as well go ahead and get a head start on the day.

Dressing as quietly as possible, he carried his lamp downstairs and, instead of making coffee, made do with a sip of water from the ladle. He wasn't hungry, anyway. Ma would be up shortly to make biscuits and fry up ham and eggs. He'd wait until then.

Outside, the tranquil night wrapped around him, the air cool against his skin, the stars in the sky above winking like diamonds in a black-velvet skirt. Kerosene lamp dangling from his fingers, he leisurely traversed the dark yard toward the barn, where his cows were likely stirring from their straw beds. He'd need to change out their water and check the bedding to see if it needed more materials. Pulling open one of the heavy doors, he thought he heard Rusty, their new puppy, whine.

"Rusty?" The door scraped along the ground as he pulled it closed. "Come here, boy."

Striding down the aisle, he glanced into the doorless stalls on either side, surprised all the animals were up and alert. He looped the lamp on a nail.

Bracing his hands on his hips, he shook his head. "Couldn't sleep, either, I take it."

A soft thump, like a rock hitting the far wall, had him swerving around. His pulse spiked. Adrenaline surged. Something wasn't right. He could feel it in his bones.

Creeping toward the last stall, footfalls absorbed by the straw-covered earth, his gaze swept from left to right. He wasn't armed, so he kept his hands free and ready to defend.

When he reached his destination, Nathan surged around the waist-high wall, half expecting to be tackled. But it was empty. No intruder here.

A horse blanket in the corner rustled, and a rust-colored head popped out. He sighed. "There you are, you little scamp."

Starting forward, he picked up the shivering dog

and huddled him close to his chest. "Next time, don't scare me like that."

"I'm afraid there won't be a next time."

Before Nathan could make a move, what felt like a shovel collided with his head and blackness engulfed him.

Chapter Twenty-Two

Nathan stirred to the sounds of coursing water and birds far above whistling to each other. His head ached something fierce, and his ribs and stomach were sore. Why—

The awful memories rushed in. Landon. The barn. The shovel.

Opening his eyes, he squinted in the unrelenting sunlight, the heat and humidity already oppressive. How long had he been out? Struggling against the metal restraints binding his wrists behind his back and the thick ropes securing him to the tree trunk, he cast around the surrounding forest for his enemy. Landon's horse munched on the grassy bank.

"Finally, you're awake." Landon entered his field of vision, brandishing a pocketknife. "I thought I was going to have to upend a bucket of water over your head."

Nathan fought the dread and panic threatening to take hold. *Think, O'Malley. There has to be a way out of this.*

His mouth felt stuffed with cotton. The remembrance

of that single sip of water hours earlier tormented him. "What do you think you're doing?"

Squatting in front of him, Landon thumbed up his hat brim, an ugly scowl marring his features. "Do you know what I've been forced to endure these past days? Because of you, Ma bursts into tears every time I walk into the room, and Pa treats me as if I'm some sort of circus freak." The blade glinted in the light. "No longer am I their beloved only son, capable of no wrong. Instead of looking on me with pride, they look at me with a mixture of pity and revulsion. All because of you and your interference."

"You've brought me here why?" He kept his gaze straight ahead and not on that knife. "To teach me a lesson?"

"No." Pushing to a standing position, Landon snapped closed the knife and stuffed it in his pocket. His cold gaze bore into Nathan's, the complete lack of emotion worrying. "I see this more as an act of revenge. You see, I'm gonna ride outta here in a few minutes, leaving you to the mercy of the elements and nature. If the heat doesn't get you, perhaps a mountain lion or bear will happen along." A sick smile curling his lips, he gestured to the stream. "That serves two purposes. Not only will it draw animals, I like to think how seeing and hearing the water will torment you as the sun gets hotter and you get thirstier. So close, yet so far away...."

Seizing the pail behind him, he dumped a heap of gutted fish at Nathan's feet. To lure wild animals?

Bile burned his throat. The man was more depraved than he'd realized. "There's no way you'll get away with this, Landon. There are too many people who can link my disappearance to you."

A fire ant crawled beneath his trousers. He shook his leg to dislodge it before it could bite him. He scoured the ground, wincing when he noticed the ant mound near his boot. Landon laughed at his predicament.

"I don't care if they do. You see, I'm leaving town. It's time for a fresh start, compliments of my folks." He patted a bulge in his left pocket.

"You stole from your own parents? They're good people. They don't deserve that." A fiery sting near his ankle meant he hadn't been successful. He pulled his knees up to his chest.

"I figure they deserve it for believing a stranger over their own flesh and blood." Sauntering over to his horse, he grabbed hold of the reins and led the large animal closer. "I'm ready for some fresh faces. A new crop, if you know what I mean." He wiggled his brows. "Ya know something though, I think before I leave town I should pay sweet Sophie a visit. She and I have some unfinished business."

Growling, Nathan strained against the ropes, ignoring how they dug into his flesh. "Don't you dare go near her," he snarled through clenched teeth.

"You'll never know if I did or didn't, will you? I kind of hope the animals stay away. It'll give you more time to worry over her possible fate."

When he vaulted into the saddle, Nathan struggled harder, but the ropes wouldn't budge. He let his head fall back against the trunk, gasping as sharp pain vibrated through his skull. "If you touch her, Greene, my brothers will never stop looking for you." He'd growled out the warning, hating the helplessness spreading through his chest.

I'm begging You, God, please protect Sophie. It's

out of my hands. I was fooling myself to think I could control what happens to those I care about. I've been no better than Caleb in that area. You are the one who holds ultimate control, as it should be.

"I welcome the challenge." He nudged his mount into motion. "Good riddance, O'Malley."

After Landon left, the solitude of the forest, the feeling of utter isolation, closed in. And just as his enemy had predicted, the unknown haunted him.

Sophie was at the laundry line beating dust and dirt from a rug when the sound of an approaching rider rolled through the meadows. Propping the cane carpet beater against the post, she walked toward the lane, smoothing stray wisps from her damp forehead. Whoever was paying her a visit, they sure were in a hurry.

When she recognized Caleb's mount, her heart skipped a beat. The youngest O'Malley rarely darkened her doorstep anymore.

He reined in Rebel, his dark gaze scanning the farm. From the saddle, he said, "Is Nathan here?"

"I haven't seen him since yesterday." Not since that unfortunate moment at her bridal shower. "Why?"

His lips thinned. "He didn't come down for breakfast, so I went looking for him. None of the horses or wagons are missing, and he didn't milk the cows. Something's happened. He wouldn't have gone off without tending to them first."

Stark fear slithered through Sophie. "You don't think—"

"I'm headed over to the Greenes' now. Josh is on his way to the sheriff's."

She worried her lip. "We were so sure he'd target

me." *Oh, Father, please watch over him. Keep him safe. Help us find him.* "I'm going with you."

"No." Rebel shifted beneath him, and his gloves tightened on the reins. "It's not safe. Take Will over to our place. Josh and I will report back there in half an hour."

"But—"

"Putting yourself in harm's way won't help bring him back, Sophie."

She stifled a groan of frustration. The adrenaline pumping through her body demanded action. "Fine." She clipped the word out. "But if you don't find him right away, I'm joining the search party. Don't try to talk me out of it."

"Understood." Wheeling his horse around, he bolted away.

Hands shaky and knees like jelly, she ran to the barn hollering for Will. He dashed outside and skidded to a stop, eyes as big as marbles.

"We're going over to Sam and Mary's for a little while," she breathlessly explained, making a beeline for her horse.

Will dogged her steps as she struggled to lift the saddle, her limbs devoid of strength. Images of Nathan, of his possible condition, scrolled through her mind. Landon was a ruthless man. He wouldn't blink twice at harming another human being.

"Why are you so upset?"

She strove to keep the fear from her face, but it proved a difficult task. "I'm concerned about Nathan. His brothers can't find him."

"You mean, he's missing?" His voice rose. "Where could he be? What if he's hurt?"

Turning from her task, Sophie placed her hands on his shoulders. "We need to pray for his safety, Will. Remember that verse we learned? 'So do not fear, for I am with you. Do not be dismayed, for I am your God. I will strengthen you and help you. I will uphold you with my righteous right hand.'"

"I remember."

"God isn't going to abandon Nathan. Nor will He abandon us. We have to trust Him, okay?"

He nodded solemnly. "Okay."

"Okay." *Lord, help me be strong for him.* "Let's go. We'll ride together."

The ride over seemed to take longer than usual. Sophie was on edge, jerking at every sound, her gaze scanning the forest in the foolish hope Nathan would come waltzing through the trees, oblivious to everyone's alarm.

That didn't happen, of course.

At the house, Mary and Kate wore matching expressions of unease. Sam was searching the property on the off chance Nathan had gone for an early morning walk and, as Will had suggested, gotten hurt and needed assistance. Ever the hostess, Mary doled out cookies and milk for Will, cake and coffee for the adults. Sophie couldn't eat. She stalked from window to window, restless for answers, until Kate came and linked arms with her, guiding her back to the table.

"You should drink your coffee. Or would you prefer tea? I can brew you some."

"No, thank you, I—"

She broke off as male voices filtered through the glass. Rushing out the door, she saw Josh, Sheriff Timmons and Sam conversing at the corner of the cabin.

"Any news?" She hurried over, spirits sagging at the sight of their hangdog faces.

Sam shoved his spectacles farther up his nose. "I didn't see anything out of the ordinary. I called for him, but got no response."

Sheriff Timmons looked around. "You're sure all the horses are accounted for? No wagons are missing?"

Josh stroked his goatee. "Nothing. Nathan wouldn't have willingly gone anywhere without first milking those cows."

"What if there was an emergency?" the sheriff suggested. "A friend who urgently needed help?"

"I know my son," Sam quietly asserted. "If that were the case, he would've let one of us know."

"So no one in the house heard any commotion this morning?"

"No."

Josh held up a hand. "Wait a minute, Caleb said Nathan's bedside lamp was gone. Maybe he got up early, went to the barn to start on chores and was jumped."

Sophie ground her back teeth. The endless posturing spiked her aggravation. It was clear who did this. Enough talking, already. They needed to go searching for Nathan. Now. Before it was too late....

Caleb rode into the yard then, and the men turned as one to wait. He dismounted while Rebel was still in motion, boots slamming to the ground.

"Landon's skipped town," he declared, thumping his hat against his thigh in frustration. "Most of his things are cleared out. Jedediah's coin stash is gone, too."

"Do they have any idea which way he was headed?" Sophie asked.

"None. I say we round up a search party and spread out across the area."

The sheriff headed for his horse. "I'll gather the men. We'll need a day or two's worth of supplies."

"My wife and daughter-in-law can help with that." Sam pivoted and made for the door.

"Meet me at my office in an hour."

Another hour of waiting and agonizing. With a frustrated groan, Sophie stalked over to Caleb, who was riffling through his saddlebag. "I'm going with you."

Beneath the low brim of his hat, brown eyes touched hers. "I know."

Having expected a battle, she fell back a step. "You aren't going to try and talk me out of it?"

"If you were any other female in this town, I would. But you're capable, an excellent shot and a so-so cook. I can live with that."

Nodding gratefully, she lowered her suddenly watery gaze to the ground. Caleb placed a finger beneath her chin and lifted her face. "Hey, we will find him. I won't accept any other outcome, and I know you won't, either." His gaze probed hers, making her feel exposed. "He's lucky to have someone who cares about him as much as you do."

She didn't deny it. What would be the point?

"I'm gonna run to the mercantile for a new canteen," she said. "I'll meet you at the sheriff's."

"All right."

On the ride into town, Sophie's mind wandered to Landon and their many encounters, the subtle signs she'd stubbornly ignored. Forcing a kiss was nothing compared to kidnapping. She'd never dreamed the seemingly charming young man would be capable of such evil....

Straightening in the saddle, she thought of their last outing and the remote location he'd led her to. "What if?"

Crossing the bridge at a fast clip, she slowed her horse when she caught sight of the young Thompson brothers playing marbles beside the barbershop. They looked up at her approach.

"Davey. Grant." She leaned over the saddle horn. "I need you to do me a huge favor."

Grant, the older brother, scrambled up. "Certainly, ma'am."

"Go to the O'Malley's and find Caleb. Tell him I'm headed up to Lookout Point. If you do this, I'll personally take you to the café and you can choose any dessert you want."

Davey's eyes rounded. "Truly?"

Nodding, she urged, "But you have to hurry, okay?"

"Yes, ma'am!" Holding their caps, they ran off.

Please, Lord, don't let this be a huge waste of time.

Her gut told her this was right. She had to pursue it. She just hoped her impulsiveness didn't cost Nathan his life.

Chapter Twenty-Three

Nathan smelled the bear before he saw him.

Resting his head against the tree—gently this time—he squinted against the early evening sunlight slanting across the forest. The scene was a peaceful one. Trees all around, a sloping mountain stream gurgling over moss-covered rocks, white and yellow flowers bobbing in the thick grass carpet. No clear sign of danger, but he knew it was there. Somewhere.

It didn't matter if he sat motionless. The predator would catch a whiff of his scent, the sweat drenching his shirt and the blood from the head wound matted in his hair. And the fish. Black bears weren't all that aggressive, but with a ready meal available, who knew what the outcome might be.

He prayed harder than he'd ever done before.

When he opened his eyes, his heart jumped into his throat. There, on the opposite bank, stood a massive animal. This was no youngster. This was a full-grown adult, his black eyes shiny, his nose bouncing as he sniffed the air.

Although it was a futile act, Nathan tugged again on

the metal restraints around his wrists, wincing at the sting of skin rubbed raw. Even if he could get them off, he doubted he'd be able to free himself from the ropes securing him to the tree.

Sophie's beautiful face drifted through his mind again, and he felt the sharp pang of regret. He prayed she was safe. That Landon's threats had been empty, intended only to torment him.

Nathan must've blacked out, for the next thing he knew the beast's rancid breath blasted his head. Looking up, he willed himself to stay absolutely still.

"Nathan!"

He jerked. Was he hallucinating?

"It's going to be okay." Sophie's voice rang with promise.

There. To the left. He glimpsed her dear, sweet face, the pucker of determination on her forehead, the glint of the battered Winchester in her steady hands.

The bear shifted closer, his plate-size paws with razor-sharp claws about a foot from his feet. The metallic taste of fear entered his mouth.

"Uh, Sophie…" She loved bears. She wouldn't—

Three quick reports of the rifle blasted through the forest. Again, Nathan jerked. The beast weaved on his feet before falling to the earth with a shudder. Nathan stared. It had been a clean shot, the second and third shots unnecessary. Guess she wanted to make certain…

Then she was there beside him, kneeling in the dirt, hands running over his arms and legs, checking for breaks. Blue eyes large and beseeching, she smoothed his hair, his cheeks. Her face lacked all color. Where she'd been cool and steady in the face of danger, she was now shaking like a leaf.

"No need to look at me like I'm going to disappear before your eyes," he rasped, relief swamping him at the sight of her safe and sound. *Thank You, God.*

"I'll be right back."

He got a little nervous when she disappeared into the woods. But she returned a minute later, leading her horse, canteen in hand. *Water.* Kneeling again, she lifted the canteen to his lips and helped him drink.

"Slow down," she murmured. "A little at a time."

Taking it away before he'd gotten his fill, she pulled out a knife and, going around to the other side of the tree, worked to free him.

"I'm sorry about the bear," he said, knowing her actions would bother her later.

The tension around his shoulders and chest went slack as she cut through the last rope. He scooted upright. Coming around, she studied the fallen animal with a frown. "It was either him or you. Besides, it won't go to waste. The meat and hide will go to a deserving family. You can help me decide who in town needs it most."

Crouching behind him, her fingers skimmed his hair. When they encountered the knot, he sucked in a breath.

"What did Landon do to you?" Outrage and horror marked her words.

"Not as much as he could have." Twisting, he studied her. "You haven't seen him today, have you?"

Her brows winged up. "No. Why?"

He shook his head. "Never mind."

Frown deepening, she bent to study his bound hands. "I can't get these handcuffs open," she lamented.

Nathan stiffened. "Did you hear that?"

"What?" Scrambling up, she skirted the bear and grabbed her rifle.

"Sounds like we might have company."

Sophie helped him stand, then aimed her weapon in the direction he indicated, prepped for danger. When his brother rounded the bend, they both sagged with relief.

"Caleb!" Sophie lowered the rifle. "I didn't know how long it'd take you to get here."

Assessing gaze taking in the scene, Caleb dismounted and strode over. "You okay, Nate?"

"I'm fine, thanks to Sophie's quick thinking."

Caleb looked at the bear, then transferred his gaze to her. "How did you know to look here?"

"Because this is where Landon brought me that day."

Remembering, Nathan felt fury burn in his gut. "We have to find him."

Caleb grunted. "That 'we' doesn't include you. You, dear brother, are going home and going to bed. As soon as we cut those handcuffs off."

"I'm fine," he protested.

Faced with their disbelieving stares, he insisted, "I'm just a little worn out, is all. And in need of a bath. After I get a fresh change of clothes and a bite to eat, I'll be as good as new."

His brother shook his head and strode to dig in his saddlebag for a pair of pincers. While he worked to cut him free, Caleb addressed Sophie. "Take him home. After I take care of this bear, I'll meet up with Timmons and the men." He clapped Nathan on the shoulder. "Don't worry, we'll find the louse and bring him to justice. We'll make sure he doesn't hurt anyone else again."

Sophie caught his wince. "Doc Owens is going to be paying you a house call."

"I don't recall agreeing to this."

They ignored him. And he wasn't really in a condition to fight the issue. He was weaker than he'd first realized. Leaving Caleb behind, he and Sophie set off.

Halfway down the mountain, as dusk descended, he remarked, "You do realize you saved my life back there."

The smile that had been absent too long transformed her face. "I guess."

"I suppose it was your turn to be the hero, huh?"

"Me? A hero?" She laughed it off, carelessly shoving her ponytail behind her shoulder. "I don't think so."

"Oh, yes, you are. Your quick thinking, your skill and bravery, saved me. You are very much a hero in my eyes, Soph."

She ducked her head, but not before he glimpsed her look of pleasure. "I couldn't have done any of that without God's help."

He smiled at her humility and firm faith. If anyone had a reason to doubt, it was her. She was one amazing woman. Why had he waited too late to see it?

Sophie waited until Doc left to go upstairs to Nathan's room.

"Your mom sent up another bowl of soup for you." She hesitated beside the bed. "Do you want it now or should I put it on the table?"

Shifting beneath the blue-and-white quilt, he eyed the steam rising from the bowl. "I'll wait for a bit."

Upon their arrival two hours ago, he'd eaten two full bowls along with three biscuits slathered in butter and honey. His mother must be trying to make up for the meals he'd missed.

Sinking into the hard-backed chair that had been scooted close to the bed, Sophie folded her hands in her lap, unable to keep from examining him with her gaze. His hair and skin gleamed from a recent washing. Scruff yet darkened his jaw. The only visible signs of his ordeal were the bandages encircling his wrists.

"I'm fine." His lips lifted in a smile meant to dispel her serious mood. "The only reason I'm in this bed is to avoid a fuss from you and Ma."

"Just reassuring myself," she quipped, grateful the sick, terrifying feeling was gone. *He was safe.*

Josh appeared in the doorway. "I have news."

"Spill it." Nathan scooted up and settled against the headboard.

"I've just come from town, where they received a telegram from Sheriff Timmons. He has Landon in custody."

Sophie squeezed her eyes tight. There'd be no more looking over her shoulder, no more worrying he'd return someday to wreak further havoc in their lives.

A warm hand covered hers. Looking up into Nathan's familiar gaze, he gave her an encouraging nod. To Josh, he said, "Where did they catch him?"

"The outskirts of Sevierville."

"I assumed he would've headed for North Carolina."

"He may have needed supplies first."

Mary's voice drifted down the hall. Stepping inside the room, she smiled and smoothed her apron over her hips. "You have a visitor. Come on in." She motioned.

Hat in his hands, Frank moved into their line of vision. Sophie froze. Could it be possible she hadn't given a single thought to her fiancé in more than twenty-four hours? Reality came crashing in like a rogue wave, her brief happiness and relief slipping away.

His gaze fell on her and Nathan's joined hands. "I, uh, heard about your ordeal, Nathan, and Sophie's role in rescuing you. She's something, isn't she?"

Nathan's expression closing, he smoothly removed his hand. "Yes, she certainly is."

"I'm glad to see you're both all right." He smiled nervously at Sophie. "Mother doesn't care that your actions were honorable. She doesn't think you should've involved yourself in what was a man's responsibility. However, I think she'll cool off by Saturday."

Sophie couldn't think of a single response. Saturday. Only four days away.

"Bonnie is a fool." Nathan's demeanor turned frosty. "And so are you, Frank Walters, if you allow her to soil your relationship with Sophie. This young woman is a treasure. You ought to treat her as such."

Sophie gaped. Josh cleared his throat, suppressing a smile. Mary shifted from one foot to the other. And Frank? Not surprisingly, he didn't take offense.

"You're absolutely right." Coming forward, he settled a hand on Sophie's shoulder. "I'm very fortunate she agreed to be my wife. I'll do my utmost to be a good and faithful husband."

She had to get out of there. Before she shook off his too-familiar touch and announced she didn't want to marry him. That Nathan was the only man for her.

Bolting to her feet, she edged toward the door. "I, um, have to get going. Will is no doubt tired and ready to return home."

"I'll escort you." Frank took a single step.

She put up a hand. "No, thank you. I'm tired, too.

I need to go home and clean up." Avoiding looking at Nathan, she said, "Goodbye, everybody."

And then she fled, desperate for solitude.

Sophie was getting married tomorrow.

The fact dominated his every waking moment, weighing him down, making him feel like a man condemned.

Lugging a crate full of crocks to be washed, he turned the corner and smashed into Caleb. The crate slipped from his hands and crashed to the barn floor.

"Why don't you watch where you're going?" he demanded, crouching to inspect the damage. He lifted a jagged piece. "See what you made me do?" he huffed, hurling it down, impatience humming through him.

Caleb thumbed his hat brim up. "What *I* made you do? I was minding my own business when you came out of nowhere."

Pushing upright, Nathan's fists clenched. "You could've warned me you were there."

Caleb's eyes narrowed to slits. "You're being unreasonable. What's with you? I know you had a terrible ordeal, but these past few days you've been a bear. Even Ma doesn't wanna be around you, and that's sayin' something."

Nathan grimaced as shame swept through him. Caleb was right. He'd been grumpy and short with anyone and everyone who'd crossed his path. "I'm sorry. I shouldn't have taken my foul mood out on you."

Righting the crate, he began to gather the pieces strewed across the straw.

Caleb bent to help. "You didn't answer my question. What's bothering you? I've never seen you this unsettled."

That's because he'd never had his world upended before.

"Is it what happened with Landon? He's in jail awaiting trial. He's never coming back."

"No, not that. It's this whole wedding fiasco. Sophie shouldn't have to marry if she doesn't want to."

Caleb frowned. "I agree. But what can we do?"

With the crate in his arms, Nathan walked back to the counter and plunked it down. "I did the only thing I could think of—I offered to marry her myself. She chose Frank instead."

Caleb rocked back on his heels. "*You* proposed to Sophie?"

"Yeah."

"I can't believe it." He huffed out a rusty laugh. "You're in love with her."

Nathan, hand poised to toss a shard into the waste bin, stilled. Stared at his brother. "No, I am not."

"Oh, yeah." Caleb nodded, grinning infuriatingly. "You most definitely are."

Laying the shard on the counter, Nathan jammed his fists on his hips. "Just because Sophie's happiness is important to me doesn't mean I love her."

"Her happiness is just as important to me, brother, but that doesn't mean I'm prepared to make her my wife."

"You're wrong." Seizing his hat from the counter, he smashed it on his head. "I'm going out for a while. Not sure what time I'll be back."

Caleb kept right on grinning. "Tell Sophie I said hi."

Chapter Twenty-Four

"I don't wanna move to Frank's." Will slumped onto the bed stripped of linens, his narrow face sullen and wan, blue eyes brimming with accusation. Watching his home being dismantled was upsetting him as much as it was her.

Sophie wished she could make this transition easier. Carefully placing Granddad's folded quilt into the shallow trunk at her feet, she went to sit beside him. "I know you don't, but Frank's mother can't take care of their farm all by herself. It makes more sense for us to live with them. Eventually our animals and things will be moved over there."

Sam O'Malley had promised to care for her animals until Frank finished the barn addition.

The pitiful way Will looked at her, like an abandoned puppy, broke her heart. "Do you have to marry him?"

"We've been over this already," she reminded him gently, looping her arm around his shoulders. "It will take a little time, but we will adjust. We'll learn to make the best of the situation." They had no other choice.

He scuffed the floor with his shoe. "I guess it beats leaving Gatlinburg. I'll still have my friends."

"That's true. You'll go to the same church. The same school." She hugged him close. "I like Frank. Don't you?"

Will scratched his head. "He's okay, I guess, but his ma's an ole sourpuss."

Sophie stifled a startled laugh. "You mustn't call her that." She searched for the right words. "Some people are hard to get to know at first."

"Like Aunt Cordelia? She used to make me uncomfortable, but now I sort of like her."

Sophie glanced through the open bedroom door, unable to see Cordelia or the Lamberts as they packed up their belongings. Hopefully they hadn't overheard that last bit.

"Yes, like that," she murmured. Although she suspected the outcome wouldn't be the same with Bonnie, she had to encourage Will to treat her with respect. Their lives would proceed more smoothly if they all got along. "You never know what's going on in a person's life to make them the way they are. We'll have to pray and ask God to help us be patient and kind."

"I suppose."

A heavy footstep on the stoop alerted her to a visitor. "I'll go see who that is."

Cordelia, who'd been stacking pots in a crate, reached the door first. "Nathan." Over her shoulder, she shot Sophie a significant look. "Come in."

Hat in his hands, he hesitated just inside the door. Sophie drank in the sight of him. His brown hair was a little on the shaggy side, and he hadn't shaved in a day or two, if the dark stubble on his jaws and chin was anything to go by. The fact that he looked a bit of a mess, and a whole lot distracted, made him that much more appealing to her.

Foolish girl. He doesn't want you. He told you so to your face. His near-death experience hasn't changed a thing.

Poised beside the cold fireplace, Sophie twisted her hands, hating that, despite everything, she still longed to throw her arms around his waist and hug him tight.

"You'll have to excuse the disorder," Cordelia said into the strained silence. "We're helping Sophie ready her things for the move to Frank's."

She winced. Did her aunt have to phrase it that way?

His molten gaze burned into Sophie's. "I stopped by to see if Will might like to come fishing with me."

Will shot out of the bedroom. "Of course I wanna go. Do you mind, Sophie?"

"Not at all."

She recognized this for what it was—a sort of farewell outing. While their move would take them across town, their relationship with the O'Malleys, Nathan in particular, wouldn't be the same.

Selfishly, she wished she could go along. That she could have one more carefree afternoon with him.

Nathan greeted Will with his usual smile, yet there was a sadness in his eyes he couldn't hide. He silently waited as her brother located his shoes and hat.

Cordelia resumed her place in the kitchen.

"I packed snacks in case he gets hungry," he told her. "We may be gone a couple of hours."

Like a moth drawn to a flame, Sophie drifted closer. "Take all the time you need."

"I'm ready." Grinning with anticipation, Will

plopped his hat onto his head and swung open the door. "Let's go."

With a halfhearted wave, Nathan turned and left, closing the door softly behind him. Sophie moved to the window and watched them go. Walking side by side, Nathan's hand resting protectively on Will's shoulder, her heart stuck in her throat. The pair could almost pass as father and son. At the very least, brothers.

Tomorrow would mark the beginning of a new life for her and Will. Mindful of everything she was turning her back on, she wondered if she was making the biggest mistake of her life.

Their outing proved to be a bittersweet experience. For the sake of the boy, Nathan put on a brave face, teasing and joking as he had in the past, chatting about nothing of consequence as they waited for the fish to bite. Inside, he was wondering how his and Sophie's lives might have turned out if Tobias hadn't died. If Cordelia hadn't interfered.

He wasn't naive enough to believe Sophie would have remained single forever. She was too sweet, too incredible, for the men in this town not to have noticed, given enough time. But they were out of time, weren't they? After tomorrow, she'd be Mrs. Frank Walters.

A strange sense of impending disaster spiraled through him, leaving him with the impression that if she went through with this wedding, his chance at happiness was lost forever.

Fanciful thinking again, O'Malley? You told her you didn't care who you married.

He glanced across at Will lounging on the opposite bank, hair in his eyes and looking content for a change. Poor kid. He'd faced a lot of uncertainty and upheaval lately.

Frank better treat him right, or he'll answer to me, he silently vowed.

"It's time for us to head back, buddy."

Will's brows snapped together. "Already?"

"Your sister will be wanting you home for supper." Reluctantly, he gathered his pail and pole. "I didn't have much success today." He showed Will the three small fish he'd caught. "How about you?"

"Me, either." He lifted his bucket.

"Just one, huh? At least it isn't scrawny like mine."

Will peered up at him with wide, somber eyes so much like Sophie's it made his chest hurt. "Will you still wanna spend time with me after Sophie marries Frank?"

Nathan stopped in his tracks. Bent to his level. "We're friends, right?"

He slowly nodded.

"Just because you're moving to a new house doesn't mean we can't hang out. I still need a fishing buddy."

An uncertain smile lifted his lips.

"And you know you're welcome at our house anytime. Ma is continually baking up batches of sweets. Caleb and Pa and I need someone to help us eat it all so we don't get fat." He patted his stomach.

Will's eyes lit with appreciation. "Miss Mary is the best cook around."

"Listen, I want you to remember that you can talk to me about anything. Anytime you need to get something off your chest, come and see me. That's another thing friends do. They help each other."

"Okay." Will appeared to be satisfied with Nathan's answer.

"Good." He straightened, taking note of the sun's lowered position in the sky beyond the trees. "We'd better make tracks."

When they approached the cabin, Nathan noticed the Lamberts' wagon was gone and his cousin's horse was in the yard. What was Nicole doing here?

As they stowed their gear in the barn, he hated to think of the Tanner homestead empty and abandoned, the buildings crumbling from neglect. Tobias and Sophie had worked tirelessly to keep the place up and running. It must be killing her to leave it.

Reaching the door a second before him, Will shoved it open and went inside to hang up his hat and wash his hands. Nathan followed closely behind. The girlish chatter ceased at once, calling his attention to the far corner of the room. He halted abruptly, jaw going slack at the sight that greeted him.

Framed by the window, the gentle light setting her hair to shimmering like burnished gold, Sophie stood modeling her bridal gown. His gaze skimmed over the details, soaking in the overall impression of pure, natural beauty. This wasn't a fussy dress. Simple yet elegant, like the woman wearing it. The soft white material clung lovingly to her curves, the sweeping neckline affording him a generous glimpse of gently sloping shoulders and creamy skin, the short puffed sleeves revealing smooth, tanned arms, dainty wrists and graceful hands.

In a word, she was stunning.

Sophie should be my bride, not Frank's. He doesn't love her like I do.

Nathan's heart knocked wildly against his rib cage.

What a crazy thought. This was Soph. His *friend*.
The friend you've fallen in love with.

Sophie was watching him intently, head tilted to one side as if trying to decipher his reaction.

"You shouldn't be seeing her like this," Cordelia chided, arching that imperious brow of hers at him, intimidating despite her casual dress and lack of feathered creation atop her head.

Crouched at the hem, Nicole gave a dismissive wave. "It doesn't matter if Nathan sees her dress. He's not the groom."

He's not the groom. The words struck him with the force of a horse's hoof to the head.

The intensity of his feelings was wholly alien to him. Like a turbulent, roaring river overflowing its banks, it ripped away his reserve, those previously held notions that love and romance were for everyone else but him, that he would be perfectly content on his own, that he and his childhood friend would never, ever, suit.

Lies. All of them.

He. Loved. Sophie. Laughing or arguing, he loved her. Happy or sad, dusty overalls or pristine skirts, he loved her.

"I want Sophie for myself," he whispered the words out loud.

Strange, the sun didn't fall from the sky. The buildings around him didn't collapse into piles of dust. The ground didn't open up and swallow him whole.

"What was that?" Cordelia asked. "Nicole was speaking. We couldn't hear you."

His fingers tightened on his hat, unknowingly crumpling it. "Nothing."

So the world hadn't stopped turning. There was just

one problem—he'd come to the realization too late. She'd made her choice. Hadn't he caused her enough trouble for one lifetime? Loving her meant he had to respect her decision. Loving her meant he had to do the right thing and let her go.

No matter how much it killed him to do so, he'd wish her well. And plead with God to help him get over her.

Nathan looked as if he'd been conked on the head with a milk pail. Not exactly a reaction to inspire a girl's confidence.

Admit it, an inner voice accused, *you harbored the hope that one look at you in this amazing dress and he'd fall at your feet and declare his undying devotion.*

That hope died a swift death.

She fidgeted, earning a warning glance from his cousin, who was attempting to shorten the dress's hem. "Stand still. I don't want to accidentally poke you."

"I need to talk to Sophie," Nathan stated, serious and determined.

What now? she wondered frantically. Another argument? More hurtful truths?

"Go ahead," Nicole murmured, black head bent to her task, "don't let us stop you."

Advancing into the room, Nathan set his hat on the sofa and slipped his hands into his pockets. "Alone." His tone brooked no argument.

"We don't have time for this—"

"I'm sure we could afford to give them five minutes of privacy," Cordelia spoke up, surprising the other women. To Nicole, she suggested, "Why don't we take a short stroll? I'm sure you could do with a bit of fresh air after the long hours you've put in. Besides, I've heard rumors of a boutique, and I'd like to hear your plans."

"Oh." Her violet eyes sparked with anticipation. Wedging the pin into the material, she stood and wagged a finger at Sophie. "Don't move from this spot. Got it?"

"Got it."

"Come along, Will," her aunt called to the bedroom, "we're going outside for a bit."

When the trio had left them alone, the cabin walls seemed to close in on her, an undercurrent of urgency vibrating the air between them.

"How are you feeling?" she asked.

"My head's a bit tender, but other than that, I'm as good as new."

Nathan approached with measured steps. Coming very near, careful not to let his boots soil her dress, his hungry gaze roamed her face. "You look like a dream."

Sophie commanded her heart to slow down.

Her disobedient hand lifted, lightly caressed the side of his head, his brown hair tickling her skin. "You've let your hair grow out."

His mouth quirked even as he grasped her hand and, lowering it, held on tight. "I look like a shaggy mutt."

With his warm, capable fingers clinging to hers, time slowed, her breathing slowed, her blood turned to sludge in her veins. His beautiful mouth was near enough to kiss.

"No, it suits you." Her voice came out scratchy. "I like the stubble, too."

He looked approachable, easy this way. Less forbidding.

You're getting married tomorrow. Or have you forgotten?

Nathan gingerly tucked a curl behind her ear, silver eyes bright like the midnight stars. "All I've ever wanted was for you to be happy." A frown tugged at his lips. Releasing her hand, he stuffed his deep into his pockets. "I wanted to tell you that no matter what happens in the future, I'll always be here for you. We've been friends for as long as I can remember, and that's not going away. Not ever."

Her heart broke a little. What had she expected? Pressing her hands against her middle, she nodded, willed away the what-ifs, the broken dreams. "I know."

"Don't forget it," he said with a fierce smile. "Promise."

"I promise." *Please, please go now. I'm not as strong as you think.*

"Good." With a slow pivot, he walked to the sofa and retrieved his hat. At the door, he stopped and looked back. "I'll see you tomorrow."

Then he left her. And she feared the words they'd just exchanged were nothing more than optimistic lies.

Chapter Twenty-Five

"I'm getting married today." On her knees in the dewy grass, Sophie splayed a hand atop the stone marker flush with the ground. She'd placed a hastily assembled bouquet of wildflowers, mostly daisies, along the top edge. "I think you'd like the idea of Frank as a grandson-in-law, Granddad. I wish you could be here to walk me down the aisle. I wish Ma could be here, too."

So many impossible wishes.

Twisting, she sat and pulled her knees up to her chest, surveying the scene sprawled out in front of her. Situated on a hill, the cemetery overlooked the quaint, one-room church and this end of Main Street, tranquil and quiet due to the early hour. Dawn was just breaking, the sun barely gracing the mountaintops ringing the valley.

Unable to sleep, she'd quickly dressed in her favorite pants and shirt and left the cabin, drawn to this last place of connection with Tobias and her ma. Will wasn't home. He'd spent the night with a friend; a good thing because she'd needed to be alone this morning.

Sophie's gaze settled on the church, the short, fat bell tower silhouetted by the pale pink horizon, the recently repainted white clapboards gleaming. Later that day, in front of the entire town, she'd walk the aisle. She'd pledge to honor and cherish and obey Frank Walters. She would bury her dream of a life with Nathan.

She forced her mind to her groom. She wouldn't allow herself to be bogged down with sorrow—it wouldn't be fair to Frank. She wondered about his mindset this morning. Was he nervous? Excited? Having second thoughts?

Thursday evening, when he'd joined her and Will for supper, he'd seemed as steady as always. Sensitive to her feelings about the move, Frank had been especially attentive, intent on pleasing her and her brother. He hadn't mentioned the scene in Nathan's bedroom, and neither had she.

"Lord, I need Your help." She pushed her loose hair away from her face. "Frank deserves my utmost respect and devotion. Please help me to honor him with my thoughts, words and deeds."

Help me forget the love of my life.

Tracing her granddad's name carved into the stone, she murmured, "It's time for me to go now, Granddad. Lots to do today."

Pushing to her feet, she tilted her face toward the lightening expanse above. *I don't know if it's possible, Lord, but I'd really appreciate it if You would tell him hello for me.*

When Nathan descended the stairs at a quarter until three, he found his parents in the living room already dressed for the wedding. Pa looked up from his task of clasping Ma's necklace, spectacles reflecting the afternoon light. Deep wrinkles appeared in his forehead when he took in Nathan's casual clothes. Ma, whose back was to him, didn't notice.

Josh, wearing head-to-toe black, emerged from the dining room, Kate following closely behind, glowing and vibrant in an emerald-green frock that matched her eyes.

"Why aren't you dressed?" Josh demanded, tugging on his suit sleeves.

Pausing on the bottom step, he saw Ma twist around. "Nathan, you're going to be late if you don't hurry. Why, you haven't even shaved!"

Josh sauntered over, speculation ripe in his expression. "Those clothes look like you slept in them." He ruffled Nathan's hair. "And when was the last time you visited the barbershop?"

Flicking away his brother's annoying hand, Nathan edged sideways. "I'm not going."

"What?" Ma gasped. Pa and Kate looked concerned.

"Why not?" Josh demanded.

His mind raced. What reasonable excuse could he give for not attending? While everyone was aware of his general distaste for weddings, this was different. This was *Sophie's* special day.

Up until that morning, he'd fully intended on going. However, faced with the prospect of sitting idly by and watching the woman he loved marry another man, he found he just couldn't do it. Not for his family. Not even for her.

When he said nothing, Ma came over, covered his hand gripping the banister. "Sophie is practically family. Your father is giving her away. How will she feel if you don't come?"

He was certain that his absence would be best for everyone.

"Have you had another argument?" she ventured, clearly upset. "After you've made up, you'll regret not going."

"I can't explain right now." His voice was gruff. "Please, just accept my decision."

Pa squeezed her shoulder, urging her to leave him be. "We need to get going, Mary. The reverend wants me there a little early." Wise eyes brimming with sympathy, he patted Nathan's hand. "Let me know if you need to talk later."

Emotion welled up. "Thanks, Pa."

For too long, he'd convinced himself he was content with his single state, determined to avoid messy, unpredictable relationships he couldn't control, that wouldn't fit into his neat, tidy world. Too late, he realized his world was awfully lonely without Sophie in it. Staid. Boring. Colorless.

He wouldn't have a marriage like his parents'. Wouldn't be blessed with a loving wife and children like his brother.

You have no one to blame but yourself, O'Malley.

Josh and Kate lingered after their parents left.

"Sophie won't understand." His brother studied him intently.

Above him, a door closed. Footsteps echoed along the hallway and Caleb appeared at the top of the stairs sporting his Sunday best, a deep brown suit that hadn't gotten much wear in the past years. He'd even shaved and slicked his midnight-black hair away from his face. His dark brown gaze rested on Nathan, his knowing smirk flashing.

Descending the stairs, he announced nonchalantly, "He's not going because he's in love with Sophie."

Nathan winced, anticipating Josh's reaction. "Thanks, Caleb."

"No problem." He passed by and, circumventing the couple, went to retrieve his hat.

But his older brother didn't laugh or act surprised. "I was wondering if you'd ever get around to admitting it to yourself."

Kate's eyes grew round. "You knew and didn't tell me?" she addressed her husband.

Pulling her arm through his, he said, "I wasn't certain, but I've long suspected. He and Sophie have a long, turbulent history. There was too much friction for there not to be something below the surface."

"That's what I told him." Caleb leaned against the door and folded his arms, observing the fallout of his treachery with open interest. "Opposites attract, I've often heard."

Nathan held up his hands in surrender. "I admit it, I love her. That doesn't change anything."

Caleb consulted his pocket watch. "She's not shackled yet."

"If you love her," Kate earnestly urged, "you have to tell her. Give her the chance to make an informed decision."

"It's too late. Everyone's expecting her to marry Frank. Guests are probably arriving as we speak." He couldn't stop what was already set in motion.

"You mean to tell me you're going to sit around and sulk while the woman you love marries another man? Don't make the same mistake I did." Josh glanced at his wife with reverence and love that mirrored what Nathan felt for Sophie. "I let my foolish pride almost rob me of the most precious gift God has ever bestowed upon me."

His sister-in-law's lips trembled and moisture glistened in her eyes. Sophie would never look at him that way. He'd blown it too many times. "You're forgetting something. I asked her to marry me once already, and she turned me down." Scrubbing a weary hand down his face, he stepped down and moved to the window, pushing the curtains aside. "I somehow doubt that after the countless lectures and set-downs I've subjected her to she'd harbor any tender feelings toward me."

"You won't know until you try," Josh prompted. "Isn't she worth the effort?"

Nathan's father was waiting for Sophie on the church steps. He smiled when he saw her and came to help her alight the buggy. "You make a beautiful bride, my dear." He reached to take her hand.

Sam was like a favorite uncle, a man of integrity who'd raised his sons to love and serve God and to respect others. He was the perfect choice to give her away. If only… But no, she couldn't allow regrets to distract her from her course.

"Hold on a second, Uncle Sam." Clutching Sophie's bouquet, Nicole descended and hurried around to her side. "I'll hold up her skirts so they don't get dirty. Can you take the flowers, Sophie?"

Wagons lined the parking area. Horses belonging to single riders shifted in the shade provided by the copse of trees surrounding the building. Had all the Gatlinburg residents turned out for her wedding?

With each step, panic built in her chest. While her

hands and feet were blocks of ice, perspiration dampened her nape and forehead.

Think of Will, she repeated again and again.

Sam swung open the heavy oak door. They entered the alcove and Nicole rearranged Sophie's skirts. Straightening, she smiled with satisfaction. "You look stunning, if I do say so myself."

Sophie focused on the young woman who'd freely given of her time and talent. Her raven hair had been swept up in an intricate French twist, random glossy curls left to sweep over her shoulders. The elegant lavender outfit enhanced Nicole's pale, creamy skin, the perfect foil for her wide violet eyes.

She clasped her hand and squeezed. "I can't thank you enough for all you've done, Nicole. If it weren't for you, I'd still be sporting a braid and overalls."

Color blossomed in her cheeks. "It's been a pleasure dressing you."

Hushed conversations died down when the piano music began. Sam extended his arm. "It's time." A hint of apology behind his spectacles put her on guard.

Nicole went ahead of them to find a seat. Sam paused in the entryway. When she caught sight of the guests packing the pews—far more than attended Sunday services—her throat closed up. Her fingers clutched his suit sleeve.

Reverend Munroe was there conversing with Frank.

Instead of observing her groom, Sophie's errant gaze swept the crowd for a dear, familiar face. The O'Malley clan occupied the first two pews. Josh and Kate, Caleb and Mary were seated together. Alice, Nicole and the twins shared space with Megan and Lucian. Nathan wasn't there. Her stomach burned with disappointment.

She glanced up at Sam. "Nathan isn't coming, is he?"
He frowned. "I'm afraid not."

"Perhaps it's for the best," she murmured, earning her a curious look. He didn't question her, however. There wasn't time. The music swelled, cuing the start of the ceremony. When the reverend and Frank left off speaking to focus on her, the guests turned as one to get a glimpse of the bride.

Sophie felt light-headed. Focusing on her little brother, handsome and grown-up-looking in his very first suit—a gift from Cordelia—and seated in the front row beside their aunt, she forced her feet to move.

I'm doing this for him. For our future.

She willed her gaze to Frank. He was smiling, a serene smile, his brown eyes full of admiration. *Frank's a good man. No...he's a great man.*

But you don't love him, her heart accused. *You love Nathan. Always will.*

By the time they reached the altar, her throat was so dry she wondered if she'd be able to recite the vows. Sam handed her off to Frank, who held both her hands. If he noticed their dampness, he didn't let it show.

"Ladies and gentlemen, we are gathered here today—"

The rear doors banging open startled the reverend, and nearly everyone in attendance jerked in their seats. Boots thundered on the floorboards. A disheveled man rounded the corner, a man whose face was set in determined don't-mess-with-me lines.

"Nathan," she whispered, heart leaping at the sight of him.

What was he doing here? What on earth could have possibly possessed him to disrupt her wedding?

Chapter Twenty-Six

Nathan shrugged off the weight of all those stares, his sole focus the beautiful bride at the altar. He strode toward her, rumblings forming in his wake.

"What's he doing?" A little girl's voice carried.

"Is that Nathan O'Malley?" Another man peered after him. "I thought he was the shy one."

Frowning deeply, Frank dropped Sophie's hands. Bonnie popped up from her seat, waving her handkerchief like a white flag. "What's the meaning of this? Aren't you going to do something, Reverend?"

Nathan ignored them all. This was *his* Sophie. *His* friend. *His* girl. He didn't know if she could ever love him, ever want him, but he couldn't let her go without trying to find out.

When he reached her, she stared at him as if he'd dropped down from another planet. "Nathan?"

Without a word, he bent and tossed her over his shoulder. What they had to discuss couldn't be done in front of the entire town. Sophie's outraged gasp was punctuated by a few of the spectators'.

He leveled a challenging gaze at Frank, who stood

watching in wide-eyed shock. "I'm sorry, but I can't let you marry her."

Swinging around, he winked at Will, who responded with a huge grin. Cordelia looked like the cat that had caught the canary.

"There won't be a wedding here today, folks. You may as well head on home." Tuning out the resulting uproar, Nathan strode for the exit with his precious cargo.

Outside, Sophie's fists pounded his back. "Put me down this instant, Nathaniel James O'Malley!"

"Your wish is my command." Reaching a nearby tree, he set her sideways on his horse and vaulted up behind her.

Sapphire eyes as wide as saucers, she sputtered, "Wh-what do you think you're doing?"

Nudging Chance into a trot, he grinned like a fool. "Rescuing you, what else?"

Her mouth fell open. Although he had his arms securely around her waist, she gripped the saddle horn with one hand and his forearm with the other. Wisps of honeyed hair danced around her forehead and temples. The scent of spring meadows enveloped him.

"Who are you?" she demanded, eyes narrowing. "Did you fall and hit your head? Stay outside in the sun too long without a hat?"

"Nope. I'm thinking more clearly than I have my entire life."

She studied the passing landscape. "If you don't stop this horse right this minute and tell me what's going on, I'm going to jump off."

There was just enough heat behind the words to make him slow Chance. They'd ridden north of town toward the river and adjacent fields where his family often picnicked and had the whole countryside to themselves. Safe enough, he surmised, given the likely chance she'd give him an earful once they dismounted.

She didn't prove him wrong. The instant her white kid boots hit the ground, she rounded on him, frothy skirts billowing around her like a bell, and shoved his chest. "What's gotten into you? How dare you humiliate me like that, tossing me over your shoulder like a sack of sugar! I'll never hear the end of it!" She shoved him again, forcing him back a couple of steps. Red seared her cheekbones. "And what about Will? Do you want me to lose him? Is that what you want?"

Capturing her wrists, Nathan circled them behind her back, a move that brought her flush against his chest. She was a radiant vision of loveliness—her skin flushed with exertion, eyes brilliant fire, fine eyebrows arched in defiance.

"Are you finished?" he intoned, face angled downward.

Tears glistened. "I was prepared to give you up." Her voice quivered. "How am I supposed to do that now?"

The abject misery in her pale countenance made his heart ache. His stubbornness and pride had caused her this anguish.

"I don't ever want you to do that," he whispered softly. "Not ever."

Overcome with emotion, he lowered his mouth to hers.

This was all a wonderful dream. A delicious, lovely dream. It had to be. Dreams didn't come true in her world.

When she wiggled her wrists, he instantly let go, in-

stead settling his hands around her waist in a possessive move that thrilled her. His lips were sure and firm
against hers, seeking reassurance, giving love. Going
up on her tiptoes, she framed his face and tugged him
closer, the light stubble on his lean jaw prickly on her
palms. A low moan slipped past his lips.

Easing back, he rested his forehead on hers. "I'm
sorry I embarrassed you. I couldn't let you marry Frank,
not without telling you how I feel."

Sophie's heart flip-flopped. Could this be real?
Could Nathan truly want her?

Caressing her cheek, he smiled tenderly, beautiful
eyes bright with a fierce, blazing love that literally took
her breath away.

"For the longest time, I couldn't see past our friendship, our history, such as it is. When you blossomed
into this amazing, lovely young woman before my very
eyes, I was blown away by the strength of my attraction.
To say that I was confused is an understatement. Here
you were, my neighbor and friend, younger than me by
several years and someone I felt extremely protective
toward. I wasn't supposed to think of you in a romantic
way. It felt wrong. I fought it with everything in me."

The insight thrilled her. He'd been as drawn to her
as she'd been to him. Assuming he was referring to
her transformation, she said, "Nicole is gifted at what
she does."

"No, Soph—" his gaze grew intense "—I'm talking
about before the dresses and sophisticated hairstyles. It
started months ago, way back in early spring. To me,
it doesn't matter what you wear or how you style your
hair. You could wear a flour sack, and you'd still be the
most beautiful girl I've ever seen."

Her lips parted. "You're serious?"

"Very much so." He nodded gravely. "Remember the night we played Blind Man's Bluff?"

How could she forget? She'd been humiliated, thinking he'd kissed her out of pity.

"I desperately wanted to kiss you for real, but I was afraid of my own reaction. That's why, at the last minute, I settled for a chaste one on the cheek."

"Then the comments started and you gave in because you felt sorry for me."

"Pity had nothing to do with it." He laughed suddenly, shaking his head. "That embrace rocked me to the core. I knew then that I was in big trouble."

Growing serious once more, he skimmed her satiny sleeve. "The moment I saw you in this dress, the truth of how I felt about you hit me like a ton of bricks. There was no more denying it. I love you, Soph."

She could hardly process the words she'd never imagined she'd hear. "That was days ago. Why didn't you say something?"

A grimace twisted his lips. "I didn't think I had a chance with you. Not after the way I've acted…like an overbearing big brother more than a friend."

No chance with her? "Nathan, I've loved you since I was fourteen years old. No amount of lectures or disagreements could've changed the way I felt about you. You'll always have my heart, my love and affection, my respect."

Eyes sparkling with happiness, he released her and, digging in his pants' pocket, produced a sapphire ring that flashed and shimmered in the sunlight. When he dropped to one knee and took her left hand in his, Sophie's heart began to pound.

"We've known each other all of our lives. There are no surprises and, after today, no secrets between us. We've seen the good and the not so good in each other, we've hurt each other, too, and yet our bond has remained unbreakable. You are vital to my happiness, Sophia Lorraine Tanner. Will you marry me? My best friend and my dear, sweet love?"

"I want that more than anything in the world." Smiling down at him, she lovingly cradled his cheek, heart bursting with a joy she couldn't contain. Nathan wanted her for his wife!

Grinning, he stood and pulled her close. "You've made me the happiest of men."

Hands curled around his neck, she stroked his hair. "I'll always have a tendency to act impulsively."

"And I'll probably always be tempted to scold you when you do." He smiled ruefully.

"We will have differences of opinion," she warned. "We'll argue."

"I figure that's standard for most couples." Arms looped around her waist, he held her snugly against him. "The fun part is making up." He waggled his eyebrows before brushing a soft, all-too-brief kiss on her mouth.

"Nathan, what about all those people? They bought gifts. They came expecting to see a wedding. And poor Frank? Here I am rejoicing over my happiness while he's left to face the crowd alone. I feel awful about that."

A line appeared between his brows. "Since I'm the one who kidnapped the bride, I'll go back to the church and explain everything to the crowd. Unfortunately, there's nothing I can do to help Frank. He'll have to come to terms with the fact that I love you, and I'm not willing to give you up."

Sliding her hands to his chest, she smoothed his shirt collar. "He's not suffering from a broken heart, I'm sure. However, he must certainly be feeling humiliated at being abandoned at the altar."

"I'll pay him for the supplies he used to add on to his barn."

"And I'll return the gifts."

"You may want to hold off on that." He smiled. "I want to make you my bride as soon as possible. *After* I've had a chance to court you properly."

"Oh? What do you have in mind, Mr. O'Malley?" she prompted, the church guests already forgotten. The prospect of being courted by him intrigued her.

"Hmm…let me see. I'm thinking picnics by the river. Chess games if you agree to allow me to win sometimes." He winked. "Flowers. I'll shower you with flowers and baked goods."

"Sounds lovely." She laughed, giddy with excitement. "This courtship, how long do you see it lasting?"

"I predict it will be a brief one."

Epilogue

Three months later

"Will, hurry up and put your coat on," Sophie called up to the loft. "We don't want to keep everyone waiting."

His face appeared at the top of the ladder. "One minute, okay? I'm almost finished with my list."

"All right. Make it a fast minute." She smiled, thinking of the O'Malleys' Thanksgiving dinner tradition. After the meal, everyone around the table took turns sharing what they were thankful for. Unlike her brother, she didn't have to pen hers on paper. Her many blessings were written upon her heart, and she considered them daily, thanking God for His goodness and grace.

Humming to herself, she retrieved the basket containing two apple pies from the counter and went outside into the crisp fall day. Above her, thick, white clouds floated in a cerulean sky. The meadows and forests bore witness to the changing seasons, the trees resplendent in hues of scarlet, orange and gold. A container of mums and daisies added a splash of much needed color to their front stoop.

"I'll take that, Mrs. O'Malley." Nathan took the basket and captured her hand, weaving his fingers securely through hers.

Her husband of two months flashed her a devastating smile, one that hinted of intimacies shared, of enduring love intertwining their hearts and souls into one. Since their wedding day—a small family affair performed on his parents' property—he'd grown more precious to her than ever before, so much so she had to sometimes combat the fear of losing him and trust God to guide their steps.

Over the course of the past months, losing Tobias and coming very close to losing Nathan, she'd learned that while she may not always understand God's ways, His plans were best. "And we know that in all things God works for the good of those who love Him, who have been called according to His purpose."

"Quoting Romans this morning?"

She wasn't surprised he recognized it. Every evening after supper, Nathan read from the Bible and, together, the three of them prayed, a most special time that brought them closer as a family.

"Just reminding myself of God's provision."

His gaze warmed, and she reveled in the affection she witnessed there. Handsome and fit in a hunter-green shirt that molded to his chest and brown trousers encasing his lean, muscular legs, he wore his brown hair a tad longer than he used to, and he'd gone to shaving every other day now, lending him a more relaxed, approachable air.

He indicated the pies. "These smell delicious."

"I hope they taste as good as they smell." Shortly after their engagement, she'd enlisted Mary to help her learn to bake. Not only did she make bread on a daily basis now, she sometimes tried her hand at desserts.

"If they taste anything like the rhubarb pies you made last month, I'll have to fight my brothers for a piece."

The door shut behind them and Will bolted past in a blur of green and brown. "Come on, you guys," he teased over his shoulder, dark hair flopping on his forehead. "What's the holdup? We don't want to be late!"

He shot off into the woods, no doubt as eager for the companionship as he was for the food. Will loved that he was now officially part of the O'Malley family. He'd taken to calling Nathan's parents Aunt Mary and Uncle Sam, titles that greatly pleased the older couple.

Following at a more sedate pace, they entered the woods that separated the properties, quiet for a moment as they absorbed the beauty of the forest spread out in all directions.

"I forgot to tell you. I received a letter from Cordelia yesterday."

"Really? How is she doing?" He guided her around a fallen moss-encased log.

"She wrote that she's glad to be home, but it sounds to me like she's lonely."

"Admit it, you miss her," he said good-naturedly, "bossiness and all."

"You know, I do. I got used to having her around." Cordelia had stayed on another week after their wedding, keeping Will with her at the Lamberts' so that she and Nathan could have time to themselves. "She invited us for a visit sometime before Christmas. Before the weather turns bad."

His silver gaze cut to her, dark brows raised in question. "Would you like to go?"

"I've never been to Knoxville," she mused. "I'd like to see her home and visit her church. Perhaps you and I could do some sightseeing while Will visits with Cordelia."

Downcast gaze on the lookout for exposed roots, he considered her words. "I like that idea. It's a short day trip. Why don't we go next week? We can ask Will's teacher to send his lessons along so he won't get too far behind."

"That would be wonderful." She smiled over at him, grateful beyond words. "Thank you, Nathan."

Casting around the forest and seeing no one, Nathan stopped and set the basket on the leaf-littered ground. Hands on her shoulders, he pulled her close.

"What are you doing?" She laughed, completely at ease with him.

"When you look at me like that, Soph," he breathed, "it makes me want to forget about my family, toss you over my shoulder and carry you back home." His earnest bordering-on-vulnerable expression triggered longing of her own.

Lifting her face to his, she kissed him, a toe-curling experience that made the day at his folks' seem very long indeed.

"You know you want to spend time with Juliana and Evan," she reminded him after a while. "They're only here for a week."

Smoothing her hair behind her ear, he nodded regretfully. "You're right."

"And—" she ducked beneath his arm and away "—think of all that delicious food you'd miss out on. Turkey and dressing, pumpkin pie, collard greens, warm, gooey yeast rolls." She ticked them off one by one, squealing when he picked her up and whirled her around.

"Nathan!"

Chuckling, he lowered her to her feet. "Okay, okay, you've convinced me, woman. Let's go before I change my mind."

Both of them grinning ear to ear, they hurried on their way.

His parents' house was, of course, chaotic. Laughter spilled in from the living room, and in the kitchen, bustling activity abounded as his ma and Aunt Alice plied Jessica and Jane with heaping platters to carry to the dining room table. Rich aromas wrapped around him, making his mouth water and his empty stomach growl.

When he reached out to snag a green bean from a nearby bowl, his ma playfully swatted his hand. "No filching. If I let all of you men do that, there'd be nothing left. Sophie, dear, how are you? Happy Thanksgiving." Ma greeted his wife as if she hadn't seen her the day before, pulling her into a warm hug.

His wife. The term still startled and pleased him in due measure.

His thumb grazed the gold ring on his fourth finger, reassuring himself it was still there. That this was real. Sophie was well and truly his, a fact that filled him with gratitude and a humbling understanding of God's goodness, the blessing she and Will were to him.

Gazing at her now, cheeks rosy from the cool air and quite possibly from their interlude in the forest, big blue eyes alight with contentment, his chest expanded with love and pride. She was truly lovely, inside and out.

Together, they drifted into the living room. Amid greetings and hugs and the shaking of hands, Nathan took note of the new additions to the O'Malley clan this year. Lucian lounged on the sofa, relaxed and content with Megan tucked close to his side. While he hadn't lost his formal manners altogether, he wasn't above joking and teasing along with the rest of them.

On the other end of the sofa was perhaps the most popular addition, six-month-old James. At present, he was being bounced on his father's knee. With his fine jet-black hair and blue eyes, the baby bore a striking resemblance to Evan, whose look of paternal pride was unmistakable.

And then there was Will and Sophie. *His* new family.

Pushing to her feet, Juliana hurried over, flame-colored hair swept up in a dignified bun. "Welcome to the family, Sophie. I was ecstatic when I heard the news."

"She's not exaggerating." Evan grinned, holding the baby steady with a large hand on his tummy. "I came in from feeding the animals one afternoon and she was jumping up and down, waving the letter around and basically scaring poor Jamey here."

Juliana didn't deny it, just laughed.

Nathan was next in line for a hug.

"Congratulations, Nate." Pulling back, her forest-green eyes communicated her delight. "I wish we could've been here for the wedding. I hear it was a touching ceremony."

It had been a perfect day. Sensitive to Frank's feelings—they'd planned to marry only three weeks after that first interrupted ceremony—they'd decided against a church wedding. And so here on his family's land, beneath a bright blue sky and with a handful of family and friends in attendance, he and Sophie had exchanged heartfelt vows.

"We understand how difficult travel must be with an infant."

"Would you like to hold him?"

"If you're sure I won't break him." He winked, waiting as she transferred her son to him. Cradled against his chest, the baby was small and warm and smelled like fresh flowers and milk, a curious combination. "Hey there, little guy," he murmured, aware of Sophie's keen interest.

Holding out a finger, she allowed James to wrap his fist around it, her eyes going soft when he smiled at her. "He's beautiful," she said wonderingly.

Juliana beamed her thanks. "Someday you and Nathan will have a baby of your very own."

Sophie's widened gaze collided with his, and they shared a smile. A baby. With Sophie. A thrill shot through him at the prospect. She'd make a wonderful mother.

"Time to eat," Mary called from the dining room, and everyone began filing around the table. It was cramped, but no one cared. They were just happy to be together.

The meal was delicious. Afterward, the sharing of everyone's lists evoked both tears and laughter, especially Will's. He was over-the-moon excited to have Nathan as a brother-in-law and was hoping for a niece or nephew very soon.

All in all, it was a great day, but as the sun sank lower in the sky, Nathan became impatient to escort his bride home. As she was packing up leftovers, he caught sight of Caleb slipping out the kitchen door and followed him.

"Hey." Nathan closed the door behind him. "Where are you sneaking off to?"

Caleb pivoted back, shrugging up a shoulder. "Just going to check on the cows."

"Too much togetherness for one day?" Nathan stepped off the porch and joined him, sensing the nervous energy his brother radiated. Sorrow overtook him as the truth sank in. Caleb was leaving.

"You could say that," he hedged, his restless gaze scanning the horizon.

"When are you leaving?"

His brows shot up. "How did you know?"

Nathan settled a hand on his shoulder. "Wasn't that hard to figure out. I'm surprised you've stuck around as long as you have."

"Figured I'd ease the workload for a while after your wedding." A ghost of a smile crossed his lips. "Give you and Sophie time to adjust to married life."

Nathan huffed a laugh. "Thanks, Caleb. I appreciate that."

"No problem."

"Are you sure you won't stay a little longer?"

Caleb's gaze darkened. "I couldn't, even if I wanted to."

What did that mean?

Seeing the unspoken question, he continued. "My presence around town bothers Rebecca. Well, let's be honest, it bothers more folks than just her. But she's the one I'm most concerned about."

"You can't let others' opinions rule your life. If

you're around more often, seeing you wouldn't come as such a shock."

Pulling away, Caleb's jaw set in a stubborn line. "I've already made my decision, Nate."

The door opened then, and Sophie joined them, linking her arm with Nathan's. "Will is staying the night with your parents again."

"Okay."

She looked from one to the other. "I'm sorry, am I interrupting something?"

Caleb shook his head. "No, not at all. I was just leaving." Pointing at Nathan, he addressed her. "You keep this one in line, you hear?"

"I—I'll try." Her frown meant she knew something was off, but she didn't comment.

As his brother took off for the barn, Nathan summoned a smile. "Ready to go?"

Indicating the basket looped around her arm, she nodded, and they headed for the woods.

"Caleb's leaving for real, isn't he?" she questioned him at the halfway point. "I thought, since he's been around for a while, that he'd decided to forego his jaunts into the high country."

"I think we all hoped for that scenario, but no. He's restless. I'm afraid he won't come around again for a long while."

"I'm sorry, Nathan," she said, her voice thick with compassion. "I know how much you miss him, how much you worry when he's away."

"Right now, the only thing we can do is pray for him."

They'd reached the cabin by now, his new home that Sophie had gone out of her way to make as cozy and comfortable as possible, and his sole wish at that moment was to focus on his wife. "Wait here."

Taking the basket from her, he placed it inside the kitchen and, rejoining her outside, led her to her favorite tree. With a playful grin, she climbed up first in a flurry of skirts, and he followed close behind. Wedging himself against the trunk, he motioned for her to scoot close and lean back against him. He anchored her with one arm around her tiny waist, thumb lazily skimming her rib cage.

He heaved a grateful sigh, a lazy smile lifting his lips. "This is more like it."

Her head beneath his chin, her soft hair tickling his neck, she held tightly to his arm, trusting him to keep her from falling. "I'm so happy I can hardly stand it," she said with a low chuckle. "You and me. Together...."

"I know." And he did. They almost hadn't made it to this place.

Twisting her head, she gazed up at him with humbling adoration. "I love you, Nathan."

"I love you, my dear, sweet Sophie." And then he kissed her to show her how much he meant it.

* * * * *

"I'm sorry I was distant before. That was just me being foolish."

Samantha didn't ask what he was talking about; she obviously knew. "What was going on?"

Corbin debated finding some intellectual way to say it, but he wasn't thinking straight enough. "I got turned upside down by that kiss."

"Yeah. Me, too." She glanced at him and then turned to put a stack of plates away.

"It was intense."

"Uh-huh."

Now that he had brought up the topic, he wasn't sure where he wanted to go with it. For him to go into the fact that he couldn't get involved with her because she was an alcoholic... Suddenly, that felt judgmental and mean and not how he wanted to talk to her.

Maybe it wasn't how he wanted to be with her, either, but he wasn't ready to make that alteration to his long-held set of values about who he could get involved with. And until he did, he obviously needed to keep a lid on his feelings.

So he talked about something they would probably agree on. "I was never so scared in my life as when Mikey was lost."

"Me, either. It was awful."

He paused, then admitted, "I just don't know if I'm cut out for taking care of a kid."

Her head jerked around to face him. "You're not thinking of sending him back to your mom, are you?"

Was he? He shook his head slowly, letting out a sigh. "No. I feel like I screwed up badly, but I still think he's safer with me than with her."

She let the water out of the sink, not looking at him now. "I think you're doing a great job," she said. "It was just as much my fault as yours. Parenting is a challenge and you can't help but screw up sometimes."

"I guess." He wasn't used to doing things poorly or in a half-baked way. He was used to working at a task until he could become an expert. But it seemed that nobody was an expert when it came to raising kids, not really.

"Mikey can be a handful, just like any other little child," she said.

"He is, but I sure love him," Corbin said. It was the first time he had articulated that, and he realized it was completely true. He loved his little brother as if the boy were his own son.

"I love him, too," she said, almost offhandedly.

She just continued wiping down the counters, not acting like she had said anything momentous, but her words blew Corbin away. She had an amazing ability to love. Mikey wasn't her child, nor her blood, but she felt for him as if he were.

If he loved his little brother despite the boy's issues and whining and toddler misbehavior, could it be that he could love another adult who had issues, too? He was definitely starting to care a lot for Samantha. Was he growing, becoming more flexible and forgiving?

He didn't know if he could change that much. He'd been holding himself—and others—to a strict high standard for a long time. It was how he'd gotten as far as he had after his rough beginning.

Corbin wanted to continue caring for his brother, especially given the alternative, but the fact that Mikey had gotten lost had shaken him. He didn't know if he was good enough to do the job.

Samantha's expression of support soothed his insecurities. He wanted love and acceptance, just like anyone else. And there was a tiny spark inside him that was starting to burn, a spark that wondered if he could maybe be loved and fall in love, even with a certain nanny.

Don't miss
Child on His Doorstep
by Lee Tobin McClain, available August 2020 wherever Love Inspired books and ebooks are sold.

LoveInspired.com

*Can saving a kidnapped child bring danger to this
K-9 cop's doorstep?*

Read on for a sneak preview of
Tracking a Kidnapper *by Valerie Hansen,*
the next book in the True Blue K-9 Unit: Brooklyn *series*
available August 2020 from Love Inspired Suspense.

Traces of fog lingered along the East River. Off-duty
police officer Vivienne Armstrong paused at the fence
bordering the Brooklyn Heights Promenade to gaze
across the river at the majestic Manhattan skyline. Her
city. Her home.

Slight pressure against her calf reminded her why she
was there, and she smiled down at her K-9 partner. "Yes,
Hank, I know. You want to run and burn off energy. What
a good boy."

The soft brown eyes of the black-and-white border
collie made it seem as though he understood every word,
and given the extraordinary reputation of his breed, she
imagined he might.

"Jake! My baby! Where's my baby?" a woman
screeched.

Other passersby froze, making it easy for Vivienne to
pick out the frantic young woman darting from person to
person. "He has blond hair. Bright green pants. Have you
seen him? Please!"

"I'm a police officer," Vivienne told the woman. "Calm down and tell me what happened."

The fair-haired mother was gasping for breath, her eyes wide and filling with tears. "My little boy was right here. Next to me. I just… I just stopped to look at the boats, and when I turned to pick him up and show him, he was gone!"

Vivienne gently touched her shoulder. "I'm a K-9 officer and my dog is trained for search and rescue. Do you have any item of your son's that I can use for scent?"

The woman blinked rapidly. "Yes! In my bag."

Vivienne watched as the mother pulled out a stuffed toy rabbit. "Perfect."

In full professional mode, she straightened, loosened her hold on the dog's leash and commanded, "Seek."

Hank circled, returned to the place at the river fence that the woman had indicated earlier, then sniffed the air and began to run.

The leash tightened. Vivienne followed as hope leaped, then sank. The dog was following air scent. Therefore, the missing child had not left footprints when he'd parted from his mother. Someone had lifted and carried him away. There was only one conclusion that made sense.

The little boy had been kidnapped!

Don't miss
Tracking a Kidnapper *by Valerie Hansen,*
available wherever Love Inspired Suspense books
and ebooks are sold.

LoveInspired.com